The Spell of
The Enchantress

Brent moved nearer to her, wanting so much to take her into his arms; but he knew that now he could not. This strange wild girl had an effect on him he'd never known before. The tempestuous set of her head, the dark mystery of her eyes . . . Brent wanted Analee more than any woman he had ever known. As he looked at her he knew that his feelings were not in vain; he knew that she wanted him, too.

"When will we meet again, Analee, is that what you wanted to say?"

"Yes," she whispered.

"We shall find a way," Brent said. "*I* shall find a way."

THE ENCHANTRESS

KATHERINE YORKE

PUBLISHED BY POCKET BOOKS NEW YORK

A POCKET BOOKS/RICHARD GALLEN Publication

POCKET BOOKS, a Simon & Schuster division of
GULF & WESTERN CORPORATION
1230 Avenue of the Americas, New York, N.Y. 10020

ISBN: 0-671-83165-8

First Pocket Books printing October, 1979

10 9 8 7 6 5 4 3 2 1

Trademarks registered in the United States and other countries.

Printed in the U.S.A.

AUTHOR'S NOTE

In the eighteenth century, when this book is set, many places in what we now call the English Lake District had different names, or the spelling was different. I have used modern names throughout so that the areas in which the action takes place may be more familiar to the modern reader.

In the spelling of the various gypsy words I have used the translation by Charles Duff of Jean-Paul Clébert's classic book *The Gypsies* (London, 1963). I am also indebted to this book as well as E. B. Trigg's *Gypsy Demons and Divinities* (London, 1975) for much of my information about the gypsy people.

I consulted many books on the English Lake District and the Rebellion of 1745, but I am especially grateful to David Daiches whose *Charles Edward Stewart: the life and times of Bonnie Prince Charlie* (London, 1973) was constantly by my side.

K.Y.
London 1978

Chapter One

Where she came from no one knew; no one asked; few cared. In the huge roving community of drovers, peddlers, tinkers, whores, gypsies, pickpockets, horse thieves and honest traders that descended on the Cumbrian town of Appleby for the June Fair in the year 1744 she was scarcely noticed.

But some there were who did notice her and ask themselves questions. The men who followed her progress through the town—surreptitiously, if their wives were watching, or with open admiration if they were not—could not help but appreciate her beauty beneath the pallor; the graceful dignity with which she walked, even though her feet were bare; the proud tilt of her head, the fierce defiance in the eyes of one who had learned to protect herself.

The women, those who noticed her, pitied her for her air of extreme weariness, her slow tired pace, the sloped shoulders, the tattered clothes she wore and the picture of poverty and loneliness that she presented.

Everyone came to the June Fair in Appleby; everyone that is who had to do with horses, cattle, sheep or chickens or who had farm produce or home-made goods to sell. Those who wanted to buy or exchange came, and those who wanted to hire servants or be themselves hired for the farms or great houses. They came in vast numbers from across the border with Scotland; they came from all parts of Cumberland and Westmorland; some even came from as far south as Preston or as far east as York.

1

But few came from the real south. It was a long way. Even by horse or carriage it was a journey of many days. On foot it would take weeks. And those who did notice or speak to the girl agreed on one thing; she came from the south; she was not one of them. But she said few words as she walked with her bundle in her hand, stopping occasionally to admire some glass beads or metal jewelwork displayed on many of the stalls in the market place, her fine eyes glinting as though in imagination she could see herself adorned in such finery. Or her fingers would tentatively feel the satins and silks, the brocades and soft cloth, her face alight at the vision of herself such richness conjured up.

But no one tried to sell her anything because it was so obvious she could not pay; and the men smiled and winked at her or made some coarse gesture, or promised her a bauble or a yard of cloth for a certain favor she might give them, while the women told her to be off so that she should not spoil the view of those who could afford to buy.

Finally, as though instinctively seeking home, she came to the tents that stood a little apart from the town where the gypsy folk set up their camp . . . those wanderers of the road who spent the year going from one fair to the next. The tents and carts clustered around smoking fires, and in the late afternoon the enticing odor of wood smoke and roasting meat filled the air.

The town of Appleby lay in the broad valley between the range of Pennine mountains in the east and the hills of Lakeland to the west. She had followed the jagged line of the Pennines in her journey north knowing that they led from Derbyshire to the Cheviot Hills that formed the border with Scotland; that they would lead her away from all that she was fleeing from, the hateful memories and painful regrets of her past life.

Boroughgate, the steep main street of Appleby, led to the huge red stone castle built in the time of the Normans. At the bottom a bridge crossed the river Eden and, asking her way, the girl had trudged wearily up the bank toward the gypsies' field. Ahead of her, almost obscured in the hazy mist of late afternoon, were the Pennines which had guided her and knowing they were still near, in sight, comforted her. They seemed to offer both a consolation and a way of escape if she needed it. But now she was hungry and tired and at last she stopped by a fire on which stood a huge iron cauldron, and her nostrils twitched as though she were already eating the savory fare.

"Eh, the lass is hungry; give her sommat t'eat."

The family sitting round the fire, huge bowls on their laps, looked up at the words of the speaker, first at him and then at the hungry girl.

"Wilt eat, lass?" The big man said, moving up as though to make a place for her.

The girl smiled with the timorousness of one who is not frequently offered kindness.

"Aye, if it pleases you."

"Margaret, give her a bowl and some of this good stew. Lass, sit thee down."

Everyone wriggled to make way for her and crossly the woman got up and ladled into the bowl a measure of stew, muttering bad-temperedly to herself.

"More, Margaret, more," the man said authoritatively. "This one looks as though she's not eaten for days."

Yes, she was very thin, he noticed, and hollow-eyed as though she hadn't slept much either; but the meagerness of her clothes seems to emphasize the contours of her young body, the firm swell of her fine young breasts. His eyes gleamed appreciatively—for Brewster Driver was not primarily an altruist and it is doubtful whether a less well endowed girl would have been offered as much as a bone.

The girl saw his expression—it was one she often saw in men—but she was not in a position to make conditions so she sat down next to him, smiling her thanks.

"You're very kind; very kind," she said, taking the bowl from the woman and hungrily stuffing great chunks of muttton into her mouth. The man watched her.

"And from the south I reckon?"

"Aye," between mouthfuls.

" 'Tis a long journey."

"A very long one."

The man continued to look at her and saw how she wolfed her food and didn't stop eating until it was all gone. Then she wiped the bowl clean with her fingers and licked them carefully one by one. Brewster Driver laughed.

"Give her some more, Margaret, she's famished!"

"Nay," the girl said quickly. "I've had enough, thank you."

She could see that the careworn wife was not best pleased at having to feed a stranger with scarce victuals, and she knew how women disliked her anyway, particularly when the lecherous look in their husbands' eyes was clear for anyone to see.

"Now some ale," Brewster said. "Alan, give her some porter."

A tall youth, like the man in looks only beardless, got up and poured ale from an earthware jug into a pot which he handed to the girl as reluctantly as his mother had ladled the food."

"Thirsty too, I see," Brewster said.

"Yes." She wiped her mouth on her arm and handed back the pot. "Thank you, thank you very much."

The girl glanced round at the faces gazing at her sullenly. She had the picture quite clear in her mind; it was so familiar. The lecherous, ill-tempered, heavy drinking father who burdened his wife with too many children and never made enough money to feed them. They all resented her; the children because she had eaten some of their food and the wife because she knew that all he wanted was to bed her.

Brewster got up, a huge man in shirt and breeches, the latter secured at the waist by a broad leather belt. From his pocket he drew a long clay pipe into which he carefully pressed tobacco from a leather pouch

4

which hung on his belt. He lit the pipe with a spill taken from the fire and gazed thoughtfully at the girl through the smoke issuing from his mouth.

"How do they call thee, lass?"

"I am called Analee."

"Gypsy stock, like us?"

"Aye."

"Not that I'd have thought otherwise with thy dark hair and black eyes . . ."

Margaret, thin-faced and haggard of body, made an exclamation of annoyance and got to her feet clattering the dishes.

"Black eyes indeed!" she muttered.

"Now Margaret," roared Brewster in a voice that instantly cowed his wife. "Let us have none of thy jealous spite. This girl is young enough to be my daughter. See, here, Analee," he pointed proudly around the fire, "there you see my fine sons Alan, Roger and John and my daughter Nelly who will be about your age, eighteen she is; and my Jane who is thirteen, and the little ones playing over yonder, Peter, Agnes and Toby."

He gazed fondly at his brood, momentarily the family man pleased with his achievement.

"You're very kind, Mr. Driver, to share your food . . ."

"And wi' so many mouths to feed an' all," grumbled Margaret; but Analee thought, or imagined, that the young-old face of the wife had grown softer, the voice less harsh. Maybe she resented at first the generous impulses of her husband, or the reason for them, but relented after a while.

Analee, invigorated by the rest and the food, got agilely to her feet.

"I must go . . ."

"Whither, lass?" Brewster's eyes were speculative. Analee avoided them.

"I must go on, from one place to the next."

"And how dost live?"

"By a little of this, a little of that," she replied flinging back her head and gazing at him with that look which was meant to be defiance, but which men found so attractive. "On kindness such as yours in the big towns, from berries and nuts in the woods through which I pass; from the clear water in the streams. And then when I can I work. I can gut a rabbit or hare, aye and trap them too, wring a chicken's neck or spear a fish. I can cook them, and also clean and scrub and make baskets of wicker. I can . . ."

"Canst ride a horse?"

"Aye, very well. I was brought up on the back of a horse." Brewster's eyes glinted. "Maybe I can give you some work."

"Here?"

Analee had a familiar feeling as to what the work would entail, and yet his tone was businesslike.

"Aye. Appleby is famous for its horse fair; everyone comes to buy and exchange. A few days work with food and a pallet on the floor. Eh?" Brewster was looking at her hard, calloused feet; between the toes brown, congealed blood. "Not so much wear on your feet maybe. What say?"

Analee followed his gaze and looked at her feet—as brown as leather and almost as hard from walking. She pushed her hair back from her forehead and gave a deep sigh.

"But where are your horses?"

"Ah," Brewster said with a cunning look, lowering his voice, "we have to find them."

It was not the first night that Brent Delamain had kept watch by the side of his dying grandfather. Since he had been so hastily summoned home from Cambridge he had taken turns with his mother, his sister and his elder brother to see the old man through the night.

But Sir Francis Delamain was stubborn, a fighter. He had been long in the world and he was reluctant to leave it. His still bright blue eyes gazed unseeingly at the wall, but his chest rose rhythmically though his breathing was harsh.

A solitary candle guttered in its holder as Brent sat

staring at the old man and pondering his own future. The death of his grandfather would make a vast difference to his life, all their lives. George was the heir. George who had been groomed since childhood to succeed to the vast Delamain estates. George, the good one, the sober, clever, industrious one, the obedient one . . . whereas Brent. Well, everyone thought that Brent was a disappointment.

Brent's stay at Cambridge was considered to be a passing visit. All the Delamain sons went to Cambridge, it was a tradition. But how long they stayed depended on their scholastic ability, and everyone knew that Brent had none.

Brent had a fine record as a boxer, a rider, a hunter and a fighter. But where did that get a man? Especially a younger son who seemed to have no aptitude for anything except chasing women and killing foxes, and losing money he hadn't got at cards. It was even rumored that Brent had fought a duel because there was a long thin scar on his cheek which he swore he had got merely fencing.

Sir Francis Delamain who had increased the family fortune, already considerable when he inherited it, three-fold by his thrift, financial acumen and industry, had no time at all for Brent. His charm may have worked on a lot of people, but it didn't impress his grandfather. Old Sir Francis was a canny northerner, and he couldn't abide to see people idle or wasting money. Brent showed no interest in the land, except for chasing over it, or the army or navy in which his grandfather would gladly have purchased him a commission. He had no appreciation of how to acquire money, or even how to keep what little he was given. He had certainly no aptitude for the study of the classics or history. What was to become of Brent, no one knew.

Now George, his brother . . . why there was a fine fellow of a man. Keen, industrious, a good scholar and what was more, he had given up the great chances he had to shine in London, in politics or the university, to help his grandfather run his estates. And what a success he had made of that! How quickly he had mastered the arts of animal husbandry, forestry and estate management.

No, George was like his grandfather, a true Delamain, and Brent was too like his father Guy, another reckless ne'er-do-well who had carelessly thrown his life away for the Stuart cause, leaving Francis to care for his wife and children and bear the shame, into the bargain, of having a son who was disloyal to the lawful government of England.

Brent knew all this and more as he gazed at the withered face of a man he had respected and feared but never loved. When he was dead George would have all. Though he did not fear him, Brent neither liked nor respected his brother. Where would Brent fit in when his grandfather finally breathed his last? Nowhere.

The candle flickered and went out. Brent cursed and got to his feet. It was a cold night for June and he went to shut the window that he had opened to try and get rid of the stench of death before finding a tinder to relight the candle. From the window of his grandfather's room he looked down on the courtyard, across the outbuildings with the stables and the bakehouse, onto the meadows stretching as far as the river which gleamed like a ribbon of silver in the moonlight.

The whole of the Delamain estate, or what he could see of it from here, was bathed in clear, golden light and Brent thought how beautiful it was, how dear to him, and how much he would miss it when, as was inevitable after his grandfather's death, he would have to go. For George had made it clear that he thought it was time he got married, and that when he did his family would have to make room for the huge number of new Delamains that he intended to breed. Mother was to go to the dower house in the grounds with their sister Emma; the middle brother Tom was a monk at Douai and safely out of the way, and Brent . . . well it was time he found gainful employment, anyway, George made clear, and now was no concern of his.

Suddenly Brent stiffened, seeing a movement by the

trees which began the Forest of Delamain at the end of the water meadow, the great forest—one of few in a mainly agricultural area—that stretched almost as far as Penrith on one side and Appleby on the other. Maybe it was the moon playing tricks, the shadow of a branch waving in the breeze. Brent peered out again, just to be sure. No, he had been right—it was a distinct, stealthy human movement; not a movement of the horses in the paddock there . . . and suddenly it was joined by another. There were two! There were at least two people in the meadow by the river, maybe more. By the height of the moon Brent knew it to be well after midnight, and all the castle servants long in their beds.

Brent opened the door and ran swiftly along the stone corridor to his mother's room. Always alert, as keenly anxious for her son and their future as he, she rose as soon as the door opened and hurriedly put on her robe.

"Your grandfather?" she called abruptly.

"No, mother, he is still alive; nothing further ails him. But hurry. I want you by his side. I have seen strange movements by the river."

"Movements!" His mother grasped his arm—the arm of this dearest, most favorite son.

"Horse thieves, mother, if you ask me. They're from the fair at Appleby I doubt not. I told George that he should lock his new yearlings up and not have them loose in the field, but of course George knows everything and I nothing. First rouse the servants for me, mother, and George and I will hasten down before they escape with all the stock."

"Oh, Brent . . ." Eyes full of love followed him. So gentle and gallant and like his father; so warm and passionate, such a good friend. If only Brent had been born first instead of George . . . "Take care." She didn't want to let him go. "They might have weapons."

"Mother, I'll take care; that's one thing I can do. Even George says that." And he kissed her lightly on the cheek, squeezed her arm and sped down the steps of the great majestic staircase that led into the long

9

galley. The moonlight was bright enough to show the way, though Brent could have found it blindfold in this beloved place. Every inch of Delamain Castle was dear and familiar to him.

He strode through the kitchens, the cockroaches scurrying away from him on the stone floor, and let himself through an outhouse into the yard where he paused and listened, his nose sniffing the air for the scent of disturbance. Brent was a countryman and knew you could smell danger before you could see it. But no, the air told him nothing. Had it, after all, been merely shadows?

Quickly he ran across the yard to the stables. Ah, yes. Here he did sense danger; he could hear the sounds of restlessness within, a few snorts and whinnies. But it would not be the thoroughbreds, the hunting mares, that the thieves would be after. It would be the young yearlings in the field, half-tamed, unshown, unknown.

Brent listened for sounds from the castle that George and the servants had stirred; but there was nothing. He would have to act himself. He grasped a stout staff that stood against a shed and opened the door of the stall of his own stallion Marcus, who had brought him home only the week before. He made a gentle familiar noise so that Marcus should recognize him and not alert the thieves on this still night. There was no time for a bridle but Brent was an expert rider and, clasping the horse's mane, sprung lightly on its back and gently urged it forward into the yard. He turned toward the field and, jumping over the gate, thundered across it.

Then it was as though hell had erupted. Simultaneously from the house came cries and the sound of many feet, whereas from the edge of the forest the shadows materialized into running people, and riderless horses tethered together or single were driven into the direction of the far gate which was open. The running figures sprang onto the horses and urged them at a gallop across the field.

Pandemonium reigned. Some horses threatened to

10

trip over the rest and the leader, who was near the gate, was cutting the riderless horses loose and urging the others to do the same.

"Break loose! Break loose!"

But already several were beyond the gate, having cut loose already. The released horses shot back toward Brent and he had to avoid cannoning into them himself.

"Hurry!" shouted Brent over his shoulder, but already he knew it to be too late and cursed when he saw the useless gaggle of servants rush into the field waving staves and sticks.

A fierce hatred of the horse thieves possessed Brent and he dug his heels into Marcus's flanks. Although it was not his property they had been after, it was certainly not theirs.

Now all the riders were away, and Brent after them, but the riderless horses still tethered together got in his way. He pulled Marcus to a halt, dismounted and tried to seize the rope that hung from the neck of the leader of a riderless group when suddenly a mounted figure swept up to him and tried to snatch the rein from his hand. Helpless as he was, and disadvantaged, being on the ground, Brent caught at the wrist that had snatched the rope from him and held it in a vice-like grip, hearing a sharp exclamation of pain.

He looked down in amazement at the slender wrist he was holding, then up at the rider. He saw bright eyes gazing fiercely at him, a full, firm mouth that grimaced in pain and a beardless chin tilted in the moonlight.

A boy! A mere boy. The voice had given him away, if not the narrow wrist and unshaven face. Well, he'd have a mere lad off his horse in a trice and he'd beat him soundly before handing him over to the magistrate, who no doubt would eventually hang him. Brent tried to spring on to the horse behind the lad but in the effort loosened his grasp on the wrist and, with the cunning of an expert horseman, the boy sharply backed his horse, causing Brent to lose hold completely and fall flat on his face.

With a laugh the boy grabbed hold of the two horses tethered together and sped off.

Now Brent was furious. To be worsted by a mere lad, a beardless youth scarce fifteen, or maybe younger since his voice was still unbroken. He grabbed hold of Marcus, sprang onto his back and kicked him into full gallop after the disappearing thief who had not only taken the horse he was on, but had had the nerve to steal two more as well, despite being pursued!

The path through the forest taken by the thieves —leading toward Appleby as Brent had suspected it would—was tortuous and narrow. It was familiar to him from boyhood ramblings, but he guessed that the riders in front of him were gypsies and no one rode as gypsies rode, especially when they were stealing other people's horses. A grudging admiration for them rose in his breast. And to employ a boy into the bargain— what nerve!

Suddenly Brent saw his quarry in front of him; he was being held back by the two other horses he was leading. Looking back and seeing his pursuer, the boy let the tethered horses go and they halted suddenly causing Brent to falter. As he turned aside to avoid a collision Marcus at the same time stumbled on a gnarled bough in the undergrowth and Brent, without a bridle or saddle, went over his horse's head and fell heavily to the ground. In front of him, the rider hearing the cry and the commotion of horses whinnying turned and paused. When he saw what had happened he kicked his horse and sped toward the fallen man.

Brent lay on his face, winded and heaving, but aware that he was not hurt. He was also aware that the rider was coming back and as the horse trotted gently up to him made no move. The rider paused for a while and then dismounted, coming stealthily toward Brent. Brent saw the feet and the legs of the rider's harsh leather boots, waited until they were a few inches from his face and then, drawing a deep breath, he gave a mighty lurch and dragged the boy thief to the ground sitting astride him so that this time there would be no escape.

The boy gasped and struggled but Brent had his waist between his knees and his hands on the boy's shoulders.

"Now my young rogue, I've got you," Brent cried, banging his head on the ground. "They hang horse thieves, you know, no matter how young."

The boy gave a cry and struggled, arching himself, and Brent's hands moved downwards to pinion him more firmly by the chest. But instead of a bony boyish frame such as he expected, his hands encountered twin mounds of firm flesh such as Brent had never felt on a male body, but many times on that of a woman. With an exclamation he drew his hands away still sitting astride, and pulled off the cap that the "boy" had worn on his head.

"My God. 'Tis a woman!"

He was so amazed that he continued to sit where he was gazing at the defiant face that looked up at him, the dark luxurious hair that now, loosed from its cap, spread on the ground. That firm full mouth, that tilted beardless chin pointing aggressively at him belonged to no youth but a full grown, beautiful—nay, voluptuous even, he thought, aware of her curved hips beneath him—woman.

"A woman horse thief," Brent continued as if talking to himself. "I do not believe it."

The woman stopped struggling and decided on another tactic, having seen the look on his face, so clear in the moonlight. And a handsome, noble face it was too—certainly the master of the house, no servant he, no clod-hopping menial sent to catch them.

"Sir," she said. "I beg you will let me go or I will be horse-whipped."

"Or you will be hanged, you mean," Brent said beginning to smile at such audacity. "Horse-whipped will be mild compared to what they do to thieves in Carlisle. You are a thief, are you not? Woman or no? A common thief."

Analee—for it was she—knew men well enough to realize when a threat was real and when it was not. And this fine lord, this nobleman whose graceful body

13

was sitting astride hers in the sort of position that, despite the gravity of the circumstances, could not help but give rise to idle fancies—this gentleman with his light bantering tone surely didn't mean what he said. There was a smile on his lips for a start and he had certainly settled his body more firmly on hers in an insinuating manner.

"I am not a common thief, sir, but a woman reduced to what I do through harsh circumstances. I beg you to free me for if they know I am caught I shall be given no more work. *Please* sir. We are to leave here soon; we shall not trouble you again."

"But be free to steal from others, eh?"

Brent was reminded how much he had hated the thieves but a short time ago; how willingly he would have given a mature common gypsy man to the sheriff to be hanged.

He stared at the girl and saw her teeth gleam in the light of the moon that streamed through the trees. He was aware of her body under his, a soft pliant body with a narrow waist, full hips and legs spread just that little bit enticingly apart. He was aware that she had stopped struggling and the look on her face was no longer defiant—it was warm and inviting, coquettish.

He sat more securely astride her, aware of the desire in his loins, the blood pounding in his temple and he bent over toward her face until he could feel her warm breath and see the glow in her dark passionate eyes.

He would lean over and kiss her and . . . oh the thrill of taking this voluptuous body in the moonlight, the crude and carnal notions the very thought engendered.

The moment passed. Her thighs were encased in breeches, her body in a thick jerkin.

"I cannot make love to a lad," he laughed and reluctantly released his sure hold on his captive, pulling her to her feet with him.

She was tall and her body was still close to his. He was aware of her round full breasts beneath her leather jerkin, even though they'd been flattened and

14

tied with some sort of cloth to make her look more like a boy. And indeed in her man's garb with her long black hair and her sinuous gypsy body, her dark flashing eyes looking so challengingly at him, he thought she looked even more desirable than she would dressed as a woman, or indeed dressed in nothing at all.

They stood for a moment—aware of each other but not speaking. There was a tantalizing body smell about her, a fresh smell as though she either washed or soaked herself in a compound of herbs and exotic spices. It was a lingering alluring smell that made him want her even more.

"I will let you go if I can see you again," he said, "if I could meet you on proper terms."

"*Terms,* sir?"

"I would not take advantage of a woman like this— you know what I mean."

"Oh I can see you *are* a gentleman," Analee said mockingly, "I'll warrant the first one I ever met."

Of course she was crude, Brent thought, what else could he expect of a gypsy? Her voice was from the south. It was not as uncultured as he might have expected; but whichever way she spoke troubled him not. She excited him.

And she didn't resist him as he put his hands firmly about her waist, drawing her close up against him. His hands moved to her breasts, his long strong fingers outlining the contours of each before he cupped them in his palms. He was aware of her long slim body pressed against his, the impress of her thighs, the sudden sharp breath as he felt her nipples harden beneath his touch. As she lifted her face her firm sculpted mouth brushed his chin, sending a thrill of tormented desire through him, and the fathomless depths of her dark eyes beckoned to him.

Her lips parted and, as her tongue flicked out to moisten them, he saw the gleam of her teeth and he clasped her to him, imprisoning her in his arms. He ran his tongue along her open lips, felt her shudder and

15

her beautiful molded mouth seemed to merge with his like a symbol of the ultimate coupling.

He could feel the pounding of her heart, hear her deep passionate breathing, smell her tantalizing essence. He felt he was drinking from her depths, a cool perfumed libation, an elixir of exotic and intoxicating spices, a syrup of renewed and everlasting desire.

He only broke away because he felt his head reeling and he had the sensation that he would spiral down into a bottomless pit, embark on a journey without end. He saw that the gypsy's eyes were closed, the lids flickering as if she too were in a trance. He stumbled, only maintaining his balance because he still clasped her, clinging to her like a rock. Brent shook his head to clear it, aware of the pounding of his own heart, the trembling of his body, the aching desire in his loins.

"I will see you again," he murmured, his voice shaking. "I will. I must."

The gypsy opened her eyes, and in them he read her own need for the fulfillment their kiss had promised. The look excited him, and he moved to take her, there on the forest floor. Why not? She wanted it as much as he did, that was certain. He had never kissed anyone before who hinted at such immediate and overwhelming passion. He grasped her hand, but Analee shook her head, regretfully, and backed away.

"Why not?" He followed her, still holding her hand.

"Not now. Not here. They might come back."

"When then, where?"

She continued to walk backwards and he followed her, looking for the chance to pinion her against a tree and seize her in his arms. As though aware of his intention Analee stepped back carefully, enjoying the game, her mouth beginning to show an enticing smile.

She was such a coquette! He reached out to grasp her, but she eluded him.

"Take care lest you fall again, sir. This time I might *not* help you to get up."

Analee knew she had to deceive him, get away from him . . . alas. Alas because he was so handsome,

16

with his blond aquiline good looks, the urgency of his throbbing lips, the meaningful thrust of his powerful thighs and his strong young supple body. It was not hard to imagine the ecstasy their union would bring. But she had to resist him, this *gadjo* with the strong, clever face, the suspicion of a sardonic smile, blue eyes set deeply on either side of a straight, broad nose. His thick curly hair was so very fair that it appeared almost silver in the moonlight, and as he had bent to kiss her a lock of it fell over his forehead enhancing the virile, dramatic quality of his appeal—someone, she felt, who was masterful and sure as a lover, yet tender and gentle as well.

As they kissed she had been aware of the thick hard bristles on his lip and chin and knew that this was no boy, but a full-blooded experienced man, maybe a year or two older than she, and possessed of the kind of animal vitality that attracted, in no ordinary way, someone as sensuous and alive as Analee herself.

She was reluctant to part with him, reluctant that he hadn't followed his instinct and ravished her where she had lain on the hard ground. She continued to look regretfully at the handsome *gadjo* as she backed away, but she knew what she must do. After their lust was spent what would he do with his gypsy woman then—the horse thief? Why, turn her over to the magistrate, doubtless, and forget he had ever seen her. She was reluctant to believe he would do such a thing; but Analee knew men . . . and most of them were not to be trusted. With a last rueful glance she turned and sprang agilely on to the horse that stood docilely where she had left him.

"We cannot meet," she said looking down at him, observing the desperation of his stance as though he would spring onto her.

"But you said . . ."

"I promised you that to get away. I like you well enough, sir. I like you very well. Were circumstances other than what they are I would with pleasure . . ."

Analee turned the horse away from him, set its head up river.

17

"Why?" Brent cried. *"Why* can't we meet? I will not betray you. I want only to see you dressed as a woman, yes, to hold you again in my arms . . ."

"Some things are possible," Analee said sadly, "some things are not. You and I are not of the same ilk. There would be no point in our meeting again. It would only bring disaster. Besides, where would we meet?"

"There are *taverns,*" Brent cried furiously, angry with himself for letting such a chance go. "I only ask to see you again, then . . ."

"Then when you tire of me you might remember the magistrate, my lord," Analee said, glancing back. "As you observed, I am but a common horse thief."

And she kicked the horse's flank and rode off through the forest.

"Women," snarled Brewster Driver, as soon as he saw her emerge from the trees, "incapable of doing a thing right. Where the devil have you been? I feared you were taken. They'd hang you."

"Aye, I know," Analee said, thinking how near to the truth he had got. "I waited in the shadows until they gave up."

"And the horses?"

"I had to let them go. They held me back. Anyway I got this fine one," and she gestured toward the mount she was riding.

"Aye," Brewster said grudgingly, "we didn't do too bad. The boys have gone ahead. Well, we have taken eight horses between us and saved our skins."

"Just," Analee grunted, thinking if he knew he'd flay her!

"They're good horses." Brewster turned toward the town. "Belong to Sir Francis Delamain, one of the most notable breeders in the county."

Analee thought of her handsome captor, her would-be seducer, of the light in his fascinating blue eyes. Sir Francis Delamain! She felt regret, but knew she had had no other choice. No time, no chance for adventure here. Besides they were moving on as soon as the horses were sold.

"Won't his horses be recognized?"

"Not with a lick of paint here, a touch of varnish there," Brewster smiled. "We'll get rid of them by first light, which it nearly is now by God, and we'll pay you and you can be off."

"Off?" Analee cried, "may I not move with you?"

"Oh no, girl," he looked at her slyly. She was a fine strapping girl and a good trouper, wonderful horse-woman too. Any other qualities he'd not been able to find out about; she was too agile, not unfriendly, just quick off the mark. But the children liked her, and even Margaret had got used to her. She cooked and cleaned and had made herself useful. "No. We don't need thee."

"You do. Tonight without me you would have had four horses instead of eight. 'Twas I enabled you to make off while I kept them looking for me. I can be the decoy."

"Ah . . ." Brewster's eyes grew thoughtful. She wanted to stay, that was a good sign and yes, she was useful. "Maybe you could be more . . . accommodating," he said, "if I allowed you to stay. Not so quick to be off, if you know what I mean."

Brewster's eyes were always watching her; she could sense that he was for ever looking for an opportunity to be alone with her. Thankfully it was almost impossible to find such a moment, living in a close community with eight children and a watchful wife hardly ever out of sight. At night Analee shared a tent with the women. On the whole Analee thought she was safe; safe enough now to give Brewster one of her flirtatious smiles—a hint of a promise she didn't mean to keep.

"I'll have to see about that," she said, "but then *if* I'm to go it's out of the question, isn't it?"

"Well, you can stay," Brewster said, excited by the bold look she'd given him, "for a while. We'll move on to Carlisle, steal a few more nags." Brewster

19

looked anxiously up at the sky. "Come let us make haste, 'tis nearly dawn."

Analee fell into line behind Brewster; she was tired and dejected, now that the excitement was over. What sort of life would she have, stealing horses, always trying to be one step ahead of Brewster, to be out of reach of his roving hands? But she'd wanted money and shelter, a rest from walking and wandering as she had been now for a year ever since . . . well, that didn't bear thinking about. Even now she couldn't think about it. That was why she'd gone back when the man pursuing her had fallen, just to be sure she wasn't leaving someone else half dead or wounded, needing help. But to have seen him again . . . no, a risk she could never have taken. Men, being what they were, turned nasty when spurned.

And she was now a horse thief, a criminal, not merely a traveling gypsy girl. One who lived by singing and dancing, eating berries or begging food, and sometimes getting pleasure in a dry ditch or a sheltered corner of a field from a wandering gypsy lad picked up on the way, who helped her just for a time to forget the memory of the love she had lost.

Chapter Two

Brent Delamain and his brother George, accompanied by a single manservant, rode out from the huge gates of Delamain Castle later that morning, well after the sun had risen. George was full of righteous indignation, a determination to see those villains hanged and his horses restored. He sat pompously on his horse and fulminated about the lawlessness of the society in which they lived.

But Brent cared little about restoring the horses or capturing the thieves. He knew something that his brother did not . . . that one was a woman. There had been something so extraordinary about that midnight encounter that he could still hardly believe it had happened. Was it a dream to find a beautiful girl wearing men's clothes, and to kiss her? But not merely a kiss—an impassioned embrace, such as he had rarely known.

No, it had felt real enough. Brent knew he must find her again; to taste once more the excitement that he lacked now and craved—an adventure with a beautiful woman, and a horse thief at that!

But she was so ordinary thief, no ordinary gypsy, of that Brent felt sure. He had had many casual encounters with beautiful women—albeit none so romantic as in a forest glade in full moonlight—and sometimes pleasure had followed and sometimes it hadn't. But whether he lay with them or not they were usually quickly forgotten, appreciated but unremembered. Some called him the will o' the wisp of love, a man whose affections were incapable of real depth or emotion.

All the women ran after Brent; he knew it. He was not sure whether it was a boon or a curse. From a very early age he had gained experience in the amorous arts, attracting one bosomy wench after another, usually servants in the castle, until he had the sort of knowledge that many an older man would envy—and this scarcely before he'd started to use a razor.

Sometimes he lost and departed with a laugh and without a backward glance when some woman rejected him out of pique or excessive devotion to a husband . . . But this woman last night, this gypsy— why, he could even feel her body beneath him now, not the nag he gripped so tightly between his thighs. She was not only exceptionally beautiful, she had a lusty earthy quality, a sense of sheer fun and enjoyment that glowed in her healthy face, shone from her

21

clear eyes filled, as he had looked at her, with a desire to equal his own. An enticing, coquettish mischievous woman. There was a vibrancy about her, a need to possess and be possessed that was a challenge to a man like Brent who, though still so young, had almost grown jaded in his knowledge of the ways of the flesh.

This was a woman he wanted desperately to know, an unusual woman . . . one he would not forget. He had scarcely slept a wink all night thinking about her. He was determined to find her.

Had his brother known what sensuous thoughts were passing through Brent's mind, he would have exploded even more. But the brothers, so dissimilar even to look at, didn't share confidences. Their inner reactions to the task ahead typified the eldest and youngest of the Delamain brothers, as different as nature could make them—George dark and thickset with a dour complacent countenance, as though he had known from an early age the importance of his place in life and intended to prevent anyone else from usurping it. This particularly applied to his younger brother, tall, fair like his mother from the noble Allenby family, and with a charm and ease of manner and a fascination for women that George so conspicuously lacked.

After an hour's ride they were at the outskirts of the town within sight of the castle on the hill, flag flying boldly, and George grimaced with distaste.

"How I detest fairs! The scum of the country gather here! A chance for whoring and dissipation and all manner of evil-doing."

"And commerce, brother," Brent said solemnly. "I believe you do not disapprove of that?"

"Indeed I do not. Some of my cattle and sheep are this very day to be sold and a stronger breed of Herdwick purchased in order to try and survive our savage winters. Yes, and I want to see for myself some new machinery about which I have heard for ploughing the land. But the rest of the fair . . . bah!"

"Let us split up then, brother. You to see about your business and I after the horse thieves!"

"Ah, *you'll* have no luck," George retorted. "If I know you you will be dissipating yourself in the tavern and among the women. You'd not recognize the nags if you saw 'em. What is to become of you, Brent, I know not. Idle and stupid!"

Brent's face darkened at these unjust and unfair remarks. Even though he knew they were partly inspired by jealousy, he also knew that his clever and astute brother had the power not only to wound emotionally, but to inflict real physical hardship on him and his mother and sister after his grandfather died. Suppressing a retort he said:

"Shall we part then?"

"Aye, and see you bring the thieves back with you!" George called back contemptuously, summoning his servant and urging his horse up Boroughgate, which was away from the main body of the fair.

Once George had gone Brent's good spirits returned. Possessing a happy and ebullient nature he was seldom depressed for long. And oh! it was such a perfect day for a fair! The smells and sounds of the market seemed to beckon to him. Tethering his horse to a post, he strolled along the streets by the river, savoring the jostle about him, the frenzied enjoyment of life. Stalls lined the streets selling all manner of goods—fine carpentry, jewelry, woollen cloth, silks, ribbons, shoes and gloves made in Carlisle. The food stalls groaned with cheeses, loaves of fresh baked bread, gingerbread, jams, quinces, jars of frumenty, newly churned butter. And the clothes and colors—everyone decked in their best; corpulent merchants and owners of land with their smiling, satisfied-looking wives parading on their arms.

Everyone tried to stop him, sell him something, but Brent walked on smiling and bowing when occasionally he saw someone he knew.

"Tell your fortune, sir, tell your fortune!"

Brent shook his head and was about to pass by the gypsy who sat on a stool by the side of the road dressed in traditional gypsy garb—long skirt and embroidered blouse, scarf tied about her head, gold rings in her ears. Her black eyes gazed boldly up at Brent, reminding him of those other gypsy eyes and on impulse he stopped and extended a palm for her inspection. The gypsy grasped his hand and studied it eagerly.

"Ah, a wealthy man, I see, a lord without a doubt." The smooth well-kept hand was a certain indication of quality, and so was the cut of his cloth and the high polish on his boots. "And a long and happy future for you, my lord, with a beautiful fair wife and many children to grace your lordship's hearth and . . ." —she glanced up at him to see how he was taking these unremarkable deductions—"other happiness too besides, my lord, for I think you do like the company of ladies . . ."

Brent smiled.

"Aye, I do that. Tell me . . ." he gave her a silver shilling and leaned forward. "Do you know a gypsy girl who works with horses? Very striking, a beautiful lass she is."

The woman looked startled.

"You ask me for a *gypsy* girl who works with 'orses? 'Tis like looking for a starling in a field of birds when the hay is being cut. *All* gypsy girls have to do wi' 'orses one way and another . . ."

"But this is a *very* attractive girl, a clever rider. Unusual I would say . . ."

"Ah," a cunning look came over the fortune teller's face, "you would not be from the magistrate would you, my lord?"

"Oh no, nothing like that!"

"But you is talking of *stealing* 'orses, isn't you, my lord?"

"No, no, leave it then. Here is another shilling for your trouble."

Brent smiled again and strode off. After all it had been most unlikely that the first gypsy he met would know his mysterious woman. On the other hand he'd heard they were a close community.

"Wait my lord, wait!"

The call came from behind him and as he glanced over his shoulder the gypsy woman was waving to him. Brent hurried back, his spirits rising.

"Yes?"

The gypsy leaned confidentially toward him.

"*If* my lord could part with a sovereign I think he would find what I have to say not unhelpful." Calmly she extended a grimy palm toward him. Brent took a gold sovereign from his waistcoat pocket and placed it in the middle of her hand watching her fingers curl greedily over it.

"Well?"

"They *say*," she leaned even closer, "that Brewster Driver had a girl working for him. No one knows where she came from or why, but she is very comely and good on horseback. I ain't seen her myself; but those who have say she is southern and gives herself airs, though what she is doing with Brewster Driver, God knows."

"She is his *woman?*" Brent cried with horror.

The gypsy gave a lewd cackle.

"Well, I'm not saying she is and I'm not saying she isn't. Brewster Driver is a law to himself; but he does have a wife and goodness knows how many children, and . . ."

"Where do I find Brewster Driver?" Brent said sharply.

"By the 'orses in the field up yonder my lord across the river. He is a big man—very strong, very short tempered. Be careful you do not pick a quarrel with him, my lord, if you value your pretty face. A *very* pretty face, my lord, it is. One the ladies love I'll warrant."

Brent, bestowing his charming smile, briefly thanked the woman and went swiftly over the bridge and up toward the field where a few horses stood chafing and whinnying, some being led off the field, some on to it. Prospective buyers poked their flanks and looked into their mouths, or watched them being paraded in a ring. Brent looked about him with dismay. There was such a clamor, combined with the smell of hay and dung, that he knew not which way to turn.

"Looking for a 'orse, sir? Fine gelding?"

A small ferrety man holding a tired looking horse by a thin piece of rope was gazing hopefully up at Brent.

"Do you know Brewster Driver?"

The man looked crafty; Brent proffered a shilling. The man bit it and put it in his pocket.

"I do know him, but he is not here."

Brent's heart sank. "Then where can I find him?"

"They say he's gone."

"Gone *where?*"

"The next place, sir, the next place. We gypsies move on. Maybe Newcastle, maybe Penrith; but you can see how few nags there are left sir. The fair is nearly over . . ."

Brent turned away biting his lips with disappointment. Of course Brewster would have disposed of his stolen horses as quickly as he could and got out.

"You could try the camp, sir. Maybe he is still there. Up yonder past the cattle pens." The man pointed to where Brent could see gypsy tents in a field. But there was an air of bustle, and many small carts piled high with goods and children were already on the move. The roads in northern England were bad and the gypsies traveled mainly on foot or by horse, steadying the narrow carts which contained their tents and other worldly possessions. He threw the man another shilling and ran toward the gypsy settlement.

Those who were left gazed with interest at this tall elegant gentleman, with the fair hair curling over his ears and fine clothes, looking about him. It was very seldom you saw such a person coming among gypsies.

Brent stared at the faces gazing impassively at him, dark, canny gypsy faces. An invisible implacable wall separated them from him. What was he doing searching for a strange gypsy girl anyway? What would he do when he found her? For the first time the ludicrousness of the situation struck Brent—what a wild, madcap thing for him to do! This was why his brother

26

George thought him such a fool. If he knew about it he would say how like Brent it was, running after a woman he'd lusted for as he'd straddled her body on the forest floor in the moonlight. How like Brent to put the needs of the flesh before anything else—his inheritance, his grandfather's death, his very existence in this uncertain world. Brent turned away back toward the town.

"Are you looking for someone, sir?"

A tiny dark-haired creature gazed up at him out of great brown solemn eyes set in an elfin face. He was no more than ten or eleven years old.

Brent smiled at him kindly, "Do you know Brewster Driver, lad?"

The boy nodded. "Everyone knows Brewster Driver, sir."

"And is he here?"

Brent's heart beat faster again; the boy was pointing. Brent followed the direction of his finger.

"Where, boy? Where?"

"That was where his tent was, sir, there in that spot. They loaded the horses and moved out early this morning."

Brent's eyes fixed on a long empty space between two other tents whose occupants were on the point of moving too. Brewster Driver had gone.

Analee walked alongside the cart as the small procession made its slow way along the road from Appleby to Penrith, some thirteen miles distant. The small children ran after the riders in front, and Brewster Driver strode at the head of the horse that pulled the cart. His elder sons rode on the horses they had kept from the previous night's forage to Delamain Castle.

To one side of them was a river and far away in the distance the dim outline of Lakeland hills; but immediately to the east were the Pennines over which Analee had come. Sometimes a low bank of cumulus cloud made the mountain range seem very high, and at others the sky was clear and the ridge of purple topped hills, some of them still capped with snow, was so clear that even the sheep grazing on them could be seen.

They had camped overnight by the side of the River Eamont which wove its way toward Penrith, sometimes narrow and sometimes broad. Nearby was the huge redstone castle of Brougham, surrounded by a moat and heavily fortified. The gypsies took care to keep well out of sight of the castle and its inhabitants, caring little for the thought of the dungeons which lay below the water level.

The second day on the road dawned fine and warm and Brewster Driver and his family set off early, while the birds were chirruping their early morning songs, to creep past the castle before the owner and his guards were awake. Sometimes wandering gypsies disappeared altogether, captured by some robber baron who slaughtered the men, raped the women and turned the children into slaves . . . or so the fearful stories told around camp fires went.

Analee felt light at heart and a little song came spontaneously to her lips. The flat, green valley through which they walked was interspersed with hillocks and copses. Well cultivated fields were watered by little streams which ran from the high ground to feed the Eamont.

The sun came up and warmed her back bringing her a feeling of luxury and ease. Suddenly, in imagination she was no longer a gypsy, but a grand lady surrounded by servants, adorned in silks and wearing fine jewels . . . Analee shook herself; for a moment it had seemed like a vision. It was the thought of the nobleman, the beautiful *gadjo* who would gladly have taken her in the forest. But what then? Would he have carried her off to his home, set her up in style? Why, no! He would have cast her aside, or at least . . .

Suddenly Brewster halted and pointed into the distance with his crop where, on the outskirts of a forest, was a large pile with crenellated battlements, gothic spires and a square Norman tower. Surrounding it were lawns and paddocks, a church and various small

28

cottages and out-buildings such as belonged to a great house.

"See, the village of Delamain and its castle! Minus a horse or two, and seeking us doubtless!"

Brewster gave a harsh laugh and Analee felt her flesh grow cold and her heart miss a beat.

"Ah, but we've put them off the scent," Brewster continued, resuming his walk. "They'll have gone off to Appleby seeking us, and see, yonder lies Penrith."

Brewster pointed ahead and in the distance Analee saw a town perched on a forested hill; they were entering wooded country.

No, he would have given her to the magistrate, the tall stranger whose passionate kiss had awakened in her desires and memories long dormant. She had never expected to be so aroused again; she thought that love lay dead alongside her loved one in the grave. Her shame and guilt had driven her hither, pursued by a terrible remorse. What right had she to be happy on a sunny day, to be remembering the intensity of the nobleman's desire, the ardor in his eyes, the yearning with which he begged her not to leave him?

And she'd *had* to leave him, even though she regretted it now. She would never see him again, and it was a long time since a man had so taken her fancy, a long, long time. Though but twenty, in her short life Analee had lived through experiences not known to some in a whole lifetime. She glanced at Nelly walking beside her, Brewster's eldest daughter with whom she had found an affinity. Nelly was a pale, almost ethereal looking girl, taller than average, and with an air of delicacy and sensitivity about her lacking in the rest of his brood.

Nelly was a dreamer, forever gazing into some imaginary world seen only by herself. Compared to sturdy Jane who was only thirteen, Nelly was considered useless by her mother and father alike, having no aptitude for cooking and cleaning and mending on the one hand, or horse riding on the other. Nelly said little, but Analee was aware of an unspoken sympathy

29

between them from the way Nelly's great sorrowful eyes followed her about.

Nelly had stopped with her father, and stood, her head on one side, her eyes fastened hungrily on Delamain Castle which looked like some fairy palace in the haze of noon.

"Imagine living some place like that," Nelly said as the procession moved on. "Even being a servant there would be a paradise. Imagine, enough to eat, a comfortable place to sleep, clean dry clothes to put on. I would settle for such an existence."

"Aye, 'tis very different from our own," Analee agreed, looking again at Nelly, noting her pale tired face—the girl looked almost sickly—her eyes great dark circles as though she slept badly.

Analee, so used to a roving life, never thought of anything different. She could have slept on a bough hanging over a lake, such was her adaptability; she could curl up under a hedgerow with only the stars for light, her bundle for a pillow and her cloak for warmth and slumber until the birdsong which lulled her to sleep awakened her again. Analee was used to a completely natural life and, because of it, enjoyed a rude health which she took entirely for granted. The pale countenance and thin body of the girl beside her awakened her curiosity as much as her sympathy.

In the weeks she had spent with the Driver family Analee had experienced her first period of stability for over a year. Until then a ruthless need to move on, to escape from bad memories, had kept her permanently mobile. But in time memories fade and motion, obsessive motion, defeats its own purpose. Analee had become aware of such an exhaustion that when she did bed down with the Drivers she realized she was at the end of her tether. Now, after two weeks of good regular meals and sleep under cover, she felt as though she had been reborn, revitalized, a new woman. She felt strong, vibrant and healthy, in contrast to the pitiful figure beside her who sometimes awoke her at night on the palliasse they shared in a corner of the tent with her pitiful weeping. But when

30

she gently questioned her during the day Nelly shook her head and said she knew not what Analee meant.

Her reverie was interrupted by a shout from Brewster who halted at the head of his horse. Analee could see a cluster of tents and carts in a field to the right, sheltering below the hill upon which lay tiny Penrith. They had reached another resting place. What would Brewster have for her here? More horse thefts? More sidling glances and groping hands? More hot passionate breathing on the back of her neck?

Analee knew she could not stay long with Brewster and his family or she would commit murder. Her situation was too precarious balanced between trying to placate and please Brewster by her petty acts of pilfering, and trying to keep his bulky, clumsy, repulsive body off hers.

"Thank God we have somewhere to settle for a few days," Nelly said. "How I hate this life on the road."

"Have you ever talked to your father about it? Maybe he would not mind if you went into service in some great house."

"You think I can talk to my father about *anything?*" Nelly said with unaccustomed spirit in her voice. "You think he ever listens to *me?*"

No. Brewster never listened to anyone except sometimes his sons if they shouted very hard. It was Brewster's loud voice and masterful presence that dominated the family, that cowed his pathetic wife and silenced his children, even the gamboling of the very little ones. Analee could imagine the difficulty Nelly would have trying to convince her father that she found her way of life unsatisfactory.

"Then you must run away."

Nelly gave a tired smile, a mirthless chuckle escaping almost unbidden from her throat.

"You think I can run away so easily? He has tied me to him for good."

"But how? How can he do that?"

Nelly's glance was enigmatic, cynical and worldly-wise. Analee was shocked to see an expression of such

31

despair and disenchantment. Further inquiries were hindered by more shouting from Brewster, who led them into the field where the familiar arc of tents and carts proclaimed yet another gypsy site.

Analee went forward with the kind of delighted anticipation she always felt when she saw her own kind gathered together. Saw the rough familiar faces of gypsy folk, heard the Romany language, smelt the wood fires and the odor of food cooking. Yes, she did belong to them; she was one of them. She helped unload the cart while Brewster and his sons, with many a foul curse, were untethering the horses. Margaret got out the food they had caught or stolen and Jane, the little housewife, started to scamper around with pots and pans, while the smaller ones ran off to gather kindling and the older boys prepared to light the fire and erect the sleeping tents, one for the men and one for the women.

Analee had her place in this familiar bustle and set to with a will. She was hungry. On their journey that day they had caught several rabbits and a few pigeons and Analee's task was to skin and pluck them while Jane cut up onions and the elder boys were sent with pitchers to draw water from the well. As soon as it was lit Nelly sat by the fire gazing into the flames, huddled over it as though to draw warmth and life from its fierce, crackling heat. Once or twice as he passed her Brewster gave her a savage kick accompanied by curses, but she appeared not to heed him and simply shifted in the direction he had kicked her.

"I don't know what ails our Nelly," her mother grumbled, her face streaked with sweat and charcoal as she placed the pot over the flames, "she is worse than usual."

"Do you think she may be sick?" Analee inquired softly, helping Margaret correct the angle of the sloping pot.

"Sick?" said Margaret wonderingly as though she didn't know the meaning of the word.

"She is so pale and listless; her eyes are ringed so darkly. Her shoulders are so thin."

"Aye, she is not a healthy girl. Never has been. It was her chest last winter. We thought to leave her in a poorhouse but none would take her as we are Romany people and do not belong to a town or village. Sometimes I wonder she did not die of the cold last winter as many of our folk did."

Analee shuddered. She remembered the cold of the previous winter too and thought of her own thin weak body, scarcely recovered from her ordeal, tramping through the snow, looking for food and shelter and every time despairing to find it. Each day she thought might be her last.

But the winter seemed a long time ago today as she looked at the sun setting over the majestic lakeland hills in the west, nearer to them now, casting its final beams in a splendid gesture of farewell. Her spirits and her hopes rose at such a magnificent sight and then, in the twilight, she joined the others around the fire to partake of rabbit and pigeon, bread and a flask of ale the youngsters had managed to steal while passing through a village on their way. The young ones were always sent off to do the petty pilfering. Brewster thought it good training for them and watched with admiration their tiny, wiry little bodies scampering craftily through the throng, to disappear and then reappear with booty skillfully hidden under their rags. Peter at seven was a particularly adept thief and Agnes at five was catching up with them.

But Nelly, Nelly had never been a good thief, showed no aptitude for it at all; had been clumsy and awkward and looked to be heading for the gallows even as a tiny child, until Margaret persuaded him not to send her any more. It might have been a good thing if she had swung, Brewster thought savagely, looking at her creased apathetic face through the flames, all the trouble she'd caused.

The chattering good-natured calls of her own folk seemed to Analee like music as she sat by the fire in the darkness, her belly feeling replete with the good fare. Her chin was propped on her knees as she stared at the dancing flames, which seemed to form and re-

33

form until they appeared to make a face—a handsome, noble face, eyes gleaming, mouth slightly curved. Analee shook herself and sat up. The picture of the man in the forest haunted her almost every night, driving out memories she thought she would never forget. She got up to collect the bowls—all licked clean except Nelly's, which had hardly been touched. Analee was aware of little Toby's eyes staring greedily into it and with a smile she quickly gave it to him and watched how his skillful thieving little hands, adept at concealment, hastily conveyed the succulent morsels of pigeon and rabbit to his mouth until, in a trice, the platter was empty and Analee proceeded on her way to the water bucket that stood by the women's tent.

Suddenly the air seemed momentarily still and she lifted her head as the clear silver tones of a flute rang out with such urgency and sweetness that she felt her blood chill because of the memories that took her back so long ago. Then the soft, subtle brush of the tambourine joined in gentle accompaniment to the flute, a haunting, vibrant, gypsy dance, that made Analee's toes start to tap and her body sway involuntarily to the sound of the music.

She looked up and saw the faces around the many fires in the camp and observed how everyone had fallen silent as if in appreciation of the sweet harmony of the music. Then suddenly a fiddle came to life and the music changed to a merry jog that quickly had youths and maids on their feet while the older ones sat and clapped in time to the music.

Analee impulsively dropped her pots and leapt into the circle formed by the dancers. Now the musicians came from out of the shadows and she saw that the man who played the flute so sublimely was a cripple and leaned on a crutch, while the fiddler was a robust hearty Romany lad and the tambourine was played by a girl about the same age as herself. They stood near the Brewster tent and, because of the closeness of the music, Brewster's sons Alan, Roger and John joined in, clapping their hands, tapping their feet and swirling with the gathering throng. Then with a roar Brewster got up and energetically mingled with the dancers until the only ones remaining were Margaret, even her sallow face transformed by a smile, and Nelly, who gazed apathetically in front of her neither seeming to hear or see.

But Analee observed none of this. It was a long time since she had danced, since she had even wanted to. She had wondered if the sound of music would ever stir her again. As she whirled, clasping first this hand and then that, the sweating happy gypsy faces passing by her in kaleidoscopic confusion, from the throng of bodies came one that caught her in his arms and threw her in the air then, as she landed, she found her feet stamping time in harmony with a young gypsy lad. Their bodies twirled and bent and spun and jumped until Analee suddenly realized they were dancing on their own, their bodies lit by the flames of fifty fires, the circle of watchers panting and clapping, beating time to the music.

Analee felt possessed as she danced, inspired to surpass herself by the agility and grace of her partner. She was unaware of the roaring, shouting and clapping, hearing only the haunting melody as the beat quickened and the stamping grew louder as she and her partner reached the climax of the dance. Then, as he whirled her finally into the air and she sank to the ground, the music stopped and she was aware of smiling faces, laughing and shouting and furiously clapping hands.

Analee remained in a low curtsey, aware of her beating heart, the agonizing shortness of breath. The youth still held hard onto her hand and then he drew her to her feet and bowed, smiling, his face very close to hers, his even white teeth caught brilliantly by the flames. He even brushed her face with his lips and drew her body close to his as the music started again, and the couples who had retired to leave the floor to Analee and her partner, began to dance, this time to the slower rhythm of a love song.

"How art thou called?" the young man whispered

35

into her ear. She was aware of his warm breath, the beginnings of a beard on his face, his hard supple male body drawing her even closer to him.

"I am called Analee. And thou?"

"Randal. I haven't seen thee before."

Analee smiled and her body began swaying to the rhythm again as Randal put his arm around her waist and led her into the throng of dancers.

Suddenly a rough hand seized her and drew her almost to the ground, a sharp painful grasp of her shoulder that made her wince from pain. Randal was pushed roughly away and Analee found herself pressed against the gross form and overhanging belly of Brewster. She could feel his hot breath on her cheeks bearing the rank, stale smell of ale and onions.

"So we have a dancer have we? An acquisition. I daresay more useful than a horse thief."

"What do you mean?" Analee said furiously, trying with all her might to strain away from his powerful clasp.

"There are taverns are there not? Gypsy dancers are much sought after in taverns, ale houses, the castles of the nobility. Aye, we could put thee to good use."

Analee tried to shake herself free from Brewster and beat vainly on his thick arms with her clenched fist but he only laughed and drew her closer to him, knowing that in the press of bodies under the cover of dark no one would notice them.

"What am I that I am to be put to good use?" Analee shouted. "Some kind of animal?"

"Aye, a bitch," Brewster said his eyes glinting lustfully, "or a mare to be put to foal." And suddenly his wide fleshy mouth came down hard on hers. He gripped one of her breasts in his huge hand and squeezed it so tightly that she would have cried out had she not been breathless and choking with the moist pressure of his mouth against hers, his tongue vainly seeking entrance between her clenched teeth.

Analee suddenly lashed out with her knee, catching him full in the crotch and Brewster, roaring with pain, released her and nearly fell to the ground. Analee felt a hand on her arm and she was being dragged through the throng to the cover of the darkened tents. She was still panting and gasping as she sought cover of the dark and leaned against the side of a van. Her mouth and her breast ached and the front of her dress was torn. She wiped her mouth on her arm and gently kneaded her bruised breast.

"Is he thy husband?"

In the dark she could see little, but she knew from the outline of the body made familiar by the rapture of their dancing that her savior was Randal.

"My *husband!* God forbid. Nay, I lodge with his family."

"But the way he took you! I thought he had a right."

"He would have the right. Tell me, Randal, do you have a tent here where I can hide?"

"Nay, I sleep rough with my brothers and sister. They are the musicians, I the dancer. We pass from camp to camp, town to town making a little money here and there."

"Oh."

Analee felt downcast; her hopes had been high; but here, on reflection, was an opportunity, of a kind, to take to the road again.

"May I come with thee?"

"With us?" Randal's expression went from doubt to pleasure. "You want to be with us?"

"I have to get away from him."

"Then he *is* your husband!"

"No, he is *not* I tell you! I promise we are not wed; but he does desire me and after tonight I think he will have me, his passions inflamed by the dance and drink. I am not safe."

"Then come with us. We can leave at first light. We have a cart and some belongings, for my brother cannot walk. He is a cripple."

"Aye, I saw it. I am sorry. I too have belongings. Look, after everyone has gone to sleep I will creep back and collect them, then I can join you at once.

37

Brewster will be too addled by ale to stir before the sun is well up."

"Away then. I'll take thee to our cart."

"You are sure your brothers and sister won't mind?"

"Nay. My sister will be glad of company, and to have another dancer—why, we could do a good turn."

Analee laughed suddenly, delighted by the prospect. To be on the road again, but not on her own, was an attractive proposition for one who had grown used to company, who needed friends to ease her solitude.

"Quick, show me where your cart is. I think the dancers are growing tired."

"Oh, it will be an hour or two yet. Come."

Stumbling through the dark after Randal, Analee wondered how she could say goodbye to Nelly, the one member of the Driver family for whom she had formed an affection. There was something about the forsaken, forlorn girl that moved her deeply. She would miss Nelly and she knew Nelly would miss her.

After a while, on the very outskirts of the camp, they came to a solitary cart with a roof of sorts and a horse standing nearby. Analee looked back and saw that the dancers were indeed thinning, and beyond them she could see the outline of Brewster's tents.

"I will go now while there are still fires burning and I can find my way," she whispered. "Do not leave without me."

"Never fear. Take care. Shall I come with thee?"

"No, no."

Analee sped away in the darkness, careful to keep to the periphery of the camp. Sometimes her face loomed up in the light of the camp fires and she was recognized as the inspired dancer. People called out to her and wished her well. Then the music stopped and the remaining dancers came straggling back to their tents. Analee imagined the musicians packing up, their surprise at learning she would soon join them.

When she neared Brewster's tents she crept on her knees, keeping below the level of firelight. It was as she thought. Alan was stamping on the embers and there was no one else to be seen. It was unusual for the Driver family to be up much after sunset. Soon there were just a few embers glowing and Alan disappeared through the flap of the men's tent to join his father and brothers. Analee waited until all was still and then she silently entered the women's tent.

Inside it was pitch dark. Margaret was lightly snoring as she sometimes did and this gave Analee her bearings to the far corner where she shared a palliasse with Nelly. She stepped gently over the bodies of Jane and little Agnes and then got on her knees, her hands feeling in front of her for her small bundle of things which she always kept ready, as though permanently poised for flight.

Suddenly a hand clasped hers and she nearly cried out with fright but stifled the sound.

"Analee! Is that you?"

"Yes."

"Thank God. Father is very angry with you."

"I know."

"He says he will horsewhip you in the morn and that you won't be able to sit down for days."

"Did he say why?"

Nelly was silent. "No, but I can guess. We can all guess; we saw him go after you in the dance."

"Well he'll not horsewhip me or see me again. Nelly, I'm going to leave. I have come to get my things and say goodbye to you."

"Oh Analee," the frail hand clasped her arm again and Analee heard her weeping softly.

"Nelly, I can't stay, don't you see? You know what your father is like. He'll . . ."

"Aye, you must go. I know what he is like; what he wants."

Nelly's sobs were quieter and she took Analee's hand and drew it down on to her body so that it rested on her belly. Startled by the action Analee let her hand trace the roundness of Nelly's belly which she found swollen and hard. It did not yield as she pressed it.

"Nelly! Are you with child?"

"Yes."

"*That's* what ails thee! Why did I never notice?"

"I am not too far gone; it is easy to conceal."

Suddenly an awful thought struck Analee and then she knew the reason for Nelly's action in placing her hand on her swollen belly.

"It is . . . oh Nelly!"

"Aye, my father. He has been doing it regularly since I became a maid. My only care is that he will soon start on Jane."

"Oh, Nelly. How you must hate him!"

"Well, it is not unusual you know among country folk such as us, or so I understand. My mother hates it, but what can she do? He used to lie with her in the tent, but then he started beating her until she could take no more. Now he catches us when he can, and others. Oh, I knew he wanted you Analee, all along."

Although Analee was a gypsy girl and knew that fathers did impregnate their daughters, and sometimes sons their mothers, she still thought it a disgusting unnatural custom. To think of the foul Brewster having carnal relations with this sweet, fragile girl filled her with nausea.

"How can I help you, Nelly?"

"You can do nothing. I can see how it is with you and you have more spirit than me, Analee, more courage. I feel my life is over in a way. I care for no one and nothing. I cared for you though. You have been my friend. Oh, I wish I could come with you!"

"Then *come!*"

"No, I dare not. I have not the strength to travel by road and he will kill me. He will find me and kill me, I know that. Maybe we shall meet again—I hope so. I wish I knew more about you now; that we'd talked more. Somehow I didn't think you would be going so soon . . . I should have known."

Analee leaned toward Nelly in the dark and kissed her cheek. She felt such love and pity for the poor girl that she would have taken her with her; but on the other hand she knew Nelly was right. Brewster, en-

40

raged, would find her and when he did he would probably do what she said—kill her.

"Nelly, I know we shall see each other again. I am traveling with the musicians. Yes! The man I danced with, Randal, those are his brothers and sister. So I shall make a living dancing after all. We shall meet again, Nelly, I'm sure of it."

She kissed her and pressed the thin hand. Then she crept stealthily from the tent, all the possessions she had in the world wrapped in a small bundle.

And by the time dawn lit the slumbering camp the dancers were on the road.

Chapter Three

"Go forth, oh Christian soul, from this world . . ."

A single candle burning by the bedside of the dying man cast upon the stone walls the sepulchral shadows of those who were gathered around his bedside.

Sir Francis Delamain, so long near death, had suffered a fatal seizure and the life slowly ebbed from his body as the priest uttered the majestic words urging the Christian soul on its long voyage from this life. It was a solemn group that surrounded the bedside of old Delamain, a solemn and divided group. There were those who thought he should be ushered from the world by a priest of the old religion—Brent thought so, and his mother, Susan, thought so. She was a member of the Allonby family, staunch Catholics, who had been steadily dispossessed of their lands and titles over the years for their faith. His young sister Emma thought so too as she fearfully gazed at her grandfather whose face and closed eyes already looked like an image carved for a tombstone.

But the heir, George Delamain, who stood some distance from the body of his family as though to emphasize his separateness from them, listened with satisfaction to the awesome words delivered in good strong English and not the devilish Latin tongue of popery. The eldest Delamain had always been on the side of the establishment, and George was no exception. The eldest Delamain had sided with King Henry against the Pope; with Queen Elizabeth against Mary Stuart, and with Cromwell against the Royalists, then when the tide turned, welcomed Charles II back to the throne. Delamain loyalty doubled about again when James II was sent into exile and the Prince of Orange and his wife Mary, James' daughter, were invited to take the throne of England. It had supported the Hanoverian Succession in 1714 and had helped fight against the Pretender, Prince James, in 1715.

And so the Delamain lands and properties flourished while the Allonby family, always on the side of opposition, had lost power and worldly wealth.

"In the name of angels and archangels . . ."

Brent was aware of George standing apart—his proud firm stance proclaiming that he was within a heartbeat of being the head of the Delamain family. George seemed already to have assumed the mantle of authority and responsibility bequeathed to him by his dying grandfather as though, in parting, the old man had assured the line of continuity by the survival of his eldest grandson. Had Guy Delamain been here in his place, Brent thought, how very different things would have been.

Brent had no recollection of his handsome, brave father who had died when he was seven, worn out by illness, misery and poverty—the lot of an exile. But the stories told by his mother built a vivid picture in his mind; stories which enthralled Brent and Emma and Tom, but to which George always turned a deaf ear, stepping aside, determined not to listen, in order to preserve his own fixed idea of his father as an outlaw.

From a very early age George had shown himself in every way to be a complete member of the Delamain establishment. He had abhorred the memory of his father, disliked his mother, despised his brothers, tolerated his only sister and developed a firm—no one could tell if it was sincere or not—affection for his grandfather.

Now George was to come into his own—the inheritance for which he had striven for so long; the vast possessions and great acres of the Delamain estate.

"In the name of Seraphim and Cherubim. . . ."

The candle nearly died, then the flame leapt in the air, blown to gigantic proportions by the keen wind which whistled through a door gently opened and quietly shut. The shadows on the wall rose and shrank with the flame and then they were joined by a fifth shadow which stood by the door as the family turned to see who had entered.

"Tom!" Brent could scarcely keep his voice to a whisper and, leaving his mother and sister, went rapidly to his brother's side. Tom smiled in greeting, but put a finger to his lips and listened attentively, or appeared to, his head bowed in silent prayer as the voice of the clergyman droned on.

The old man's hands which had occasionally plucked the coverlet of his bed were now still, his face waxen, his cheeks sunk. His pulse had stopped, nothing stirred. Long before the exhortation was finished Sir Francis Delamain had joined that company to which he had been called. He was dead.

When the voice ceased no one spoke, cried or uttered a word. If anyone grieved for the old man they did not show it; not even George showed it. He stood staring at the dead countenance and then as the minister removed his stole and closed his book, George, Sir George, turned to him and bowed. Only Tom remained, with lowered head, his lips still moving. Tom in his own way, in the Latin of the old faith, was bidding the soul of Sir Francis Delamain prepare itself for its meeting with its maker.

George opened the door and announced to the servants assembled outside that his grandfather was dead. They bowed or curtseyed, acknowledging his succession, and then they entered one by one and stood or knelt by the master few had loved but whom they had served for so many years. One or two of the women, overcome by the solemnity of the occasion, even wept.

Tom raised his head, inclined it again in the direction of his grandfather and then went up to his mother and kissed her. She embraced him, leaning her head for a moment on his shoulder and then she groped for his hand and allowed him to lead her from the chamber. Brent and Emma followed while George remained until the last of the servants had paid their respects.

When the last one left George closed the door and went up to his grandfather's bed. He gazed for a long time at the immobile body, his face showing, by the spasms that passed over it, more expression than for many hours.

In so far as he was capable of the finer emotions that uplift the human spirit George had loved the old man. They had been two of a kind—unimaginative, unemotional, thrifty, hardworking, respectful toward lawful authority. Both cherished a long-held goal; the aggrandizement of the Delamain estates, the glory and enhancement of the name Delamain.

The old man had spent too much time in Cumberland, not enough circulating in the court and business circles in London. George Delamain intended to make good this omission—he would work doubly hard, at home and at court. He was determined that before many years were out the King would ennoble his family with a barony and to this end he would spend any amount of money, devote any amount of time. George intended to establish a great baronial family, a power not only in the county but in the land.

"You have served the family well, old man," he

said in a whisper. "Be sure I will extend the fruits of your stewardship until the name Delamin rings through the length and breadth of the land."

George took the still, dead hand and lifted it to his lips. Then he placed it on the old man's breast and raised his own hand in a gesture of farewell before snuffing the candle and striding purposefully from the room to claim his inheritance.

In the privacy of her own chamber alone with her children, Susan Delamain broke down at last, having maintained so impassive, so serene a face during the long agonizing hours of the old man's death. This was all changed by the arrival of Tom, whom she hadn't seen since she made her furtive journey to France for his solemn profession as a monk of St. Benedict seven years before, in 1737. She had pretended to be visiting her home, her brother John and his children at Furness Grange in Cumberland, but a desperate voyage from Whitehaven to France had followed and two treasured days with her son until the Church had claimed him forever.

Now she gazed at the tall lean figure of Tom, his ascetic countenance, the hollow eyes. Why, he looked like a saint already, though his hair was long and untonsured and he wore the clothes of a sober merchant, a man perhaps of small property, and not those of a priest.

"Tom, oh, Tom." He held her in his arms, his head resting on hers, his eyes gazing at his brother Brent and sister Emma who stood behind her.

"There, mother. There, it is all right. No need for tears. I am safe and well or is it . . ." He stood away from her and looked into her eyes, "or is it my grandfather you weep for?"

"Oh, Tom! How can I mourn that evil old man? No, it is you for whom I weep. My second born whom I have not seen since you forsook the life of man for that of God. Oh, Tom, how has it been with you? You look tired and weary; has the life been too hard for you?"

Tom's face was transformed by a boyish smile.

"Why no, mother! I am weary because I have been traveling for a week, ever since I heard the news that grandfather was not expected to last the month. But I am very happy, both as a monk and . . ."

"Yes?"

His expression grew secretive and he glanced at his mother as though wondering how much he could tell her in front of Brent and Emma. Of his mother's devotion to the old Faith and the Stuarts he had no doubt; but what had the years done to his younger brother and his sister? He knew quite well what they had done to George.

"Is it something you would not have Brent and Emma hear?" His mother saw the direction of his eyes.

"Well . . ."

Brent, who had also been delighted to see his brother, looked puzzled. What news could Tom have for his mother's ears only? What secret that was unfit for him and Emma?

"If you would rather . . . we will leave the room, Tom," Brent said beckoning to Emma who clung to the side of the brother she hardly knew, but about whom so much was said, as though she could not bear to leave him. She looked dismayed as Brent gestured to her.

Tom sensed the solidarity that bound his brother and sister to his mother; they were united; as one. Surely his secret would be safe with them?

"It is just that . . . I have been in Rome."

Brent was the first to react and stepped forward.

"Rome, brother? You are no longer a monk of Douai?"

"Oh, yes. You know that a Benedictine monk joins a particular community, not just the Order of St. Benedict. My allegiance is to Douai. However, I was sent by my superiors on a mission of the utmost importance at the request of the King . . ."

"The King!"

"His Majesty James III of England," Tom said solemnly, watching the reaction on the faces of his listeners to his words. The expressions, at first puzzled then fearful, suddenly became transformed with understanding, even joy, and Susan went over to clasp Tom's arm.

"Oh, Tom. The King! You are serving the true King of England?"

"I have that honor, mother. You do not disapprove?"

"Disapprove? Oh, Tom never fear. We are loyal servants of the same King—Brent and Emma here, and I. All my family too of course, John and Stewart with the exception of . . ."

Susan bowed her head.

"I know, mother," Tom said gently. "You do not need to say more. George. I know well how he feels about our sovereign Lord, King James."

"He has allegiance, like his grandfather, only to King George. He even announces that he will spend more time in London at the Hanoverian court in order to further his ambitions."

"And I am sure he will be successful, mother! The Hanoverian Elector needs all the supporters he can get. People are restless, now that Walpole has gone and England is at war on the Continent. They are tired of the German influence at court, the licentiousness of the Hanoverian Prince and his mistresses."

"By 'prince' you refer to the King I presume?" Brent ventured.

"We never acknowledge the Hanoverians as kings of England; they are Electors of Hanover, Princes of Germany. But rightful kings of England? Never. Anyway, to resume my story. I was sent to Rome as Chaplain to Prince Charles Edward. I am a contemporary of his and the names Delamain and Allonby are well known and loved by the Stuarts. Of course I was loath to give up my monastic life, but my superior is a staunch supporter of the Stuarts and he has hopes that, with their Restoration, the Benedictines will be allowed to return to England and re-establish their houses there. Then I will become a proper monk again. So much does the father Abbot have this as his prayer that he was determined to have me further the cause by proximity to the rightful house.

"Thus I went to Rome just at the time the French were defeated by a force commanded by George II at Dettingen and the spirits of the Stuarts were low. However, since then the French prime minister, Cardinal Fleury, has died and been succeeded by Cardinal de Tencin who is very sympathetic to the Stuart cause, despite the disinterest of the French King Louis XV. The cardinal was once helped by His Majesty King James and is now anxious to be of assistance to the Jacobites.

"So, in January this year, His Royal Highness, Prince Charles Edward, journeyed to Paris and since then he has been actively engaged in preparations for the conquest of England."

"Aye, we heard of it," Brent said dispiritedly. "How in February this year a French fleet under Marshal Saxe embarked from Dunkirk only to be dashed to pieces by a storm in the Channel."

"I was there," Tom said, his grave tones echoing Brent's. "We were on the same ship as the Marshal and succeeded in returning safely to port. It was a bitter blow. The French seemed to lose interest after that and Marshal Saxe was sent to Flanders. His Royal Highness was for sailing to Scotland alone in a fishing boat, but we dissuaded him. He even wanted to serve with the French troops against the English, but we said what folly that would be! It would disgust the English that the rightful heir to the throne was taking arms against them.

"It was Murray of Broughton, who arrived in France last week to find out the truth for himself, who informed me of grandfather's illness. John Murray is one of His Majesty's most ardent supporters in Scotland and, on learning that I was to come to Delamain to see my grandfather, he bade me appraise the strength of support for the King here and in northern parts of England."

"Among the Catholics and the old nobility support

is strong," Susan said, "but our merchant classes have grown too satisfied and rich under the Hanoverians. They do not yearn for the old way of life as we do. You will find very small support here."

"Why, brother," Brent said, his eyes gleaming with excitement. "Let us *engender* support. Let us whip it up. If we have a small active number surely support will grow? We have connections from here to the border. Oh, Tom, is it really possible His Majesty will land in England?"

"Not His Majesty yet I fear," Tom said smiling. "He is an old man and he looks to his son to capture England in his name. No, it is Prince Charles Edward, scarce twenty-four years of age and as handsome, as upright and as fearless a man as ever you could wish to see—he already saw fighting at 14 years of age—whom we shall welcome to these shores, and before very long, I'll warrant you. He kicks his heels in Paris and will do anything to board ship for England; though his advisers would have him land first in Scotland where support is greatest—some of the Scottish clans having been long persecuted by the Hanoverians because of their devotion to the Stuarts. From the north the Prince will journey with an army to join up with supporters in the south and the Elector will be packed back to Hanover where he belongs, you mark my words."

"May it please God," his mother said, bowing her head.

"But Tom, you know how it goes with George? If word of this were to come to his ears you would be dragged off to prison in Carlisle, brother or not. What you do must be very secret."

"It cannot be done from here, mother," Brent said. "This is no longer our home; we are unwelcome here. George said that the moment grandfather died you and Emma would be banished to the dower house and I must be about my way . . ."

"And where to, pray?" Tom demanded, his eyes narrowing. "Are you not a gentleman? Does he expect you to work like some artisan?"

"I think he would have me in the Hanoverian army or the navy. George thinks I am good for nothing, Tom, and it is partly true, I must confess. I lack direction, I . . ."

"What is it you want to do, Brent?" Tom said softly, his eyes betraying warm affection for his brother.

"Why, nothing better than to serve the King. Do you think I may?"

"Come to France?"

"Why not? With you? When you go back. Let me come with you, Tom. Oh, please."

Tom paused and looked at his mother, his face doubtful. He knew how much she had suffered already. Her life had been one long martyrdom to the Stuart cause, first husband and brother, now maybe her two sons. But Susan's head was proudly raised and her eyes shining.

"I know of nothing that would make me more proud, Brent my son. I know how restless you have been; how you have kicked your heels and wanted for direction. In the service of the King your talents can find a home, and then when he comes to his own country he will reward you by ousting your brother and bestowing on you the lands that should rightfully have gone to your father—Delamain, village *and* Castle."

Her voice rang out proudly and Tom felt his eyes moisten. His mother was like the woman in the Bible extolled in Proverbs: "She hath put out her hand to the strong things; and her fingers have taken hold of the spindle . . . Her children rose up and called her blessed; her husband, and he praised her."

Tom clasped his mother's hands and held them to him. "Mother, you will be on your own . . ."

"I . . . I will be with her," Emma cried. "I will take care of mother while you and Brent bring back the King to England."

Tom looked at his sister, grown so comely, so tall since he last saw her. She was a maid ready for marriage, for adorning the house of some great noble. But what future did eighteen-year-old Emma have? What future did any of them have unless the Stuarts were restored to the throne of England?

"You are a noble girl indeed," Tom said, kissing her. "I know you will take care of mother and she you. We shall not be far away and we shall see you are both protected. Scotland and the south of England are well taken care of. It is here in Cumberland and Westmorland that we seek support for our cause."

The silence at dinner the following day was uneasy. Apart from the stealthy movement of the servants, their soft murmurings as they served, no one spoke. At the head of the table George sat wrapped in thought. Next to him his mother kept her face expressionless. Brent and Tom applied themselves to what was on their plates. Emma hardly ate at all.

It had been a difficult day, getting the old man laid out and ready for burial. Taking his body to the vaulted Delamain church that stood in the grounds with the family tomb among the gravestones, listening to the prayers intoned over it. Tom, Brent and George took it in turns to stand guard with the male servants. People came and went, some to pay their respects, others on business.

Now the Delamain family was alone, restless in its solitude. After the last course had been served George motioned to the servants to leave and, as the heavy doors closed behind them, apprehension seemed to hang heavy in the air.

At last George, who had appeared to be warring with some inner turmoil, lifted his head, took a draft of wine and leaned over the table.

"Let us not mince words. Tom, you are not welcome here. Brother you may be, but you have turned aside from your family to an alien cause, a foreign faith. You have forfeited the name of Delamain and I am glad you are known only as Father Anselm. Once grandfather is in his tomb you must go, Tom. I do not want the authorities to hear of your presence among us. They know it already, but there is a reason. Once grandfather is buried that will have gone.

I do not want you another night in the castle after tomorrow, the day of his burial."

Tom seemed about to reply, but observed the caution in his mother's eyes and he bowed his head in acknowledgement biting his lip. George then turned to Brent.

"Brent, for other reasons you too are not welcome here. You are idle and good for nothing. You do no honor to our family name. You are twenty-two, without fortune or prospects. I cannot keep you. I refuse to. You are to go for the army or navy or find some other suitable occupation as befits a gentleman. I have no room for you on my estates."

Brent too seemed about to speak but on seeing his mother's eyes upon him held his peace.

"Mother, the dower house is being prepared for you and Emma. I have told you I wish to marry and to this end I want the castle prepared for my bride. Of course I will not marry until a suitable period has elapsed after grandfather's death."

"Have you anyone in mind, George?" His mother inquired with a trace of mockery in her voice. It was not lost on her son who replied with asperity.

"There are many women in London, mother, who would consider it an honor to have me ask for their hand. I do not anticipate any difficulty. Indeed I am much sought after as a dinner guest and to accompany young ladies to fashionable balls. You may expect an announcement quite soon."

George nodded and sipped his wine, the fingers of his left hand drumming the table.

"But all of you know why I am so anxious to be rid of you. You have always in your hearts adhered to the old faith, the Stuart cause. You are a danger and a hindrance to my advancement. Your family, mother, has brought shame on the Delamain name. I do not care to be tarred with your brush. Would that the Allonbys, one and all, were safely over the water with their beloved Pretender. Tom, you openly espouse the old faith and, Brent and Emma . . . I know well you are with mother rather than with grand-

52

father or me. I want to be rid of you, once and for all. I cannot wait to start a new life."

Brent rose to his feet and crossed to where his brother sat.

"Gladly, George, will we absent ourselves from our home. For it is our home whatever you may say. Even grandfather let us know that, however much he deplored the fact of father's exile. You have abused that sense of hospitality that has always been a mark of our family name.

"As for Tom and I, we shall go, and willingly. As soon as grandfather's remains are laid to rest we shall take ourselves to people who do value and respect us, the Allonbys whom you so despise. We shall not lodge a night longer than necessary in a place where we are so unwelcome."

"Good," George said with satisfaction. "And when the militia come to disperse what is left of the Allonbys, God grant they take you off too and fling you in some loathsome dungeon where you are best forgotten . . ."

"George!"

His mother rose to her feet, eyes blazing.

"I am still your mother, though God knows I sometimes wish I were not, for you disgrace me and the memory of your father. It is you who have caused this rift in our family, brought us to shame. You with your greed and your petty spite, George. I will stay in the dower for that is my right; but I will have as little to do with you as I can and Emma likewise. For if you cut us off we scorn you too. In your own family, George, you have this day made implacable enemies. Be it on your head, my son."

George faltered and looked at his mother as though wondering if he should retract his words. He seemed to be once more the victim of warring forces as he stared at his mother and sister, his brothers whom he had just dispossessed.

But George Delamain—Sir George Delamain—had trained himself to eschew emotion from an early age. If momentarily he regretted the force of his words he quickly overcame such a sign of weakness and, without glancing backwards, strode purposefully out of the room leaving the great doors open behind him. His heavy footsteps echoed along the stone corridors as his family, still shocked at the abruptness of his words, gazed at each other wondering what the future would bring.

Chapter Four

Analee felt instantly at home with the warm-hearted troupe of brothers and the sister, Selinda, who welcomed her to their ranks. Selinda, who played the tambourine, was the most reserved, as her brother explained to them what had happened as they came back exhausted, from hours of playing. Each carried a large bag of coins which clinked satisfactorily together, indicating that there would be enough to eat for several days to come. Randal spoke hurriedly to them, bidding them pack up and be ready to start before dawn. By the time Analee had rejoined them they were all asleep curled up in the shadow of the cart, all except Randal who advised her to get as much rest as she could.

Now they were on their second day away from the gypsy camp wandering around the countryside near Penrith.

"There we may bide the winter," Randal said, "for when the snow and the winds come 'tis no place to be wandering on the roads."

"There is not enough work for us to bide there all

winter," Hamo the fiddler said, " 'tis best we go up to Carlisle and stop there."

Hamo and Randal took turns leading the horse, and the girls walked by their side. Benjamin, the cripple, rode in the cart, entertaining them with his flute. Benjamin was like the runt of the litter compared with his tall strapping brothers—lean, wiry men with jet black hair and dark brown eyes. Selinda resembled her brothers, being dark and slim but only medium height. Her skin was whiter than theirs and there was an air of fragility about her, unusual in one who spent her time on the road. She had none of the sturdy robustness of Analee who swung along, easily keeping up with the men. From time to time they would halt to give Selinda time to rest or travel for a while with Benjamin in the cramped cart.

Benjamin was short, having suffered damage at birth and one of his legs was completely bent at the knee so that he had to hobble on his stick. He had a thin, emaciated frame and his arms and legs looked as though they would snap if any pressure were applied to them. His cheeks were hollow and his hair was sparse, unlike the thick thatches of his brothers, the luxurious raven locks of his sister. But the size and quality of his eyes, their luminosity as they blazed with amusement or affection made Benjamin's face almost beautiful. His skin had the transparency of fine porcelain and his mouth betrayed a sweetness of disposition as though he found himself permanently at peace with the world; in love with life.

Thus it was a gay troupe that Analee found she had joined as they walked briskly along chattering and laughing. Yet once on the road they were busy. There were rabbits to snare, hedges to explore for berries and ditches for hedgehogs, the odd fat pigeon to stalk, pounce upon and kill. There were herbs and grasses to gather to flavor their soups—mushrooms, nettles and wild garlic. Occasionally a lone fowl or chicken wandering on the road was seized and its neck wrung before it was plucked and roasted on a stick over a fire, its belly filled with rosemary and garlic.

At nightfall they sought the shelter of a wood or rocks and Randal and Hamo would make a fire while Selinda and Analee cooked whatever they had gathered during the day. Sometimes they had caught a hedgehog and then they made the favorite gypsy dish of *hotchi-witchi* by wrapping it in leaves and baking it in earth. They would take the prickles out with their fingers and divide the succulent flesh before cramming it into their mouths. More often than not, however, it was a rabbit or pigeon, or sometimes it was no meat at all but a soup made from berries and herbs in the gypsy way.

The other thing they did to pass their time on the road was to tell stories, and here Benjamin the dreamer excelled. They would gather around the little cart in which he rode and listen as he told tales about gypsy lore, or invented new ones himself about those far-off days when the gypsies had come from the east and dispersed all over Europe. There were so many legends about the Romany folk handed down from generation to generation that no one knew whether they were true or false. The true ones were embellished in the telling and the false ones came, in time, to be regarded as true.

They skirted the town of Penrith and its surrounding hamlets and villages, moving all the time across that flat plain to the hills that proclaimed Ullswater and the range of lakes, valleys and mountains that stretched to the sea. At times hills appeared out of a haze, as though floating on cloud, and then they reminded Analee of some enchanted land such as she had heard her grandmother talk of in her far-off childhood. When the sun rose or set behind the hills and the sky was streaked with reds, purples and many shades of gold, Analee would be spellbound by the sheer beauty of it and yearn to be among the peaks, clambering along the narrow passes, roaming through the bracken and short wiry grass or sleeping in some sheltering cave.

At the head of Lake Ullswater they played in the tavern of the tiny village of Pooley and the next morning Analee crept out of the tent she shared with Selinda just as dawn was breaking. She stood by the side of the lake which, it seemed to her, was so large it must lead to the sea for it disappeared out of sight hidden behind the high fells on one side and the thick woods on the other.

There were one or two tiny islands on the lake, and the calm water with scarcely a ripple disturbing its surface was so enticing that impulsively Analee stepped into it wading out until it was almost up to her knees. She held up her skirts and nearly cried at the bitter cold of the water which came from high in the ice-bound hills.

All that day the troupe wandered along by the side of the lake with its wooded bays and rocky inlets, through the tiny villages nestling on its shores and across the broad valley of Patterdale with truly gigantic peaks towering on either side. One or two remote farmhouses were tucked in the folds of the steep fells upon which the hardy Herdwick sheep incredibly found purchase with their nimble feet.

The valley seemed to be the limit of their journey and when they came to the small lake at the end of it they bathed their weary feet and gazed upwards seeking a way out. Although beautiful and fertile, it was an empty desolate place with no more hamlets with taverns to play in.

A crofter, passing the time of day with this curious group, told them that there was a bridle path over the mountains to Ambleside and Windermere but he shook his head at the pony and cart and the sight of the cripple and the pale tired girl. Selinda tired easily and sat on a stone shivering, her arms pressed to her chest for warmth.

"Them mountains terrify me," she said. "If you go on, I go back."

"Aye and me too," Benjy said, remembering the crofter's piteous glance, "You cannot get the cart over there and I cannot go without it."

Analee held her hand over her eyes and looked toward the massive mountain range which hemmed them in. They didn't terrify her; they thrilled her. Were she alone she would take off along that narrow winding path that soon disappeared out of sight among the jutting crags. It was a ravaged, harsh wilderness with the individual alone among the elements.

"We could perish in the mountains and none be the wiser," Hamo grumbled, and Analee looked at him with contempt; there was a soft side to Hamo and, more than anyone else, he was always grumbling and complaining about the lack of comfort.

Randal was whittling at a stick, frowning, indecisive for once. She knew he wanted to go on, and yet he was aware of the drawbacks. He glanced at her as though to say why did they not venture on alone and leave the others? She knew what was in his mind, had been for some time. All that prevented him was the presence of his brothers and sister.

He didn't displease her; on a cold night she would rather have his body hugging hers than poor Selinda whose thin frame brought no warmth. But she liked things as they were; the dancing, the adventure. If they made love she would have to leave, for she never stayed with casual lovers for more than a night or two. If she wanted to ease the yearning of the flesh she saw nothing wrong with it; but her affections could not be engaged. Her heart was ice-bound like the mountains. It was not to be taken, certainly not by Randal Buckland.

"We best turn back," Analee said. "We have not eaten well for days, Randal, and Selinda grows even thinner."

Analee looked at her with pity; yes, a puny, delicate girl with large eyes black-rimmed with fatigue. She was ill-suited for the road, for the harsh life they led.

Randal threw his stick into the bushes and took the reins of the pony, circling the cart so that it faced the way they had come. Analee didn't know why, but the gesture filled her with foreboding and she glanced behind her at the massive wall of rock they were forsaking as though there were something about it that would protect her. Somehow she felt there was some symbolic meaning in the act of turning back, that it was the wrong thing for her to do. She wondered if she should abandon them and go on, press on ever toward the sea?

Randal was looking at her. He smiled and held out a hand beckoning her on.

So they turned their backs on the heart of Lakeland, and returned the way they had come toward the flat countryside lying between Ullswater and Penrith. Their spirits rose as they found more nourishing food to eat, sometimes given them by crofters or a kindly farmer's wife.

In many ways it was an idyllic life in that fine hot summer. Sometimes they would stop in a village and Hamo would get out his fiddle and Benjy his flute, and Analee and Randal would link arms and begin the measured steps of a saraband, Analee accompanying herself on the castanets and Selinda throwing her tambourine high over her head. At the end of an hour or two when the whole village had gathered and some were beginning to drift away, Benjamin would limp around with a bag attached to a stick going one way and Selinda going the other so that the whole circle of onlookers was encouraged to give a coin or two. Then they would buy food in the village and that night they would eat well.

Thus they made their way back to Penrith, the town perched on a hill, so high that from parts of it you could see into Scotland. The great castle in the center towered over the narrow streets and houses, which clustered together so that in some places they almost seemed to lean over and touch one another.

As soon as she came into a town Analee was aware of a constriction that made her long to be away from it again. She hated the feel of cobbles beneath her bare feet, the noise and shouts of those who thronged the streets going about their business. Selinda seemed aware of her fear and moved closer to her.

59

"We know several of the tavern keepers here and always do a good trade. Sometimes we are asked to one of the great houses in the area. Twice we have played and danced at Lowther Castle; but at night we go to a field outside the town to make our camp. Do not fear."

Analee smiled and grasped Selinda's hand. "I do not fear; but I hate towns. Would we could always keep to the open road."

Selinda glanced at her companion about whom she was curious because she said so little about herself. With the gypsy's respect for an individual's privacy neither Selinda nor her brothers would have dreamt of questioning Analee. They knew she was not from the north like them. Like them she spoke in the *Romani* tongue, but her accent was not theirs. At first they had thought she was foreign; she was so tall and her skin was of an olive cast like their brother and sister gypsies they occasionally met from Italy or Spain. But at night as they sat around their fires Analee just listened while they spoke of their experiences or joined with them as they quietly sang the gypsy lullabys which were universal.

They stopped outside a busy hostelry and Randal went inside, emerging after a time with the tavern keeper who knew them and welcomed them. He looked with open admiration at the lithe form of Analee, noting with approval her brightly colored gypsy skirt, her loosely tied bodice with her big firm breasts carelessly exposed in the gypsy fashion. Yes, he thought, she would put his customers on fire. Now that she was more rested, her skin had burnt to a deep olive brown with exposure to the fine weather, and the sun had given her black hair a lustrous sparkle.

The innkeeper grunted and nodded toward her with satisfaction.

"A relation?" he queried.

"We are all brothers and sisters," Randal replied, his brown eyes flashing a little with jealousy as he saw the looks the innkeeper was giving Analee. Almost from the moment he had seen her coming to him in

60

the light of the many fires that night in the camp, Randal had felt that here was the woman for him, the promised one, the *tomnimi*. Because he and his brothers and sister had moved outside the formal tribal structure, and as no one knew where Analee had come from or to which tribe she belonged, an elaborate courtship was not necessary. However, strict customs governed gypsy life and these were inbred enough in Randal for him to want to adhere to them.

But he was always close to Analee, helping her, trying to show his feelings by his presence. However, not by so much as a glance or a smile did she indicate whether he had succeeded or not.

But the way the *gadjo* innkeeper had looked at Analee enraged Randal, the way he'd ogled her breasts which, in true gypsy fashion, she did not try to conceal. The important parts of a gypsy woman to keep concealed were her midriff, her thighs and her legs and, in accordance with custom, Analee kept these very well hidden indeed by her long skirt and the several petticoats she wore underneath.

Selinda noticed the fire in her brother's eyes; she had been aware of Randal's feelings from the beginning. The Buckland family, orphaned when they were young, were very close, and Selinda had often wondered when her brothers would start finding brides for themselves and what would happen to her when they did. What would happen, above all, to Benjamin? No one would ever find a wife for him. Selinda dreaded the breaking up of the family, even though she knew it was inevitable, and she always felt a sense of panic when Hamo or Randal betrayed an interest in some woman they met. Even now they were old not to be married and she, Selinda, the baby at seventeen, was considered ripe for marriage and would be soon past it if she did not look out. A prize no longer.

Analee became aware of the tension as the innkeeper's red face, after staring at her bosom, peered into hers. It had happened to her too often for her to be affected by it. But what surprised her was the way Randal's face grew dark and his chest heaved; for a moment she thought he would strike the innkeeper. And then she understood. Randal wanted her.

But before she had time to weigh these implications, the innkeeper stepped aside and, in a gesture of benevolence, motioned them into the inn where there was a roar as soon as they were seen and a space on the rush and sawdust strewn floor was made for them.

Hamo had seen his brother's wrath and was disturbed by it too. But he put his fiddle to his chin and started a merry gypsy zorongo. Benjamin lifted the flute to his mouth and Selinda shook the tambourine above her head while Analee, impatiently clicking her castanets, her head raised expectantly, her body taut, her feet tapping time, waited for the cue to enter. Then, as Randal, excited as much by the sight of her preparing to dance as by the music nodded to her, his eyes gleaming, she lifted the edge of her skirt, her other hand curled on her hip and made the zarandeo, or swirling movement of the skirt, that preceded the dance. Then his hands on his hips, Randal came in from the other side and, their bodies so close together that at times they almost touched, they went through the intricate movements of the dance.

Such was the atmosphere, the appreciation of the crowd that all, musicians and dancers, gave inspired performances. But perhaps it was Randal who worked the hardest because he was trying, through the proximity of his body, the messages sent from his eyes, to tell Analee how he felt about her—how much he resented the amorous glances of the *gadjé* who leered at her flying breasts, trying to catch a sight of her legs as the skirts whirled and twirled about her lissom form. And then when each dance finished they would crowd around her, trying to touch her with their hands, offering her drink and food.

Selinda, at the edge of the crowd, was aware of the charged atmosphere, a feeling that had been absent from their previous performances since Analee had joined them. For the first time, she felt apprehensive and wished that they and Analee had never met. Somehow she felt she would bring an unwelcome change to their fortunes. Randal had admired women before, may have loved some of them, but he had never quite reacted as he did with Analee so that he seemed hardly able to bear her to be out of his sight. His temper had not improved either since she had come among them. He was short and snappish with them and everywhere Analee went his eyes followed her.

Selinda sighed as her body swayed and her knuckles tapped the tamborine or she shook it above her head in a long trill. She knew that compared to Analee she was an unformed slip of a girl. She was neither as tall as Analee nor as well built; she lacked her swaying hips, the full bust and the luxuriant black hair that fell over her shoulders. And Analee's eyes . . . by any standards they were beautiful as they either flashed bold or were modestly concealed by lowered lids while her thick lashes curled up even more enticingly, if that were possible, on her cheeks.

Of the many gypsy beauties Selinda had seen, none were quite like Analee; she certainly far eclipsed her, Selinda, and she had been told many times she was beautiful. For the first time in her gentle life Selinda realized she was jealous—jealous of another woman's beauty, and afraid of what she might do to the close-knit family with whom she roamed the northern parts of England.

Suddenly Selinda saw a tall, well-dressed man step out from the back of the tavern and join those who pressed forward eagerly, scarcely able to restrain themselves, in the front row of the crowd. But, unlike the heaving lascivious men whose tongues had lolled out and whose foreheads perspired as their lustful eyes followed the leaping shimmering body of Analee he merely stood, his pot of ale in his hand, and gazed at her thoughtfully, his face unsmiling. There was something about the intensity of the look that intrigued Selinda and made her feel sure that Analee and the graceful young man with a fine broadcloth jacket and breeches and a crisp white cravat, had met before.

Then the music stopped again and, as the crowd once more pressed toward Analee, the man, who stood a head taller than the tallest man there, gave an imperious gesture with his hand and stepped forward. Analee, who had been about to turn and seek refuge with the musicians, stopped in her tracks and gazed into the face of the blond stranger.

"So we meet again." The man's eyes bored into hers, but he was not smiling. Analee's heart gave a lurch and she stepped back.

"I know you not, sir."

"I think you must remember if I remind you . . ." he glanced round, his expression now roguish, and put his mouth to her ear. "The first female horse thief I ever encountered."

Analee felt her face redden under her dark tan despite the heat. She had recognized him immediately; the unforgettable sight of his young vibrant face lit by the bright moonlight peering into hers as he straddled her body.

"My lord, I . . ."

"Don't disturb yourself. I shall not betray you. I want to talk to you!"

"But, my lord, I'm dancing. I cannot!"

"After. Meet me outside. I'll wait for you."

There was a commanding note in his voice and Analee found she was impressed, despite her dislike of authority. Her mind in a whirl she turned to join her companions. What bad luck! But what did he want, this young nobleman? Surely not to betray her, *now?* No, she knew what he wanted. She could feel the press of his body as his thighs imprisoned her, the urgency of desire that he had transmitted to her in that forest glade transfigured in the shadows cast by the moonlight.

And Analee had responded. She had almost wished he would take her there and then as he'd wanted to. She was sorry that his good breeding had held him back.

And then his face had come out of the crowd, so different from the coarse, brutal, lecherous faces that leered at her, seeming strangely evil and cruel in the light of the glittering candles. His had come out of the crowd, aloof, unsmiling; but as he had looked down at her she noticed the tenderness in his eyes, the hint of a smile on his curved aquiline lips.

Randal had seen it too. As he came up to them the joy, the ecstasy of the dance, had vanished from his face and she saw it was sullen and suspicious.

"Who was it?" he whispered. "What did *he* want with thee?"

"Like all the rest I suppose," Analee said nonchalantly, gratefully accepting a jug of ale from a serving maid and putting it thirstily to her lips.

"I thought you knew him?"

"Me? Did you see the cut of his clothes, the elegant way he walked? *I* should know a nobleman like that? I'd be lucky indeed!"

Randal looked at her doubtfully. He was sure she was lying, but her face turned to his was so innocent and beguiling. Randal's heart flooded with love for Analee at that moment and he knew that he must have her: an overwhelming desire for her possessed him. Yet he knew she didn't return his feelings; her attitude to him was just the same as toward the others. He would have to find a *drabarni*, a herb woman, to make him a love potion with which to win Analee.

The crowd of drinkers started calling for music and dancing again, but Randal and his companions were tired. Analee had been on her feet, twirling and swirling, for over three hours. It was getting late and they had to find a camp for the night. Analee wondered how she could get away from her companions to meet the lord—because meet him she knew she must. In him, from the beginning, she had felt an unusual challenge; someone with the power to hold her, to make her cease her wandering.

Analee had suspected Randal's feelings for her; he made them so obvious, poor youth, as he hovered around her. She could feel him following her everywhere with his eyes. But she had known many men like Randal, many gypsy lads with whom she had lain for a night or maybe two before going on her way. If she was to stay with Randal and his troupe of musicians she could not allow herself to become involved with him. If she did she would have to leave, and as for a wedding, why, it was out of the question.

Analee glanced round the crowded tavern and could see no sign of the nobleman. Then she saw that Randal and Hamo were engaged in a harangue with the tavern keeper, doubtless about payment. Most tavern keepers kept a proportion of what the gypsies took —some of them demanded as much as half, and it was best to keep in with them or else you would not be welcome again, either to the tavern or maybe even the town. There were still those who would harry and persecute the gypsies, as happened in parts of Europe. She had heard that, in places like Spain, at the sound of the *tocsin* the local population of a town set about hunting the gypsies like animals; they were even rewarded for each gypsy they captured.

Analee slipped outside and went round to the back of the inn. The sun was sinking. Horses were tethered to the posts and grooms went back and forth saddling one here, unsaddling another there where the owner had come for a night's rest or entertainment. Analee looked round and then, feeling conspicuous in her dress, knowing how she stood out among all these men, turned to go back inside again when a hand gently grasped her shoulder and she could feel warm breath on her cheek.

She turned around and looked up at him. He was now dressed in a traveling cloak, a tall hat on his head. He looked even more elegant and awe-inspiring.

"Sir, what is it you would have with me? I am but a wandering gypsy, not fit for the likes of you, milord."

"I sought you the day after we met in the forest and you were gone," Brent said, smiling down at her. "I felt we were destined to meet again, but my grandfather died and I could not come and look for you. Now I am bound for Keswick with my brother, and chance has let me find you again. What is your name?"

"Analee, my lord."

"I am not a lord, Analee, merely a gentleman— Brent Delamain by name. My brother is now Sir George Delamain and, having come into possession of the great Delamain estates, has sent me packing."

"*Packing,* my lord. You?*"

Brent laughed bitterly. "Aye. But my brother Tom has come from France and we journey to our cousins who will give us food and shelter. Analee, I may go to France with Tom, my brother. How can I see you? How can we meet?"

He came close to her and looked into her eyes. Unlike other men, other *gadjé,* the non-gypsies, he was not groping and fumbling for her bosom as soon as he had the opportunity. Although he was tall she did not feel dwarfed, as she too was tall. She remembered how easily their bodies had seemed to merge, as though made for each other.

"I am on the road," Analee said, "with the musicians you saw. We earn a living dancing and singing . . ."

"Then dance and sing for my cousins! Analee, that is a capital plan. They dwell near Keswick . . ."

"But sir, we are bound for Carlisle. To go to Keswick is to turn back. We have just come from Lakeland—'tis too remote, there are too few people, the nights are too cold. The troupe does not wish to go to Keswick. I cannot do that."

"Then come by yourself, Analee. What happened to the people you are stealing horses with?"

"Oh, I left them in our last camp. I cared not for the father of the family I was with. But here, with these people, I have a nomad life which I like and money, so that we can eat well and occasionally buy materials for new clothes."

There were footsteps behind them and Tom appeared, also caped and hatted like Brent.

"Brent, what ails thee? Why . . ." Tom's eyes opened wide in wonder to see his brother in such intimate conversation with the wild gypsy dancer. Even though he was a monk and dedicated to celibacy Tom was still a man; and both as a man and a monk he had admired the grace of the gypsy dancer, felt the power of her supple sensuous body as she had danced before him, her hands high in the air, her skirts whirling about her body, her bare feet moving so fast over the floor that at times he could scarcely see them.

"Tom, this is Analee. We have met before. Analee, my brother Tom Delamain."

Analee dropped a small curtsey as Tom bowed his head. She felt shy in the presence of this stern-looking stranger; like Brent, yet not like him—there was distance about him, something forbidding.

"Brent, we must go. We shall never be there before dark."

Brent glanced at the sky.

"Tom, it is already getting dark! Let us stay here for the night in the tavern. We cannot risk the horses over the paths to Keswick. 'Tis too far, Tom," he pleaded. Tom smiled and glanced at the gypsy. It was an hour or so to darkness yet. Still, Brent was right. They had tarried too long in Penrith. Tom felt awkward in the presence of the girl.

"Brent, I'll go and seek rooms for the night. They may be hard to find if it is market day, as I think it is."

"You go in, Tom, and I'll join you."

Tom smiled at Analee and inclined his head, while she gave a brief bob.

"Analee! Come sup with us! Surely you will not say no?"

"But my friends . . ."

"They will sup with us, too. Say yes."

"Oh, I know not . . ."

Analee couldn't remember when she had last eaten indoors. The thought of the succulent roast pig, barons of beef and fowl that she had seen in the dining room tempted her . . . Surely Randal would not mind, for once . . . But what then? Analee knew of the strange bond that had been established between her and the nobleman, however far apart their stations in life were. She knew that Brent wanted more from her than to dine with her, and although she wouldn't be the least reluctant to give it—she wondered how.

"Well . . . I will sup with you, though if my friends will or no I can't say. But . . ."

"Yes . . . ?"

Brent moved nearer to her, wanting so much to take her into his arms; but he knew that now he could not. This strange wild girl had an effect on him he'd never known before. The tempestuous set of her head, the dark mystery of her eyes . . . Brent wanted Analee more than any woman he had ever known. As he looked at her he knew that his feelings were not in vain; he knew that she wanted him, too.

"When will we meet again, Analee, is that what you wanted to say?"

"Yes," she whispered.

"We shall find a way," Brent said. "*I* shall find a way."

All during the meal Randal was aware of the glances between Brent and Analee even though they did not sit together, but gazed at each other across the table. For the Buckland family it was a new and strange experience to sit on a chair and have your food put on a platter before you on a table. Randal was at first suspicious of the food and asked a servant what they were eating so as to be sure it was not horse or cat or dog, food abhorred by gypsies. Brent laughed uproariously at the very idea and patted Randal on the arm assuring him that it was bullock and pig and fine fresh chicken.

Tom didn't laugh. He knew well the strict customs of the gypsies. He had come across many of them in his journeys through France and Italy. His monastery had often sheltered them as they fled from persecution. What worried him was the fact that his brother clearly had designs on this gypsy girl, and he remembered his mother's letters. Brent had always been wild, as if part gypsy himself. But as far as anyone knew no Romany blood ran in the Delamain family. Brent would never conform, or do the expected thing.

69

He was foolish with women, had been since he was a boy and the first hairs had appeared on his face. There had been escapades not only with the young servant girls at home, but also at school and at university. Yet he was impervious to the charms of the nicely brought-up girls that his mother had introduced to him.

It seemed that where love was concerned Brent had a reckless foolish streak in him. Tom could see it now, and grieve for it.

Tom had the cripple on one side of him and the shy young girl on the other. A very different type she was from the bold Analee who, aware of her charms, flaunted them in front of his enamored brother—surely her bodice was too far down, even allowing for lack of gypsy modesty? To gypsies the breasts were purely functional, for the purposes of rearing children, not for alluring men. Yet Analee would know how the *gadjé*, the non-gypsies, reacted to that portion of the female anatomy. But she was a beautiful woman, Tom thought—there was a proud, almost aristocratic tilt to her head, a disdain in her eyes that he had seen in noblewomen far, far better born. Was she perhaps half-gypsy? The daughter of a gypsy woman and a nobleman, or the other way round? If the sin had been known the gypsy parent would have been an outcast from the tribe, particularly if it was the mother. Any gypsy having anything to do with the excluded member would have been polluted, *marimé*. No, it was fanciful, Tom decided; he had seen her dancing. That magic, that special skill, came from a pure bred gypsy, little doubt of that.

Still, she was a puzzle. She was different from the troupe she was with, that was clear. She was taller and spoke good clear English. Her fingers were long and thin, and there was an air of breeding about her that was certainly at variance with the Romany life—the hard life of the road. Only her calloused feet and her tanned complexion betrayed that.

Tom saw Randal's dark glances as he listened to the prattle of Benjamin, the engaging little cripple,

70

or tried to induce the shy Selinda, who kept her eyes on her plate, to say a few words.

Brent and Analee didn't need to speak—their eyes did that for them. Brent found it difficult to stop looking at her, although as the host he was aware of his duties. He was also trying to seek a way of seeing more of her. But how could he? He was bound for Keswick and then France. He was dedicating his life to the service of the King. What place did a wandering gypsy girl have in that?

The genial landlord appeared at the table, honored to have served their lordships but indicating that the hour was growing late.

Tom got up, looking at Brent who rose reluctantly, his heart heavy. If only he could think of a way. He walked with his guests to the door aware of Randal just behind his shoulder, Analee a little in front of him.

"Will you stay at least as my guests for the night at the inn?" Brent said desperately.

"No thank you, my lord," Hamo replied. "We have found a place just beyond the town up by the forest. We gypsies do not like to sleep under a roof. It is foreign to our natures."

Brent nodded, keenly aware of Analee's receding back. Soon he would see her no more. Outside the moon had risen, as round and as bright as on the night they had first met. Analee was looking at it, too. Randal and Hamo paused to bid farewell to Tom and thank him and Analee, looking up at Brent, whispered.

"Our camp is in the forest up the hill."

"We can meet . . . ?" Brent could hardly believe his ears.

"When they are asleep. Say within two hours . . . I will stay on the edge of the wood looking for you. Take care not to get lost. You will see the cart and the horse in the field nearby. Take care."

Without another word she walked swiftly away from him and waited for her companions in the shadow of the inn. Then, after farewells were said, they turned and walked out of sight.

Brent and Tom watched them go, Brent's heart still thudding from the excitement of the unexpected initiative.

"I see you were fascinated, Brent," Tom said cautiously.

"She is a fine woman," Brent said, then frankly to his brother. "Tom, we have met before. I am very taken by her."

"Oh, folly," Tom said aghast, "but, Brent, 'tis absurd."

"I know it is absurd. But it is a fact. I am taken by Analee the gypsy girl and I think . . . I think she is not indifferent to me."

"But what can you do? She is a nomad, a wanderer . . ."

"Do you not detect something about her, brother, that is not like a gypsy? She has breeding and refinement such as the shy young lass with her has not. Analee is not true gypsy if you ask me."

" 'Tis odd you should say that . . ."

"Then you feel it?"

"There is . . . *something*. Has she said aught to you?"

"No. We have hardly spoken. But I will find out."

"How? We leave on the morrow. By next week we shall be in France. Brent, you must not let this passion, this folly, hinder you from serving the King. It is not the time for indulgence."

Brent gazed at his brother, that good man, that ascetic monk. How could he understand the awakening of desire, the burning of the flesh? Tom had put this aside from him, but Brent could not. However much he tried, the thought of Analee, the desire for her, obsessed him. How it would work out he did not know. He turned away from his brother, his head bowed.

"Nothing will hinder me from serving the King, Tom." Brent stretched and yawned. "Right now I'm for my bed." Tom smiled to himself with relief. At least Brent had got his priorities right. For a moment Tom had thought he was going after the girl. He clasped his brother round the shoulder as they climbed to their respective chambers and bade each other goodnight.

Brent felt his skin tingling with excitement. The town below was bathed in moonlight and above it lay the thick forest. Brent went up the steep slope of the main street and on the outskirts of the town, following the brief directions given to him by Analee, saw the field and the wood beyond. In the clear light he could see in the distance the cart and the horse grazing beside it. Suddenly a shadow appeared from the trees and Brent walked quickly toward it.

It was Analee. The moonlight was behind her, nearly obscured by the tops of the trees, but it seemed to make a halo round her head so that she looked of almost ethereal beauty. Brent gasped and the blood pounded in this throat; his chest felt tight and constricted. As he drew near her she put a finger to her lips and, turning, disappeared quickly into the trees. He followed her, terrified of losing her because she wore a big black cloak and was guided by the path of light made by the moon glinting through the trees.

When they were in the heart of the wood, surrounded by trees, she stopped and turned to him. He saw they stood on a smooth green sward about the size of a bed and beyond that everything was dark. It was so magical that Brent felt he must be possessed by some sort of gypsy spell and he drew her toward him pressing his face into her hair, murmuring into her ears.

Analee was trembling and as her mouth sought Brent's he clasped her round the waist. The cloak she was wearing slipped from her shoulders exposing her beautiful rounded breasts, the nipples erect like tiny rose-buds.

As they kissed the rest of the cloak fell to the floor revealing that she was naked underneath. Brent lowered his hands to her rounded buttocks and pressed

73

her to him, aware that she was eagerly loosening his shirt and clumsily attempting to unfasten the top of his breeches.

With a cry Brent held her away from him and gazed at her vibrant body shimmering in the moonlight. Her taut erect breasts cast shadows across her flat stomach and, below, the thick dark hair of her *mons veneris* glistened as though covered with fresh dew. As he quickly completed the undressing started by Analee, Brent leaned and kissed her, first one breast and then the other, fondling each rounded nipple gently with his tongue until it seemed to spring out of his mouth. Then he bent lower and, half kneeling, let his tongue flick over her belly, lingering on the little dimple at her navel and then progressing further down, until he knelt naked like she was, before her. Analee rose above him like some glorious primeval goddess, her skin moist and glistening with the impress of his tongue, her legs slightly parted before him.

Then she knelt too so that she was level with him and they embraced again, his hands cupped over her breasts, hers caressing his back so that she could draw him to her until his throbbing manhood pressed against her, urgently seeking entry. His hands moved from her breasts to the small of her back and, still locked in a deep embrace, she slid gently backwards, supported by him until she lay back on the soft grass, her parted legs raised to receive him, and Brent, now on top of her, gained immediately that entry they both so earnestly desired.

Brent thought he would never know the depths of that woman sufficiently even if he were given perpetual life. She was possessed of such artifice, such consummate feminine skills that her turning, writhing, moist body seemed completely to engulf him at one time, so that he felt he would be forever lost in its depths, and not care. He achieved a climax of rapture, not once but several times first with her beneath him, then on top of him, then finally lying side by side, her legs clasped around his body. The moon had shifted so that they were in its shadow, but he had been aware only of Analee during their lovemaking.

Now they lay facing each other, the intimate parts of their bodies still in contact, their mouths almost touching, their eyes open, gazing at each other.

"I love you," Brent whispered.

Analee continued to gaze at him, her eyes smiling but said nothing.

"Ever since that moonlit night when we met, when we kissed so passionately, when I merely felt the outline of your lovely body I have wanted this. I have thought of nothing else."

Analee touched his lips with her finger pressing them together.

"Do not say it. It is not love."

"It is love. For me it is."

His heart grew cold at the thought that, for her, it was not so. Was this just some ritual at which she was particularly adept?

"Love grows with time," Analee whispered. "This is passion. It is good of itself. It needs no other commitment."

"I am committed," Brent said, "to you."

Analee turned over on her back and gazed at the sky, dark blue velvet above the trees. Despite the hour they were not cold. Brent saw how her belly and thighs glistened with the outpourings of their mutual passion, her throat and breasts gleaming with sweat. He placed a hand on her stomach and could feel the steady dull pounding of her heart.

"How did you learn this skill, Analee?" For he knew that he was far from being the first man that she had lain with. Analee turned to stare at him gravely.

"That is a story I will tell thee, if we meet again."

Brent sat up, leaning back on his hands.

"*If* we meet again! I cannot give you up. From now on . . ." Analee lay where she was and he saw that her face had grown sad.

"Brent, you know it is not possible. I am a wan-

75

dering gypsy . . . you a nobleman. I must go one way, you another. I . . ."

"I have nowhere to go. No home. Analee, let us go together. I am free. Come with me!"

Analee's face twitched with amusement; the sadness had gone. "And what will your brother say?"

"My brother? He will be going to France. I can stay here with my cousins. I can serve the King *here*. Analee—"

Analee suddenly gazed sharply over Brent's head, her eyes filling with horror. He saw how, petrified, she was about to speak and turned quickly to try and see what it was that had so terrified her. But the blow fell too soon, and the darkness when it came was sharp and sudden. The moonlight was extinguished completely.

Chapter Five

The cart jogged along the narrow road that wove through the flat country between Penrith and Carlisle. The mountains of Lakeland receded into the distance the further north they got and soft undulating hills had replaced the high Pennine range.

Analee lay in the back of the cart, Benjy humped up beside her. There was now no room for Selinda so the troupe of formerly gay musicians had to make frequent stops so that she could rest. No longer gay . . . indeed it was a melancholy group that strode silently beside the lurching cart and the tired old horse.

All Analee could see as she lay on the floor of the cart was the lowering sky, for it had begun to rain and nothing protected her from the soft insistent drizzle. Her feet had been loosely bound so that she could not leap over the side and run away; those who had seen her dance had no doubt as to her ability to perform this feat. They had left her hands free and she used them to pillow her head against the rough planks of the cart.

Sometimes she sat up and propped herself against the side, straining to see the peaks of Lakeland now well to the south; but they were scarcely etched in the mist and even as she looked they disappeared altogether. There was no hope for her, no comfort or solace; no beauty around her, no bright skies or singing birds. She closed her eyes as she once again recalled the awful events of that night. She had seen Randal coming. He must have been skulking in the woods, watching her and Brent making love. Indeed, he had confessed that it was that sight which had driven him to such madness, made him pick up the huge stone and crash it down on Brent's head. Whether he was dead or not Analee had no means of knowing. It had been nearly dawn, and immediately Randal had ordered his family to pack up. Within half an hour they had left the field and the still figure lying face down, the back of his head a tangled mat of blood and hair.

Randal had gone about his business very deliberately, saying nothing, giving no explanations—his brothers and sister meekly obeying him. Analee, too shocked to react, let alone protest, was bound hand and foot and tossed in the cart like a trussed sheep. No one thought to explain anything to her or say a word, no one asked what had happened. Randal had thrown her cloak at her in the forest and until nightfall when they stopped this was all she wore. Selinda had quietly and unquestioningly packed her few things —her brightly colored skirt, her petticoats and her stiff white bodice with the black lacing up the front.

They knew something had happened, something terrible; but no one asked what.

Analee was used to this taciturnity—the instinctive

obedience of the gypsy to the head of the family. They would not question Randal's motives or his right. He was the head of the family and that was enough. Even Analee fatalistically thought he had a right to behave as he had. He had wanted her, had been prepared to court her in true gypsy fashion and then he had caught her making love in a forest glade to a non-gypsy, a *gadjo*. In some gypsy tribes a maid would have had her head shaved, be an outcast and forced to wear a headscarf knotted under the chin, rather than at the nape of the neck as was the custom, so that everyone would know of her sin.

Before her own downfall, her own exclusion from her tribe, Analee had seen—sometimes, not often, because although the gypsy code of sexual ethics was strict, it varied from tribe to tribe—wrongdoers punished in this way. More often she had seen on her wanderings old gypsy women without an ear, or a nose, or an eye missing—mutilations carried out for transgressions committed in their youth. Men of course got off much more lightly; but didn't men anywhere?

Even though Analee was free, belonged to no tribe and conformed to no custom, she accepted Randal's right to behave as he had. Now he was claiming the ancient gypsy right to marriage by abduction. He was taking her bound to the gypsy camp where he came from, to the *phuri-dai*, the head woman, or to the chief of the tribe who would offer them the bread and salt which were the traditional elements of gypsy marriage.

Randal had explained it to her on the night after her abduction. Until then he had said nothing at all. After the meal he had motioned to the others to leave him and Analee alone and then he had squatted on his haunches, stirring the embers of the fire with a long stick while Analee, hands free but feet firmly bound, sat helplessly before him.

"You knew I wanted you, Analee. I had never wanted a woman like you . . ."

Analee said nothing at first, her eyes smouldering like the embers of the fire. She wanted Randal to know with what contempt she regarded him and what

78

he had done. But he just squatted there stirring the burning wood, his dark, lean face reflective.

"So you take me by force . . ."

"It is the only way. The *phuri-dai* will have to marry us because I have captured you for my bride. If the *phuri-dai* knows you have lain with a *gadjo* your head will be shaved, maybe your nose cut off."

Analee shuddered. Not only had she seen its effects, she had seen it done. One swift stroke . . . Analee was proud of her beauty. Randal she might one day be able to get rid of; but a lost nose or an ear or an eye could never be recovered.

"You know I will not be happy with you, Randal. Why don't you let me go? I have been free for so long, on my own. I belong to no tribe . . ."

"You do now," Randal said firmly. "You belong to me. I have captured you."

With that he got up and stamped out the fire, then went to join the others. Analee had lain down where she was and tried to sleep, aware of the family coming back and bedding down for the night, of the watchful eye of Randal or Hamo gazing at her every time the bonds cramped and she woke.

The cart rolled on and Randal and Hamo steadied it on either side, taking care to see that Benjy was alright, but having no regard for her at all. She was a chattel, a piece of merchandise tied with string. Even Benjy gazed at her with contempt and Selinda avoided her altogether. She had lain with a *gadjo*—she had committed grave sin. They knew it, somehow they knew it.

On the third day they came to the camp outside the old town of Carlisle not far from the Scottish border. This was where the Buckland family had its roots. In so far as they had a home this was their home. Those too old to travel lived here permanently and the young ones came and went.

In the distance, as they approached the camp, Analee could see the smoke rising from the many fires, the tents and one or two wooden huts that gave the nomadic camp an air of permanence. Usually when

79

Analee saw a gypsy settlement she felt a sense of belonging, of homecoming—a rest from her wearisome wandering, a reminder of former, happier days. But now she looked at it with terror. What would happen? Would Randal, full of vengeance, report her misdeeds? She would be taken before the *kriss,* an assembly of the elders who meted out justice, and without a doubt she would be punished. No, at best all she could hope for was marriage to a man she didn't love, who had killed her lover, or at least maimed him.

Brent. How often had Analee thought of Brent during that slow tedious journey along the narrow road. They had been attracted from the beginning, and it was fitting that they had come together in the moonlight, in a forest like they had first met. She thought of the way their bodies had fused and melted and, although she had known many men, she had never had an experience that gave her such an overpowering sense of belonging, of the realization of ultimate satisfaction.

She had known that it was meant she and Brent should make love and in her heart, even now when it seemed hopeless, she had a feeling she would see him again and that it would happen again. How this would be achieved she knew not. It was the power of her gypsy's second sight, a gift she knew she possessed. She had known that she would wander and then there would be a time of great difficulty, a dark cloud in her life. Then she would be happy again. All this she knew, but how and why were veiled from her.

This was the time of the dark cloud. How long would it last?

As Randal and Hamo led the cart into the camp, ragged children ran toward them, hands were raised in greeting. Some called out. One or two looked curiously into the cart. Randal neither smiled nor responded to greetings but, with his face set, led the horse to the large tent that stood in the center of the field. Outside a swarm of children played happily and women bustled backward and forward between tents and fires preparing the midday meal. The men were busy mending pots and pans, or grooming beyond recognition for resale horses they had either stolen or bought very cheaply. Outside the large tent an old woman sat puffing a clay pipe and beside her sat a man younger than her by many years, but old just the same. Randal left the cart where it was before the tent and with Hamo went over to speak to the couple sitting outside. The old woman's toothless mouth cracked in a joyful grin and her hands reached up to clasp and embrace him. Then they listened carefully while he pointed to the cart where Analee sat alone. Benjy had been helped down by his brother and was now hobbling toward the large tent where he was also greeted and embraced. Then the old man got stiffly to his feet and leaning on a stick walked slowly with Randal over to the cart. He gazed at Analee, saying nothing, then he chuckled. "You have captured yourself a fine bride, son. Well . . . does she consent?"

He spoke in *Romani* and Analee caught the nuance in his voice. Randal didn't reply but looked at her. Analee thought of the face without a nose, the hideous one-eyed crones . . . She nodded.

"Good."

The man seemed satisfied and Randal's face relaxed. He smiled at Analee and helped her out of the cart. She stood cramped on her tied legs, unable to move and Randal picked her up and carried her over to the tent placing her roughly on the ground in front of the tent, almost throwing her in fact.

"This is Rebecca . . . the *phuri-dai*," he said motioning to the old woman. "This is Lancelot her son. My father Rander Buckland was married to Lancelot's daughter's sister-in-law. We are all Bucklands and all related. Lancelot is the head man of the tribe."

Analee nodded she had understood and tried to sit up. Her legs were stiff. The old woman was looking at her enigmatically—not unsympathetically, but in a way Analee didn't completely understand.

"Untie her, Randal," Lancelot said. "You have her consent."

"Oh, she has consented?" the old woman said in a voice firm despite her years.

"She nodded," Lancelot said, "when I asked her if she consented."

"You must hear her say it," Rebecca said. "Then we have her bond and can untie her feet."

"Do you consent to be the bride of Randal Buckland who has claimed this right by capture?" Lancelot intoned solemnly. Again Randal looked at Analee, his face impassive, his chin tilted, his stance proud. It made him feel a man to have captured Analee, like a gypsy brigand of old. Even though he had tied her up and had given her no chance she was still his by right of capture. Forced capture. She was reluctant, Randal knew. How she must hate him. Her eyes burned with resentment and her nostrils flared like a horse that refuses to be broken in. He had seen that stubborn refusal before in the eyes of an untamed horse; but he tamed them in the end. Oh yes, he did; and I think it was sweet to see how meekly they submitted—as Analee would to him. In his mind's eye he could see her body glistening in the moonlight responding to the demands of the *gadjo,* giving willingly of herself. His eyes grew bright with desire at the memory of the sight—which mentally he had dwelt on many times. Analee was a fitting prize to capture—stubborn, untamed, but—oh—what booty for the man who lay with her.

"You must say it, woman. Say the words," Lancelot said. Analee looked at Randal, at Hamo, at Benjy . . . they all gazed stonily at her. Even Selinda had no pity in her eyes . . . She had sinned with a *gadjo*. If the tribe knew she would have her hair cut off, at least, perhaps worse . . . Analee saw the look in their eyes, the unified hostility and knew they would all condemn her. She fingered her nose . . . "I consent," she said.

All those who had gathered around to witness the strange ceremony clapped and shouted. The expression in Randal's eyes and that of his family changed from suspicion and hostility to relief, even to gladness.

She had submitted. There would be no more trouble from Analee now.

"Let us have the bread and salt at once," Randal said bending to untie Analee's legs, "and we can be wed." Rebecca looked surprised.

"You wish it so? You do not wish a proper gypsy wedding with dancing and feasting?"

"We can feast later," Randal said laughing, chafing Analee's ankles to make the blood run through. "Now that I have this prize I do not want her to escape me again!"

Analee, astounded, gazed at Randal. How could this man force her into a marriage when he had hardly spoken a civil word to her in days? Randal who had been so kind before, so adoring, seemed to hate her . . . but he wanted her, she knew that. He had seen her make love in the moonlight; goodness knows how long he had watched, maybe he'd seen everything. He'd been inflamed. Randal wanted her as Brent had. All men were the same. Well, it might as well be got over. There was an inevitability about it. Marriage to Randal would not be forever; she knew that. Her second sight had told her that this was just a dark cloud, a bad time. One day the cloud would pass and the sun would shine again . . . and Analee, the wandering gypsy, would be free.

The gypsies in the camp were excited by the unexpected news of a wedding and immediately ceased the tasks in which they were engaged to run to the tent of the *phuri-dai* who would perform the marriage. Most of them had seen Randal and his family come in with the cart, and many had seen Analee unceremoniously taken out from it, her feet bound, and dumped on the ground in front of Rebecca.

It was a long time since there had been a marriage by capture in the camp. What they did not know was whether the captured bride was willing or unwilling. If she were willing it meant that she and her *tomnimi*, her betrothed, had met secretly, had been denied permission to marry by her father. The man had thus made a show of forcing her, but in fact she had gone willingly to stay a while with him and consummate their union. Now the marriage would consecrate this physical union that had already occurred, and then the bride and groom would return to the girl's father and a reconciliation would take place. But if the bride were reluctant, if she had been forced against her will, then after the wedding the bridegroom would do his best to woo her, to win her love—for true love was an essential element in gypsy lore. He would go to the *cohani*, the sorceress, and obtain from her spells to win the heart of his captured bride.

Now, as they hurried to the tent looking forward to the feasting and dancing that would take place later in the day, the tribe did not know what was the case with the bride that Randal Buckland had brought home tethered in a cart.

Although Lancelot was the leader of the tribe, the undisputed head was his mother Rebecca, the *phuri-dai*. She did not know how old she was, but some thought over a hundred years of age. She, his mother, knew how old Lancelot was and he was nearly eighty. She was said to be able to remember as far back as the Civil War and the execution of the King and that was nearly a hundred years ago.

Rebecca had held dominance over the Buckland tribe gathered outside Carlisle for so many years that there were few who did not remember her as *phuri-dai*, even the very old ones. In her youth she had been a great beauty, something of a *cohani* herself, a weaver of magic spells, a fortune-teller of reknown. She had been married three times, all to members of her own tribe—maybe more, she couldn't remember—and she had had fifteen children, at least; she couldn't be quite sure of that now.

Everyone in the tribe was related to her one way or another and as she waited, a new rug around her shoulders for the ceremony she was about to perform, her old eyes still bright, still piercing, noted where everyone was and what they were doing.

Rebecca, in her long life had seen many enforced

marriages—and knew every variation of betrothal and marriage within gypsy lore. She had seen willing brides and reluctant brides, passionate brides and those whose feelings toward their husbands were cold. On the whole gypsies wanted warm romantic love to bless the marriages but, being human, Rebecca knew you could not always have what you wanted.

Randal's bride, she had known from the moment her wise old eyes saw her tossed on the ground, was very reluctant, very unwilling. Randal may perhaps have done better to have thought again; but she knew what Randal was—headstrong, a law unto himself. He had wanted this woman and he had captured her. God knew from where. She looked foreign; she was so tall that Rebecca felt she could not possibly have hailed from these parts where the women were medium or small in height. Maybe not even from England. She had a glowing olive skin and dangerous-looking dark eyes. She was a beauty alright; but she would give Randal a bad time if she wanted to.

Soon he would come to her or to Reyora, the *cohani,* and ask for spells to bind his bride to him. Rebecca slowly shook her head. Even strong spells would be difficult to tame that one, she thought.

Standing quietly by the tent Analee too was watching the preparations, noting how everyone put down what they were doing and hurried to where the old *phuri-dai* was sitting. And the *phuri-dai,* she saw, was watching her—an old, old wise-looking woman, and shaking her head.

She thought she saw sympathy in those knowing old eyes, friendliness and, for the first time for days, Analee lifted her head and smiled. Rebecca seemed to nod her head as though she understood, and then she turned to take the bowl of salt and the large piece of bread offered her by a young boy of the tribe, one of her great-grandsons she thought.

Suddenly the babel of noise stopped at a signal from Lancelot and everyone was quiet; nothing moved except the tops of the trees, beside the field, which rustled gently in the breeze. Autumn was in the air; one or two of the leaves were falling already. Winter came early in these parts. Rebecca nodded at Randal who stepped over from where he had been standing with his brothers and sister and held out his hand to Analee. Analee stared at him, her face a stubborn mask.

"You have consented," Randal murmured menacingly under his breath and slowly she put out a hand and took his. Then he led her before the *phuri-dai* where they both knelt, hands clasped.

Rebecca leaned forward, her bent arthritic hands carefully breaking into two halves the large piece of freshly baked bread. Then from the bowl held by the boy she took salt and, sprinkling it on to each of the two pieces, gave one first to Randal then one to Analee. At the same time she murmured according to custom, "When you are tired of this bread and this salt you will be tired of each other."

Analee took the bread and gazed at it for a long time, then at a nudge from Randal she gave her piece to him and took his.

"Eat," Rebecca commanded and she watched over them as they consumed the bread and salt.

Then she took a pitcher handed to her by Lancelot and poured over the heads of the kneeling couple grains of wheat that had been freshly gathered in the harvest. When she had finished and the newly married couple, the yellow grains spilling all over their dark hair and bright clothes, still knelt before her she gave the pitcher to Lancelot who dashed it to the ground, keeping the handle for himself. Then the boy who had helped to officiate in the ceremony carefully picked up the broken pieces, gave one each to the bride and groom and handed the rest to Randall's family and those who, nearest the couple, eagerly reached out for these good luck symbols.

It was over. A babble of voices broke out and Randal helped his bride to her feet, dusting the grains off his clothes, shaking his black curly hair. He smiled at Analee but she looked coldly past him at the *phuri-*

dai because she had sensed that the wise old woman knew she was married against her will.

Then a man stepped forward and held up his hands. This was Sacki the son of Lancelot, grandson of Rebecca and father of young Gilderoy who had helped his great-grandmother with the ceremony. Most of Lancelot's sons were now dispersed over the kingdom, but Sacki had remained in the camp to help control tribal order. As a boy he had been forced into the army and had the lower part of his leg shot off at Malplaquet when Marlborough and Prince Eugene defeated the French in one of the wars of the Spanish Succession—though little did Sacki Buckland, a boy of 14, know what the war was about or who was in command. He was lucky to come home alive. The gypsies, being considered the lowest of the low even in the scum of the army, were not deemed fit to treat and were normally left to die where they fell. It was only because the leg was clean shot off and one of his fellow gypsies had applied a tourniquet to staunch the blood that Sacki had lived to tell the tale. In fact his life had surely been saved by the brotherhood of gypsies who had spirited him away from the army and nursed him in France until, on a makeshift wooden stump, he was fit to return home.

Sacki had a loud firm voice which seemed to make up for his physical disability and everyone stopped talking and listened to him.

"Now that we have Randal and his bride married according to our law we shall gather in the afternoon for feasting and dancing. So hasten to your tents and make preparations."

The throng cheered and smiled and, breaking up, some gathered round Randal and shook his hand or clasped his shoulder. Few took notice of Analee—the men because it was not allowed to ogle a new bride and the women because they knew that, to have been married in such a fashion and so quickly, she had offended against gypsy honor—she had lain with Randal and could not be a virgin. She was *marimé*, unclean, a woman to be scorned and pitied even among themselves. So they moved away looking at her over their backs and one or two made signs to her that meant they despised her.

Analee saw the dark glances and knew the reason for them. She knew how much the gypsy women enjoyed a conventional wedding where everything was agreed beforehand, the bride known and preferably a member of the tribe. They would enjoy preparing her for days, making her clothes and gradually building up to the climax which was the wedding ceremony and the feast. But the focus of interest, above all, was the physical union of the man and woman which took place during the feast in a tent set aside for the purpose.

The ceremony of the *dichlo,* the official deflowering of the bride, was an essential part of the gypsy marriage ritual and it was enjoyed the more by those who had undergone the humiliation of it rather than by those for whom it was yet to come. At a sign from the new husband four matrons would go into the tent to inspect the newly deflowered bride, and emerge bearing a white silk handkerchief soaked in her virginal blood which they would take round for the inspection of the members of the tribe gathered outside.

Analee thought the ceremony of the *dichlo* was disgusting and degrading and she did not regret that on her wedding day it would not be performed, even if the women slunk away pretending to despise her because she was *marimé,* unclean. They thought she and Randal already had carnal knowledge of each other. What would they have thought if it was revealed that her most recent experience with a man was with a *gadjo,* a non-gypsy—and scarcely a week before at that!

Analee suddenly recalled to mind Brent and the way he had lain. He must have been dead or mortally wounded. How long ago it all seemed, how trivial life was for events of such importance to be over and others to happen so quickly. Within a week she had made love to a *gadjo* and married a full-blooded gypsy, a member of a tribe.

So be it. She would bide with him as long as was necessary; she would be a wife to him because she had promised; she had eaten the salt and the broken bread and seen the pitcher smashed to smithereens. In gypsy symbolism this meant she was bound to respect him for as many years as the vase had been reduced to pieces. Seven pieces she'd counted—seven years. Was it possible that she could live with a man who had forcibly wed her for seven long years?

For the rest of the day the camp resounded to laughter and the sound of voices raised in song. A wedding was a good thing and even a reluctant bride—and she clearly had been, anyone could see that by the way she never looked at her husband all during the ceremony—better than no bride at all. Randal was popular and they wished he had found someone who obviously loved him. But beautiful as his bride was she was foreign-looking and proud. The women could see that the men secretly admired her and they despised her the more that she had given herself easily, that she was no virgin, *marimé*. Pah! Well maybe the *cohani* would give Randal a potion and his bride would fall madly in love with him. It had happened.

The *phuri-dai* took the newly wedded pair into her tent and they drank ale or herbal teas. The men gathered on one side and the women on the other. No one talked to Analee; few even looked at her.

Then the curtain over the tent parted and a woman came in and everyone momentarily stopped talking. The woman looked at Randal and then, for a long time, letting her gaze linger, at Analee. Then she went over to talk to Rebecca. Analee knew without doubt that this was the *cohani*—she could tell by the way that her eyes turned up like those of a bird and the peculiar intensity of her gaze as she stared at Analee; also by the way everyone stepped respectfully aside for her to pass.

The *cohani* could exercise magic for good or ill; she could tell fortunes, weave spells and provide potions. She could cure and she could kill. Every tribe had a *cohani*—someone who from girlhood had developed special skills, learning the craft, often from their mothers or a near relative.

Some said that, while still in her childhood, a demon had penetrated her as she slept and when the girl awoke she was aware of her special powers and that she was *cohani*.

In her youth many had considered Analee to be *cohani*—they had sworn she had magical powers and, in fact, she knew that she had the gift of second sight and that sometimes things which she said would happen, did. But she knew she was not a real *cohani*— she knew a lot about herbs and spells having learned about them from her grandmother. She had the gypsy's respect for the influence of the *cohani* and especially for her prowess when she was also *drabarni*, a woman skilled in the medicinal use of herbs. In some tribes one woman was both *cohani* and *drabarni;* in others they were different—the *cohani* was primarily concerned with black magic and with evil, the *drabarni* with good.

Reyora the *cohani* was a great-grandmother of Rebecca and she had learned many of her powers from her great-grandmother and assumed her mantle when Rebecca grew too old. She was the daughter of Rebecca's grandson Spartus and she had married her first cousin Wester Buckland, the son of Rebecca's granddaughter Zia.

Everyone had known from her early childhood that Reyora had *cohani* powers like her great-grandmother. She had known so much about potions and spells and had saved a new-born baby from death merely by incantation. People came to fear Reyora because she could exercise her gifts both for good and ill; they took care not to cross her path.

When Reyora married it was well known she had chosen Wester Buckland and that he wanted to marry someone else. He was even *tomnani*, betrothed, and then his beautiful bride-to-be, a big strong healthy girl, suddenly sickened for no apparent reason and died. Reyora had been asked to help her, but she would do nothing and even Rebecca, who was *cohani* until a very advanced age, would not interfere.

Wester was terror-stricken when his *tomnani* died so young, so unexpectedly, and he immediately took Reyora for his bride, as she wished, however reluctantly. Reyora was not beautiful, not good-looking even by gypsy standards; but she was not ugly like many *cohani*—she was arresting, with her slanted eyes and the quiet determined way she had of moving like a bird of prey about to strike its victim. Reyora was now thirty-three.

As soon as she entered the tent and looked at Analee she realized she was not in love with Randal, that she had not wished to marry him and that she bore a grudge against him and his tribe. Reyora had four sons and no daughter which was a disappointment to her because she would have liked the *cohani* powers to have continued in her branch of the family. Try as she had to weave the right spell she had been unsuccessful in bringing a daughter to herself and Wester.

After talking to Rebecca and greeting her relations and Randal, Reyora walked slowly over to Analee and smiled at her, the first person, the first woman to show her kindness apart from Rebecca, since she had come to the camp.

"How are you called?" Reyora said softly, seeing the fear and the despair in Analee's eyes.

"Analee."

"I am the *cohani*."

"I know."

Reyora smiled a mysterious smile, aware that her powers had been instantly recognized by someone who, Reyora sensed, had some *cohani* gifts herself.

"I am called Reyora. Rebecca is my great grandmother. Were you ever *cohani, drabarni?*" She added casually.

Analee shook her head.

"Your mother?"

Analee's eyes were veiled. She didn't intend to reveal her past to anyone, let alone the *cohani*. But she knew the *cohani* could divine much that she couldn't see. Analee felt already that Reyora knew all about her.

"I have some *cohani* powers. I have been able sometimes to predict the future; but herbs, and spells . . . no."

Reyora noticed that Analee lingered on the word "spells." She knew Randal would be looking for a spell to make her love him.

"I hope you will be happy with the tribe now you are among us," Reyora said, "and that you will count us among your friends. Even though you came unwillingly, and I know how unwillingly, we here are now your family to love and help you."

Analee didn't reply, and Reyora could tell from the smouldering look in her dark eyes that she would do all she could to resist the love spells, all the magic, all the incantations that she could perform.

From outside came the sound of the flute and, looking around, Analee saw that none of the musicians were present. They had gone to play at the wedding feast. Randal came up to her and, smiling at her, took her hand.

"Will you dance at our wedding?"

Analee stared at him, her gaze meeting his.

"You have accepted," Randal murmured. "We are wed."

Analee tilted her head, her feet tapped time to the music, her body swayed and she allowed him to lead her out of the tent.

Outside, the field had been transformed in a few hours into a spectacle of color and gaiety. Streamers and banners had been hung from the tents and mats spread on the ground for the food. A pig was slowly being turned over a huge fire, its succulent smells reminding Analee that she had not eaten properly for a week. The hedgehogs were being wrapped in clay and laid in the red hot ashes under the slowly turning pig. On another spit a sheep was roasting and on yet another a young heifer. The smell of baking bread mingled with that of roasting meats, and cakes, sweetmeats and jellies were also being prepared.

The young men had taken a cart into Carlisle and now came back with flagons of ale and some wine for the chiefs at the wedding. The children, half naked, were running about playing with their dogs or hoops and wrestling with one another in the grass.

Looking at the scene Analee felt grow in her an approximation of happiness that she had not expected. Here she was with her own people, accepted into a tribe again, a member of the Buckland family. She belonged; she was Randal's wife and related to Rebecca the *phuri-dai,* head of the tribe. She could, if she liked, settle to a life of ease bearing children for Randal and establishing herself as one of the matriarchs of the tribe, a power, a force.

Unless she wanted to she need never go on the road again, wandering from town to town, eating berries, making out with men like Randal to sleep with, or being chased by others less pleasant like Brewster Driver. Yet, unlike the others who had been content with a night or two, Randal had wanted her forever. He had cared enough to take her by force, despite seeing her in the arms of a *gadjo.* Why, he might have killed them both on the spot. Analee's eyes sidled to the face of her bridegroom who was now presenting her to the gathered tribe, who called out and clapped. He was a handsome man, no doubt; tall and well built despite the slight wiry frame of a dancer. There was a savagery in his eyes, a pride in his mien that she had not noticed before as he had followed her about, trying to please her in order to gain her attention.

Capturing a bride, taking her by force, had transformed Randal; given him stature. She thought if he had behaved like this before she might have been more interested; might have been indifferent to the advances of Brent Delamain. Now he firmly gripped her hand and led her into the circle made by the tribe and Benjy struck up a theme on his flute and Hamo on the violin and Selinda raised her tambourine into the air. At a signal Randal lifted his arms above his

93

head and slowly circled his bride, his eyes flashing, his belly thrust forward in a primitive erotic gesture. For this was an ancient dance, the *alborea,* which had been brought all the way from Spain, a dance full of meaning and significance and much performed at weddings.

As he circled her, his hips undulating, his fingers clicking and his chin tilted proudly and aggressively forward, his eyes never leaving hers, Analee felt rising within her an unexpected surge of excitement, even of desire such as she had never dreamt she would feel about Randal.

He was, after all, a good-looking man, a gypsy like herself, a Romany, a wanderer, above all a dancer— a superb, excellent dancer who understood the rhythms and cadences of the gypsy dances which they performed so well together. In time with the music Randal stopped suddenly and then Analee slowly began her part of the intricate courtship dance, first stepping slowly and deliberately, then raising her hands above her head, her breasts thrust forward, her hips swaying as she gently circled her partner. Their eyes never left each other's and, as she revolved he turned on his axis and slowly smiles broke on their faces in mutual accord and their teeth gleamed. As though sensing that her hostility was breaking the crowd warmed to the magic of the dance and began to tap and clap and sway to the rhythm of the music.

Then the pace of the dance increased, sweat pouring from Hamo's brow as he frantically bowed the strings of the fiddle, his fingers appearing to have magical properties of their own. Analee and Randal were now stamping their feet together, their torsos almost touching, each with a hand nonchalantly on a hip, the other raised above the head, Analee clicking her castanets, Randal his fingers. Their bodies moved together and parted, their hips gyrated and, because it was a wedding dance, it seemed to anticipate the act of love intended to cement the ceremonial vows they had just made.

But, as the rhythm increased and the blood pounded

in their temples and their bodies grew fevered and hot it was instinct that spoke, not thought or words, not memory of violence committed or love lost.

Randal and Analee danced until their feet were bleeding and their bodies ached. They danced while the bold sun sank low in the sky and the moon timidly appeared over the horizon, so that at one point night and day merged as their bodies fused in the dance. Then, at last, in front of one of the myriad fires they sank exhausted to the ground and ate pork and beef and the delicacies which were offered to them.

For a long time after they were replete they sat staring into the flames, not speaking, watching the other dancers, the other musicians who had taken over, their own bodies limp with weariness.

Then quietly and without being noticed, when the merriment was at its height, at a gesture from Randal they got up and silently stole away toward the tent that had been prepared for them.

At dawn some gypsies were still dancing and feasting and fires still flared to meet the rays of the rising sun. Inside the nuptial tent Analee lay on her back aware of the light glimmering though the curtained entrance, of the man asleep beside her, of his heavy regular breathing.

Randal had thrown himself on the palliasse prepared for both of them, too exhausted to stir or say a word, to make any attempt to take her. And Analee had lain throughout most of the night thinking, reviewing her life, trying to see into the future, trying to decide what would happen, what would be best for her to do.

Randal was her husband now; he had captured her, but not won her. It would take a long time to win her heart; but her body he could have as many others had. As Brent Delamain had. But if she did see Brent again, ever, it would not be for a long long time. Analee meanwhile had her life to lead, a life difficult enough without moaning over the thoughts of a great love that might have been. Or might not. He had looked for her, yes, and wanted her; but so had many men. So did Randal. He had wanted her enough to capture her; make her his bride by force.

As the sunlight filtered through the tent flap Analee looked at his face, softened in the half light, dark with his beard, the hairs on his chest still matted with sweat. He looked very handsome as he slept, manly and virile, his dark hair tumbling over his brow. Suddenly he groaned and turned over so that he lay on his belly with his head facing hers. Looking at him she could see his eyes were wide open, staring at her, at the mound her breasts made, at the sweat trickling between them on to her own flat stomach. It was very hot inside the tent; they were both panting a little.

Randal put a hand on her thigh which was exposed to him as she had moved back the coverlets because of the heat. She felt a tremor, but she did not resist him. He was watching her as he let his hand work itself inside her thigh and she was aware that something other than the heat was making her heart pound. She desired Randal, who was now caressing the inside of her legs so that she parted them for him to make what she wanted easier.

He raised himself still holding on to her thigh and for a moment she saw his dark intense face, his brow glistening with sweat, leaning over her. His eyes were a strange color, a reflection of herself, and then his mouth pressed hard down upon hers and she could feel his even white teeth against hers, and she bared her mouth with a savagery which equaled his. Then they began twisting and turning as though playing out once again the slow preparatory rhythm of the wedding dance. She could feel the heavy weight of his chest as he positioned himself on her, his thick black hair like soft fur against her breasts, her hard erect nipples. She moaned and parted her legs wide and arched her hips so that with a sudden and violent movement he came suddenly and easily into her.

The dance was played out again as they settled down to its rhythm, its easy gyrations, the yielding and thrusting. She thought at one time that he would smother her with his mouth, the probings of his tongue and that his weight, as he ground her into the floor, would stifle her. She gripped him with her thighs and raised her legs to lighten the burden and, sensing her discomfort, he supported himself with his elbows, digging his toes firmly into the ground and taking the weight off his hips. He understood her completely. They were fully in harmony, attuned as they had been in the dance. She half-somersaulted for him so that she almost touched her head with her feet and, gasping with delight, he plunged into her again and again and she thought he looked like some young heaving bull, fecund and potent, the veins standing out against his temple, his face transfigured like a demon's.

She strained upwards to receive him deeper and he gave a great cry as the frenzy mounted, the rhythm increased. As she pushed and urged herself toward him he gave a mighty shudder and poured his seed straight into her as though she were a great vessel and he was filling her to the brim. Then the eruption exploded within her and she seemed lit by a thousand fires. She crossed her legs behind his back as he slowly lowered himself onto her until they lay flat and contented, heaving, joined in mutual passion.

Then they both slept and when they awoke it was because the curtain had parted to let in the light and old Rebecca stood there, a bowl in her hands, her old face cracked in a smile of satisfaction. Randal was still lying on Analee, his head resting on her breast, her legs crossed over his as though still to imprison him.

The old woman gazed at the naked bodies covered with sweat, glistening, and she smelt the air with satisfaction. She still thought it was a wonderful sight to see two nubile, fertile bodies coupling, easy with replete desire. She had noticed the change in the dance, saw how well suited they were, and the sight in front of her pleased her the more.

There would be no need of spells now.

She put the bowl of scented herbal tea beside them and silently withdrew, closing the curtain behind her.

Randal had seen the old woman, the satisfaction on her face, and now gazed at the face of his half sleeping bride. Now she was his. He had taken her many times and he would again. And how well she received him! She was a fine creature, an earthbound human being and now his; his seed inside her; the mother-to-be of his children. He had conquered Analee as a stud conquers a fractious mare; he had tamed her and molded her to his desire. She opened her eyes and saw his gaze, understood it, and his lips brushed hers. Then he raised himself, suspending his body over her for an instant as though he would plunge in and take her again. He saw her quivering flesh beneath his, the dark gleaming pubic mound, the incandescent thighs, the parted legs, the big quivering firm breasts. Her smile was enticing; but instead of lowering himself on her again he lay beside her, placing a proprietorial hand on her breast.

"Well?" Randal said, the first words, almost, they had spoken since they had been married.

Analee smiled lazily back.

"Well?"

"We are wed then."

"Truly it seems. Well and truly." She looked at their bodies and smiled.

"I will be a good husband to you, Analee. I know I took you by force; but I felt there was no other way. I . . ." He looked uncertainly at Analee and she turned her gaze from his. "The *gadjo*," he said at last, his voice bitter.

"I know. What you did was wrong."

"I was beside myself. To see you with him . . . and I wanted you so much."

"I know. Don't speak of it. It is finished and over. You captured me and I accepted it and now, well we are wed . . . and we are right well bedded."

"Aye, thoroughly," Randal said with satisfaction, and he took her to himself again while outside the noon sun climbed higher and higher into the heavens.

Chapter Six

In medieval times much of Lakeland belonged to the great monastic foundations established mainly in the twelfth and thirteenth centuries. One of the greatest, founded in 1127 by Stephen, Count of Boulogne, nephew of the reigning monarch, Henry I, was Furness Abbey. Here in a sheltered valley overshadowed by steep cliffs of red sandstone and surrounded by green woods, the Cistercian foundation had for 400 years acquired and controlled lands and possessions that amounted almost to a kingdom. The abbots were nearly as mighty as the marcher lords who wielded such power from the reign of William Rufus onward.

The abbeys controlled wool and pastures, sheep and cattle and they built earthen dikes that wound across the moors and pasturelands as boundaries to show the limits of their properties. In 1209 the monks of Furness bought the greater part of Borrowdale from the heiress to the Barony of Allerdale, Alice de Rumelli. The boundaries of the property reached from the Head of Derwentwater to the Sty Head Pass. Most of this land was used for the grazing of sheep and cattle, but to the west the Forest of Copeland arose from the Buttermere fells and was kept as a deer reserve.

Grange-in-Borrowdale was one of the chief monastic settlements of that beautiful valley. The name *"grange"* meant a farm belonging to a monastery and from the Borrowdale settlement the monks ran their estate, *"grangia nostra de Boroudale."*

The monastic lands were broken up at the time of the Dissolution and parceled among the local nobility or gentry. Some were acquired by right of tenure by the yeoman farmers—"statesmen" as they were called, who formed the backbone of the population in northern England. But now in the first half of the eighteenth century a new class was developing, thanks to the opening of trade routes, new inventions that were improving industrial techniques, and the prosperity brought about by years of peace under the first Hanoverians and their able Prime Minister, Robert Walpole. The rich yeoman farmer now might also dabble in business, become an ironmaster, a forgemaster or a dealer in wool. The pack-horses plied between the coastal ports of Cumberland and the hinter regions of Lakeland where the sturdy Herdwick sheep gave of their wool and the mines yielded their rich ores—iron, copper, lead, plumbago and tungsten.

The Allonbys were part of the old nobility, part of the Lakeland heritage that went back to the Conquest, yet they had not acquired the new skills of making money by commerce. Maybe the intrinsic awareness of their class held them back; the knowledge of the statesmen they had sent to Parliament in London, the soldiers and sailors to the wars, the monks to the abbeys and the scholars to the universities.

Several members of their family had been monks of the Cistercian Order at Furness and two of them abbots. Now, stripped of their lands and great possessions by successive monarchs and rulers bent on vengeance, all the Allonbys had left was their lovely house, Furness Grange, which stood on a tree-covered promontory jutting into Lake Derwentwater.

The promontory was known as Catsclaw because it sprang out from the steep smooth slope of Catbells mountain which swept downward to the lake. And in deed the jagged rocks and stones of the peninsula did resemble those of some massive predatory cat and the spiky coniferous trees its fur. Rising from the trees Furness Grange, largely an Elizabethan construction, was built of warm, pink sandstone—maybe quarried from the hills surrounding Furness Abbey or, at the Dissolution, the abbey itself—with black crossbeams and narrow mullioned windows.

But the most spectacular thing about the Grange was its view of the lake and the surrounding fells and mountains covered with heather or green woods. Occasionally there were stark, gray, rocky crags whose sharp teeth rose unevenly above the lake like those of some monstrous giant.

In the mornings when it was fine a mist rose from the still waters of the lake, and when it cleared the rosy tops of the hills and mountains could be seen in all directions from massive Skiddaw at one end to, at the other, towering Castle Crag which almost blocked the narrow opening known as the Jaws of Borrowdale. Opposite were the wooded precipice of Walla Crag and the sharp tongue of Friar Crag, above which the rough, rocky ridge of Glaramara could just be seen, topping the hills on the east side of Borrowdale.

Every morning Brent Delamain, from his bed by the window on the first floor of the Grange, could look out on the peaceful scene. The hardy permanence of the rocky crags, the calm immutable serenity of the lake not only consoled him for his misfortune, but seemed to give him strength so that every day he felt a little better.

After being found in the copse near Penrith by a farmer on his way to milk his cows in a nearby field, Brent was taken to the town mortuary where he was left for dead. The surgeon found no pulse and no breath and he was put on an icy slab, the blood on his head already congealed into a sharp black rock-like substance. It was thought that he had been the victim of some jealous husband for he had been found naked, his fine clothes neatly folded nearby. From these it was deduced he was a gentleman who had seduced the wife of a farmer or some person of lowly station.

It was the mortuary attendant who recognized Brent and probably saved him from death. He had once been a servant with the Delamain family, moving to

Penrith on his marriage to the daughter of a shopkeeper. Even the blood and dirt could not disguise that noble brow, that fine aquiline face. Out of respect for his late master the attendant, Norbert, covered his naked body with warm blankets and set out to seek someone who might know what Brent Delamain was doing in Penrith. It was but a short step to the hostelry where Tom was staying, already having alerted the town authorities about his brother's disappearance.

For the rest of his short life Tom Delamain thought that God had intervened to save his brother. The form had indeed seemed lifeless as Tom bent to inspect it and then knelt to say in Latin the prayers for the dead. As he gazed through his tears on the still waxen face of his brother he saw color slowly steal into the white lips and, imperceptibly, a small pulse began to beat at his neck.

Quickly the surgeon was called and Brent was removed to the tavern and placed in a warm bed and everything that could be done to bring him to life was done. But although Brent breathed and his pulse grew stronger he did not recover consciousness and remained in that state for nearly a week. In that time his cousins, John and Stewart Allonby rode over from Furness Grange and a coach was hired which, under their escort, went very slowly along the narrow road to Keswick. There the coach was abandoned and the rest of the journey was made across the lake by water to the landing stage at Catspaw.

It was a sad arrival for Tom who had not seen his Allonby cousins for years. He felt closer to this other branch of the family than to the Delamains because their loyalty to the Stuart cause was legendary abroad, in those places where exiles waited and plotted. He had a fierce, proud love of the Allonbys and what they had endured, still endured, for the rightful king and the old faith.

How different was the arrival on this cold day in September of the year 1744 from the one he had planned. True Brent was there, but unconscious and, some thought, unlikely to recover. There was a sadness about the house for days as those around prayed and waited for a sign of change.

But Brent was a young, vigorous man and whether it was the result of all the prayers offered up for him or the skill of the doctors who were called from as far away as Preston and Carlisle to attend him, or his own robust constitution, none knew. But one day, as Tom sat beside his bed, saying his Office, he looked up and suddenly saw Brent's blue eyes, a little faded because they had been shielded from the light for so long, gazing at him with the uncertainty and confusion of a new-born baby. They were unable to focus properly, and they scarcely seemed to recognize Tom. Brent found difficulty in talking and could not move his limbs and for the first few days it was hard to tell whether his recovery was to be desired or whether it were better he had died; whether he would be a normal human being, or a lifelong invalid.

But gradually Brent started to recover; his eyes cleared and remained fixed when he looked upon a person. He started to form words that made sense and his limbs began to move. Then one day, as Mary Allonby was sitting by his bed reading, he looked at her with a clarity that was startling and smiled.

After that his recovery was swift. There was no impairment to the brain or the limbs, as far as the doctors could tell. He could make a complete recovery; he would live to father children, if God wished it, and serve the King. And then, knowing all was well, Tom set out one morning and, accompanied by Stewart, made his way to Whitehaven where he took a ship for France, alone. He could delay no more.

Every morning Brent was a little better, but he loved to lie in his bed looking out on the lake watching the mist break and, if it was fine, the sun rise above the purple slopes of Skiddaw. He could feel the blood flowing strongly in his limbs and he would twitch each muscle to be sure it still worked. Then he would turn and look toward the door with anticipation, waiting for his cousin Mary to bring him his breakfast.

Mary Allonby, fair-haired and oval-faced, petite, very like his mother, her aunt, had become indispensable to Brent. Like a good angel she was to be observed sitting quietly by his side, reading to him, or keeping a companionable silence if he did not feel like it or wished to sleep. At first she had fed him, preparing his food herself, making it delicate and tempting for the invalid and spooning it gently through his cracked parted lips.

She was the first thing he saw in the morning and the last thing at night as she gave him the gentle smile he had come so much to love, kissed his brow and blew out the candle. He would watch her close the door, the soft light in the corridor outside gradually receding, leaving him in darkness and he would think of her moving quietly along the corridor, her braided hair gleaming in the glow of the candle she carried in her hand, the soft fabric of her dress swirling around her slim figure.

Four weeks after he had been found and left for dead Brent Delamain gazed with anticipation at the door, waiting for it to open and Mary to come in with her tray. Today he would get up and dress and go for a walk; just a short one, as far as the lake. Usually he dressed for part of the day or sometimes he didn't dress at all, but stayed in his nightshirt with a warm shawl about his shoulders, a rug over his knees as he sat by the window.

But today he felt so well and vigorous. Why, he could run up Catbells and down again. He wanted to be well to go and join Tom in France, prepare the way for the conquest by the King. There was a tap at the door and Mary came in with the tray in her hand. Brent stretched his arms over his head in an expansive gesture.

"Mary, I feel so well today. I could walk over Honister. I could . . ."

"Brent, Brent," Mary laughed, placing the tray with fresh rolls, Cumberland butter and hot coffee on a table by the bed. "Mr. Lorrimer said only *short* distances first. He has been a good doctor, done you well and you must abide by what he says."

Brent shrugged and turned to butter his rolls. "Maybe you're right. The Allonby common sense my mother always called it. We'll go to the lake and throw stones. What say, Mary?"

Mary smiled shyly, looking into his face, so thrilled he was recovered, and that she had helped in some small way to bring it about. Mary Allonby had always been half in love with her handsome cousin, who was four years her senior, but he had never seemed aware of her, in that way, behaving toward her like a brother, fond, chiding, but never at all loving. Mary, a gently nurtured country girl, was well aware of Brent's reputation with women—that at a very youthful age he was even rumored to have fathered a child on one of the Delamain maidservants. That he ran after women in London and at Cambridge and they ran even faster after him. That the women with whom he associated were never nice, well brought up ladies like Mary, but the sort who frequented taverns or were to be found on the boards of theaters or, worse, who sold their favors for money or gain.

Mary could never believe it of her handsome, fastidious cousin, that he could associate with women of this kind. Why, to his very finger-tips he was the epitome of an English gentleman with his proud, erect carriage, his lean aristocratic face, his easy manners, his soldierly bearing on a horse. But Mary had known some of the young women in whom his mother had tried in vain to interest her son—and they had all said the same thing with a woeful shaking of the head; Brent was not interested.

Even the reason Brent was here in this sorry state was supposed to be due to a woman, though no one knew for sure. Tom had breathed the awful truth to John, and John had told Stewart and Stewart had whispered it to her—Brent had been found in a forest without his clothes on; not robbed, for his clothes and wallet were nearby. It all looked as though Brent was up to his old tricks again, but this time with more serious consequences. It had nearly killed him.

Was this why she had detected a change in his attitude toward her? She was sure his glances were becoming loving rather than friendly, his touch amorous rather than brotherly. Had he realized at last that this sort of woman was no good for him, got him into trouble, nearly killed him? Mary didn't know. All she did know was that the late September days were golden with happiness, and rich with promise. For her hope was that the cousin whom she had loved for so long was returning this love.

Brent was aware he had met death, maybe lingered in its shadows. He seemed to have emerged from a long dark passage in which mists had swirled and fearsome odors prevailed. Thus to open his eyes on scenes of such natural beauty as Derwentwater in the autumn; and such feminine physical beauty as his gentle cousin Mary doing her needlepoint beside him, was enough to make him fall passionately in love with life all over again. Maybe for the first time really to value being alive.

He had never really looked at Mary properly before, appreciated the grace of her long, white throat, the depths of her clear blue, almost violet, eyes, the soft swell of her young virginal bosom. Her dull-gold hair was braided around her head and little wisps which had escaped the pins fell engagingly about her forehead. When she was near him her face was always transformed by a soft smile and when she looked at him it seemed to deepen into something very special.

Gradually Brent came to be used to Mary beside him, quietly reading or sewing. They would look over the lake together and their eyes would meet and he would think it must always be thus; he and Mary Allonby were made for each other.

But what of the future? Brent's heart grew cold at the thought of the war that would ensue in his wake if Prince Charles should ever land in this country; of what it would do to his and Mary's tranquil life together. But he knew it was his duty; honor before love, and as he grew stronger and the days shortened into October he knew he would soon have to sail to France and keep his promise to join Tom.

Brent ate quickly as Mary moved about the room straightening the books; freshening the flowers with bunches of autumn leaves she had brought with her. She was happy just to be in the same room as Brent, to have him near her. Would it could be so always.

Brent finished his breakfast with a clatter of cup on saucer, wiped his lips on the napkin and swung one leg out of bed. Mary looked quickly away because his nightshirt had ridden up and one long, brown, hairy leg had a great tuft of even darker hair at the top.

"Mary, send up James to shave and dress me and we shall walk to the lake. I feel better than ever to-day! Come, get your shawl and wait for me in the hall."

"But Brent, I have a lot of mending to do. I promised myself that today . . ."

"Pah! Today you will leave the mending and the darning and walk with your cousin. We will not have many such fine days before the winter sets in."

It was true. Winter could come with awful suddenness in Lakeland, fine skies one moment became gray and heavy with snow the next. Besides, her eyes sparkled at the thought of a whole hour with Brent; maybe two.

"All right. I'll send up James with hot water and make my excuses to my brother as to why I cannot housekeep for him today."

Because of the burden of taxes and fines they had had to pay over the years the Allonbys were considered poor by some standards. They had relatively few servants, and John and Stewart put in a full day in the fields or supervising such small possessions as they had left and which could still be worked, mainly forest and pastureland. Mary was the housekeeper since her elder sister Sarah had married a prosperous merchant from Cockermouth and moved away from home.

Not given to her were the amusements, diversions and follies of other well brought up young women of her class. From an early age she had learned to make do with the solitary comforts of home and life at the Grange. Her mother had died years before and there had been a sick father to nurse, brothers to care for, servants to feed and a house to run. At the age when young ladies of the nobility and gentry were going to balls and parties or decking themselves with fine clothes, Mary was getting up at four in the morning, working all day and falling exhausted into bed at dusk. Although only eighteen she was already old in knowledge, and the harsh experience of a life where one didn't hope but simply existed, knowing that the following day would not be much better than the one just over.

But now her cousin Brent had come, and her life had been transformed just by nursing him and seeing the expression of fondness and gratitude with which he greeted her turn, she thought, into something more profound.

"Aye, you'll not housekeep today. Maybe bring some ham and bread and a bottle of ale and we'll sup by the lakeside!"

Mary fled down the stairs as Brent started to remove his nightshirt, apparently unaware of the unseemliness of it in her presence. He was so natural he was like a young animal, she thought, both liking and fearing what she'd seen. She had washed him as he lay almost naked many times when he was half conscious; but somehow there was something different about the sick body compared to the healthy one. As he'd stood there his nightshirt half on and half off, turned in profile away from her, the sight of his vigorous maleness, the muscles of his lean calves, inspired in her an awareness of a sensation that hitherto she had known little about. This young male cousin was an awesome as well as a desirable creature.

Brother John was passing through the hall as Mary flew excitedly down the broad staircase. Despite his cares he stopped and a gentle smile illumined his tired face at the sight of her animated features.

"Where art thou off to, lass? Escaping from thy cousin?"

"Oh no, John! He is feeling so well he wants me to go for a walk with him, take a picnic. May I, John?"

"Of course, lass. I can't recall when you had a day off last, seeing to your household duties and nursing Brent as well. 'Tis well deserved. Fetch some pie and ale from the kitchen and make a day of it."

"Oh, John, may I? That's just what Brent suggested."

"Did he? Good. But take care he does not go too far; he is not well yet."

"Of course I won't. I'll see he doesn't tire himself."

Mary threw her brother a smile and was about to dash into the kitchen when John gently clasped her arm and gazed at her gravely.

"Take care, Mary. Don't let him play with your emotions. You know that Brent . . ."

"Oh I know, John! Of course I won't!"

"But I see you looking a lot at him lately, in that fashion, and him, too . . ."

So John had seen it. Then it was true. Her cheeks flamed, and she put her hands to them, both to attempt to disguise the color from her brother and to cool them.

"Much as I love Brent, when it comes to women," John said gravely, "he is a philanderer. You know how he was found . . ."

Mary's eyes grew solemn.

"But would he philander with *me*, John? I am not the sort of woman . . ."

"You are a *very* pretty girl, Mary. Alas, because of our solitary life there are not enough about to tell you so, but any man would be inflamed by you if he was in his right mind. Imagine the effect on someone who had become enfeebled by illness. But when Brent is recovered, and 'twill be soon, he will be off to France, Mary. Do not let him trifle with you here."

"Be sure he will not, John. He is not like that, really."

"Take care, my little sister."

Impulsively, John Allonby, a man older than his thirty years, whom misfortune and worry and the loss of a beloved wife in childbirth had prematurely aged, bent toward his baby sister and kissed her softly on the cheek.

The woods that surrounded the house on Catspaw stretched along the length of the lake toward Keswick. At times they thickened, and at times there was a clearing either in the midst of the wood or by the side of the lake. It was this fine timber that helped keep the Allonbys out of the debtor's prison, and it was Stewart who was the expert woodsman, who knew when to cut and when to plant and when to trim back.

The larks sang that fine October forenoon as Brent, walking slowly and still with a slight limp because his left leg had not quite recovered its full use, and Mary a little ahead of him, paused and looked about for a green sward on which to sit and eat their picnic. Brent pointed to a place where the trees fell back from the lakeside and a grassy stretch reached down into the water protected from view of anyone, other than a boat on the lake, by a hillock. Mary, the hood of her cloak falling backward from her head, had been gathering fir cones for the fires that needed to burn so brightly in the large cold house in wintertime, and on her arm she had a large basket, half full. Brent had carried the warm bread and large ham pie in another basket and when they stopped he took out the flagon of ale and put it in the water to cool.

It was quite warm so he removed his greatcoat and laid it on the grass for them to sit upon. Underneath he wore the jacket and breeches of good broadcloth that had been found by him on the night of his attack, and a fine linen shirt, that Mary had freshly laundered for him with her own hands, open at the neck.

Mary's cloak slid to her feet and Brent took that and placed it alongside his, aware as he did of her neat ankle just visible beneath a dress of locally woven cloth that was of a becoming blue, particularly complementary to Mary's coloring. Brent's heart beat a little faster at the sight of the ankle, and his mind was a confusion of thoughts and desires and of women remembered long ago.

What puzzled Brent was that he could remember none more recently than Joan Shuttleton, a whore he'd taken up with during his last days in Cambridge. He'd met her in London and taken her with him to live openly as his mistress, which was one of the reasons that his brother had summoned him home even before it was clear that grandfather's last seizure would kill him.

Even the memory of Joan Shuttleton was hazy, as though that part of him had somehow become involved in his injury. He could remember very clearly his family and events and the death of his grandfather and the arrival of brother Tom; but the women who had formed part of so many of his amorous adventures were unclear in his mind, and particularly the one whom Tom had sworn was responsible for the state in which he had been found.

Tom had been quite blunt in describing to Brent the circumstances. How, even after many hours lying in the forest and on a slab in the mortuary, the traces of lovemaking were still evident about his body, quite apart from the fact that he had been found naked.

It was hushed up of course, Tom said. Norbert knew the family, and the doctor was bound by his medical oath not to tell. But Tom had no doubt his brother had an assignation in the forest with the gypsy he had met that night in the tavern and of whom there was no sign, of her or her troupe of traveling musicians, afterward.

Gypsy? Brent's face crinkled again as his eyes moved from the well-turned ankle of his gently nurtured cousin toward the lake. Gypsy? Brent had no recollection of a gypsy dancing in the tavern as Tom

111

had said, flaunting herself before him. He had apparently told Tom they had met before. Brent closed his eyes and tried to reform half remembered impressions in his mind. But no . . .

"Brent, are you all right?" Mary had seen the spasm as his eyes closed and bent anxiously forward.

"Yes, yes, dear cousin. It is the light on the lake. What a splendid day we have here. Look how old Walla Crag dips into the water yonder, and Skiddaw, is it not a picture? First thing this morning you could not see it for mist. Here, come sit by me," he looked up and reached out a hand and saw that Mary was gazing at him timorously, not offering him her hand, her eyes almost fearful.

"Why, Mary, don't be afraid. I shall not harm thee!" He laughed and her eyes met his and she saw all the strength and gentleness in them, not the fearful animal young male she'd caught a glimpse of in the morning and of whom, as he'd looked up at her and stretched out his hand, she'd instantly been reminded. After all, she was a grown woman. Her mother had been wed at her age. It was quite common hereabouts even at 16 or 17; some were no longer maids but matrons at 15. That she had been protected was due to the presence of her brothers and lack of close female company. Sarah was almost as old as John and they had never been close. Certainly Sarah had never confided in her about womanly things, never told her her thoughts on her approaching marriage to Ambrose Rigg.

Mary had grown up in an all-male household for so long, except for a few women servants and none of them close. Unlike richer friends of hers she had no maid, no old nanny to enlighten her about the things between men and women. All she knew, Mary surmised, and when she saw it as exactly and as explicitly as she had seen Brent that morning, boldly outlined against the window, she'd been frightened and disturbed.

And now here he was turning to her smiling, patting the ground beside him. Was her whole world about to change? Take on new meaning?

They ate hungrily; the fresh air and short walk had restored Brent's appetite and Mary's face glowed with pleasure as she saw him making short work of the pie, the freshly baked bread and the strong ale he had fished out of the lake.

"It is so good to see you well again, Brent."

"And good to be well, cousin. I think Old Man Death thought he had me, but I thwarted him!"

"Don't speak like that. You are but a young man. 'Twas an unfortunate accident . . ."

Mary faltered, thinking of what Stewart had told her. She looked at Brent from under lowered lashes.

"Accident? You think it was an accident? I know not how I came to be there nor does anyone else. Ah, I see you looking at me, Mary. You have heard that they said it was the fault of a woman. Well . . ." Brent shrugged, " 'tis the first time being with a woman was such a dangerous thing."

He laughed and she saw the expression in his eyes change as he looked at her and moved closer. It became bolder. Her mouth went very dry and her heart started to beat quickly in her chest. As he moved closer his arm stole about her waist and she could feel his hot breath on her cheek. "Women are not so dangerous are they, Mary?" he murmured, his big hand pressing her slim waist.

"I think it is *men* who are dangerous," she managed to whisper, aware of his hand, his presence, his warmth, "or so I heard tell."

"And you heard it of me, I'll warrant. Well I'll not deny I love women. Ever since I was a young boy I was chasing the maids. I have had some of my best moments in a woman's arms—every man will say the same if he is honest, and yet . . ." He moved away from her, his arm resting now on the ground.

"I am not a womanizer, Mary. I am looking for someone perfect to whom to give my love. I know what people say about me, that I am idle, no good.

113

But I have a good sword arm, a steady seat on a horse. I can box and run, and fight . . ."

"Fight?" Mary looked up at him startled.

"I mean fight in battle, Mary. 'Tis true I never have; but . . . Mary, can you keep a secret?"

"You know I can."

"Then this is why Tom was here; not just to see grandfather. Tom is . . . you are sure you won't tell?"

Mary looked at him enigmatically, her eyes steady. Her heart had ceased its hammering.

"I know why Tom was here. While you were so ill upstairs Tom and John and Stewart spent many hours talking—about the King. That is what you were going to say?"

Brent sat back, resting his weight on the palms of his hands, and looked across the lake. The sun had risen high over the opposite hills whose brown and purple reflections shimmered in the clear water, so that they seemed to form one very steep continuous range. The thick, wooded slopes of Lodore led up to Ashness Fell whose jagged rocky outline formed the horizon against the clear, blue sky. If he looked to the left he saw the spires and roofs of the little town of Keswick diminished by the huge Skiddaw range which towered protectively over it. To his right the lake narrowed and Castle Crag and King's How loomed up on either side of the Derwent River as it meandered past Grange into Borrowdale.

The islands, too, reflected in the water so that the fir trees seemed to point up to the sky and down to the depths at the same time. From where he sat he could see St. Herbert's island and Rampsholme, and up toward Keswick, shadowed by Friar's Crag, the home of the Earls of Derwentwater, firm supporters of the Stuart monarchs. It was from here that one had gone to fight for King James in 1715; from here that his brave wife, fleeing by night up by Walla Crag, had tried to save his life by selling the family jewels in London—all in vain.

The exquisite poetry and magic of the scene vied with the practical reality of the fate of Lord Derwentwater. One who had died for the man for whom Brent was prepared to sacrifice his life: King James III of England—languishing in Rome and exile.

"Yes, about the King, Mary. I should have known you would know. And how do you feel about it?"

"Why of course I am for it, Brent! My family, as you know, have always been staunch supporters of the Stuarts. I am with them heart and soul."

"Even to death?"

Brent gazed at her and she solemnly met his eyes. She felt then a bond with him that was stronger than death and wondered if he felt it, too. It was not just a desire for him as a man, a husband, a lover; but a feeling of union with him as a person, a fusion of their lives. What did it matter that Brent went with women of ill repute, that he was considered idle—though she had never considered him such? He was half Allonby, her first cousin, and the same blood flowed in their veins, the same obsession for a cause—the Restoration of the Stuarts, as nearly one hundred years ago another Stuart, Charles II, had been restored to his rightful throne after years in exile. It could happen again. It would.

"Even to death, Brent; my brothers', and mine and," she paused and her voice trembled, "even yours."

Brent drew her to him and his arm encircled her once more. His cheek for the first time touched hers and he whispered into her ear.

"The Cause is my life, Mary. My salvation. I will be a man and a warrior and show those who despise me that I am as bold as they are. My brother mocked me because I had no money and no occupation, no calling, he said. Now I have! I am going to France to be with Prince Charles, to fight for him unto death."

"Oh, Brent!" Mary turned to him and threw herself into his waiting arms, pressing her face against his chest. Huge tears rolled down her cheeks, wetting the fine lawn of his shirt. "Brent, do not die! I cannot bear it. Do not speak like this, I beg of you."

"There, there." Brent patted her back and pressed

her closer to him, sensing her womanly smells, her soft clinging body. He wanted her violently, to take her on the ground where they were now and make her sweet girl's body his, see it yield its secrets for the very first time to any man—and how many women had done *that* for him? Precious few, if any. Certainly no one had done it as Mary would because he knew so well, had known for a long time, that she loved him, that she would do his bidding, even now. He held back her face and removed the tears with his fingers. Then he kissed the wet path they had made from her eyes to her mouth very gently like the pecking of a bird. Her head was held back and her eyes were closed as his mouth came very softly down on hers in a kiss that was tender at first, but became more passionate as he felt her response, saw her open her eyes and look at him, saw the longing in them, the desire matching his.

He pressed her back on the grass and lay beside her, his mouth still fast on hers as he slipped a hand through her bodice to feel the soft young breasts beneath. She didn't stop him, but moaned as though the action pleased her. Surprised that she had not resisted, and excited by her passion and his own headstrong need he grew bolder and unlaced her bodice and exposed her breasts completely. He gasped with wonder as he saw how soft and yet voluptuous they were, how the tender pink nipples, like plump raspberries, grew erect, either from the sudden exposure to the cold air or from her own desire. He knew not which as he bent his head and caressed them gently with his tongue, first one and then the other.

Mary, awakened for the first time, had never believed that such physical pleasure was possible. She didn't resist or even mind as he felt beneath her bodice and then unlaced it. As his mouth left hers to caress her exposed bosom she opened her eyes to gaze tenderly at him, so proud of her gentle lover, that he wanted her and had treated her with such delicacy. She would have given herself completely to Brent then if he had asked it of her. She wanted to. She was not afraid and felt in her loins the need to merge with him. And there was a moment as he looked at her breasts and she gazed at him that it could have happened. She was aware of her nudity, and the sight of being so gazed upon by a man, seemed to inflame her own desire. But suddenly Brent drew her bodice close again and then lying down beside her, panting a little, took her head into the crook of his arm and kissed her hair.

"Not now, Mary. I could never forgive myself."

"I am willing."

"I know; but I want you and your family to know that I am an honorable man, not a rogue who will even seduce his young cousin. I know what they say about me . . ."

"They *love* you, Brent."

"I know, but they still think I am a rogue. I want to win you, Mary. Show them I am worthy to be your husband."

He could feel her stiffen in his arms and he turned her face and saw the expression in her eyes, the tears that lurked in the corners. "That is, if you will have me, Mary?"

"*I* have you! Oh, Brent, can you mean it? What can I give you? I am a simple country girl, completely unused to the ways of the world, inexperienced. How can I be a fit wife for you?"

"Then neither of us thinks we are worthy of the other. Capital! 'Tis a good start." Brent broke the charged atmosphere by sitting upright and slapping his knees with laughter. " 'Tis the oddest proposal I have heard."

"Did you make many?" Mary said slyly, echoing his mood.

"Not of this kind. Not honest proposals. In fact," Brent looked mildly astonished at his own admission, "I have never asked the hand of a woman before."

The laughter went out of his eyes and he looked at her again, noting how her hair stirred in the soft breeze that came from the lake, saw the grave look in her eyes, the sweet dimple of her upturned mouth.

She looked a picture of English womanhood at its best in her soft blue dress enhanced by the wonderful background of the lakeland scene. At that moment Brent Delamain who had never hitherto doubted himself, his prowess or his abilities as a lover did wonder if he was fit for her, good enough for her. Could he possibly deserve such a creature?

The look in her eyes told him that whether he deserved her or not she was his. He bent toward her again, sliding his hands once more under that bodice still enticingly unlaced, cupped the small breasts in his big hands and drew Mary toward him, seeing her parted mouth and feeling beneath his palms the warmth of her skin the pounding of her heart.

As they kissed the breeze from the lake grew stronger and a cloud obscured the sun. Mary trembled and Brent, unsure whether it was from fear or cold, broke from her, solicitously covering her with her cloak. He drew her up to her feet and held her for a long time in both his arms to warm her, until they turned to go back together to the house.

Chapter Seven

Susan Delamain and her daughter, Emma, were among the first to come over at the news that Brent and Mary intended to be married. In all her wildest dreams Susan had never hoped that her tempestuous wild rogue of a son would be taken by his cousin's delicate beauty. She loved her niece almost as much as her own daughter and had tried to take the place of a mother to her in the years since Sarah Allonby had died.

Susan was glad to get away from Delamain Castle and the cramped dower house where she had lived since the death of Sir Francis. Her eldest son had immediately left for London; but even his welcome absence did not quite compensate for the loneliness and unease she felt without Brent. And there had been the terrible suffering while he was ill, and her inability to travel to his side because Emma had developed a fever that the doctor feared might be the pox and, although it was not, she had taken a long time to recover.

Brent went in the boat over to Keswick to welcome his mother, leaving Mary to supervise the preparations for the feast that was to solemnize the betrothal that night. Sister Sarah—named after her mother—and her husband Ambrose Rigg were also due to arrive with their young son Henry and the baby Elia just six months old.

It was the longest trip Brent had made since his recovery and he was glad of the presence of Stewart because he still felt nervous, in case he should falter on his left leg which was still lame. Each day, accompanied by Mary, he walked a little further but nearly always they stood at the spot where he had asked her to marry him, first awakened her woman's desire, and they embraced all over again.

Brent and Stewart waited by the Moot Hall in the old market place for the coach to arrive from Penrith. It would be put up in the town while they made the journey across the lake. There was still no proper road, or one big enough for a coach and four, from Keswick to Catspaw. Transport was either by horse or boat and the latter was both the fastest and the prettiest way.

Although it was only two months since he had parted from his mother, in the interval he had nearly died, his sister had been ill, and it seemed an eternity to Brent as he anxiously paced up and down waiting

119

for the coach to appear. Stewart laughed at his impatience.

"Why, Brent, you would think you had not seen your mother for years."

"It seems like it, Stewart. Think what has happened. I have nearly died and I have got myself a bride."

Stewart, nearest in age to Mary and close to her, like her too to look at with his clear deep blue eyes and very curly blond hair, grew suddenly solemn and the laughter abruptly ceased. Brent knew why. Stewart thought he was a philanderer and unfit for his sister. Neither of the brothers had been very enthusiastic at the news, but Stewart the least. Stewart had been taciturn and had not offered Brent his congratulations. Brent wanted very much to convert his cousin whom he so much admired, to have his approval. Stewart was a solid countryman, an expert in wood and tree felling. He was close to the soil and his values were good earthy ones. He smiled seldom and, like his brother John, seemed bent with the cares of the last years.

Fortune had rarely smiled on the Allonbys since anyone could remember. John's wife had died with her baby after an agonizing birth and soon after that their father, stricken with grief at John's bereavement, so like his own. His wife had died giving birth to Mary. The brothers toiled and hoped for better times, praying that the Stuarts would one day return, restore their lands and recompense them for their losses. It was their only hope. That and, maybe, a good match for Mary. And now Mary had decided to throw her heart at her cousin, a man they loved but whose attitude to life was so unlike theirs, so casual and reckless. For the last thing they had wanted when Tom had brought the stricken Brent with him was to have him end up betrothed to Mary.

"You like it not, Stewart, do you?" Brent said quietly. Stewart shrugged and looked away.

"I like you well enough, Brent, you know that. But as a husband for Mary . . ."

"I have no fortune."

120

"Oh it is not that . . . well, not only that. It is . . ." Stewart avoided his cousin's eyes and banged his hands against his thigh.

"You think I am not steadfast?"

"Well, Brent, up to now . . ."

"True, I have used women ill, Stewart—or they me, I know not quite which. I have played with them, and dallied with them. But Mary I love truly. As I have no woman before . . ."

"Brent, you hardly know her . . ."

"Hardly *know* Mary! Of course I know her. I have known her since she was born!"

"Yes, but as a wife . . . I mean you did not think of Mary like that before."

"She was young."

"She has been a maid for many years now; but you never looked at her before, Brent, as other than a friend."

"Is it so wrong that I learnt to love her?" Brent said defensively.

"No, of course not. But in such a short time, and most of that you have been ill . . ."

"And not in my right mind, is that what you want to say?" Brent said harshly, now stopping his pacing and staring at his cousin.

"I don't say not in your right mind, of course not, but emotionally. Mary has nursed you and you have become dependent on her. I say you should wait . . . to be sure, Brent."

The pleading look in Stewart's eyes moved Brent as no words had done. He was well aware of the misfortune that had dogged the Allonbys; of the suffering of the brothers and the concern for their youngest sister. The only one who had done anything was Sarah, and it was doubtful if she was really happy with the pug-faced, pompous Ambrose Rigg. She had married beneath her and she had married for money, for security and possessions and all the things she had been without for so many years. And now she had a fine house and her own coach, and a personal maid and a nursemaid; but whether or not she was happy no one knew. Sarah was a woman who kept her own counsel. In many ways she was more a Delamain than an Allonby, shrewd and calculating, like George.

Brent's thoughts were distracted by the thudding of horses' hooves, and the coach with the Delamain arms blazoned on the doors swept into sight. His heart filled with joy at the thought of seeing his mother and, as the coach stopped and the groom jumped down, Brent bounded ahead before him to open the door for his mother and sister. When Susan saw him she remained in her seat and Brent saw that tears were cascading down her face as she reached out her arms for him. He leapt into the coach and sat beside her, folding her in his arms, hugging her to reassure her all was well. Beside her mother Emma stared out at Brent through her great brown eyes, also filled with tears. She looked pale and thin. Thank God it had not been the pox, but she had been very ill.

"I am here, mother, all is well."

"Oh Brent, they told me you were dying and I thought I would never see you again. God is good, God is good."

"God *is* good, mother. But for my left leg which moves a trifle slower than its fellow I am in good health, and in love, mother! The best tonic for recovery."

Susan gave her son a wry look and offered him her hand. "Of that I am not so certain. Help me out, Brent, and take care with Emma. She is delicate, too."

Outside the carriage Stewart bowed and kissed his aunt's hand and then gallantly that of his little cousin, a year younger than Mary and her equal in good, though very different, looks. Emma was dark like the Delamains, brown hair, brown skin and eyes that were an enticing tawny color like those of a wild bird. Even her recent ill health had not dimmed her beauty and Stewart, who had been smitten since she was fourteen, once again felt his heart turn over.

But Emma, unaware of these emotions, and certainly not reciprocating them, smiled at her cousin and pecked him on the cheek in sisterly fashion.

Emma liked exciting young men like Anthony Webber or Lord Borfield, whom her brother occasionally entertained to dinner or invited to escort her to balls. They danced well and spoke entertainingly and made bold glances as she partnered them in the quadrille. Stolid cousin Stewart was too silent, too clod-hopping to attract such a one as Emma Delamain. The trouble was he knew it, but he continued to hope and his devoted gaze followed her as she tripped out of the carriage and instructed the maid she and her mother shared to unpack her things, and help the boatman load them into the boat.

It was a merry party that took to the boat for the short journey to Catspaw. Brent sat in the stern with his mother while Emma tried to draw the taciturn Stewart into a conversation on the prow. She was vexed at having to come to Furness Grange which she considered the most boring of backwoods, and her earnest cousins the Allonbys were very hard going. But her mother had insisted it was good for her health and as Emma hoped to persuade George to give a season for her in London, the restoration of the color to her cheeks was essential.

Besides, Emma was intrigued at the speed with which Brent had declared himself for Mary and wanted to know what was behind it. The quiet and serene Mary was the last person Emma would have expected her dashing, willful brother to be attracted to. She knew all about the sort of things he got up to —the servants who had to leave suddenly, to say nothing of the story about the mysterious gypsy who apparently nearly caused his death. Mary Allonby of all people . . . Emma was agog with interest.

"You also think I am not fit for Mary, mother?" Brent inquired as the noise from the oars and the prattling of Emma on the prow drowned his voice.

"Of course I think you are fit, Brent. In every way a desirable husband. But for *Mary*, Brent? She is so quiet and docile, so serious. The last person I would have supposed you to be attracted to."

"She is an angel, mother. Sitting by my bedside . . ."

123

"That is what I was afraid of," Susan said, pursing her lips in the Allonby fashion of being sensible. "I wish I could have come to nurse you. You grew dependent on her, saw her in another light. Brent, is it wise? Shouldn't you wait?"

That was the second time someone had said the same thing to him in an hour, Brent thought, the excitement suddenly draining away. He felt tired and uncertain. Of course they were related, his mother and Stewart; both sober and careful Allonbys. But they had both asked him to wait—until he was sure. Was he being fair to Mary?

"The future is so uncertain, mother. We thought we should have some happiness before . . ."

"In case there is war?"

Brent nodded.

"I might die, like Uncle Robert . . ."

Susan's eyes flew shut in a spasm of grief for the premature death of her gallant brother on the scaffold beside Lord Derwentwater in 1716—a young man so full of charm and promise. Now to think of her son, not unlike Robert in looks and temperament. She wrung her hands in an involuntary gesture of despair and looked over the lake, her eyes scanning the high peaks crowned by Glaramara that crowded together at the end of Borrowdale and stretched as far as the eye could see. How different, how serene the mountains were from a distance than when you were close to them or cowering under them, attempting to climb them as she had when a girl, with her father and boisterous brothers.

Happy days of her childhood in the red house on the lake surrounded by the protective fells and woods. It had seemed to pass too quickly, and to give place to uncertainty and anxiety as she reached womanhood and had waited for the war to come, dreading what it would do to her brothers and to her husband Guy.

Only they had been wed, they had some years of happiness together. Was it right to deny Brent and Mary? Was it right to deny *Mary* the happiness for, in her lonely solitary life away from civilization, she scarcely met any young men at all, let alone suitable ones? She could see Brent's attraction for Mary quite clearly; but Mary for Brent . . . it was as she had feared, an infatuation based on need and, being Brent, it would not last once the need was past. They were very different people.

"I know not what to say for the best," Susan clasped Brent's hand and squeezed it. "I would not deny you or her. But, Brent, what if there is no war, if the Prince does not come? He has tried to come often before you know."

"He will come, mother. This time it is sure. In a year we shall have the Stuarts again on the throne."

"Oh would it could be. How different everything might be. But I cannot bear to think of what is going to happen until then. Oh look, Furness Grange, and there is Mary on the jetty with John." She clasped Brent's hand again and turned to him, her eyes shining.

"For you I *will* be happy, Brent. We may have so little time."

There had not been such a feast at Furness Grange since anyone could remember. There had been little enough to feast about and few resources with which to do it. But the family reunion as well as the betrothal of Brent and Mary was considered sufficient reason, and extra servants had been engaged from the neighboring hamlets to prepare the succulent food and serve it.

The long dining table was set with silver marked with the Allonby crest, crystal goblets stood by each place setting and white linen napkins. The feast was already spread on the sideboard as Brent sat down, on the right of his cousin Mary, and he wondered how much they had sacrificed to prepare this repast for them—a great baron of beef, sides of ham, chickens, pies and crisp newly baked bread.

While they dined and the servants moved around the talk was kept to generalities about the weather, the state of the soil, the quality of grazing land and the bad winters they were having and which had taken off so many souls in recent years.

Brent knew that they had to talk with care because of the presence of Ambrose Rigg, that worthy merchant from Cockermouth who gave Sarah fifteen years and already had a paunch and the heavy-jowled look that comes from excessive fondness for food and drink and the good things of life. But it was not his appearance that worried the Allonbys, but his politics. It was men such as Rigg who ensured the survival of the Hanoverians, who had benefited by years of peace since George I came so wrongfully to the throne. Rigg's ancestors had been serfs, then "statesmen," yeoman farmers. Ambrose himself had broken away, gone to Whitehaven as a youth and slowly built up a fortune from very humble beginnings, first as a sailor, then as a ship owner and merchant.

But no amount of money could make up to Ambrose for his lack of breeding, his coarse ways and uncivilized manners. He had looked for a wife to remedy these defects and had found one in the impoverished Allonby family from whom he bought wood to build boats and houses. The history of the Allonby family was well known, how they had once been among the greatest in the county, but how foolish political involvements had reduced them almost to penury. But nothing could take away a good lineage and fine manners and Sarah Allonby, already well over twenty when he met her and looking for a husband, and a fortune, was just what he needed.

There was no question of love on either side, or even of much respect, at least on Sarah's. Ambrose was nearly forty, an uncouth old bachelor who picked his nose and scratched his behind in company. His face was already purple and his eyes had the rheumy look of the drinker; but as he began to come increasingly over to Furness Grange on his fine horse accompanied by a groom, she knew the reason was not to buy more wood from her brothers, though he did, but to court her.

126

Then he had invited the family to his new house in Cockermouth, built in extensive grounds with two floors and outbuildings. He had taken them to Whitehaven to inspect his ships and his warehouses and then, while they were still gawping at the scale of his wealth and possessions, he offered for Sarah's hand. Although her brothers were aghast she had known what to expect and promptly accepted. Not only would she no longer be an old maid, she would be a wealthy woman, too. What did Ambrose's origins, looks and disgusting manners matter?

Over the years they had been married Sarah had improved both his manners and his appearance. He was still paunchy and florid but he did not drink so much; his clothes were well cut and of good cloth and he no longer broke wind at the table. He had also sired two exceptionally beautiful children and although Sarah found the process of the siring disgusting, she was willing to put up with almost anything to achieve the status in life she now enjoyed. Let Ambrose get her with as many children as he wanted; she was able, and the more she had the more secure was her station in life, the more certain her hold on his possessions and wealth for her progeny.

Susan thought that night, as she looked at her niece from across the table that you could see from the set of Sarah's mouth that she had sold herself for money. The mouth was turned permanently downward as though in a sneer and there was a hard calculating look in her eyes. She had never been a beauty, but had looked well enough and she had the robust good sense and cheerfulness of the Allonbys. But now Sarah looked every inch a Rigg—the wife of a rich Hanoverian merchant of low origins but great ambition.

Sarah was as much taken aback by her sister's betrothal as anyone, but at the dinner table she saw quite clearly the reason. Mary was infatuated by Brent's animal charm—he had nothing else, no money, no prospects. Well Ambrose would not provide for him, that was for sure. Nor a dowry for Mary either. He bought enough wood and produce from her brothers that he did not need and, besides, his own family would increase and his duty lay with them.

"Now then," Ambrose was saying, his face florid with the abundance of good claret he had drunk. "This war in Europe is doing us no good. 'Twas a mistake to embark on it in the first place. What care we who reigns in Austria? Get out of it, I say. Let us have the peace good Walpole brought us in his day."

"If we have foreign kings they will concern themselves with foreign parts," John said, clearing his throat. "We need English kings on the throne."

Brent looked at his cousin with alarm, but Ambrose frowned and tapped his goblet on the table.

"I do not have any love for the Germans," he said, "as you know, John, but I have no love for the Stuarts either if I follow your meaning. I would favor the sort of government this country had under Cromwell. I would do away with kings and such wasteful nonsense and have a good honest republic."

Sarah smiled at her husband, not fondly, but as one cynically amused. The only thing that mattered to Ambrose was the amount of money that he could amass in the shortest possible time. Politics or who reigned in London were of not the slightest interest.

"My husband thinks that his coffers would swell greater with a man of business at the head of the government," she said. "Isn't that true, Ambrose?"

"Aye, 'tis," Ambrose nodded. "No frippery, no nonsense, mistresses and the like, such as I hear they have at court. A good man of business."

"Some say," John said slowly looking at his brother-in-law, "that the war is good for certain business."

"Oh?" Ambrose looked interested as though he might have missed something.

"Illicit brandy, tobacco, silks from France."

Ambrose's frank, shrewd expression which he had when discussing business grew guarded. Although it was well known that the smuggling trade thrived through successful respectable business-men like himself it was still unlawful, punishable by confiscation of property, fines and imprisonment. It disturbed him to think that John, in whom he did not confide, might have heard something of his activities in this connection. Many of his ships ran a profitable line in smuggled goods through the large entrepôt depot on the Isle of Man, plying from Roscoff and Nantes in France and Port Rush in Ireland.

"I know naught of illegal business," Ambrose said blandly. "I am a good honest merchant and I pay my duties and taxes. Now, wife, it is late; we should make an early start in the morning . . ."

John was quite used to Ambrose's habit of assuming he was the head of the household at the Grange. He did everything but sit at the head of the table, calling for food when his platter was empty and wine when he needed it. Now he had announced that the dinner was over and it was time for bed.

It was late; the candles had grown low in the sconces and some had even been replaced by the servants. Mary and Brent had said very little, preferring to excite each other by sly amorous glances, or the quick clasp of hands under the table.

But Ambrose had been looking surreptitiously at Brent throughout the dinner, noting that he was a fine strong man, broad shouldered though slim hipped. A fast mover. Without a home too, Ambrose had heard; a wastrel, kicked out by his brother. He did not look a wastrel, though, to Ambrose who had only met him a couple of times in his life whereas his brother George he knew quite well. They did business together and he knew that George despised him because he was of yeoman class, ill-mannered and self-made. George Delamain had always made it very clear how he felt about Ambrose Rigg: he would take his money or his goods but he would not sup or dine with him, or invite him to his castle—Sarah or no Sarah Allonby for a wife.

Ambrose was a man who nursed grudges. He was conscious of his origins and ashamed of them. His ancestors had been serfs for generations, serving the needs of the Allonbys and Delamains and such folk. Nothing was guaranteed to inspire greater enmity in Ambrose than to be patronized and snubbed by such as George Delamain, now Sir George, and the like. He had, therefore, looked at young Brent with interest; there would be no love here between the brothers. What a good way to pay George back for the humiliations he heaped on Ambrose—he had once made him wait outside the kitchen door when he called in person for payment, Ambrose not being a man to extend credit for too long.

"Aye," John said, echoing Ambrose, " 'tis late. But let us drink to the health of Brent and Mary." John got up and took his glass and the rest of the assembly joined him. "Brent and Mary . . . Brent and Mary, health, happiness."

Brent stood up and made a graceful, short little speech of thanks on behalf of himself and his betrothed and then everybody clapped and, at the signal from John, the servants appeared and drew back the chairs.

Ambrose went over and stood with his back to the fire getting out his pipe and filling it with fragrant American tobacco newly smuggled via Nantes.

"A word with you, Master Brent."

Brent was passing, his arm through Mary's, and stopped as Ambrose called to him. He bowed to Mary who continued with her sister into the drawing-room, and went over to where the tall broad merchant stood with a proprietorial air puffing his pipe as if he owned the place.

"Yes, sir?" Brent said, respectful of the years between him and his cousin's husband.

"Now lad, what do you do with yourself?"

"Well . . ." Brent faltered. He had done nothing and it was hard to say what he was about to do, especially to someone as much of the Establishment as Ambrose Rigg.

"Turned out of the castle, I hear."

"In a manner of speaking, yes sir."

130

"What are you going to do then?"

Ambrose spewed smoke right into Brent's face and gazed at him, chin slightly tilted, his hands behind his back.

"I thought of going to ... abroad."

"Ah, to seek work?"

"Yes."

"The colonies maybe, America ..."

"Yes, yes you could say that."

"But you don't have anywhere in mind?"

"I thought ... the West Indies," Brent improvised.

"You have connections there, of course?"

"No, sir." Brent began to realize he was sounding like an idiot. This man was trying to find out if he was suitable for his sister-in-law and clearly the answer would be no, at this rate. "I mean to try and find my own way, sir," he said, raising his head and meeting the level gaze of Ambrose.

" 'Twill be difficult with a wife."

"Oh, Mary will stay here. I have ... today given her brothers and my mother a promise not to marry her until I am able to support her."

Brent still choked at the thought of the solemn family conference that had taken place in the library just before dinner and made him so silent during it. As yet Mary knew nothing about it, which was just as well.

"Ah ... pity." Ambrose tapped out his pipe on the chimney piece and belched, looking quickly around to be sure his wife had not observed him. "Look here, young Delamain ... I hardly know you but I like what I see. A capable strong lad with a good pair of shoulders, and a good head ... Cambridge I hear? Oh don't worry, not much of a scholar I know, but neither am I and I've done well enough. How would you like to be taken into employment by me?"

Brent wondered if his ears were deceiving him. To work for Ambrose? Doing what? Keeping accounts? The idea was horrifying.

"Oh sir, 'tis kind of you but I have set my heart on abroad ..."

131

"You'll get there well enough, boy. I'll put you on one of my ships. Learn to be a captain, a master mariner maybe. Learn all the business; be my right hand if you're good. My son is far too young and will take a long time to catch up wi' me. You're about the right age."

Brent's senses reeled from the impact of what Ambrose was saying. Here he was about to embark for France on adventure and he was being offered a job as a merchant! The bile in his throat nearly choked him. But he knew Ambrose was far too important to offend out of hand—the Allonbys depended a good deal on business with him and, besides, there was Sarah, a sour piece and going sourer, but an Allonby all the same.

"Sir, you make me a very generous offer. May I have time to think about it?"

Ambrose's clap on his shoulder nearly sent Brent staggering. He was a powerful man, almost as tall as Brent and twice as large, though most of it was fat.

"Think on't lad, do. Not too long, mind. Talk it over with Mary. A few months in each part of the business, at sea, the warehouses and so on and then maybe a nice house in Whitehaven to bring the bride home to. You'll have a secure future within a year, Brent. I don't give a penny for your chances in the Indies or seeing Mary again before five years are out. Besides, are you not lame?"

Ambrose looked curiously at Brent's left leg which even now was hurting Brent through standing too long.

"Only temporarily, Mr. Rigg. It was injured in an accident."

"But they take time to heal, boy. I heard about the 'accident' too which makes me think you should hasten to the altar before she fetches you another one and dispatches you for good!"

Ambrose leaned back roaring with laughter, his red face puce with merriment, his eyes watering. Here was a lad of spirit! A seducer of every woman he

132

came upon apparently, and bold to boot. Brent's face was nearly as red as his.

" 'Twas not like that . . ."

"Oh, I know you can't remember. Knocked cold. No lad, wi' your hot blood you need a good woman and a steady job. Take my advice. There will be plenty of time for dalliance when you are wedded and your wife bedded with an infant or two." A roguish look came into his eyes, "I can show you in time one or two places in Whitehaven, and not just for sailors of the rough type either; but well kept, nice girls . . . don't worry, when you are well settled there is no need to become a dull fellow!"

Ambrose winked broadly and roared with laughter again and Brent began to understand why the perpetually sour look had transformed Sarah's once not unpleasing face. "There now, come and see me in a day or two. Talk it over with your family. 'Tis a fair offer."

Brent slept badly that night, tossing and turning in his bed. The thought of working for Rigg was abhorrent to him, yet one thing did trouble him and continued to do so. He *was* lame; his leg seemed the one part of him which refused to get completely better. If he walked or stood too long it hurt, not just a mild pain but an agony that precluded long hours marching, for the time being anyway.

Also there was Mary. She expected to marry him almost at once. She wanted to and so did he; but tomorrow he was going to have to tell her of his promise to John and his mother after that fearful family scene when they had both accused him of being a philanderer—too easy with women. The only way to show his sincerity was to wait, to prove to himself and them, and, above all, Mary that he was a man of honor, someone who kept his word, capable of giving and receiving true love.

They were immune to his arguments about the war, the question of losing his life. Who knew when the war would come? The Prince might stay in France forever, for all they knew. No, a year.

Brent gave a promise for a year. Now he would have to tell Mary.

Brent arose with the dawn and, dressing quickly, went to look for his eldest cousin who was always about at that hour doing his accounts or walking in the grounds. He found John in his study hunched over his ledgers, the room still lit by candles because the dawn light outside had scarcely penetrated the thick mullioned windows.

John looked surprised as Brent came in and rubbed his hands.

" 'Tis cold. The winter will come early. Could you not sleep, Brent?"

"No."

"I thought as much. I know how keen you are to wed and I know why. But you owe it to Mary . . ."

"It is not that only," Brent sat down, legs apart, hands on the arms of his chair and gazed at his cousin. "Ambrose wants me to work for him. He wants an answer, not today but soon."

"Work for Ambrose?" John said, echoing Brent's own sense of amazement. "Doing what?"

"Learning the business, being his right hand."

"But you don't want to do it, do you?"

"No."

"Then say no and that's it. Say it today before he goes." John cocked an ear. "I think I hear them stirring now. See, 'tis dawn." John blew out the candle and gazed at his cousin in the half light.

"John, I have been thinking a lot during the night; plans tossed about in my head like a bobbin on water. My leg is much worse than I admit . . ."

He saw a skeptical look come over John's face.

"Oh? I thought it was mended."

"Well not quite. It gets very painful if I walk far. Well that is a factor about going to France. If I become a fugitive I shall have much walking to do. How can I serve the Prince . . ."

134

He left the sentence unfinished noting the steady unfriendly gaze of his cousin.

"Aye. 'Tis as I thought. You do not wish to join your brother because, as always Brent, you put your heart first. You want Mary and by God you will do anything to have her—even renege your duty . . ."

Brent rose from the chair, his face white with fury. "John, how can you say such a thing! You think I am a renegade? I tell you I'll not touch your sister whether I go to France or no. I'll not see her or have ought to do wi' her, just to *prove* to you that I am not what you think, a craven rogue. Whether I go to France or whether I stay in England I will *not* abide a moment more at Furness. You have worked me up right proper, John."

And before his astonished cousin could say a word or intervene Brent stormed out of the room and took the stairs two at a time to where Ambrose was just emerging from his bedroom door fastening his cravat.

"Why, Brent, you're abroad early, lad!"

"I'll work for you," Brent said. "I'll come with you today. If you'll have me. I can start at once."

Ambrose's taciturn morning face broke into a grin. He put out an arm and drew Brent into the bedroom where Sarah was putting the finishing touches to her toilet.

"Excuse us, my dear," Ambrose said, observing that his wife was fully dressed and decent. "But Brent and I have business to discuss."

"I have the children to see to," Sarah said shortly and gathering up her shawl and putting it over her shoulders against the chill morning, left the room.

"Now, Brent," Ambrose said turning to the light so that he could see his face, "you've reached a decision overnight?"

"I have."

"Why do you look angry then? You look as though you were in some sort of temper."

"Well . . . I told John and he . . ."

"Thinks you're too good for me. All the Allonbys do, lad, aye *and* the Delamains . . ." Ambrose reached out and patted Brent's shoulder. "I am well used to their contempt; but I could buy and sell them all, you know, maybe even your brother although I do not take his property into account. No, I'm used to the scorn of the Allonbys—John and Stewart—I know what they think. But they take my money right enough and they tolerate me because I am wed to their sister. Oh, not worthy of it, I know . . . don't think she doesn't make me feel that too, rather she tries; but I take no notice. An Allonby woman in bed is like all the rest, I find; and once you've lain with a woman that's all you need to know about her . . . as I don't need to tell *you*, lad!" Ambrose gave him the same obscene wink as the previous night. "Oh no, what they say don't worry me . . ."

Brent felt he should defend his cousin but didn't know how. To tell him what John had said was to betray the cause. He bowed his head in shame at his inability to tell the truth.

"No, it was not like that exactly, Mr. Rigg. John thinks I stay here to be with Mary. That is why I want to come with you today, to get right away."

"Oh good. Capital. Pack your bags, boy, and you can come with us. Sarah and the children go with the maid to Keswick and back by coach, the way they came. I have to be in Cockermouth by dinnertime and it is hard riding over the hills. Be off now." He took Brent to the door and shook his hand, well satisfied that the day had started so well.

Brent hurried to his room and began to put together his possessions. The mist from the lake was gradually being dispersed by a wintry sun whose weak beams played across the floor of his room. Brent suddenly stopped and looked about him. He had come to love this room; it was his home. How could he have known this time yesterday as he waited for Mary to enter with his breakfast, and the brief kiss she allowed to go with it, that today he would be gone?

Everyone told him he was too quick off the mark, too sharp tempered. He'd hardly given John a chance . . . but what chance had John given *him?* Accusing

136

him of philandering, of reneging, of pretending hurt, of forsaking the cause, all for a maid.

His wounded pride made him angry again and he hurriedly crammed his things into a small leather bag that stood in the corner. Then he cast a final look round and strode to the door which, just as he reached it, burst open and Mary flew in, her face ashen.

"Brent, Brent, what is this? You are going? What is Ambrose saying?"

She hurled herself into his arms and, putting down his bag he folded them about her and hugged her to him, caressing her hair with his lips. Suddenly he felt too uncertain, too broken-hearted to speak. He felt a rare idyll was coming to an end. She leaned away from him and looked into his eyes.

"Is it true?"

He nodded.

"*Why,* Brent?"

"I have to prove myself . . . for you."

Mary broke away and stood back, a finger pointing incredulously toward herself.

"For me?"

Brent observed how pale she was, how her thin frame trembled and his heart went out to her in pity, and remorse. But he was still too angry, too stung with John's remark. He drew Mary to him and kissed her hungrily, pressing her body roughly against his until he felt her shudder with pain and try and draw away. Brent roughly let her go.

"Ask thy brother! He has taunted me this morning and I have had enough, Mary. I have sworn not to see you or to have aught to do with you until *they* think I am worthy. Ask *them!*"

The look of anguish she gave him told him she did not understand—the reason for his sudden departure, his brutal and passionless embrace. He felt tears of frustration and rage sting his eyes as he ran down the stairs, aware that she was not following him.

He did not see Mary again. As he quickly broke his fast and said his farewells she remained upstairs. John did not try to make him change his mind, did not know what to say, but shook his hand and wished him well. His mother, so lately reunited with him, only sorrowed to see him set off so quickly again; but she knew the reason. Had she not herself helped to contribute to it? She kissed him sadly, her eyes half filled with unshed tears.

"Go well, my son. Thank God you are recovered. You know where I am when you need me and, Brent," she looked gravely into his eyes, "I *do* trust you. I know you will do what is right and in time you will think that what we did was right."

Brent turned from his mother, kissed his sister, still half asleep, shook the hands of his silent cousin and mounted a horse lent to him by Stewart. Then with Ambrose Rigg panting on his horse behind him he set off along the narrow track that led over Catbells, across the Newlands Valley, and up over tree-covered Whinlatter to the prosperous little town of Cockermouth.

Chapter Eight

Analee lay in the dark next to Randal. She was cold and she pressed up against his body to draw warmth from it. Randal stirred and sighed in his sleep; she was conscious of his hard buttocks against her stomach, her breasts against his lean hard back.

It was two months since Randal had bound her hand and foot and tossed her in the cart, taken her off and married her. Two months and the weather had turned from a warm and mellow September into a bitter November. But more than that, Analee had turned from a free wandering gypsy into a settled married woman who cooked for Randal, kept the tent clean and chatted endlessly with the other women of the tribe while the men squatted together mending pots and pans, smoking and drinking beer.

At night she and Randal came together and made love but, apart from that, apart from knowing that she was his woman and he was her man, they had very little knowledge of each other; they had very little to say. It had not been like that with her last real love, the reason for her wandering—they had talked the day and night round, yearning continually for each other's company, the touching and the hearing of sounds.

Analee knew it was not usual for women and men to want to be together so much, to have so much to say to each other. She had observed enough around her, experienced it in her own life, to know that the sexes were very different. Except for making love, or dancing, they kept apart even in the camp. She and the women chatted and gossiped; the men talked in low tones about what they were doing. Men and women had really nothing in common at all, except for this one thing—the need to communicate with each other bodily in order to breed.

And that was what worried Analee this bitter November night as she lay awake pressed against Randal. She knew she was with child. It had happened to her before and it was happening again; she knew the signs —the absence twice of her woman's monthly time when, in some tribes, women were considered unclean, *marimé,* and had to go into a separate tent and sleep apart from their menfolk until it was over. In addition her breasts pained her and she felt tired and listless.

Analee didn't want a child. She was already feeling constricted living here in this camp with the chattering women and the swarms of children who ran around their feet every day. The thought of a baby and then another, until she was fat with heavy pendulous breasts and a perpetually tired and harassed expression . . . it didn't suit her at all. Analee already wanted to be off on her travels. The compulsion she'd had ever since the tragedy was with her again: to be tied to Randal as his wife and the mother of his child, children . . . she shuddered. She couldn't take to the road when she had children. She would be trapped.

Her movement made Randal stir again and he turned toward her in his sleep and the *kar*, the part of him that bred children—regarded with veneration by gypsy folk—pressed into her again, even though he slept. The touch thrilled her and awakened her desire, and she held it with her hands until it grew and throbbed and swelled and erupted its effluence all over her belly. She rubbed it into her skin with her hands because it was such a beneficent enriching substance, the source of life, making children as well as beautiful soft skin. She rubbed it on her face, her nostrils flaring at the pungent smell, and she stroked the *kar* tenderly as it lay against her thighs because it was a giver of such good things, a source of such strength, such beauty.

Analee felt very close to Randal because of his emission onto her in the night. In a way she did love him. He was one of the best looking men in the camp. He was tender as well as proud and vigorous, and a satisfying if inexpert lover. But he had not had much opportunity. Gypsy men were chaste, and that was why he had been so anxious to find a wife; to assuage the torment and the heaviness of unsatisfied lust.

But Analee was a good lover, and over the weeks she had taught Randal how to contain his urge so that he satisfied her too and, in doing so, made it even better for himself. She showed him how to make it last, how to concentrate the mind on something else while the postponed climax made the desire more pleasurable, and the result even more rewarding when it came. She showed him what things a woman could do to excite a man besides lying on her back; how she could lie on top of him; or sit astride him showing him the full beauty of her figure, her breasts above his head, her stomach level with his eyes. Or she could sit with her back to him, and he could observe the marvel of her straight back and round buttocks; or he could approach her from behind and, as he leaned over her or lay on her, grasp her rounded breasts or her soft yielding buttocks.

Then she showed him all the things a woman could do to a man to please him even more; caress his nipples or his *kar,* or show herself to him in different ways —and she taught him what he could do to give her pleasure and bring her to the point of frenzy without entering her.

All the nuances of love-making Analee taught Randal, to his increasing pleasure over the weeks, until he could hardly wait for the sun to go down when they could make their way to their tent and begin the delights of making love all over again.

But the one thing they had not done, which most gypsies did not do, was try and prevent the fruits of their love-making from developing into a child. And this was because Randal wanted a child; wanted to make Analee his own even more than she was already.

But Analee, because she had second sight, because she was experienced in these womens' things as well, knew the child was not Randal's. She knew the cycle of the woman and that when she had lain with Brent she had been fertile; she knew the signs of fertility— the cramp in the abdomen, sometimes the tiny spot of blood on the underskirt. She'd been like that the day she'd lain with Brent.

Brent Delamain was the father of her child. Even if she had not known the physical signs; she knew in her gypsy's heart it was so. She with child by a *gadjo,* not by her husband, and the child might have blond hair, a white skin and an aquiline aristocratic face— just like Brent Delamain and not like Randal Buckland at all.

Analee felt heavy-hearted as she lay in the dark waiting for the glimmer of dawn to appear through the entrance to the tent. She thought with tenderness of the beautiful *gadjo,* of their two meetings in the moonlit forests—one to meet and kiss, and one to make love. That was all. Oh, but she had danced for him. When she had seen him in the tavern standing looking at her darkly from the shadows, it was for him *alone* she had danced, flaunting her body and offering herself to him as only she, Analee, knew how.

Randal stirred and his *kar* grew big against the hair of her thighs. She felt her breasts swell and her heartbeat quickened with desire. She slid onto him so that she lay on top of him and she pressed her face into his thick black hair. The *kar* swelled inside her and she rode him gently up and down while, still half asleep, his face lit up with the intensity of the pleasure and he groped for her full, pointed breasts above him. Then he woke completely and he drew her down and crushed his mouth on hers, and licked her face with his tongue all over as she increased the momentum of her heaving thighs until he spent his seed inside her.

Randal could feel her beating heart above his as she lay flat on his chest, having timed her climax with his. He stared with wonder at her face pressed up against his; it was a dream of beauty and womanliness such as Randal still didn't feel he deserved: that she'd come so reluctantly and then given herself so completely. He knew that it was meant to be so with women; after all, they did belong to men, it was the way of nature. And yet Analee was different; she was like no gypsy woman he had ever met or hoped to meet. All the women in the camp said she was foreign, but she refused to discuss herself except to say she came from the South.

He whispered into her ear that he loved her and she opened her eyes and smiled into his. He wanted to hear her say she loved him; but although she said many things to him she never told him that.

"I want us to have a child, Analee," he whispered, there in the dawn, knowing how many times he had put his seed deep inside her, knowing every time as he thrusted deeper and deeper with more and more force, that he was aware of his urgent need to create.

"Water her well," old Rebecca had cackled, knowing his desire, "and she will bring forth in time like the good earth."

"In time," Analee said, sliding off him and lying by his side, "there is plenty of time for a child."

"I want many children. Maybe move away and start our own tribe."

Analee was silent. She felt pity and sorrow for Randal knowing that what he wanted so much was inside her, but it was not his. She couldn't tell him. She would have to see Reyora the *cohani* and do something about it.

"It is not Randal's child," Analee said, deep inside the *cohani*'s tent.

Reyora nodded as though she'd known already. She looked very wise, squatting on her haunches with her shawl round her head half obscuring her face. On every finger she had rings, and on her bare ankles Analee could see the glow of gold bands. She'd sought out the *cohani* after the noonday meal when Randal had gone off with the men to look for hedgehogs and pigeons. The women would think she was asking the *cohani* for a spell, maybe to make her fertile. They would not know the reason.

But Reyora had been waiting for Analee to come to her; she had not known why, but she had known it would be Analee and not Randal who would come. Everyone could see that after the wedding they had been happy and could not wait to go to their tent at night. They would creep away from the fire even before it was dark.

"It is the child of a *gadjo*," Reyora said after a pause. "A blond, handsome *gadjo*. Maybe a lord?"

Analee looked at her, marveling at the skill of the *cohani* who could tell not only the past but the future as well.

"You see I cannot have the child of a *gadjo*. Randal would kill me if he knew. If the child is dark as we are, then . . . but I will not know until it is born."

Reyora nodded again. She was often asked for potions of philters to abort gypsy women, usually when they were with child before marriage or when they had too many. Such was her skill that she did it for the *gadjo* women too, and often would depart for Carlisle in answer to an urgent summons carrying with her her bag of herbs and ointments.

"If you do it now, early, he will never know," Analee said, "and then we can have his child."

Reyora looked enigmatic and, for a moment, Analee thought she was going to tell her to clear out, to expose her before the whole camp. She had lain with a *gadjo* and then married a gypsy. But Reyora was merely looking at her, swaying backward and forward on her hips, her face leaning sideways on her hand.

"You are not full gypsy, are you, Analee? You are *didakai*—half gypsy?"

"You have known all the time?"

"Pretty well," Reyora said, swaying. "There was so much about you that I did not understand. You look like a full blooded gypsy and behave like one, but I know."

"My father was not a gypsy," Analee said slowly, quietly, fearing that anyone should hear. "That is all I know for my mother died when I was born. Her mother brought me up and all she would say was that my father was a *gadjo,* but that as he was dark like my mother no one could tell. It was said I was her child, my grandmother's, because otherwise my mother would have been cast out from the tribe. My mother was only sixteen when I was born. That is all I can tell you."

"And now you have a child by a *gadjo,*" Reyora smiled softly. "Was it someone casual you met, or do you love him? That was why you were so reluctant to wed Randal."

Reyora nodded, rocking back and forward slowly. It was all making sense now.

"I knew him hardly at all; we met in an extraordinary way. But we had affinity; it was like love."

"Then the child was conceived in love, that is good."

144

"But I don't want the child . . ."

Analee looked with bewilderment at the *cohani*. Surely she realized that?

"You are sure?"

"I don't know where the *gadjo* is, or even if he is alive. Randal injured him when he saw us together. I cannot have his child. I know nothing about him."

Reyora got up and went to the corner of her tent. She took a taper from a box and went outside to light it from the fire that burned in front of the tent. Then she came back and, lighting the candle, put it on a box beside the palliasse on the floor.

"Come and lie here," she said to Analee, and she busied herself with a box that stood by the palliasse.

Analee felt frightened but she did as she was bid. She lay on the straw and watched the *cohani* taking powders from different boxes and mixing them in a bowl. Then she spat into the bowl and said some sort of incantation over it and left it in front of the candle.

She took a jar from some vessels by the box and brought it over to Analee.

"I want you to make urine in this for the spell," she said passing her the jug. Analee obeyed and got onto her haunches squatting over the jug while the *cohani* gazed at her. Analee knew quite well the power of urine in gypsy magic. It was sometimes used for weddings when the man and the woman urinated into the same bowl, and the produce was mixed with brandy and earth and used in the ceremony. Diseases of the lung, it was said, were often cured by the drinking of urine and it could heal skin and eye diseases. Some women even washed their faces in it to have good skin, much as Analee had rubbed her husband's semen into hers during the night for the same effect.

Reyora took the jar and bade her lie down again. She poured a little of the warm liquid into the bowl and added some more powder until she had a paste.

Then she took it to Analee and told her to spit into it and the paste became runny like thick syrup.

Reyora brought cushions over to the straw and put them under Analee's buttocks.

"Now roll up your skirt," she said, "and make yourself as high on the cushions as you can."

Analee did as she was told until her buttocks were suspended up high, her legs stretched wide in front of her. Reyora removed her rings and washed her hands in water, then she knelt by Analee and put her hand gently between her legs into the cavity Analee had made for her. She smiled encouragingly at Analee to still her terror and told her to relax, but Analee's heart beat fast and the groping caused her pain and made her uncomfortable. She could tell by the slow delicate way that Reyora probed and her solemn expression that she was very experienced, that she knew what she was doing.

Reyora drew out her fingers and bade Analee rest. She washed them again in the water.

"You are already big," she said, "have you had a child before?"

Analee was silent wondering what to say. She felt hot and uncomfortable and there was a little pain inside her.

"It is not like the womb of a woman who has not given birth," Reyora said turning to her, "it is soft and slack like a womb that has already been stretched in childbirth."

"I did have a child," Analee said. "It died."

"Ah."

Reyora nodded, as if in understanding and knelt down again. Then she told Analee to be as she had before, and raised her buttocks as high as she could, gently forcing her legs apart. She stirred the ointment in the bowl with a wooden spoon and gently, slowly poured it between Analee's legs. Analee felt it fiery and burning inside her and cried in pain; but Reyora went on relentlessly, holding Analee with one hand while she poured with the other until all the liquid was gone or had spilt over onto Analee's stomach. Then she held her firm looking at her, while Analee sobbed with the pain and she bit her hand to hold back the screams.

Suddenly the burning stopped and Analee felt calm. She looked at Reyora and took her hand out of her mouth. The hand was covered with the marks of her teeth, where she had bit deeply.

Reyora removed the cushions and gently lowered her legs onto the palliasse and wiped Analee's belly with a cloth, then she pulled down her skirts and covered her with a rug.

"Now you will feel tired for a while," she said. "Rest."

"When will it work?"

"*If* it works," Reyora said, "it will be within two days."

"And if it doesn't?"

"Then you will have a child." Reyora turned to her blandly and smiled. "That is the strongest philter I have. But you are a hardy woman, Analee, good and strong for child-bearing, and it will be difficult to dislodge."

Analee felt her eyes closing with drowsiness; as she went off to sleep Reyora was kneeling beside her, smiling and stroking her face.

That night as she lay against Randal pressing again for warmth, Analee felt a searing pain in her belly. She cried out and bent up her legs to try and ease it; then she felt something sticky and wet come out from between her legs. She started to sweat and, putting her hand there, knew it was blood. The philter had worked. She felt both relief and dismay; a curious emotion she had not expected—not the dismay. Then the pain started again, only twice as bad and she called out to Randal to help her. Randal turned and clasped her.

"What is it, Analee?"

"I have a terrible pain in my belly."

"But what is it?"

"I . . ." Analee nearly screamed with the pain and thrust her legs up to her chin. Randal jumped off the palliasse, and hastily putting on his breeches flew out of the tent without another word.

Within minutes he had returned with a candle and Reyora who had her little bag of ointments in her hand. She looked at Analee stretched out, her body gleaming with sweat, her legs alternately wide apart and then pressed against her chin. She covered her naked top part and knelt down putting her hand again between her legs, just softly to feel at the entrance and then, squatting, she tried to see into the parting she had made.

Randal hovered anxiously by, the candle guttering in his hand as the thin wind blew around the tent. Reyora finally completed her examination and sat back on her heels, her hand on Analee's belly.

"Have you had any movement in the belly? Any cramps?" she asked. Analee shook her head.

"I just get the waves of pain . . . you think?" She looked at Reyora, her expression a compound of fear and hope. "The blood . . . ?"

Reyora looked onto the palliasse.

"There was only a little blood, there is none now."

"Blood . . ." Randal said stepping forward, "she is injured?"

"She is with child," Reyora said shortly, "maybe losing it. It is hard to tell."

Randal gave a cry that nearly put out the candle and knelt beside Analee.

"Oh, Analee, a child. Do not lose our child."

Reyora looked away and Analee pursed her mouth grimly through the pain. Her eyes caught those of Reyora.

"Is there anything else you can do?" she said. Reyora knew Analee was asking her to do more to remove the baby. She shook her head.

"I can relieve the pain in your belly, but inside . . . I can do nothing."

She opened her bag and took an ointment that smelt strongly of dung which she massaged on Analee's aching stomach. The strong firm hands went back and forward and slowly Analee began to feel a delicious relief, a calm that swept away the pain and left her free. Randal grasped her hand and cradled her head in her arms. "Do not lose our child, Analee. Reyora, stay with her . . ." Reyora nodded soothingly and went on rubbing up and down, from side to side. Then she crooned a little song and Analee's eyes drooped and her head lolled against Randal's arm.

Two hours later the dawn came and still Analee slept while Randal held her head and, from time to time, clasped her in his arms. Reyora sat watching them, occasionally swaying back on her haunches, getting fresh ointment and soothing the flat brown belly.

Analee sighed and opened her eyes. She stared at Randal and her eyes looked at her stomach and then questioningly at Reyora.

Reyora smiled and shook her head, ceased the rubbing and drew the covers back over Analee's naked thighs and legs. Then she got up and looked down at her and Randal. "You will be all right now. There will be no more pain. You will have the child. It is ordained."

Analee didn't know whether she was happy or sad and pressed her head into Randal's arm, so that he should not observe such confusion.

On a cold January morning in the year 1745 Sir George Delamain set out from his newly acquired house in Essex Street for the long drive to his northern home. Sir George was pleased with his visit to the capital. Not only had he acquired a home which was well fitted to the important station he intended to assume in life from now on, but he had made an inroad in Whig politics by dint of skillful social climbing. He had made the acquaintance of the Prime Minister, the Duke of Newcastle, and had almost got for himself a bride.

Almost. Sir George Delamain had been introduced a year before to Lord Dacre who had immediately selected him as a fitting escort for his daughter Henrietta who, although plain, had much to commend her for marriage. She was an heiress. Her mother, Constance

Dacre was, like Henrietta, an only child and had brought with her all the wealth of her family, the Farthingales, on her marriage to the third baron Dacre.

The Dacres had an estate on the borders of Lancashire and Lord Dacre and old Sir Francis Delamain had been acquaintances, but George and Henrietta had never met until George was asked to deliver a message to Lord Dacre in London some months before his grandfather's death.

In George Delamain Lord Dacre saw a marriageable proposition for his plump, gawkish daughter. The Delamains, Dacre knew, did not lack wealth or possessions and they had the acquisitive instinct—that is, they always wanted more than they had already. It was a well known Delamain trait. Henrietta, married to George, would be free from the adventurers who courted her solely for her prospects, aimless good-fornothings with nothing but the sort of dashing good looks which appealed so much to someone as ill favored by fortune as poor Henrietta Dacre.

In his way George Delamain too would be a fortune hunter, but Henrietta would have as much to gain: a husband with an old family background, large estates and plenty of ambition. Lord Dacre knew of George's singular wish for a barony; he felt he could help George in every way.

It was he who had introduced George to the Prime Minister and leading figures in Whig politics, who had given balls and soirées at which George was an honored guest. Above all, it was he who had warned George about the danger of a Jacobite rebellion; the effect it would have on their fortunes, possible confiscation both of the Delamain and Dacre estates if the Stuarts were restored to the throne. London was full of rumors of a Jacobite invasion. The Earl of Traquair, known to be sympathetic to the Stuart cause, had been in London that very winter sniffing out the support among suspected Jacobites. There was intelligence of his activities, and the fact that he had gone to France to see Prince Charles to bring—who knew what tidings?

The Delamain connection with the Stuarts was well known; above all their close relationship with those traitors the Allonby family—Robert Allonby who had been beheaded on Tower Hill and Guy Delamain, his brother-in-law, who had died in exile in France. George was perpetually anxious to shed this painful association with the Stuart cause—he thus became more pro-Hanoverian than the King himself, and did everything to make his own antipathy toward the Stuarts clear to all concerned. Had he not expelled his brother Brent, and his more notorious brother Tom, from the house the instant his grandfather died? Had he not hastened to London to establish a house, ingratiate himself with the Hanoverian politicians, with the court itself? No one was more anxious to stamp out any trace of Jacobitism than George Delamain and he was thus regarded, perched as he was at a strategic point in the north of England, as an important recruit by those who intended to preserve the Hanoverian succession at any cost.

Looking out of the windows as his coach rumbled mile upon dreary mile northward, George had plenty of time for reflection, for planning the future. There were frequent stops to change horses, and five nights were spent in inns on the way as the roads got worse and more narrow and the journey more tedious.

Yes, he was well pleased with his visit—Dacre had become not only a prospective father-in-law, but a good friend. He was a powerful man. He would help to remold George's image from that of a farming squire to a land-owner and politician of importance. The part George did not altogether like was the role that had been urged upon him to spy. Even he, a man of few scruples, did not relish having to ingratiate himself with his Allonby cousins to try and discover what was afoot in France. But he had promised not only Dacre but the small circle of serious-minded men, men of power and political importance, who had gathered at Dacre's house in Covent Garden to discuss the importance of the visit of the Earl of Traquair and the threat of Jacobite invasion.

George, they had pointed out, was a pivot—through no fault of his own he had access to traitorous elements. Why, by getting the information they sought he could not only pay a lasting service to his country but, who knows, maybe elevate himself to the peerage at the same time?

Baron Delamain—*The* Baron Delamain—George rolled the name round his tongue. It suited him well . . . Baron Delamain in the county of Cumberland, and Baroness Delamain . . . George felt a little less easy when he reflected on the charms, or rather lack of them, in his intended bride. He made no bones about it either to himself or Dacre—it was a marriage of convenience. It suited Dacre and himself that he should take Henrietta for a bride: what the girl herself thought about it was of no concern to either of them.

She would breed well, George reflected. She had ample girth, too much in fact, and good broad hips. The trouble was there was a history of only children in her family, and girls at that . . . but still, the woman was merely the vessel, it was the man who decided the nature and sex of the progeny and everyone knew Delamain men were good breeders, breeders of sons.

Yes, it was time he had a son, got rid of the menace of the whippet Brent taking over the title and estates should anything happen to him. Pity he had recovered from the injury that his folly had inflicted upon him . . . hit over the head by a gypsy! Even George, who seldom laughed, smirked at the thought. Thank goodness no one in London knew, or could ever possibly find out, about *that* peculiar piece of idiocy.

The coach rumbled northward and no one, neither Allonby, nor Delamain nor even the Buckland gypsies in their camp near Carlisle knew what a momentous year 1745 was to be for them, and how fundamentally the fortunes of so many concerned were to change.

Chapter Nine

From the distance Brent Delamain could see the outline of the slate cliffs that meant Maughold Peninsula and journey's end—or nearly journey's end. From the beginning he had proved a good sailor. "A natural affinity with the sea," Ambrose had proclaimed proudly when Brent was the only man still on his legs after a particularly severe voyage from Port Rush. But this comparatively short journey from Whitehaven in Cumberland to the Isle of Man had provided seas such as Brent had never before seen or wanted to again.

Once again he was the only man on his legs and, because the hold was almost empty, the boat had rolled about until at one stage he had thought it would turn turtle, and that would be the end of them.

Now the waters were calmer and the sailors started to stagger up from below, all except the master who had drunk himself into a stupor through sheer fear and was out cold in his bunk. Brent had just been down to see. He would have to bring the ship into the cove himself with the help of the mate, a dour fellow called Quiggan.

The ship rounded Maughold Head and then turned inland following the rugged coast to the harbor at the north end of Laxey Bay. Brent was grateful that it was wide and shallow because he had only been a sailor for three montths and his knowledge of navigation was elementary.

They tied up at the jetty at Laxey and, leaving the master in his berth, Brent made for the narrow main street of the town which lay in the shadow of Snaefell, the highest mountain in the Isle of Man.

Brent had been glad to take to the sea and get away from the watchful eye of Sarah Rigg with whom he lodged in Cockermouth. He had proved an adept apprentice and pupil and had soon justified Ambrose's confidence that the man was no idler but possessed of a good brain as well as a hardy body.

Indeed, a curious and unexpected friendship had grown between Brent and his employer, who proved not only fair and hardworking but curiously honest in his rough-necked kind of way. Brent had discovered how much in awe of his wife Ambrose really was; how he resented his humble ancestry, his lack of manners and how he looked to Sarah to turn him into a gentleman.

It was too late to turn Ambrose Rigg into a gentleman, Brent knew that. As he listened to his outpourings over the port when Sarah had gone to bed, he tried to persuade him that the things Ambrose considered important were not—that using a napkin and developing fine airs were of far less consequence than charity, kindness and honesty and the sort of diligence and business acumen that Ambrose so successfully displayed.

Brent envied him these things and he told him so and as Ambrose listened to this young lad, his eyes were opened and he developed a sense of self-respect for his own innate attributes that were God-given and not acquired.

Consequently Sarah Rigg, seeing how affected her husband was by his association with Brent, how less respectful toward herself, was eager to have him out of the house and gladly concurred when it was suggested that Brent should leave clerking in the warehouse and take to the sea.

Brent went to sea at a very bad time—mid-February, a month of storms and gales; but he found his sea legs quickly and also a sense of survival. He learned rudimentary navigation and the storing of ballast, and how to stow the sails with the maximum of speed when the storm winds blew up.

He had survived a battering three month's apprenticeship. Now it was May and the seas were calmer. The trees and hedgerows were abud with new life in the lanes of Cumberland and the Isle of Man, and he felt a lightening of the heart as he climbed up the steep main street to Laxey. His object was to see to the new cargo for Whitehaven of lead and copper ore, products of the mines at Dhoon north of Lazey, the purpose of this trip. At other times he put into the creeks nearer Maughold and Bradda Head to take off zinc and galena. In return he brought timber and wool and food for the Isle of Man was very dependent on the mainland of England from which it had been ruled since 1300, the Dukes of Athol having recently taken over from the Stanleys who had been Lords of Man for three hundred years.

It was a fine clear day, a breeze blew in from the sea and Brent came to the house of John Collister, a ship's merchant and chandler with whom he had had commerce before and who was one of Ambrose's agents on the island.

John Collister, a bluff handsome man of fifty and an ex-sailor who had acquired a wooden leg in the wars against France, was waiting for Brent, sitting at a table piled with bills and ledgers. He got up as Brent came in and called for his daughter Harriet to fetch some ale.

Harriet, wearing her best bonnet and apron was pleased to answer her father's summons: she always had a glad eye for Brent Delamain whenever he came to Laxey—but he only gave her the most casual of glances, polite but nothing more. Not that Brent was unaware of Harriet's charms or her obvious intention of bestowing them on him, freely, for the asking. She made it quite clear by the way she flounced in and out or lingered by the door gazing slyly up at him. Once she had even followed him on some pretext or the other; but all to no avail. Since he had wrenched himself from Mary Allonby, Brent was a different

155

man. He was determined to make a fresh image for himself from that of a philanderer and idler: to work hard and preserve his virtue in order to be worthy of Mary.

For a man of Brent's disposition the work was no hardship, but the maintenance of chastity was, especially with Ambrose forever suggesting a visit to the local bawdy house and making it clear that he frequented the place often himself.

"Art a puritan lad?" Ambrose would chide suggesting he had expected better. But it was the only complaint he had against Brent, so he decided to keep a wise counsel, say no more and continue to visit the bawdy house by himself.

Brent and Mary had made up for the force of the separation by an exchange of letters. He had written, on reflection, to explain his behavior to her and asked her to show the letter to her brothers as a sign of his good intentions. After a short interval Mary had replied indicating her acceptance of the situation and her happiness at the sacrifice Brent was prepared to make to woo her.

From then on they corresponded chastely every week, but they never met. Brent had imposed on himself this condition: their next meeting would be to be wed.

He well knew the meaning of Harriet Collister's glances as she brought in ale and oat cakes. He smiled at her in his detached friendly fashion, willing enough to exchange the time of day with her; but John seemed anxious for her departure and waved her away. His face was serious as he poured out the ale from the jug into a tankard of thick pewter and pushed it over to Brent.

"Good voyage?"

"A devil for the time of year. We were very light and bobbed about like a cork."

"And Dinward?"

"Drunk."

John nodded. Dinward was the master and seldom sober, good sea or bad.

156

"Ambrose should get rid of him. He is a menace and a threat."

"He is a good sailor when sober, and I am learning fast."

"So I hear."

John got up and, with his tankard in his hand, hobbled over to the window looking through the thick panes which gave on to the harbor. He turned and glanced at Brent as though to say something and then turned away again. Brent knew the signs of restlessness.

"You have aught to say to me, John, and cannot?"

John turned round, quaffing his ale from his tankard so that a line of fine white froth remained on his upper lip.

"I know not where to begin."

"John, if it is your daughter, I am promised . . ."

John gave a hearty laugh and wiped his lip on the sleeve of his coat.

"Oh, you observe how she hankers after you. No, I told her she had no hope there, a nobleman . . ."

" 'Tis not *that!* I am promised to my cousin. Harriet is a fine lass."

"Aye, aye and she'll get wed soon enough; but it is not of Harriet I speak. Brent . . ." John sat down heavily and put his large hand squarely on his good knee. "I wonder which way you are?"

"Which way . . ." Brent looked at John in bewilderment.

"Because if I speak out of turn I am undone."

Collister stared at Brent as though willing him to understand what he was saying, and then Brent did understand. It came to him suddenly and clearly.

"Which way . . . politically?"

"Aye, aye." Collister sat back with a sigh of relief; now he had no need to fear compromising himself.

"You are only asking me for one reason, John. There is much unrest abroad, much talk of revolt. You are asking me if I am for the Stuarts?"

"Aye." John gazed at him, mouth half open, eyes glinting.

"Of course I am for the Stuarts; you know our family."

"I know they are divided, that much I heard. That one of your brothers is a popish priest and the other a Whig baronet. It was through the priest that news came of you . . ."

"From Tom? You have heard from Tom?" Brent jumped up, his face glowing. "I have tried so hard to contact Tom since I came to Whitehaven; but he has gone aground."

"Not gone aground. He is with the Prince, but the Prince is now surrounded by many men. Most wish him well; but some harm. He has to be careful. It is hard to tell who the traitors are—disaffected Irish soldiers, men of all descriptions and every nationality you can think of surround him. Not all honest men. But now . . ." John leaned forward, his eyes gleaming, "the Prince has made up his mind to sail."

"For England?"

"For *Scotland*. The recent defeat at Fontenoy by Marshal Saxe of the combined British and Hanoverian force under the command of the Duke of Cumberland has determined the Prince that the time is ripe. He is preparing to sail this very instant."

"But surely it is *folly*."

"Aye, folly and a grand one at that. All Scotland will flock to such a brave Prince and then all England, too. You will see, in a few months the Stuarts will be again on the throne."

"Then how do you know, what part do you . . . will the Prince land *here?*"

"Nay, in the north of Scotland where all is prepared. But men close to Murray of Broughton, one of the Prince's right hand men, have been in touch with contacts of mine in Scotland and Cumberland. We are to get as many provisions for the Prince as we can from France and Ireland and America, muskets and cannon and gunshot and swords—and smuggle them into England."

Now the light dawned. Brent stood up and refilled his tankard.

"And you want me to help?"

"Can you?"

"Can I not!" Brent shouted. "John Collister, I was born to live for this day. You have made a man of me. I was sworn to serve the King and the Prince, but I had an injury that has affected my leg. But for it I would have gone to France with my brother, been by his side and that of Prince Charles this very instant. But I could not go and Tom, perforce, left without me. He left no message and nowhere to find him. Then Ambrose offered me work and he is well known for his Hanoverian sympathies, though sometimes I wonder . . ."

"Oh, he is Hanoverian all right," John said grimly. "Make no mistake about it. That is why he must never know of what is afoot, that we are using his ships to smuggle arms into England."

"Then how shall we do it?"

"Easily. You know Fleswick Bay close by St. Bees?"

Brent nodded.

"We will have a boat waiting to rendezvous with you; a small craft capable of traveling over shallow water. You will get the Captain drunk, put out the anchor and it will all be done. Then you proceed to Whitehaven with your ore."

"A smuggler!" Brent exclaimed excitedly. "An arms smuggler."

"And a price on your head if you are caught."

"My family have already died for the Stuarts."

"I know. I heard. But I had to be sure."

"Oh, John, you can be sure of me." Brent went over to the older man and clasped his shoulder. Then they solemnly shook hands and downed the rest of their ale. "Now tell me how it is to happen."

"I have the goods here in my barn," John said leaning toward Brent and lowering his voice. "We will load the ore this afternoon and the arms tonight. Then you set out with the morning tide."

"But Dinward. He will be sober by then."

"He will be sober to see the ore loaded on board.

Then the hatches will be closed and he will be taken to the town by one of my men."

"And sloshed with ale."

"Precisely, while we load the ship with arms. By first light if he is sober he will not know what he carries in his ship. You should approach Fleswick at nightfall tomorrow. That will be the difficult time; so you must ply Dinward with enough drink to ensure a good slumber and tie him up in his cabin. Our men will rendezvous at midnight."

"But if Dinward wakes? He has a good head."

John looked at him, his face grim. "Then you must kill him."

Brent stared for a long while at the old mariner. It was the first time that the prospect of death as a part of the forthcoming battle had become a reality. He had talked about it often enough with gallantry and without any real understanding. He had made it romantic in connection with Mary Allonby. But now it might mean a blade through the back in the small hours of the morning and the dumping of a weighted body out at sea. Now it was reality.

"Could you *kill*, Brent?"

Brent considered before answering.

"In cold blood I cannot think of it; but we are engaged in war . . . I have considered it often enough. I could do it."

"Good. Dinward would be not such a bad thing to start on. He is a good-for-nothing rogue and I believe he has no family so you would not be leaving a widow and orphans."

"Let us hope it does not come to that," Brent said. "But what of the crew?"

"They are stupid men, also fond of drink. Quiggan the mate is fond of money and him we can bribe. He will help you."

"Good, then give me the details—who I am to meet and how."

Later that night Brent stood on the deck smoking a pipe. The great crags rose up toward Snaefell which looked as though it was snow-capped in the white light of the moon. It had been a bad night for loading dangerous goods; too bright and too mild, too many people strolling on the quayside. But now it was done and Brent leaned over the side of the ship gazing into the clear water, hoping for a calm run on his first mission as a servant, albeit a humble one, of the true King.

And indeed at first all went well. Dinward was brought aboard drunk and slept all night; but at dawn he was wide awake, alert and on deck. The trouble with Dinward was that he got drunk easily but he recovered very quickly. Brent could see that a problem would occur in twelve hours time as they anchored off Fleswick Bay.

But problems occured before that. The promise of good weather did not hold and it was a rough voyage. Instead of drinking, Dinward stayed on deck eagle-eyed, directing the passage of the boat through the high waves that pounded from the west.

That night, after a stormy voyage the seas still pounded against the ship but, before dark, the welcome coast of Cumberland came into sight, first as a thin line on the horizon. Then, as the boat got nearer, Brent could see in the distance the mountains of Lakeland topped by great Scafell rising from the flat coastal stretch. He thought of Mary so near and yet so far, whom he could not see. She would be getting the supper now or reading a book by candlelight, or gazing into the twilight as night began to fall upon beautiful Lake Derwentwater.

The nearer they got to the coast the calmer grew the seas and Brent went down to the galley to eat, a scratch meal at sea consisting of chunks of bread and salted beef and pots of warm ale. The five crew members, who included the mate Quiggan and the master Dinward, sat around already well into their food. Brent was glad to see that Dinward was also well into the whisky, of which he kept a private store. Dinward looked on suspiciously as Brent sat beside him, steadying himself against the rolling sea.

"Ye're a lot on deck this voyage."

" 'Tis to keep away the sickness," Brent said. " 'Tis too stale for me down here."

" 'Too stale for me,' " Dinward mimicked in Brent's voice. "Oh dearie me." The crew tittered.

There was no love lost between Brent and Dinward. Dinward objected to the fact that Brent was somehow in the place of his master, Ambrose Rigg. He felt he was being spied upon. He resented his breeding and what he thought of as his fancy manners. Brent was no swearing seafaring man but, because he was the captain and in charge, Dinward did all he could to make it hard for Brent, to make him do the basic unpleasant tasks at sea and teach him as little as possible.

But Brent wasn't slighted. Although he didn't like Dinward he knew what was behind his treatment of him, the reason for the dislike. He did as he was told and said little. Now as Dinward went on taunting him Brent doggedly ate his food and drank his ale, grimacing because it was sour.

Quiggan the mate munched solidly, not looking at Brent. He had been easily bought, having little liking for Dinward. He, too, knew about the cargo, only he thought it was silk and tobacco. It was his job to get Dinward drunk. It was also up to him to suggest the ship should halt before Whitehaven.

"Best anchor over night, Dinward. Stop the rolling. Too rough to approach Whitehaven."

Dinward gazed at him cannily but drained his whisky straight from the bottle, one rheumy eye on his mate.

"Aye. Drop anchor by St. Bees. We can have a good night's sleep."

Brent's heart leapt. Dinward was playing into his hands! But he made no movement or comment apart from glancing at Quiggan who had started to sing. The fact that they were going to anchor made the company relax and everyone, except Brent, got down to drinking in earnest.

Brent was on watch and after he had eaten went

up on deck again. It was a cloudy night, no stars and no moon. He looked toward the shore but could see nothing. After a while Quiggan joined him.

"That was well done," Brent said. "Fleswick is just past St. Bees Head."

"I don't like it somehow," Quiggan said, and Brent could see him scowling in the light of the lantern that hung from the mast.

"Why not?"

"That he suggested St. Bees. Don't it seem weird to you?"

"No. Should it?"

"Fleswick nearby is known for smuggling. Why should Dinward suggest it?"

A cold finger of fear momentarily touched Brent's heart, and he looked in the gloom toward Quiggan.

"You think he knows?"

"I just think it odd, is all. He's well into his second bottle of the hard stuff, but I still don't like it," Quiggan said, stamping his feet in the cold air. "I don't like any of it. Best abandon it if you ask me. It was done in too much of a hurry."

"But we can't! We'll have the customs on to us in Whitehaven. They know well what is afoot in France. They'll open the hatches and that will be that."

"Overboard then?"

"All those guns and gunpowder?" Brent whispered hoarsely. "Are you mad? They are badly needed, and the money for such is not easy to find. We'll have to chance it. Go below and see they all get drunk. We can manage ourselves."

Kelly at the wheel shouted.

"St. Bees, sir!" Quiggan called Brent and they ran together to the fo'c's'le to let down the big anchor. As it slid into the water the boat shuddered and stopped but it was still tossing like a cork on the sea.

"Bad light for smuggling," Quiggan said quietly.

"Shh. We do not rendezvous until midnight."

163

"They won't make it in a small boat in this weather."

Brent looked anxiously down at the swirling sea.

"Can't we get further in?" he asked Quiggan.

"Too dangerous," Quiggan said, "too shallow. Best drop it all overboard if you ask me and get a good night's sleep."

Brent turned angrily away and began to regret accepting Collister's mission so easily. It *was* badly and hastily planned. He had been too enthusiastic and too thoughtless. He hadn't even begun to wonder, as he did now, if it was a trap. It was difficult to trust Quiggan and what did he know of Collister, after all?

After a while Brent went below and found the entire crew including Quiggan singing and drinking hard. He couldn't bear the noise and the stench and went to deck again. He had on a heavy seaman's cloak which he clutched around him for warmth. His eyes peered into the darkness toward Fleswick looking for the light that was to be the signal.

Brent leaned over the bulwark and gazed into the sea. They were just round the Head from St. Bees, within sight of Fleswick Bay. He could see the phosphorescent white foam on the crest of the waves. To his relief the sea was growing calmer, the wind was dropping and in the sky he could discern a few stars. He realized that from below deck all was quiet and he stepped to the top of the ladder that led into the galley. Dinward had rolled off his bunk and lay snoring on the floor; beside him the remains of a bottle of whisky soaked into the floor. Two of the crew were drunk but still awake and Quiggan sat in a corner, apparently half asleep. Brent, satisfied with the scene, signaled to Quiggan who lurched unsteadily to his feet and came across, staring up at Brent.

"Quickly," Brent whispered sharply, "I calculate 'tis near midnight."

Quiggan appeared to have difficulty in focusing his eyes and Brent cursed him for being a drunkard like the others.

"You will not get the rest of your pay!" Brent

164

hissed. The thought of money seemed to make an impact on Quiggan who began to shin up the ladder. At the top he shivered in the wind and shook his head.

"I still don't like it."

"Come on, man, open the hatches."

"Have you seen a light?"

"Not yet, but the light will be the sign that they are ready. Quick."

They unfastened the hatches and Brent leaned down to make sure the cases they had loaded aboard were still intact. Then when the canvas was loose he went to the port side of the ship which lay parallel to the shore. There was still no sign of a light and he started to despair. They would not come; the cases *would* have to be dumped into the sea.

Suddenly Quiggan grasped his arm and pointed. To Brent's astonishment a light came not from the coast as he had expected but from the sea, close to them.

" 'Tis a boat," Quiggan said.

And there it was, bouncing below on the choppy waves. Brent leaned over the side and flashed his own storm lantern, heartened to see an answering wave.

"Quick," he cried, "they will not be able to lie alongside of us for long in this sea." Running to the nearside hatch, he cast back the tarpaulin and heaved up the first case, staggering with it to the side of the the ship. Just as he came to the bulwark the boat drew alongside and faces peered up at him in the darkness. One man, standing up and balancing in the boat, addressed Brent.

"I'm Macdonald. Do you have it all?"

"Aye," Brent said, and began to lower the case which Macdonald caught with the help of another man and stowed in the boat.

"Quickly," Brent called behind him to Quiggan, "the boat is swaying horribly."

Quiggan was slow. Brent cursed and ran to the hold expecting to pass him on the way.

But of the mate there was no sign. He'd probably fallen down drunk. Brent would have to get one of the Scotsmen to help him if they were to despatch this lot. He grabbed another case and, staggering to the rail with it, dropped it over calling out:

"I think my helper is too drunk. One of you will have to come aboard."

In the gloom Macdonald gave a broad smile and grasped the side, about to heave himself aboard. But suddenly his eyes glanced beyond Brent and, before he could call out, Brent felt sharp steel in the small of his back.

"Caught you red-handed," Dinward said in a flat sober voice. "You bastard."

"Quick, get away," Brent called and, seeing the confusion on Macdonald's face, cried out again, "as far as you can. Get away."

Macdonald jumped back into the boat and, carrying only two of the score or more cases of guns that were aboard the *Lizzie,* they grabbed their oars and made off into the darkness. The point of Dinward's knife dug deeper and Brent winced.

"Get below, you scoundrel. Think to trick the master, would you? Think I didn't know what you were up to? Think you could *trust* Quiggan? Came to me as soon as you talked to him. He knows better'n to trick me."

He shoved the point of his knife again into Brent's back and Brent stumbled down the ladder into the galley. The drunken sailors gaped at him but said nothing. Dinward shoved Brent forward into his small cabin screened from the galley with a curtain. There Quiggan sat dejectedly on a stool.

"You traitor." Brent spat at him, and at that Dinward's knife cut into his flesh and he knew he had drawn blood.

"He's no traitor, only doing his duty to the master, Mr. Rigg. You think we don't know a good job when we see one? Years we've worked for Mr. Rigg and a fancy upstart like you thinks you can bribe us with gold."

Quiggan hung his head avoiding Brent's eyes.

"What is it you've got there? Silks, is it? Tobacco?

Well Mr. Rigg will see. We'll leave it all for him when we dock tomorrow. Best he should know what sort of man he's grooming for his successor."

"Take care of the customs," Brent said shortly, knowing that further words were useless.

"Oh, we'll take care of them all right. Mr. Rigg *always* takes care of the customs."

He laughed and Quiggan sniggered. Suddenly Brent remembered what he'd heard about Rigg. That much of his fortune came from smuggling. Only as yet he had seen no evidence of it himself—nothing in the ledgers, nothing in the warehouses, nothing on the *Lizzie* which plied backward and forward with the minerals, wood and wool. Yet he had only been on the *Lizzie*—Rigg had more ships and a small fleet of fishing wherries as well.

"Tie him up!" Dinward snarled and Quiggan moved toward Brent.

"There is no need, I'd not get far," Brent said.

"Tie him up!" Dinward roared and Brent felt the sharp cutting edge of a rope round his wrists. Then Quiggan shoved him roughly on the floor and bound his ankles. Like that Brent remained until dawn when the *Lizzie* raised anchor and set sail for Whitehaven harbor.

"Guns, is it?" Ambrose Rigg said, gazing down at Brent from what seemed a great height. "For whom I wonder?"

Brent was stiff and his back ached. His blood had run down onto the floor, but it had only been a flesh wound and had soon congealed. The boat had tossed all night and what with that and the stench of drink and sweat Brent had felt sick. He had not slept and at first light the *Lizzie* had made a rapid run into Whitehaven harbor. As usual Ambrose Rigg had been on the jetty to welcome back one of his ships. It was this attention to detail that made Rigg such a good businessman. He met them and saw them off; even the fishing boats that plied along the coast.

Brent had heard Rigg's steps on the deck, listened

to voices, knew that the tarpaulins were being drawn back and the contraband inspected.

Then Rigg's huge bulk had come carefully down the ladder, and he'd stood for some time gazing at Brent lying trussed like a hen in the corner.

Brent didn't reply to his question but lay looking up sullenly at his master, his thoughts too jumbled and fragmented to control. At his first task he had failed; let everyone down—betrayed Collister and, probably, Macdonald. He would bring shame on the Delamains, on the Allonbys. For this he would be hanged. All he wanted now was for death to come soon.

The only thing that surprised Brent was the expression on Rigg's face. He had expected harshness and hatred, maybe a kick in the ribs. But Rigg looked thoughtful. He stroked his whiskers and scratched his head, tipping his hat back on his head. He even seemed to have a smile of sorts on his lips.

It was very strange.

"No answer? Untie him." Rigg motioned to Dinward who was grinning with self-satisfaction and hastened to do his master's bidding, undoing the heavy sailor's knots that had bound Brent.

Brent sat up and rubbed his wrists, his ankles. Then he tenderly felt his back, the congealed blood, the torn shirt. He got unsteadily to his feet and stared at Rigg. To his astonishment Rigg winked then, turning round, said slowly to Dinward and Quiggan:

"One word of this gets round and your bodies will be fished unrecognizable out of the sea. I'm warning you."

He held a fist under Dinward's nose and both he and Quiggan cringed.

"You have done what you thought was right. 'Tis all I can say at the moment. Come to my office after you've unloaded, and take care those cases are well out of the way."

"Aye, sir." Dinward touched his cap and Quiggan backed away looking at Brent with bewilderment.

Brent, bewildered himself but giving no sign of it, assumed an air of injured innocence, glared at Dinward and Quiggan and ordered the latter to fetch his cloak and be quick about it. Quiggan and Dinward stared at each other in amazement and, giving them a surly look, Brent followed his unexpected savior up the ladder. On deck he saw that the tarpaulin was over the hatches again, neatly battened down, and there wasn't a custom's man in sight.

Rigg didn't speak but walked quickly down the gangplank to the jetty and Brent, wrapped in his cloak against the morning chill, followed him to Rigg's office, which overlooked the harbor, and indeed the *Lizzie* as she lay at her moorings, and was soon reached over the cobbles of the narrow quayside. On the ground floor Rigg had his warehouse, and the office was reached by means of a back staircase.

Brent had spent many hours crouched on a stool by the window transferring figures from one ledger to another. Now there was no sign of the clerk who had taken his place. A fire burned in the grate, flames leaping up the chimney and on either side were great leather armchairs in one of which Rigg ensconced himself after removing his coat and pouring two glasses of brandy. One he offered to Brent, the other he nursed in his large calloused hand—the hand of a man who had made his way up by dint of sweat and his own hard work. He still hadn't spoken, and Brent found the experience unnerving. Now as he stood uncertainly grasping the balloon of brandy, Rigg pointed to the chair opposite him and smiled.

"Sit, lad. Warm yourself. 'Tis no way to spend the night on a floor bound hand and foot, is it now?" Rigg gave a short explosion of laughter and his red face creased like that of a squealing new born infant.

"I understand you not," Brent said at last. "What . . . ?"

"What am I doing, eh? Condoning smuggling, eh? Guns, eh?"

"You *knew* about it?" Brent began incredulously, and stopped as Rigg shook his head.

"No, no. I knew nothing. At first I thought it might be silk or brandy, tea or tobacco but one glance and I saw the gleam of metal . . ." Rigg paused and looked severe. "Nay, that is very serious indeed. For

169

brandy and tea you could spend years in jail, but for guns you could swing. You knew that?"

Brent nodded.

"It is for . . ."

"Oh, I know what it's *for*," Rigg said abruptly. "I am not married into the Allonby family for naught you know. It is for the Stuarts; they say the unrest in France will bring the Pretender back to this country. Everyone is expecting it. Am I not right?"

"Are *you* for the King?" Brent began hopefully.

"I tell you I'm not for any king!" Rigg banged a large hand on his silk-covered knee. "I thought I made that clear. I'm for business and making money and peace and prosperity. I'll have no trafficking wi' politics."

"So why don't you mind? I can't understand you." Brent put the glass to his lips and took a draught of brandy. It was so smooth and fiery that it caught in his throat and made him choke. Then suddenly Brent understood. He lowered the glass and looked at the amber liquid glowing at its base; the pungent, exquisite aroma of the finest French brandy assailed his nostrils. Contraband.

He looked up at Rigg and a slight smile hovered on his lips.

"You're beginning to understand," Rigg said, also smiling and saluting Brent with his glass.

"Fine brandy," Brent said.

"The best, and the silk of my breeches . . ." Rigg plucked at his knee and smoothed the arm of his finely cut coat. Then he took up his pipe and reached his arm out for the tin of tobacco that stood on the table by the side of his chair. He contentedly began stuffing it into his pipe and glanced over at Brent.

"All smuggled?"

"You never knew? Oh, I can see you didn't. I took care you should not find out until I knew you better—to see whether you were with me or against me."

"You needed me for smuggling?" Brent said with astonishment. "Not business?"

"Smuggling *is* business ain't it? It is the best part of my business. I keep one or two clean ships like the

Lizzie with clean crews who know not of my other enterprises. Dinward and Quiggan are simpletons. I can only employ bright men on my smuggling ventures."

"Did you set out to trap me then?"

"Not at all. I know naught of gun-running, nor want to neither. Very dangerous *that*. You will tell me how you got air of it. No, Brent. I need a good bright lad to help me expand my smuggling enterprises. I needed *you;* but I had to get to know you better first. I could see you were not like your brother George. *Sir* George, by God . . ." Rigg threw back his head and laughed with irony. "He will fancy himself now. All set to marry into the Dacre family I hear tell."

"Really?" Brent said without much interest. "I didn't know that."

Rigg leaned forward. "Well, *I* know Lord Dacre is a committed Hanoverian. I have done business with his brother the Honorable Timothy, and I know just how committed Lord Dacre is to King George and his descendants.

"So, what did I know about *you?* I knew you were a rebel, a womanizer, that you didn't fit in. I saw you were a fine, tall lad, athletic and brave. I saw the love of adventure in your eyes and I knew you had courage. 'Aye,' I thought, 'he's for me. But can I trust him?' So I gave myself a year to find out. But you've beaten me to it, Brent. Only six months gone and already I see you have a smuggler's heart."

He got up and gave Brent that friendly shove on the back which, for Rigg, was a term of endearment. He refilled his glass and poured one for Brent. But Brent was struggling, his mind bewildered.

"You mistake me, Mr. Rigg, sir. I am a patriot, not a common smuggler. I do this for the Cause, not for gain."

"Ah," Rigg sat down again and nodded, his chin on his chest, his eyes on Brent, "a patriot, I see. A *criminal,* my lad, it is if the authorities come to hear of it. I suppose it all depends from which vantage point

171

you observe it. Now *I* see my business activities as a man of business, for gain. I see the taxes imposed by Sir Robert Walpole and his ilk, may they rot in hell, as against my interests. First it was tea, coffee and chocolate, then a year or two later tobacco and wine. The Tories could do nothing against the government. So what happened? A lot of honest businessmen decided to take the law into their own hands, myself among them. The stuff was run into the Isle of Man or Ireland where taxes were paid so we did not offend against those countries; but then we brought it here where *no* tax is paid and honest men can make a profit."

"That's why you've got no truck with politics." Brent smiled at the virtuous indignation shown by Ambrose Rigg, whose face grew redder as he recounted the iniquities of the government.

"Aye. Tax us out of existence. But wars? No, I don't want wars. We've had enough, if you ask me. I want peace and stability and prosperity."

There was a silence and, as a log fell smoldering into the grate, Brent stirred it with his boot.

"I am beginning to understand you, sir."

"Good."

Ambrose got up and stood with his back to the fire, his hand beneath the tails of his coat. First of all he looked at the ceiling, then he looked at Brent.

"I don't like saying this, but I have got a hold over you, young Delamain. Aye, and you've got one over me an' all. I've spilt the beans. I'm a smuggler and you're a smuggler. If you betray me to the authorities, then I'll betray you . . ."

"I will *not* betray you, sir! I would rather clear out and go to France where my business may be legitimate."

Rigg's face clouded and he cleared his throat, looking darkly at Brent.

"Oh no, young man. You're not getting out of this one so easy. I *need* you. I *like* you. You're not clearing out to France and spilling your blood in a wasted cause; not yet. I'll make a bargain with you." Rigg

172

drew himself up and stretched a forefinger toward Brent, shaking it vigorously as he spoke. "You aid me and I'll aid you. You join my smuggling fleet, organizing and assisting, planning and helping to control it, and I'll turn a blind eye to your gun smuggling. I'll not actively assist you, but I'll not hinder you either. As long as you work well for me I'll not inquire what else goes into the holds of my ships, and I'll see you're troubled neither by the customs nor any of my men. That's a promise."

Brent sprang out of his chair, his face alight. He only thought of the help he could give to the Cause, the amount that could be smuggled in with the extensive fleet owned by Rigg. And no questions asked! Why it was a fantastic, unlooked for, unhoped for, opportunity. He thrust out his hand toward Rigg who took it and ceremoniously pumped it up and down.

"I see we have a bargain," he said. "A true partnership is based on mutual need. You and I need each other, Mr. Delamain."

Chapter Ten

Now that the spring had come Analee only looked forward to the time of her delivery. She was big and the baby was heavy, kicking inside her, making it difficult for her to move easily, to sleep at nights. She would lie on her back, her hands on her belly, gazing up at the roof of the tent, Randal snoring or breathing heavily beside her, and her thoughts were full of dread for the future.

She still didn't want this child, Brent's child or

Randal's or any other. She wanted the child that had given one cry and died as it was born, its first cry in the world its last. She could still hear the tiny cry and see the small limp lifeless form attached to her by the cord. The child had been too thin to survive, it had been born too soon—for Analee had been cold and hungry and full of grief, and it had been a bitter winter. An old woman, a *gadjo,* had looked after her as she'd lain in a barn giving birth to the baby who died so soon; an old woman who worked on the farm and felt sorry for her. The woman had held her hand and wiped her dry mouth, and then she'd cut the cord and tied it, severing the lifeless child from its mother.

She'd given it to one of her sons to bury, as though it had been an animal, and Analee had been forced on her way.

Now this brought all those memories back and although she tried to be happy and wanted to be, she could not. She had nothing to say against Randal; he was a good man, though limited and set in his ways. Now that they no longer danced or made love he seemed to have lost his love for her; he was no longer as tender as he had been and soon she would be put in a tent by herself, away from the others, to await the baby's birth. For a woman in labor was *marimé,* unclean, and the husband could not be with her or else he would be contaminated too.

There was so much in Analee that would not conform, that had lived for such a long time away from the formal gypsy tribe, that she resented this treatment still meted out by the gypsies to women. She would often sit near the labor tent when other gypsy women were giving birth and listen to their cries, and then imagine that soon it would be her turn. Some of the women cared, but most of them did not. They had endured it and expected others to do the same. When you were very near your time the *cohani* came and assisted the new baby into the world. But even then the father didn't come near for days. Both mother and baby were *marimé* until the child had been baptized by immersion in water and thus made itself and its mother clean.

Analee could see how Randal accepted the customs of his tribe. He neither knew nor cared that she feared to be alone and needed him, because it reminded her of the time she had lain alone in an evil-smelling barn and had given birth to the child who had died with its first cry.

But she knew already that the tent was being prepared for her and that very soon she would be moved into it. She would not be allowed to come out, and there she would be on her own or occasionally with the *cohani* or Rebecca.

In the long months of her pregnancy Analee had come to realize that she could never be a true member of the Buckland tribe. She no more belonged here than she had anywhere else. She was a nomad, born to wander. The thought of the baby, of a life with Randal, was stifling and the way Randal had so quickly adapted himself to being a husband, had become just like any other gypsy of the Buckland tribe who squatted for hours smoking or chewing tobacco and mending pots and pans brought from Carlisle. His sister and brothers had soon gone off to make music without him and he no longer sang or danced as he used to. He was content to let his wife become as other wives, to sit with the women and cook and mend. Soon he would expect Analee to be just like them, with a baby in her arms and another in her belly. He had told her so. It was her duty.

He no longer seemed to remember the glory of their love-making, or the magic of the dance. He gazed at her dully because she was just a wife, an object, and it was her duty to look after him and bear children.

Randal turned in his sleep and Analee moved away from him. Though they no longer made love she didn't even want him to touch her. Already he was beginning to think of her as unclean. He showed it by the way he looked at her.

Although there had been much suffering and sadness in those days spent wandering over the hills and through the fields there had been moments of happiness too. There had been freedom and laughter with wandering gypsies encountered on the way, or with *gadjé* who liked to lie with her in a field and pay her with some food or money. She had always washed herself very carefully after this in a nearby stream or pool so that she didn't get herself the way she had with Brent. But then she'd had no chance to wash. She'd simply been trussed up and thrown in a cart.

And when she'd had the baby before she'd wanted it; she hadn't washed but had lain night after night with her lover as she had with Randal.

Analee wondered why Randal had changed from a lover into a husband so quickly. Was it because of the baby or had he tired of her beauty and her charms? Reyora had become a friend to Analee who tried to ask her the reason for this, but Reyora would smile and shrug and say it was the way with men. They quickly tired. Randal would want her again. He would be tender with her again after the baby, only then they would be kept awake by its screams. It would never be quite the same again as it had been after they had married. It could not be. It was not the way with men and women.

Reyora saw that Analee didn't understand. She was not true gypsy; she was romantic. Sometimes Reyora, who could see certain things but not everything, wondered what would become of Analee.

One beautiful June day Reyora beckoned to Analee after the noonday meal and bade her come over to her tent. Analee had been walking restlessly around the camp in the morning, too uncomfortable to remain sitting and had even followed a footpath toward Carlisle until fear drove her back. She was heavy and tired and to be near her own people was important.

The smell of the hedgerows in early summer, the wisps of pale clouds in the sky, the thick burgeoning leaves, the spring of the grass underfoot, made her yearn to shoulder her bundle and steal away—to make for the sea or to go deep into the mountains and regain her true freedom.

Reyora told Analee to lie down and lift up her skirts. Analee did as she was told and studied the huge distended mound of her belly as she waited for Reyora to complete washing her hands. Sometimes the baby moved and the mound sank in one place and rose in another. Reyora placed a hand on the belly and then prodded it gently all over. Then she put her ear to it, resting her cheek on the bulky flesh. She told Analee to part her legs and gently, with one hand pressing down on the pelvis she probed inside, her mouth pursed, her eyes gazing up at the roof of the tent thoughtfully.

"The head has dropped right down," she said with satisfaction. "It will be soon," she leaned back and pulled down Analee's skirts. "You must go to the birth tent."

She looked at Analee's face, her own expression enigmatic.

"I'm frightened," Analee said, "I don't want to be on my own."

"I will be near you," Reyora said tersely, "though I have other things to do, people to take care of, my own family to see to. It is the custom that our women are with their mothers when they give birth. As you have no mother, or mother-in-law, you must be on your own."

"Please," Analee begged, "don't leave me on my own."

"If you were a true gypsy woman you would not speak thus," Reyora said contemptuously, "that is the trouble with you *didakais,* especially with you, Analee. I have observed how you dream and wander away. You are more like a *gadjo* in spirit than a gypsy."

"That is not true!" Analee said spiritedly, getting to her feet with difficulty and smoothing her skirt over her swollen belly. "I have the heart and the looks and the blood of a gypsy! But I cannot abide this life. It is like death to sit around all day chewing nuts and gossiping

177

about nothing with the women. The men live their lives and we live ours."

"That is the way it is," Reyora said smoothly, her eyes flashing. "You must go now to the birth tent and wait there. You must do as a gypsy woman does. Get your things and do not let your husband near you: you are very close to your time."

Analee walked slowly from the tent across the field to the one she shared with Randal. In the distance the birth tent looked forbidding. Then she thought of the pain and terror she would have to endure alone. She wished even now she could leave and have her baby in some remote field or barn as she had the last time; but she was too afraid. The baby would die and there would be no one to cut the cord.

When she got into her tent Randal was sitting on the floor mending a shoe. He gazed at her with indifference as she came in and made no attempt to move or let her past.

"I must go to the birth tent," Analee said. "It is nearly time."

"Then get thee gone," Randal said. "It is an evil time and you must not come near me until you're clean again. Be quick."

"Will you at least help me?" Analee said, because it was hard to bend and get her possessions from the floor.

Randal's answer was to get up and look at her. There was no love there, or desire or even pity.

"You are on your own now, Analee, as you have always wanted to be. There is no place for a man in childbirth, you know it is our custom."

Analee stood and looked at him, panting slightly because it was so hot in the tent. Was this gaunt unbending man really the tender lover, the passionate wooer who had made love to her so many times a night when they were first married? Whose *kar* was never still but straight like a rod ready to go into her, always seeking entrance?

"I am still Analee, Randal," she said quietly, "the

woman you loved. I have not become something else, something disgusting."

Randal looked at his toes, a blush on his handsome face.

"You are not as other women, Analee, you know that. Everyone says you are different, not of our people. You do not behave as the other women, your ways are alien."

"You *brought* me here," Analee said bitterly getting awkwardly to her knees to gather together her things, "by force. You forced me to become your bride."

"It was the heat of the moment," Randal said still not looking at her. "It was a madness in me. I didn't know you, like you really are. You are not happy, not settled, not a true gypsy woman. But," he moved closer to her only not too close lest he touched her and became *marimé,* "you are my wife, Analee, wedded according to gypsy law. You are the mother of my child and it is you who must change, must become obedient and docile. Rebecca says that having a child will calm you, make you want to wander less. Then we will have another, and another, and then, Analee, you will become a true Buckland gypsy, one of the tribe. That is what I intend. To do that you must learn the hard way, and go now to the tent and have your child."

Analee knew it was useless to say more to this man who had become a stranger. Now that there was no lovemaking there was no bond, nothing. To him she was a possession, a vessel for childbearing; it was her business to cook and clean and be obedient.

Without another word, no endearment, no caress, not even a glance of sympathy or compassion Randal Buckland turned on his heels and left the tent. Analee gave in at last and, lying on the ground, her head pressed to the earth, gave vent to a spasm of sobbing such as she had never done before in her life.

After a while she grew quieter and lay there listening. There were sounds outside, shouts and the noise of horses. She crawled on her knees to the entrance to the tent and looked out, the canvas framing her face. What she saw astonished her. Brewster Driver

179

and all his family were arguing with Rebecca and Lancelot, pointing to a figure who lay on the ground and then gesticulating, arms raised to the heavens. Yes, there he was and Nelly and all the children gathered round; but the person on the ground was his wife Margaret; she was pale and still.

Analee didn't want to see Brewster Driver now, but she had no option. She had to pass by him to get to the birth tent and already she felt a cramp in the lower part of her belly, a dull ache across the back. She got slowly to her feet and tied her things, her few things, in a bundle. Then she crept out of the tent hoping to avoid being seen.

But she was unlucky. For as she came out there was a stillness and she realized that everyone had seen her, had been waiting for her. It was an event to give birth, envied by the ones who hadn't, pitied by the ones who had. They all knew, too, that Analee was different, reluctant, no true gypsy. It was even noised abroad that she was *didakai,* no real gypsy at all, and Randal Buckland had made a mistake marrying her. Normally the pregnant woman was led by her mother; there were murmurings and a few sympathetic glances as she made her way to the birth tent. But this time Analee was alone. Most of the looks she got were hostile.

The stillness on that hot day in June was unnerving. Analee was aware of the flies buzzing around, of the horses flicking their tails in the heat. Then suddenly someone cried out and came running over to her.

"Analee!" An arm was thrown round her neck and she felt hot tears on her cheeks. But the tears didn't come from her, they came from Nelly Driver, thin and sallow, ill-looking but with her face shining with joy, "Oh, Analee, it *is* you. It *is* you. Analee?"

She stood back and looked at the large misshapen form before her. Analee attempted a weak smile.

"Of course."

"And . . ." Nelly's eyes fell to her belly, so heavy that Analee had to support it with an arm.

"I am with child, as you see, about to give birth."

"You are wed?" Nelly exclaimed with astonishment as though not particularly expecting an affirmative.

"Yes, to Randal Buckland," Analee said boldly so that all could hear. "He abducted me. I was a bride by capture shortly after I left you last summer. Nelly, I must go to the tent, my pains are starting. What ails your mother?"

Everyone had begun talking again and the shouting and gesticulating went on outside Rebecca's tent.

"She has a fever; she has been sick for weeks. Father wants to rest here; but they said it is no common gypsy camp but only for the Buckland tribe. Father is talking to them about the gypsy traditions of hospitality."

Nelly's eyes lit up in a wry smile.

"And the baby, Nelly. Yours?"

"It was born dead. I don't think it ever had a chance. 'Twas as well . . . Analee, you are all right?"

A fierce pain shot across Analee's abdomen and she nearly fell. She clutched Nelly's arms.

"Could you see me . . . there?"

"Of course."

While the women of the Buckland tribe idly watched, Nelly Driver helped Analee over to the tent and came inside with her. She assisted her on to the palliasse and loosened her clothes to make her comfortable.

"I will stay with you, Analee."

"No, you must not. It is not allowed," Analee said weakly, but Nelly saw how her eyes pleaded with fear, contradicting the firmness of her voice.

"But you have no mother. Does your husband have a mother?"

"No. The *cohani* will come from time to time. She is a good sort. Go to see to your own mother. She needs you."

Nelly got up and looked around fearfully. "It is so dark here, so lonely."

Analee was about to reply when the pain came again, sharper this time. She cried out and grasped Nelly's hand, holding it tight until the spasm had passed. Then the curtains of the tent parted and Reyora came in, glancing at Nelly and motioning toward the entrance.

"Go. Your mother can stay until she is better. I will come and see her after I have attended to Analee. I see you know each other?"

Nelly nodded. "Analee was a good friend to me when I needed someone. May I not stay with her?"

Reyona shook her head and knelt down by Analee producing a long sharp knife.

"You know the custom. She is a good strong girl. She will be all right on her own."

"She is afraid."

Reyora looked at Nelly and sneered.

"I think you are no true gypsy either."

Reyora leaned toward Analee with the knife and not knowing what to expect, Analee shrank back afraid. Reyora grasped the knot of the loose tie of the belt at Analee's waist and cut it; then the knots of the laces of her bodice. She hacked at each one until the bodice fell loosely open.

"There," Reyora said getting to her feet. " 'Tis the custom to cut all knots on the clothes, as a symbol of cutting the umbilicus. It is sympathetic magic." Then she cut the skirt from top to bottom and opened it exposing Analee's belly and thighs completely. Before she could protest at the destruction of her lovely skirt, bought in the happy days with money earned from dancing, Analee felt the pain again, stronger this time. It went round in a tight circle from her navel to her back. She arched her back compulsively and bit her knuckles to stop herself screaming.

Reyora leaned down and felt her belly which was now a seething rippling mass. She knelt beside her and massaged it gently with her long supple fingers. The pain went and Analee gazed gratefully up at her.

"Do not leave me alone."

Reyora said nothing but continued with the soothing massage, right over the belly, between the legs, across the back, easing and helping. Every time there was a pain it did not last so long. But suddenly

Reyora got up, leaned over and gave Analee a piece of cloth. "Bite on this if the pain is too bad. I must go." Then she left the tent, drawing back the curtain so that it was quite dark inside.

Analee sweated now in fear and pain, her breath grew shorter and her whole body seemed alive with one long agony. The pain went, but never for long and never completely. It was dark in the tent but outside she knew it was day; soon it would be dark outside as well, pitch dark. Then inside the tent it would be black. Analee wished Reyora had left her knife so that she could plunge it in her breast and kill herself.

But somehow she survived; even when the night fell and it was so black she could not see the rest of her body. Then suddenly when she had almost despaired there was a soft voice, a hand pressed hers.

"Analee, I have come back to you. I can't leave you by yourself. I care not what the *cohani* says. I know what it's like when I had my own baby, and my mother and sisters were there. I waited for nightfall so that no one could see."

Analee pressed her hand and, drawing the thin face down to hers, kissed it.

"You will be my friend forever, Nelly."

"I have brought water and some bread. How *can* they leave you like this?"

"It is the custom," Analee smiled bitterly in the dark. "Also they don't like me. Randal captured me and they have never accepted me. Even Reyora, who is not as bad as the rest, wants to let me suffer, tame me and teach me a lesson."

"She is kind. She was very good with my mother— gave her a potion that immediately brought the color to her cheeks."

"She is limited by what she is and who she is and where she is. She—"

The pain stabbed again, this time ten times worse across the small of Analee's back. She twisted and would have screamed but for the rag Reyora had left her, now wet with her saliva. The pain in the back was so bad that it seemed to consume her entire body, and her stomach felt hot as though there was a fire inside it.

This continued through the night, and the misery of the long hours was only relieved by the presence of Nelly who comforted her with soothing words, and assuaged the pain by rubbing her belly and back with a cloth soaked in water and then moistening her lips.

At dawn the curtain parted and Reyora entered again. She stood for a long time gazing down at the tormented face and twisted body of Analee. Then she knelt and prodded her abdomen with her hands, and felt gently inside. Her face looked worried. She ignored Nelly.

"The pain, it is all in my back," Analee gasped.

"The baby has turned," Reyora said shortly, "the head is the wrong way. It will be a long labor. The waters should have broken. I will fetch the *phuridai*." She got up and went quickly to the entrance.

"What does she mean?" Nelly whispered.

"I am going to die."

"No you are not!"

"I cannot bear the pain any more. The baby has turned: it is trapped."

Analee arched again and this time the spasm was unbearable. She screamed aloud, forgetting about the rag. She knew the scream would be heard by the whole camp and the women would be glad that she suffered so, and maybe Randal would be glad because it would teach her a lesson and tame her.

"I cannot bear it . . ." she gasped and the curtains parted again and Reyora came in, followed by old Rebecca.

They both stood for a long time looking at Analee, watching her twist about, trying to stifle her screams.

"I am dying," she called to them, pleading to them to help. Rebecca shook her head and held aloft a round object between her forefinger and thumb, which, in the dim light, Analee could see was an egg.

Reyora bent toward Analee and took her legs, opening them wide. Then she looked up at Rebecca and nodded. Muttering an incantation in *Romani,* Rebecca dropped the egg so that it fell on the ground between Analee's legs.

> *Anro, anro hin olkes*
> *Te e pera hin obles*
> *Ara cavo sastovestes*
> *Devla, devla, tut akharel*

(The egg, the egg is round . . . all is round . . . little child come in health . . . God, God is calling you.)

Reyora scooped up the broken yolk of the egg and rubbed it against Analee's thighs, across the entrance to the birth passage, up over the heaving belly.

"It is a spell, an incantation," she said, "to help with the birth when it is slow. See, you will soon be better."

She leaned over Analee, staring into her dark pain-filled eyes, the eyelids heavy and drooping with weariness. "It will be soon," she whispered.

Suddenly Analee felt a rush of liquid between the legs and cried out again, thinking it was blood. She was dying. Reyora saw it too and smiled, nodding her head with satisfaction.

"The gypsy spell has worked; the waters have broken. Soon, soon now, the baby will come."

Analee looked into those dark mysterious eyes and suddenly the pain went and she felt at peace. Reyora gripped her hand and with the other massaged gently the belly round and round. Then Analee felt a sharp tugging, a feeling that she must push and she grasped Nelly with one hand and Reyora with the other and pushed. The urge kept on coming and she pushed and pushed again but nothing happened. The pain was over but there was no baby. It was stuck inside her and she and the baby would die.

Reyora opened Analee's legs wide and put her hand gently into the passage feeling and probing. Then she knelt so that she faced Analee and put both her hands in. She too was sweating. "I have it," she called, "I have the head. Here I am twisting and . . ."

She gave a pull and Analee shut her eyes thinking of the child who had been born before, who had cried and died.

Suddenly her whole body arched convulsively and the final push left her feeling empty and free, and then there was a long loud wail and then another and another.

Analee jerked up her head as Reyora knelt upright, her hands clasping a pair of crumpled bloody tiny legs. She smiled broadly and laid the baby on Analee's abdomen. Then she skillfully cut the cord with the knife and tied it.

Analee gazed at the baby lying on her belly crying lustily. Nelly had reached over and was wiping it gently with a cloth, removing the blood and the yellow sticky protective covering. Analee looked at the baby and suddenly the crying ceased and her newborn infant opened a pair of eyes and seemed to look into the eyes of its mother—a beautiful, large, perfectly formed blue-eyed baby girl with a thatch of bright golden hair.

Reyora took the baby from Analee and gave her to Nelly. Then she called for hot water, and one of the boys brought a bucket and left it outside the tent, running quickly away again lest he should be tainted by the birth.

Nelly gently washed the baby all over, noting its beautiful white skin and blue eyes, its fair hair and rather imperious face even at this early stage. It was the loveliest baby Nelly had ever seen, and so sturdy and well formed with chubby dimpled limbs. No wonder Analee had had trouble in bearing her.

While Nelly washed the baby and wrapped it in swaddles Reyora delivered the afterbirth, which she put in a bowl to keep because the afterbirth was very useful for unguents and lotions. Dried out in the sun and ground to powder it helped infertile women to conceive and made impotent men virile.

She bathed Analee all over and rubbed her with a sweet-smelling balsam made from pine and essence

186

of roses. She covered her with a blanket and left her to sleep. Then she sat for a long time by her side gazing alternately at Analee, then at her baby, her face very thoughtful.

Nelly was perplexed by Reyora. She knew enough about *cohani* to know that they were usually very brusque and always in a hurry. Why did Reyora linger, now that the birth had been accomplished? She crooned over the baby in her arms. Like her mother the baby slept.

After a long time Reyora sighed and held out her arms for the baby. She looked at her, tenderly tracing her finger over her perfectly chiseled features, noting the deep cleft of the mouth and the long straight nose and the determined chin.

"It is not the child of a gypsy," she said at last.

"No?" Nelly was puzzled. Never having seen Analee's husband she did not know what the *cohani* meant.

"It is the child of a *gadjo!*"

"A *gadjo!*" Nelly was appalled.

"A blond, handsome, aristocratic *gadjo*. A lord."

"A *lord!*"

"It is not Randal's child. Randal is Analee's husband. I thought if the child were dark it would pass for his child, but it won't. Like Analee, Randal is very dark and swarthy; so is all his family. All the Bucklands are dark; there is not a fair one among them."

"Maybe in Analee's family . . . ?" Nelly said helpfully, beginning to understand.

"No. She is olive skinned. Besides, Randal knows about the *gadjo*. He saw them lying together. It is why he married her. Oh, don't look like that, child!" Reyora said impatiently, noting Nelly's uncomprehending expression. "I don't know why he did it. The way men behave is past my understanding. He thinks the child is his now, but when he sees her he will remember the *gadjo* and he will know. He will be very angry."

"What will he do?"

Reyora shrugged. "Maybe kill it, or them both. He

will be forgiven by the *kriss* because of his rage and grief."

"Oh no," Nelly looked at the beautiful baby in Reyora's arms, thinking of her own puny little dead one buried now under some stone on the wayside—unwanted, unlamented.

Reyora clasped the baby closer and sighed. A plan was forming in her mind whose seed had been there ever since she knew that Analee had conceived by the *gadjo*. It could be done and only she, the *cohani* could do it. The only chance the plan had to succeed lay in the gypsy laws of *marimé:* that a mother and child were unclean because of the birth, until baptism had driven away the evil spirits.

The father would not come near the tent for days, maybe a week. He would not know the child was blue-eyed and blonde. Only Rebecca would see the child apart from herself and Nelly, and Rebecca was very close to Reyora; she knew her longing for a daughter. How she had tried and how she had failed. Reyora knew that only she could save this child; only she could give it respectability, make it acceptable to the tribe. Otherwise it was as good as dead or, at the very best, an outcast.

Reyora closed her eyes because she too was tired, and she hugged the beautiful baby girl very closely to her bosom, wanting it, cherishing it.

Rebecca came in that night as Analee, rested and recovered, was preparing to feed her baby for the first time. Attended by the devoted Nelly and the experienced Reyora she was trying to ease the large engorged nipple into the baby's mouth; but she was clumsy and the baby kept turning its head away and crying.

Reyora showed Analee how to nurse the baby pressed to her stomach, so that the bellies of mother and child touched, and to cradle the head in one hand while offering her the breast with the other.

"Here, you have fine big breasts bursting with milk," Reyora said, encouragingly. "Though it will be a thin stream at first, 'twill be sufficient. See here . . ."

She took Analee's nipple between her fingers rubbing it to make it taut. Then she pressed it against the baby's tightly pursed mouth, teasing it gently up and down until, eyes still tightly closed, the baby grasped it between her gums and began vigorously to suck at it.

Analee experienced a surge of joy at the feel of the baby's mouth at her breast, the fact that milk was flowing from herself to her child, and she pressed her closer and put her face against the soft little head.

Yes, she was Brent Delamain's child. There was no possible doubt about that. It made her remember the night she and Brent had lain in the forest; she could see in imagination the moonlight and feel the breeze on their bare flesh. It had been good and beautiful and the baby was lovely . . . a love child. She smiled at Reyora over the baby's head and she saw that Reyora knew what she was thinking.

Then Rebecca came in and she knew, too. She stared for a long time at the baby, contrasting its very white skin with the olive skin of the mother, the full brown breasts and the big splayed nipples the color of russet crab apples.

Reyora had said nothing to her but now Rebecca knew. She said nothing to Analee, but beckoned to Reyora and, talking quietly together, they left the birth tent and walked slowly over to Reyora's where they spent a long time together.

Reyora waited for almost a week before she told Analee about her plan. Randal was becoming anxious to see his child and the preparations were being made for the gypsy baptism. The baby and Analee would be immersed deep in the waters of the river that flowed nearby, and then all the objects used for the confinement would be burnt, all her clothes and dishes and bowls, and Analee and her child would be judged fit to be admitted to gypsy society.

Even Reyora, who was not a hard woman but not a soft one either, didn't know how she was going to say what she had to to Analee. She saw the delight Analee had in her baby; how she fondled her and dallied with her. With what care she washed and nursed her and the intense pleasure she had in feeding her, watching the milk froth up at the mouth, forming little bubbles when the baby had had enough.

Analee thought she had never known such happiness as she had that week, seeing her sturdy well-formed baby girl, noting how easily it fed, how contentedly it slept, what a happy loving child it was. She held her to her last thing at night and, when she opened her eyes in the morning, she was the first thing Analee saw.

It was a gypsy custom that the mother gave the baby a secret name, that was not known to anyone, even the father. In her heart Analee called the baby Morella, because that had been the secret name of her own mother. Whatever name the baby was eventually given, only Analee would know the real name, the name given to deceive the spirits, Morella.

Nelly helped her all week; her mother was recovering well with the potions prescribed by Reyora. Her only fear was that they would be tolerated only for as long as her mother was ill. Brewster was not popular with the men of the Buckland tribe; he was forever after their women.

A week after the birth Nelly knew that they would soon have to leave. Margaret was walking, and Brewster had begun to make preparations to go north to Scotland.

She broke the news to Analee, interrupting a time when Analee was playing with the baby, tickling it under the arms and in the groin and making it reach out its hands toward her as though it wanted more. Its large blue eyes were unfocused, but Morella seemed to know her mother, even to smile for her, though this was scarcely considered possible.

"We have to leave next week."

Nelly stood at the entrance to the tent and Analee, half naked over the naked baby because it was so hot in the tent and no one saw her anyway apart from

Reyora and Nelly, looked up sharply. Her expression changed from one who had come from a fairytale, delightful world into the real harsh one.

Nelly thought how beautiful Analee looked with her shining olive skin, sweating now in the heat, her elongated breasts full of milk drooping over the baby, with the baby's hands grasping up as though any moment she would grab one of the long fruitful breasts and put it to her mouth. Analee's face was no longer haggard with pain, but rested and rounded with contentment and fulfillment, and the good food she had been eating. Her hair which fell about her shoulders shone and the clear eyes sparkled with good humor and the love of motherhood.

Nelly, undeveloped, emaciated with spotty skin and mousy hair venerated Analee. She thought she loved her in so far as it was possible for a woman to love another. She wanted to reach out and touch her breasts, and let her hands run over her silky supple skin.

But now she had to leave. She choked with emotion as she looked at Analee.

"To the border, to Scotland. We all have to go."

"Can't you stay? Just you?"

"No. They don't like us here. The boys have been run out of the town for stealing and Lancelot says they give the camp a bad name. Father is always drunk and abusive and they say he is after the Buckland women. He is lazy, too."

"But just *you*. You can stay with me."

"I cannot. Oh, Analee . . ."

Nelly threw herself against Analee who clasped her against her naked breast, stroked her thin hair and let her hands run gently over the plain pock-marked face. She felt that Nelly, too, was like a child who needed her as much as Morella did. Nelly was trembling, and then she turned her face to Analee, aware of the heavy brown breast beneath her mouth, the dark mantle of rich black hair on which she rested her hot head. She kissed Analee's bare skin, the top of her

191

breast, and then she wept and let the tears flow unchecked.

Analee felt the hot tears against her skin, the soft caress of the lips on her breast. She knew Nelly loved her, but like a mother. Nelly had never known a real mother's love. Margaret Driver had always been too harassed by a thousand cares to love or pay any attention to this plain unappealing delicate girl who though a maid and, briefly, even a mother, was unformed and immature.

Reyora saw them like this. Noted how Nelly clung to Analee. She entered quietly and drew the curtain shut behind her. Analee looked over Nelly's head toward Reyora and thought she saw something like jealousy in her eyes, but maybe it was anger or disapproval. She gently pushed Nelly away and reached for a shawl to cover herself. Then she tossed her hair back over her shoulder and smiled at a woman she had come very much to respect and admire. Reyora had compassion. Of few women she knew could Analee say that.

Reyora sat beside Analee, placing between them a dish of sweetmeats she had had brought from the town. She looked at Nelly and wondered if she should ask her to leave, then thought better of it. Analee would need some support.

Briefly Reyora played with the baby, tickling its tummy and seeing it dimple, then she smiled at Analee and took her hand.

Analee was surprised at the gesture and stared at Reyora, answering the pressure of Reyora's hand with her own.

"It has been a happy time, Analee, with the baby."

"Oh yes!"

She looked closely at Reyora's face and saw how solemn it was. Her heart began to beat quickly and she put a hand to her breast.

"Why did you say it like that?"

"I have been thinking, Analee, about all this, not only since the baby was born, but long before. What if

192

it should be blue-eyed and golden-haired and fair-skinned?"

"And . . ." Analee began to understand.

"What would happen when Randal saw the baby?"

Analee sighed and let her hand fall from Reyora's. A weight seemed to press on her heart.

"I know. It must happen soon. He sent a message with Nelly that he was preparing the baptism."

"When Randal sees the baby he will not let her be baptized. He will kill her."

Analee's hand flew to her face, her mouth felt dry; her heart started to pound and she thought she would faint.

"What are you saying?"

"You know Randal Buckland, or rather you should. You have been married to him for nine months. He is a proud stubborn man; a real gypsy. He will know this child is not his and he will not want her."

"But they would not let him kill her!"

"They might not be able to stop him. They might not even try. You know his temper; his passion. Imagine his outrage, his humiliation at knowing it is the *gadjo's* child. That you were carrying it all the time he made love to you. Maybe he will kill you, too."

Now Nelly, listening to everything from the corner, cried out.

"Oh, *cohani,* do not let this happen to Analee and her baby."

Reyora looked at Nelly and then at Analee. It was difficult to put into words what she was thinking.

"Analee, you must go, leave the camp, Analee—tonight. I will take the baby. I will bring her up as my own and once I, the *cohani,* have said as much, no one will dare touch her. She will be special and apart."

Analee felt an involuntary spasm shake her body and suddenly she was looking into a great void. There was just darkness in front of her eyes, emptiness. Somehow she had known it would happen. Such joy was not meant. She had tried to get rid of the baby which she now wanted more than anything on earth—and God was punishing her.

This was the vengeance of God and Reyora knew it—a blonde, blue-eyed baby when it could just as easily have taken after her and been dark.

But this had been intended from time immemorial. Analee knew that. She was never meant to be happy, to have a lover or a husband who was tender to her and stayed with her, to have a baby of her own or to belong. She was meant to wander until she died; to roam over the face of the earth, over the mountains and across the valleys just as her people always had. Harried on from one place to another; never allowed to rest.

Some said it was because the gypsies had offended God, had blasphemed Christ, that they were doomed thus. And she, Analee, without a name, was one of these.

The darkness disappeared and the faces of Nelly and Reyora became clear again, tender, unsmiling, concerned. The baby Morella gurgled and smiled and reached out for its mother.

"One more time," Reyora said, "then you must prepare to go. You must go under cover of dark and take the road to the west, over the mountains. You are stronger now, but you must not weary yourself. Rest well."

"And the baby . . . ?" Analee could not bring herself to look at the child she was leaving.

"I will be her mother. I will look after her well. I will even feed her myself . . . I know how to make it possible even though it is years since I have given birth. It will take a few days, but the baby will not starve. I will protect her, teach her to be *cohani*. I said you had *cohani* powers and I will develop them in your daughter. She will be very special."

"I have called her Morella," Analee said brokenly, "after my mother. It is her secret name."

"I will remember it," Reyora said, "and you will know that she will be safe with me; but make a new life for yourself, Analee. Try and find the *gadjo*—make

194

a new life with him. He loved you and you loved him.
You are not a full gypsy and you will never settle with
a tribe. You will not adapt to our ways. I think you
were meant for other things, Analee. But start afresh
with the *gadjo*. Do not come back to take your daughter. That is all I ask you. I will not allow it. From
the moment you leave this place, she is mine. Do you
promise that?"

Analee could not bear to look at Reyora. She knew
she was helping her, was doing it for her sake, but it
was a hard, bitter bargain.

"It is that or her death," Reyora said. "You must
understand and make me a promise."

"I promise," Analee said and then she lay with her
head on the ground near to her baby and wept.

After a while she grew calmer and she sat up and
bared her breasts. Very gently she gave her baby the
nipple and pressed her close knowing that it was for
the last time.

There was little to do once it was dark. Just the familiar bundle to make up and a new skirt from Reyora to
replace the one that had been cut in two before the
birth. In the light of the candle Analee waited for the
signal from Reyora that all was clear. Morella slept in
her crib and she tried not to look at her again. Instead
Analee stared slowly around the tent which had been
her home for over a week—a place where she had
known great pain and great joy, great hope and now
great sorrow. She was off again into the world, with a
bundle and no more, no more than she'd had when
she'd come to the Buckland camp—but this time she
was leaving a husband and a baby behind.

Nelly helped her get ready and then sat with her
trying to support her with her presence, saying nothing.

"I could have taken her with me," Analee said at
last gazing despairingly at Nelly.

"Nay; think of the harm she would come to."

"Yes." The scraping for food and berries, the
scratching for a living, the cruelty and curses of people

she met on the road. Morella would have no chance on the road. Here she would be protected; groomed to be a *cohani,* to succeed the powerful Reyora. Marry well, be a full member of the Buckland tribe.

Suddenly Nelly rose and came to kneel before Analee. She brought her hand up to her lips and kissed it. "Let *me* come with you, Analee!"

Analee stared at her, gazing at the hand holding hers as though it was some kind of amulet.

"No, no, Nelly. What chance would *you* have on the road?"

"What chance have I got now? I hate my father and he hates me. He leaves me alone since I had the baby, but who knows how long that will last? I cannot bear it. Please let me come with you. I will look after you, be your friend."

Analee gazed tenderly on the poor thin young girl, so like a child herself; who stayed by her and helped her. Maybe they did need each other—she Analee as much as Analee needed her. Why not?

"You will have to come as you are."

"Who cares? I have nothing of my own anyway. Oh, Analee—may I come?"

Analee gazed at her baby and then at Nelly. She knew which one she'd rather leave behind, but she had no choice. She smiled at Nelly and nodded.

When Reyora came to say all was quiet Analee didn't dare glance back at her baby for fear she would break down. She grasped Nelly's hand and stole out of the tent, across the sleeping camp toward the path that led to the town.

It was a half moon and there was enough light for them to pause and glance back to where Reyora stood like a sentinel outside the tent, one arm firmly cradling the sleeping baby. Then she raised her other hand in a gesture of blessing and farewell.

Chapter Eleven

Brent watched the longboat make for the shore in the faint light of dawn. It was cold even for late September and in the far distance beyond the fells the mountain peaks of Cumberland were white-capped. All around the coast the land was flat, broken only by the copses of thickly covered trees with here or there a solitary farm or cottage.

Brent stood on the deck of the small fishing wherry of which he was the sole crew. The captain was Matthew Clucas, a Manx-man, an ex-pugilist and a supporter of the Stuarts. Ambrose Rigg had kept to his bargain and Brent had kept to his. After that memorable day in May when the two men had confronted each other in Rigg's office there had been no going back.

In order to deceive Dinward and Quiggan, Rigg had appeared to be disciplining Brent for his misdeeds by transferring him to the fishing fleet as a deckhand. There was no dirtier, smellier or harder work than as a deckhand on one of the small fishing wherries which, on account of their size, were tossed about on the sea like flotsam in a storm.

It had given Dinward a good laugh to think of the fastidious Mr. Delamain getting in the catch on a wherry, and every time he saw him he grinned and made an obscene gesture with his fingers.

But the plan had worked; the small fishing boats needed a small crew, sometimes only two or three at the most. Brent only caught a token catch which went on top of the cases and barrels he smuggled in from the Isle of Man, and two men were enough.

Matthew Clucas was a friend of John Collister and even had a mind to make Harriet Collister his wife, if she would have him. But the bold Harriet was hoping for better things than a former boxer with a hard square jaw, a broken nose and blunt manners.

Clucas and Brent had got on from the start. Brent never shirked hard work or long hours and his diligence as well as his devotion to the cause were infectious. He had no airs or fuss about him, but slept on the deck among the nets, ate the same food as they and became an expert at scaling and gutting the fish when time was against them.

Brent wiped a wet hand across his forehead with satisfaction as he turned and prepared to swab the deck. He felt hungry and thirsty, but rewarded. It was good to be alive. Now the dawn, once begun, came very quickly over the mountains in the east and the calm still sea, which could be so treacherous in its many moods, shimmered in the pale morning sun, a light haze drifting over it. "Come, Matthew. Let us make for Whitehaven. I am half starved."

Matthew smiled and gazed with affection at the man with whom in only three short months he had shared so many adventures. They plied continually between the creeks and bays of the Isle of Man and the coast of Cumberland. Sometimes they went north to Scotland, but Brent had developed a route that was considered safer, whereby the guns were landed in one of the many small bays of Cumberland and ferried across the steep mountains on pack horses. Then there were depots all over the north—at Carlisle, Penrith, Lancaster, taking the route followed by the Prince's father, King James, in 1715. Many thought the rebellion then had failed for lack of arms; for lack of depots and storage. This time it was going to be very different. Brent had rapidly become acquainted with the hard core of Jacobite sympathizers in the north-west, those who were prepared, as he was, to risk all, to lose all.

Only this time they would not. They were going to win. The Prince had landed in Scotland in July accompanied by only seven men. All the promises made by the French to provide arms and men had been broken. But such was his calm, his presence, his determination, his sheer magnetism that all Scotland was flocking to him. The faithful were rewarded, the waverers converted. He had raised his standard in August at Glenfinnan, proclaiming himself Regent in the name of his father King James III, and before it a body of 1400 Highlanders had assembled. Even from the beginning he had won small skirmishes against Hanoverian forces taken by surprise, and his progress south had been one of triumph.

Brent heard all this through the Scottish connections who ran arms to the border from the coast. Across the north of England and Scotland there was a line of information that stretched to the Prince and back down again. And the tales that were told of the Prince—of his gallantry, determination and wisdom for one so young. Of the way he had with the ladies and how he could melt the heart of the strictest Jacobite dowager. Now he had come as far as Perth and, according to the latest information received by Brent, was about to take Edinburgh.

The tide of enthusiasm that had swept Scotland had now crossed the border and was rolling remorselessly on as far as London. Some said the government was in disarray, others said it was not and that several large armies had been despatched north. Where they went would determine the Prince's strategy. Either he would come south by Newcastle, or he would come via Carlisle as his father had done in '15.

Brent, who wished so much to see the Prince, hoped it would be Carlisle; but above all Brent wanted to be in at the fighting. He was not content just to smuggle arms.

The quay at Whitehaven was already lined with wherries putting in their catch or going out. Brent could discern, as always, the broad figure of Ambrose Rigg and waved to him. Rigg was on the deck of another of his boats, a genuine fishing smack groaning with herring and mackerel. Only about half of his fleet actively smuggled, it was the understanding he had with the customs men whom he paid well.

Rigg bounded off the boat he was on and came aboard the *Sarah,* named after his wife. He shook Brent's hand and Matthew's and the smile on his face indicated everything was all right. As well as arms, Brent was also carrying, as usual, brandy and tea that had come from the big smuggling port of Nantes in France and carried in bigger ships to the Isle of Man and Port Rush. The little wherries which scampered across the North Sea were ideal for the sort of smuggling that Rigg did on such a large scale.

"Sarah bids me bring you home for dinner, Brent. She has a surprise for you."

"Oh?" Brent was lifting out the baskets of fish from the hold, helped by Matthew and a young lad who worked on the quay. His mind now was on fish, but from time to time he thought of the crates of guns on their way across the mountains or paths of Lakeland. He alone had smuggled in enough to equip a small army.

"And Matthew, will you join us?"

"No I cannot, thank you, Mr. Rigg," Matthew said. "I promised my mother I would be home for dinner. She complains she never sees me."

"We've been busy," Brent said, "hardly a night's sleep for ten days."

"I know. That's why I thought a day or two resting, maybe, at Cockermouth. It can be done?"

Brent glanced at Matthew, saw how tired he looked. He guessed he must look the same. Well, nothing would be gained if their health broke down. Not that he'd ever felt better; just tired.

The devil of it was that his leg had never healed. He walked with a very slight limp and sometimes it impeded his work. It didn't pain him so much; but it angered him. Still, he put it to good use at sea and he never complained. What worried him was what would happen if he had to march. He put it out of his mind; but when he was tired he was conscious that he limped more. Sometimes when he was fit and rested he didn't limp at all.

Now he limped badly down the gangplank, his leg stiff from too much exercise and Matthew and Ambrose noticed and exchanged glances.

"I have my coach waiting," Rigg said. "You can rest in that."

Brent looked at him and burst out laughing.

"I'm no maid you know, Ambrose! You'll be dosing me with laudanum and *sal volatile* for the vapors!"

Ambrose laughed and smacked him on the shoulders leaving one hand companionably around his neck. Sometimes he felt like a father to Brent.

After sluicing himself in the yard and a hearty breakfast of beef-pie washed down by plenty of ale at the tavern on the quayside, Brent and Ambrose walked to where the coach was waiting at the back of the town, the driver of the pair well wrapped up against the cold.

It was a small coach because the road from Whitehaven to Cockermouth though important and busy was narrow in places.

As soon as they settled in Brent fell asleep, his long legs on the opposite seat. After his large breakfast he felt so tired and stupefied that he had not even asked Ambrose what surprise Sarah had in store for him.

Ambrose Rigg's passion, besides the acquisition of wealth—which was an obsession—was extending his home. It had once been a yeoman's low stone house, whitewashed and extending only along one floor with a direct entrance to the barns. Indeed at one time, though Ambrose could not remember it, the cattle used to mix freely with the inhabitants of the house, being considered just as important.

This land and the house had been in the Rigg family since anyone could remember. After rising from serfdom the "statesmen" had acquired a special status. The inheritance had passed from father to son though the property still belonged to the lord or squire, monastery or landowner for whom they worked. However, they could not be dispossessed and the yeoman farmer acquired a special role of his own.

But Rigg now owned the house and the land around it outright. It stood on the hill above Cockermouth which gave a fine view not only of the town but of the Lakeland hills to the south and east. For Cockermouth lay flat in the valley of the River Derwent which entered the sea near Whitehaven twelve miles away. The imposing Rigg Manor was halfway up a bracken-covered fell and on either side was a forest of tall fir trees. Ahead was the center of Lakeland, the mountains and fells surrounding Crummock Water, Buttermere and majestic Ennerdale, and the tips of Hen Combe, Great Borne, Starling Dodd and High Style towered above the soft, undulating folds of the lesser hills.

To the west even Skiddaw could be seen and on a clear day Lake Bassenthwaite glimpsed beneath it on the main approach from Cockermouth to Keswick. Sometimes the hills were obscured in the haze of high summer or the mists of winter and they appeared mysterious and even menacing; but on a clear bright day like this day in September they stood out sharply against the sky and seemed to roll on forever—some high, some low, some hidden or only half revealed— resembling a land of enchantment.

Rigg had bought this imposing site from the descendants of one of the barons to whom it had been given after the dissolution of the monasteries in 1538. There was still a village of Thursby and an Earl of Thursby, but, like the Allonbys, they had not always been wise in their support for the ruling party and had lost a great deal of land as a result. Lord Thursby was never to be seen in Lakeland; but his son and daughter-in-law lived in Castle Thursby and were on nodding acquaintance with the Riggs, largely because of Sarah, needless to say. The Honorable Mrs. Rose Thursby would never have had anything to do socially with the former "statesman" family of Rigg, no matter how well they'd subsequently done in business.

Like the Riggs the Thursbys had a young family. It had already crossed the mind of Ambrose that, if he worked harder and the Thursbys stayed as they were, in time his own progeny, half Allonby and therefore socially acceptable, would not be a bad match as far as the Thursby family were concerned.

Ambrose was a contented man as the coach, after climbing the hill, turned through the large gates he had just had installed after being wrought by an iron-smith in Cockermouth. They provided an important link in the wall he had had constructed around his extensive property.

They swung open to a long drive which had formerly been part of a field where his father grazed cows. Now it was being turned into soft lawns and gardens. Shrubberies and flower beds were appearing everywhere, and a fortune was being spent transporting plants and vegetation from the south of England.

The drive ended in a circular sweep in front of the building that had been grafted on to the small humble home where the Riggs had their origins. Just a little croft house it had once been. In fact the original building was now part of the extensive stables, and a graceful mansion built by an architect who had studied with Mr. James Gibb, architect of St. Martin-in-the-Fields and other notable London buildings, had risen beside it.

Like its humble predecessor it was a house built of white stone, but its fluted Doric columns supported a Grecian-style arch not unlike that which graced the front of the church of St. Martin in London. The porch was wide and was approached by five steps. Double doors led onto a large hallway, showing a tall winding staircase, and a high ceiling from which hung a grand chandelier made of thousands of tiny crystals. It was a rich house, an elegant house, a big house and, if Ambrose had his way, it looked like being one of the grandest houses in this part of Cumberland, rivaling even Castle Thursby itself.

And there, dutifully on the porch to welcome him, were his wife, his two small children and his brother-in-law. John Allonby stood behind his sister, thus composing what seemed on that beautiful mellow September noon a very charming family group.

There were even one or two retainers hovering in the background to make sure that the master was immediately served, and barking dogs scampered up to the carriage as it drew into the broad forecourt. A servant ran down the stairs to open the door and Ambrose nudged the sleeping Brent in the ribs.

"Wake up. We're there. 'Tis dinner time."

Brent, startled, looked out of the window.

"We're there already?"

"You slept the entire length of the journey, my boy."

Brent looked out of the window, rubbing his eyes.

"My God. 'Tis John. Is *that* the surprise?"

"Aye."

"I hoped it might be Mary." Brent said quietly, "I have not seen her for nigh a year."

"Ah but that's who it might be *about*," Ambrose said winking and consulting the timepiece stretched on a gold chain across his large stomach. "You may have earned your spurs."

Brent jumped down and sprinted along the courtyard to where John was coming down the stairs. The cousins clasped arms.

"John, how is it with Mary? No trouble?"

"No, no, none at all. My, Brent, but you do smell."

John retreated a yard or two and looked at his cousin with dismay.

"Smell? Oh, fish. 'Tis a good healthy smell and in the basket behind the coach we have some fresh herring and mackerel for our breakfast tomorrow."

Ambrose climbed the stairs slowly because they were affecting his breathing more and more. Prosperity was making him put on too much weight. He greeted his wife with a kiss on the cheek, aware that her belly was nice and rounded. She was presenting him with another child, or so he hoped. She had miscarried earlier in the year and this had worried him, not so much for her health, as lest she should shirk her side of the bargain to provide him with a fine large family to rival the Thursbys.

But no, he had got her almost immediately with child again despite her protests and the doctor saying that she should rest. Doctors knew naught about it in his opinion; not as much as a healthy virile man like himself, even if he was on the stout side.

"All well, my dear?" he inquired letting his hand casually caress the mound of her stomach. She blushed and looked about to see if anyone had seen his gesture.

"Of course, Ambrose. Desist," she said agitatedly pushing his hand away from her stomach, and moved away to greet Brent. The smell that had offended his cousin preceded Brent up the stairs and Sarah too backed away, but only with mock dismay on her face. She knew that the Rigg fortune was too well founded in fish to make any real protest about it.

"Why, Brent . . ."

"I know I stink. I declare I had a good wash in the yard of the tavern before we came hither."

"Not a good enough one apparently. There is a fire in your room and I will have one of the servants take a tub thither and give you a good bath and fresh clothes."

Brent laughed.

"If you will."

Then he bent to greet his little cousins, four-year-old Henry, and Elia, who was just one year old and in the arms of her nurse. Brent loved children and they responded to him. He knew he would enjoy being a father when he and Mary had children of their own.

Brent went up the stairs two at a time to his room which was at the back of the house overlooking the fell that rose behind. The lower part was green pastureland, but higher up the forest began which eventually skirted Lake Bassenthwaite.

As Sarah had promised a good fire roared in the grate and soon Thomas the head servant appeared with another, carrying a big iron bath between them. Into this they poured jug after jug of steaming hot water brought up the back stairs by a succession of giggling scullery maids.

Brent sat in his bath and, after Thomas had scrubbed his back, said he would wash himself. As he got out and toweled himself before the fire he was aware of his long muscular body, his sinewy calves which had not lain between a woman's legs for a year. Brent stopped drying himself and thoughtfully looked into the fire.

How had he known that? That he *had* a woman a year ago? Suddenly there was a stirring in his mind, a recollection of trees and moonlight . . . it was like a vision or a dream. Or had it been reality? He remembered what they'd said about the accident. How he had been found. Nothing had disturbed Brent's amnesia since the blow on the head; but now the mists were starting to part. And she . . . He shut his eyes trying to recall who he had been with. He could somehow see her translucent flesh, smell a singular odor, a pungency. She was someone very special, he was sure of that. So why, how had he forgotten her? There was a knock at the door.

"Who is it?"

"Brent, it is I. May I come in?"

"I am naked as nature made me; but enter."

Brent wrapped a towel round his body as his cousin gently turned the door knob and came in. On the big fourposter bed clean clothes were laid with fresh stockings and on the floor newly polished shoes with shining buckles.

"I think we are to have a party," Brent said smiling. "If this finery is aught to go by." He reached for the fine white linen shirt and pulled it over his head. John sat on the chair before the fire and crossed his legs, looking at the fine upright figure of his cousin.

206

Brent had improved. It was true, hard work and abstinence were good for a man. His body was thicker but with muscle not fat. His face was tanned and lean, and had not that dissolute sensuous look about the mouth that came with too great an acquaintance with the fleshpots. He wore an expression of almost puritanical severity and his eyes were hard and clear. John liked what he saw and was glad that Brent was going to marry his sister.

"Well, Brent, it is almost a year," he said.

"Aye," Brent said, getting into his breeches, knowing full well what John meant.

"And you have kept your word."

"I have that—no women, not one, and hard work."

"And you still want her?"

Brent stood up straight and gazed at his cousin.

"Want her? *Want* Mary? Do you doubt it?"

"You haven't seen her for a year."

"Has she changed so much then?"

"No, lovelier than ever, a little fuller maybe. Ready to be married, Brent."

Brent's heart beat a little quicker. Suddenly those months of chastity seemed an intolerable strain. The thought of Mary, already beautiful, now grown maybe a little plump and more comely; her hips perhaps had filled out a little, and her breasts . . . those small virginal breasts he had gazed upon with the tiny rosebud nipples. He looked at John. It would not do to let her brother know that he had more acquaintance of Mary's body than a chaste kiss. His expression grew sober.

"Well, I am ready if you will it, and she. Let it be done quickly, John. I am still of a mind to serve the Prince, and he is here. He has come."

"I know," John said. "That is in my mind. Stewart is to join him for sure when he comes to England whether it be Newcastle or Carlisle. We have been in touch with your brother Tom. Oh, 'tis all arranged."

"Then I will go with him."

"You know, Brent . . . you could make Mary a widow."

"Aye." Brent went to the mirror and began the delicate process of tying his cravat. The more he served as a seaman the less delicate his fingers became. "That is why we wanted to wed a year since. We could have had a child by now."

"Well, we didn't know what was to happen. Besides, I think your mother and I were right. We had to be sure. You have done well, Brent. We are proud of you. You have kept your principles, kept the faith . . ."

Brent looked at John, his expression not altogether as warm or friendly as John would have wished.

"I hope for your sake you were right, John. It appeared you thought not of Mary or myself when you sent me out of the house . . ."

"*I* sent you? You left of your own will, aye, and in high dudgeon if I recall."

"No, *you* sent me as much as if you had pushed me. You taunted me, that I was a womanizer, a coward. Well, 'tis done. I have served my apprenticeship, John, but I don't know if either Mary or I are in your debt for it. A year has passed when we have not seen each other; have been denied each other's company, wanted each other. Now she could be a widow by Christmas, that is even if we marry at once. I suppose that is what you have come about."

He shrugged on his coat and looked at the set of his shoulders in the mirror. Then he attended to his hair. He did not wear a wig or powder it. He was glad to hear that Prince Charles did not either. He tied a ribbon at the back and then combed away from his forehead the damp locks that straggled over his brow.

"Mary wants to marry at once," John said tersely, "if it be your pleasure."

"Then let it be her choice. That is decided. My pleasure it certainly is—or will be."

John hadn't expected this harsh attitude from Brent and he looked into the fire. Maybe he had been wrong after all to forbid the marriage; but on the other hand Susan, Brent's mother, had felt the same way as he had. And Brent had improved. If he survived

208

John knew he would make a fitting husband for his sister.

"*Must* you join the Prince? Is not your work at sea just as important?"

"I have done my work. The arms are there. Now we must use them. No, I am going to fight. Never let it be said that a Delamain refused to take up arms."

"You may be fighting against your brother."

"Aye, likely. I hear he is wed, too."

"Yes, this summer. In London. We were not asked. It appears we offended your brother when he came visiting us soon after Christmas or thereabouts."

"Oh? How did you offend him?"

" 'Twas nothing said, you understand. Rather 'twas what was *not* said offended him."

"I don't think I understand you." Brent put on his shoes and decided his feet had broadened at sea as well as his body. They pinched.

"I think George was after information. He was very friendly, polite, trying, if you ask me, to gain our trust."

"He left it late if he wanted you to like him. He has not tried very hard before."

"That's what I thought. Always surly and contemptuous of us, was George, because we had no riches. This time he came bearing presents, a side of beef, a whole sheep—some silk for Mary. He wanted to know Tom's whereabouts and what you were up to. He had heard you were still in this country. When we told him we knew nothing, then it was what were we doing, what did Stewart do? Did we know aught about Jacobite movements in these parts? He was so thick about his intentions they stuck out a mile."

"Spying?"

"I think he was *pretending* to a change of heart. It deceived no one."

"You were right. Well, fancy George . . ."

"I think his father-in-law-to-be was behind it. Lord Dacre is a gentleman-in-waiting to the King. It was just after George had offered for his daughter's hand. Anyway he parted in a temper and never came again. He would make a poor spy."

"Aye, he would; he has no subtlety. Still I am surprised that even George would think to betray his own relatives. And saddened by it, too. It is odd what folk will stoop to. And did you see him again?"

"No. Only your mother and sister went to the wedding. I hear George brought his bride to Delamain Castle in August. Henrietta she is called, an heiress I understand. The only child."

"An heiress? George will like that. Is she pretty?"

"They say very plain."

"Ah, then George has made another business deal." Brent dusted his sleeve and settled the lace at his wrists. "Shall we go and dine, cousin?"

Everyone knew what John had come about and the table downstairs was set for a feast. Ambrose was already at his place carving the beef as Brent and John came through the door; but when he saw them he put down his carvers and took up his goblet already brimming with good red claret.

"Well, Brent. Are you to be a bridegroom?"

Brent smiled. "Aye, it appears so. At last."

"Then let it be soon, lad. Let it be soon."

Suddenly Sarah clasped her head in her hands and burst into tears. Ambrose looked at her with consternation and left his seat to go over to her.

"There, my love. Is the emotion too much for you? The thought of having this scoundrel for a brother-in-law?"

"Nay, it is not that," Sarah sobbed. "It is only that I fear they may have left it too late."

Brent stared at her and a feeling of foreboding suddenly overcame him. It was not the war he was afraid of, but, in his mind, he saw moonlight falling in a forest glade, a dark female body twisting beneath his. He closed his eyes to shut the vision out of his mind. Instead he saw the hazy outline of a face, but all that was clear to him was the long dark hair that framed it.

He was puzzled and his frown was seen by Ambrose who took his shoulder in that familiar bear-like grasp.

"Now then, lad. 'Tis her woman's time, you know. They get funny when they are wi' child. Of *course* it's not too late ... Even if there is a war—and I'll wager they'll contain those unruly Highlanders in Scotland —it doesn't mean to say you will be in it. My ships ..."

Brent, his lips pressed together, stared at Ambrose.

"You know, Ambrose, I must go. You know it and have always known it. I know you care nothing for politics, but I do. I've always said I must support the rightful King and now it is the time. I have my duty to my father and uncle before me."

Ambrose nodded and went solemnly back to his seat.

"Well, so be it. I will keep your place for you, and God knows you might need it. Aye, for you and your wife. For you never know, Brent, when you might be glad of work and somewhere to go with your bride, to hide maybe. There'll always be a home for you. Eh, Sarah?"

Sarah had dried her eyes and was serving the vegetables. The servants had been sent out of the room as soon as she had burst into tears, except for the nurse who had the baby Elia on her lap. The nurse was a young girl related to Ambrose and regarded as one of the family.

Like her husband Sarah had eschewed politics. They had brought neither unity nor happiness to her family and her aunt's family. Whereas thrift, hard work, independence and non-conformity had made Ambrose very rich.

These things mattered to Sarah as much as they mattered to her husband. His values and hers were the same. The last thing she wanted was a war, with her family divided, fugitives maybe. Both sides couldn't win. The thought of Brent throwing himself away was what had made her burst into tears. Sarah was fond of her little sister, not close but fond, and she had grown to like Brent. Admired him for his hard work and dedication. The folly of the possible war was too awful to contemplate.

Sarah Rigg thought it more advisable at this stage not to answer her husband. Instead she gave Brent a watery smile and made a pretense at gaiety.

"Let's not be solemn," she said. "Let's talk about the wedding. When is it to be?"

"The very moment we can arrange it," Brent said robustly, spearing a piece of prime English beef and raising it to his mouth, "if not before."

Chapter Twelve

In the large stone-floored kitchen at the back of Furness Grange Mary Allonby was rolling dough on the baking board. As she bent energetically over her task her face grew flushed and tendrils of blonde hair escaped from the tidy coil at the back of her neck. She kept a firm hold on the rolling pin and she stretched the pastry as far as it would go, for the crust on the pie should be light and thin.

"Now, miss, the oven is ready for thee." Betty Hardcastle, who had been with the family since before Mary was born and had served in every capacity from scullery maid to nursery nurse when the children were small, was now primarily in charge of the kitchen. She was one of the few servants left in the house, and most of these were employed in other capacities on what remained of the estate.

Her son Nathaniel was bailiff to Mr. John, and her other son Francis combined duties as a boatman on the lake with doing tasks around the house. Her daughters had married and moved away and her husband Sam had died of consumption many years before.

Betty was past middle age now, but her lean gaunt figure was almost as precious to the Allonby family as the house itself.

Mary nodded and, cutting the pastry with a knife, put it carefully over the pie dish, draping it round the pie funnel in the middle. The ends she tucked under the dish and then she moistened her fingers and pressed down very firmly. A smaller piece of pastry she kneaded and began to roll again, this time for the apple—the first pie was made of succulent pieces of pork and beef from home-killed cattle, stored in the larder until they were well hung.

Mary sang as she went about her duties in the kitchen and the sound gladdened Betty's heart. For too long there had been sadness and gloom in the Allonby family, which meant that young Mary had grown up in a harsh and bitter atmosphere unsuited to the formation of a pretty young maid.

John Allonby had always had the brunt of the hardship, which had made him naturally quiet and taciturn. His grief he kept to himself, but it showed only too clearly in his mien and the stoop of his shoulders.

As Stewart, naturally robust and cheerful, had grown to manhood he too took on something of the taciturnity of his brother. But Betty always remembered Stewart as a young boy and how full of mischief he had been—always in trouble, always laughing and tumbling about.

Mary's birth had been the cause of unhappiness to the household. Her mother had taken puerperal sepsis after it and died. Almost at the same time her uncle, Guy Delamain, had died abroad and the sadness that had attended her birth had seemed to leave its mark on Mary who grew into a gentle girl but always with a slightly wistful air—except when in the presence of her cousin, Brent. Betty, if no one else, had noticed how the burgeoning of young love had changed Mary, how a light had come into her eyes and a spring into her step and how she sang as she went about her work.

When Mary was small Betty had been busy with her own family, and it was not until now that she had grown close to the girl, become her confidante and companion.

It was to Betty she had turned when, nearly a year before, her brother and aunt had put paid to her hopes of marrying Brent Delamain. Betty would never erase from her memory how Mary had wept—why, she had thought the tears would never stop. The girl had shut herself in her room and refused to come down for days despite the pleas of her brothers and her aunt. The only person she would admit was Betty, and then it was to hurl herself on that comforting bosom and weep all over again.

In vain had Betty tried to comfort her. That it was for the best, that if he loved her he would wait, he would come back. But Mary seemed convinced that the possibility of attaining happiness had left her; that her chance to have Brent had gone forever.

"Don't they understand, Betty," she had sobbed, "I would have had him on *any* terms whether he loved me or no, whether he would be faithful or not."

And Betty, wise though she was in the ways of the world, had been surprised to hear such passion, such uncontrolled yearning from so young, so inexperienced a maid.

In time Mary's tears stopped and she went quietly about her household tasks again. But it seemed to old Betty that she had never forgiven her brother John for what he had done, or her aunt Susan who used to be like a mother to her—never had or never would forgive either of them.

All Mary waited for that year was news of Brent and the short stilted letters she had from him in which he protested his undying love but not much else. She was dutiful and obedient as always, went diligently about her household tasks, cooked and baked and made jam; but her relationship with her brother John subtly changed and became cold and distant, while that toward Stewart grew closer.

Mary put both pies, the apple and the meat, into the oven, the heat from the huge fire in the grate, causing her already hot face to flush. The sweat poured down her cheeks as she backed away and closed the big iron door. "There!" she wiped her hand on her apron and smoothed her hand across her brow. "That is our dinner! Now Betty, what else is there for me to do?"

She smiled at Betty whose heart filled with happiness at the sight of the smile, the genuine good humor that had pervaded her young mistress since her brother John had told her of his intention to combine business at Cockermouth with a visit to their sister, to try and see Brent. And now John had left, that very morning —and why, he might even bring Brent back with him!

"Why, miss, don't you go with your brother to the wood? Nat is there with him and you could take them some dinner. 'Tis a lovely day and it will take your mind off . . ."

She paused and looked at the young girl because there was, she knew, despite Mary's happiness, a question mark in their minds.

Supposing Brent had changed his mind? Supposing the wind that had fanned their love by the side of Lake Derwentwater had grown cold? His letters were like those of a schoolboy, awkward and ill-spelt; they conveyed nothing of the mysterious animal warmth that was Brent—Brent to whom she had been prepared to give herself regardless of convention, whose every glance, whose very touch thrilled her. Who had been wrenched away from her by the strict, overprotective attitude of her brother.

"Betty, do you think he will come back?"

Mary, eyes shining, clasped her hands to her hot face. She knew he would come back. Without any question, any doubt. She only asked again to hear Betty reiterate the words.

"Aye, Miss Mary, I am sure he will, when he knows you are eager for the wedding."

In the end John, worried by his sister's abstracted

manner, her almost permanent air of brooding and silence, had relented. He would go and see Brent; a year had almost passed. Anything might happen now that the Prince had come—and if Mary was willing to grasp even at brief happiness, why, he would go at once and see what he could arrange.

Wedding . . . marriage to Brent. Was such happiness possible, conceivable? That it would happen maybe in a few days, this week. All at once her life had been changed beyond recognition. She felt she was on the brink of momentous happenings in her own life and that of their country for, if the Prince did reach London and seize the throne, who knew how it would affect her family for so long persecuted and dispossessed? And Brent, if he fought for the Prince and they won, with what honors might he and others with him not be showered by a grateful sovereign?

It never occurred to Mary Allonby on that bright day in late September 1745, when the world seemed at her feet and her long years of waiting at an end, that the Stuarts might be rebuffed and the Hanoverians remain on the throne. It never occurred to her for a single moment that things could possibly be worse than before.

Mary packed bread and goat's cheese, apples and a flagon of ale into a basket, looked once more at her pies in the oven and ran upstairs to get her outdoor cloak, humming a song as she tripped up the stairs, two at a time.

Stewart and Nat had been hard at work since early morning. They had marked all the trees for cutting during the previous weeks, and now was the time for felling over the long winter months before the sap started to rise with the spring.

Stewart, as he worked alongside Nat Hardcastle, was happy too. He had made his preparations well. All the trees were marked and Nat could work all winter with the help of his brother Francis the boatman. And by the spring Stewart was sure he would be riding back to Furness with maybe a new horse and a fresh suit of clothes, money in his pocket and the prospect of the Allonby fortunes being restored, after so many years of trial, by King James III. At last, Stewart was convinced, the Allonbys would be on the winning side. Why, the frenzy that had taken hold of Scotland had spread as far as the Midlands; some even said large numbers were defecting to the Jacobite cause in the south, and that those who had kept their colors hidden for so many years now displayed them openly.

John, more cautious and controlled, less swayed by passion, had pointed out that few really important Englishmen had so far declared for the Prince, in fact none that he knew. All the nobles who owed their wealth and possessions to the Hanoverian succession stood firm by the King in London and not the one over the water.

But John was like that. He had sunk too far in gloom and a kind of stoical resignation that seemed to suggest he thought his lot had always been an unhappy one and always would be.

It had already been decided that John would not go to the war. He would remain in his important position of linkman between the borders and the northwest, sending note of the Prince's triumphal progress to all concerned, supervising the supply of arms so admirably speeded up since Brent had unexpectedly made an alliance with their brother-in-law. That industry alone had been enough to convince John that Brent had stopped drifting and mended his ways, that he had fitted himself to marry their sister.

And it was the thought of Mary's happiness that made Stewart sing as he and Nat chopped away that morning. To see how lightly Mary trod and how her eyes sparkled and how, overnight, the dark shadows thought his brother and aunt harsh about Brent. Nurs-under her eyes had vanished. Stewart had always ing, as he did, a hopeless passion for Emma he knew for himself the misery of love unfulfilled. When both willing adult parties were forcibly torn asunder in such uncertain times as this, why, it had seemed wicked to him, though he had never told John so. Never dared. John had replaced their father in authority and was a law unto himself.

Nat was chopping at one side of the stout fir that had stood for years, Stewart at the other. When their blades almost converged, at a prearranged signal Stewart, who was broader than Nat, would push the tree while Nat stood aside and they would watch it go crashing to the undergrowth. It was a very difficult moment to judge because, if it was not done correctly, the tree could come bearing down on one or other of them.

Stewart was just about to give the signal to Nat to jump clear when he saw a movement in the undergrowth, and thinking it was his sister who had been so foolish—she who should know to keep well clear of tree felling—he called out with a curse:

"*Mary*, remove yourself quickly from the path of the tree!"

But it was too late, maybe he had misjudged the timing and, with a crash, the tree fell, pinioning the young woman under its top branches. The noise of the tree drowned her cries and all they saw was the still, apparently lifeless form lying on the ground.

A sob rose in Stewart's throat as, casting aside his axe, he rushed over to where she lay; but even as he approached his step faltered. It was plain to see it was not Mary. It was a slight girl of about the same age, only dark, not so comely as Mary, a ragged gypsy-looking girl. But she breathed! As he knelt down beside her he could see that, although her face was deathly pale, her chest rose rhythmically and that her eyes fluttered and gazed about her as he bent over her. Then he saw that the branch had missed the upper part of her body and pinioned her by one leg only. She had had a narrow escape.

As he gazed at her, having sprinted ahead of the slower-moving Nat, he saw yet another movement in the trees and another figure running, this time calling out:

"Nelly, Nell . . ."

Stewart raised his head to see running into the clearing made by the fallen tree a woman of such remarkable beauty that his mind was momentarily taken off the poor victim who lay on the ground.

He didn't know whether it was the sculptured classical lines of her face he noticed first, or the tall, slender but very womanly body. Her skin was of a soft olive brown, her mouth firm but full, the center of the lower lip deeply dented, her nose long and straight and her thin black eyebrows imperiously arched. But it was the eyes set deeply into the face that had such an arresting quality; they were quite black so that the pupil was almost invisible. Her lids were half lowered even though her eyes were wide open and framed by luxurious lashes that looked like a fringe. She reminded him of the classical portraits he had seen of an Italian madonna; there was a remote, haunting, vital yet intangible quality about her that made people want to stop in their tracks and stare, as Stewart did then, ignoring the girl pinioned under the tree.

But the face was only a part of this vision. Her long neck swept down to a deep full bosom which was contained in a tight fitting bodice just visible under her cloak, which fell back from her shoulders as she knelt opposite him. A small neat waist broadened into voluptuous hips, and the long shapely legs under the skirt were left to his imagination. He only then observed that she was shoeless, and had the hard calloused feet of one who lived on the road.

Her hair was black as jet and curled down over her bosom as she kneeled beside the girl on the ground, and at the same time looked up at Stewart, her lustrous eyes gleaming dangerously.

"What have you done?"

" 'Twas an accident. She ran right across our path."

"You should be more careful."

"She had no business here."

Stewart rose to his feet dusting his hands. He was aware that he was talking to a gypsy, or someone part gypsy, because surely no lady walked on her bare feet and had such brightly colored clothes? Yet, this was no ordinary gypsy girl, of that Stewart was sure. There was something of the aristocrat about her, an indefinable air that his sisters had, his aunt Susan and Emma Delamain had: an absolute certainty of one's heritage regardless of one's circumstances.

She might be poor and barefoot; but she glowed with health and an innate superiority of manner that almost made Stewart feel he was being put in his place.

"*I'm* the owner," he said, "of this wood. People trespass here at their peril. Still, I regret . . ."

"I hope you *do* regret," Analee said with asperity, getting to her feet. "Lucky for you she lives and apparently is not badly hurt. Now get this tree off her with this fellow here instantly and let me look at her foot."

Obediently Nat and Stewart picked up the trunk of the stout tree and, with a heaving and groaning, lifted it clear off Nelly's leg. Analee at once took it tenderly in her hands and examined it, stroking it carefully, noting how the skin was broken but how no bones appeared to be.

"Nelly, are you all right?"

She gazed into the pale face of the girl who had become her only friend and was relieved to see a faint smile, a nod of reassurance.

" 'Twas the shock. I think I am all right."

Nelly tried to raise herself and Nat immediately gave her support, gently putting his broad hands under her armpits and helping her to sit upright. Then Nelly winced with pain and Analee realized this was because, in sitting up, she had moved her leg and something hurt.

" 'Tis the ankle," Nelly said, bending and clasping it, "I think I twisted it under the tree."

Stewart was palpably relieved. What was a twisted ankle when the whole thing could so easily have ended in death? He even smiled at the girl and her bewitching companion, whose expression too had turned from severity to one of gratitude that Nelly was not hurt.

"We are near the house," Stewart said. "She can rest there and we can bind up her ankle and tend her scratches."

He nodded to Nat who lifted the girl in his arms as though she were thistledown. Stewart pointed the way for Analee and they followed Nat toward the house.

It was before they came within sight of the pink walls that they met Mary coming gaily toward them with a basket. It was a strange sight to see appearing from the trees—Nat with a girl in his arms, followed by Stewart and a woman who seemed to Mary, seeing her in the half-light cast by the trees, like some sort of fleet-footed wood nymph. She was so beautiful, with her flowing dark hair, her step so springy, so tall for a woman, that Mary was more puzzled, more disturbed by her than the sight of the casualty in Nat's arms.

Analee knew that she invariably made an impact at first sight on all who met her and she was used to these reactions both on the part of women as well as men. They usually stared, or shifted their stance, or exchanged glances one with another. And then they all settled down, as most people do, and came to accept her except for the men who fell in love with her, the women who took a dislike to her or the Buckland tribe who had never welcomed her.

All she was concerned with now was Nelly's welfare, not this curious trio—a blonde pretty girl and a handsome young man, and a fellow who was obviously the woodman.

Hearing the commotion, the barking of dogs, Betty had come into the yard to stare, and, observing the procession, promptly crossed herself, the instinctive gesture of a good God-fearing Christian when seeing a gypsy. Her first thought was to direct the gypsies to the barn, but she thought better of it when she saw the expression on Master Stewart's face and she hurried ahead into the kitchen.

But to her surprise Stewart directed that Nat should take the girl into the drawing-room overlooking the lake and then he called for Betty to bring water and ointment and strips of clean bandage from the cupboard. In Betty's opinion barefooted gypsies, whether beautiful or no, had no right inside a decent home, let alone the best room. She hoped Miss Mary would impress this clearly on her brother who was obviously distracted by the tall gypsy—very dark she was, so clearly a foreigner—and had temporarily lost his sense of proportion.

But of course Miss Mary wouldn't send the gypsies to their proper place, the barn. She was much too kindhearted and tender. Indeed she even instructed Betty to bring some food to the table because instead of a picnic in the forest they would now eat indoors. She obviously intended to share her bread with a common gypsy!

Mary followed Betty into the kitchen, having already detected her mood.

"Now, Betty, we cannot receive guests other than with hospitality, apart from the fact that it was our tree fell on her."

"No right to be in our wood," Betty grumbled as she took loaves of bread from the bin and meat from the larder. "Gypsies!"

"I have naught against gypsies, why have you?"

Mary was smiling as she placed the beer on a platter from which Stewart would serve it.

"They are thieves and rogues. They know not manners or what to do in a house; they are ill at ease in one."

It was true, both the women had looked around them as though there was something constricting about four walls, something unfamiliar about a floor made of wood.

"We cannot refuse them succor. Besides it is a diversion. It gives me something to think about besides what my brother is saying to Brent."

When she got back it was obvious that Nelly's foot was swelling and she was feeling a degree of pain now that the reaction had set in. Although she smiled bravely she was pale and Mary could see a glimmer of tears bravely held back.

"You must go to bed," she said immediately, "and rest your foot. I shall give you some laudanum to ease the pain."

"Bed?" Nelly said faintly.

"Yes, a bed, to lie in and rest. When you are recovered you can be on your way to where you were going. Not before."

She looked at Analee, who, she saw, was fascinated by the room and the view of the lake from the long low windows overlooking it. She had turned from Nelly and was gazing across at the forest of Lodore, and her face was temporarily transfigured by a look of sheer elation.

"Very beautiful to live here," she said softly, "always within sight of the lake and the fells."

"Yes, we love it," Mary said gently. "Would you like to come up with your friend? Nat will carry her and you could help her into bed."

Nelly stopped struggling and Analee gave in. Besides, she liked the house; it was not the sort of alien place she longed to get away from as she did nost times when she was indoors. She felt a welcoming here, almost as if in some way she belonged to it. She was glad they were staying at least for today.

She followed Mary up the stairs into a beautiful room that overlooked the lake. In it was a large four-poster bed and furniture that sparkled and shone from age and care. Analee loved the room immediately.

"There," Mary said, "we had another invalid here and he recovered, though he was much more badly hurt. He said the view of the lake soothed him. Would you come downstairs and eat with us when you have finished . . . How do you call yourself?"

She looked at Analee awkwardly, the sentence uncompleted.

"Analee. I have no other name," she said simply, "just Analee the gypsy, and this is Nelly."

"I'm Mary, and my brother is Stewart. Now we know one another. Pray come and eat. There is a chemise in the drawer for Nelly and the sheets are clean and aired."

She smiled and shut the door behind her. Analee and Nelly gazed at each other.

"I don't think I ever slept in one of these," Nelly said looking doubtfully at the bed. "Why is it so high?"

"So the rats don't clamber up," Analee said laughing. She was suddenly possessed by a feeling of light-heartedness, an irrational sense of happy anticipation as though something nice were going to happen. "And this chemise is not for over your skirt. You take it off and put this on."

"Altogether?" said Nelly incredulously. "I don't remember when I last bared my skin."

"The *gadjé* do it every night—yes, they change their clothes and lie in a bed like this."

"And these drapes," Nelly said wonderingly.

"Sheets—one on top and one underneath."

"Well, I never."

"It may be the only time you will sleep in a bed," Analee said, "best make the most of it. Here, stretch out and I'll help you."

Quickly Analee divested Nelly of her clothes and assisted her to put her head through the long white chemise; then she drew back the sheets and helped her inside. Once or twice Nelly winced but finally there she was, covered by a sheet, propped up against the white pillow. She looked so ill at ease, so comical that Analee burst out laughing again. She gathered up Nelly's things from the floor and put them across a chair. Then she took her cloak off and looked at herself in the mirror.

Analee hardly ever saw herself, being unused to mirrors in her wandering life. Occasionally she saw her face in the shiny surface of a tin or the clear waters of a lake when she leaned down to drink or wash.

She was surprised now, as she looked in the mirror,

to see how unfamiliar her face had become. It looked to her much older, and more knowing in the ways of the world, since she had seen it last. But the sight did not displease her. She saw the way her hair shone and the healthy glow in her face. She bared her teeth and they were even and white, and when she smiled her full red mouth dimpled at either side.

She stroked her bust with her hands and noticed how firm it looked, much smaller now that the milk had gone. For days after leaving the baby she had to pump herself dry twice a day, for the pain was unbearable and her breasts were swollen and hard. But then the milk had dried up and now her breasts were as they had been before Morella was born.

The sight of her breasts reminded her of her baby, her loss, and Analee's face became solemn. She lost interest in the sight of herself in the mirror and turned away. She saw that Nelly's eyes were closed. Sleep would do her good.

Quietly Analee tip-toed out of the room.

There was an atmosphere in the house that Analee couldn't comprehend. She who hated walls and stone and wood felt at peace here. She came down the staircase and into the broad hall. No one was about. She wandered into the long room overlooking the lake and stood gazing at the portraits of the family, hanging on the walls. There was definitely a strong family resemblance that ran through the line. But in the place of honor over the mantlepiece was a portrait of a man with dark beard and moustache, black piercing eyes. It was head and shoulders only, and the head was turned toward the painter so that the full force of his gaze, the sad expression in his eyes, made the viewer almost painfully aware of great, inexpressible suffering.

Analee stared at the portrait for some time, almost spellbound by it. But the sad man bore no resemblance at all to the tall, well-built, blond Allonby ancestors.

"It is Charles the Martyr," a gentle voice said behind her. "King Charles who died on the scaffold."

"Oh."

Analee knew little about kings and politics, and nothing about Charles the Martyr.

"We are supporters of the Stuart Kings of England here. It is King Charles' great-grandson, Prince Charles, who has landed in Scotland to reclaim the throne."

"Oh?" Analee looked at her with the interested expression of one always willing to learn. "I know naught about kings, and take care to keep clear of the law."

"Well," Mary said taking a seat by the window, her eyes looking alternately at Analee and the portrait on the wall, "England was ruled for a long time by the House of Stuart when King James VI of Scotland came to be James I of England . . ."

"He was from Scotland?"

"Yes, but he was related through his mother, Mary Queen of Scots, to Queen Elizabeth I of England who had just died. It was ironical because Queen Elizabeth had Mary beheaded to keep her off the throne. Elizabeth was not married and had no heirs of her own body, or others close enough to succeed her. 'Twas her aunt, Margaret Tudor, sister of Henry VIII of England, who married King James IV of Scotland and their son James V of Scotland was the father of Mary Queen of Scots."

Analee was listening intently. Mary had a very musical voice and her grave expression and earnestness somehow compelled attention.

"Thus!" Mary laughed, "if you will pardon the history lesson, it was that the Stuarts came to the English throne in 1603. Ever since the Norman conquest our kings have always been succeeded by heirs of the body and so it continued until in 1688 there occurred a revolution in our country, and the rightful King, James II of England, brother of Charles II—the merry monarch they called him—and son of our martyr King, fled abroad. I need not trouble you with the reason for

226

the revolution, Analee, for 'twas complex. King James sympathized with the Catholics, like all the Stuarts, but ever since Henry VIII and the Reformation the Catholics have been persecuted in this country and no monarch was allowed to be a Catholic . . ."

Analee looked at the picture on the wall.

"Oh, King Charles I was sympathetic to our faith and they say Charles II converted on his deathbed. But King James was very influenced by his mother Henrietta Maria of France and he openly advocated that the Catholics should have the same rights as everyone else.

"Well, he was succeeded by his daughter Mary, a Protestant, and her husband William of Orange and they in turn by his second daughter Anne. Queen Anne was the last of the Stuarts, for Parliament had passed a law decreeing that only Protestants should ascend the English throne so that the Catholic Stuarts should be excluded, and the nearest heir was a fat old German prince called the Elector of Hanover whose mother had been a daughter of Elizabeth of Bohemia, daughter of James I of England and sister of King Charles I. So you can see how far back it went, how tenuous was the connection. The Prince could neither speak nor understand English and came with all his court to occupy the throne of our country . . ."

Mary was near to tears, and Analee moved over to her but feared to show too much familiarity by touching her.

" 'Twas a scandal. King James II had died, but his son who was born here and was openly a Catholic living in France was the rightful heir to the throne of England, and we who supported him call him King James III."

"And is he still there?" To Analee it did not appear right at all; gypsy rules of succession were very strict too.

"Yes, an old man now, living sadly in Rome because even the French King who used to support him would do so no longer. He it was who took part in the glorious rebellion of 1715 in which our family suffered

227

so much, and it is *his* son Prince Charles Edward who has come now to act as regent and fight for his father's throne!"

"Oh, may he succeed!" Analee cried clasping her hands. "I can see it is so right!"

"Yes, it is, it *is!* We will drive these odious Germans back to Hanover from whence they came. Oh, Prince Charles is but twenty-four years of age, so bold and so handsome, it is said. He came with only seven men and now all Scotland has flocked to him, and so will all England when he crosses the border and marches to London."

"Will he not be resisted?"

"Oh, there will be some resistance," Mary said casually, "but they say that his charm and skill and also the fact he is undoubtedly the rightful heir will carry the day."

Analee looked at the picture and suddenly there was a whirring sound in her head and she closed her eyes. She could hear the clash of swords, the sound of musket shot, the rasp of cannonballs. There were screams and cries . . . she put her hands to her ears.

"What is it, Analee?" Mary grasped her arm, her face pale with concern. "Are you ill?"

Analee swayed and the sounds abruptly stopped. She was looking steadily at the face of the King, as though nothing had happened. Then she turned to Mary and said gravely: "There will be much suffering . . ."

"Because of him? The Prince?"

"Yes. For a moment I seemed to hear the rage of battle, cries and screams . . ."

Mary gazed at her guest with wonder—this tall, strange gypsy woman with the bare feet and proud eyes. She had already seen how Stewart had been affected by her, how they all had been.

"Can you see into the future? Can it really be true?"

Analee shook her head.

"I sometimes can see things, foretell them; but I am not *cohani,* that is a gypsy witch or woman of magic.

228

But things that I often feel strongly about come true . . . in my vision just now I seemed to see much distress for our own people, the gypsies."

She put her hands to her face and looked at the picture again.

"He was a good man?"

"Oh, he was. Some say a foolish one, stubborn one; but far far better than any Hanoverian."

Analee smiled at the young girl, noting the set of the mouth, the hint of passion in her eyes. She was beautiful, and the brother was handsome, too. Analee wondered about the brother and sister living apparently with so few servants in this large house.

"Would you like to walk by the lake?" Mary said. "I can see it fascinates you."

"Yes, it is very beautiful; and the mountains . . ." Analee looked across the water to Walla Crag. "You see I normally see everything from outside, not from the point of view of being inside a house. If you are always out of doors things look very different. That window is like . . ." she pointed to the pictures on the wall, "well, as though that scene is framed like one of those."

"Yes, I know what you mean. Like a picture."

Mary led Analee into the hall and out of the wide front door. Almost immediately they could see the lake between the firs. It sparkled as though a handful of jewels, diamonds and sapphires, had been thrown carelessly into it and Analee shaded her eyes against the glare. It was a beautiful day; calm, gentle, serene, no cloud in the sky; not like autumn at all.

"You live here alone with your brother?"

Analee was reluctant to appear curious and glanced at the girl walking beside her.

"No, we have an elder brother John, who is not here today. He will be back soon. Our father died a few years ago. My mother when I was born . . ."

"Oh." Analee stopped and looked directly into Mary's face. "My mother, too, died when I was born. You know I felt a strange harmony with you as soon

229

as I saw you. Now maybe that is the reason. We have never known the love of a mother."

Mary gazed at her strange companion and clasped her hands.

"Oh, do you think so? Is it possible? Tell me about yourself, Analee, why you lead this life. There is something about you that is . . . unexpected. You are not, for instance, like Nelly."

"I *am* a gypsy," Analee said simply, "a wandering gypsy woman. I have nothing special or secret about me. Maybe I have traveled more than someone like Nelly."

"Are you from overseas?"

Analee paused and looked toward the water; it was a question that people often asked her.

"I? No. I was born here in this country. But as my mother died so young I was brought up by my grandmother and, yes, they came from overseas, from some far distant country—I know not which."

"From Spain or Italy. That is why you are so dark-skinned."

"Maybe," Analee smiled.

"I have spent all my life by the shores of this lake. I never went further than Carlisle and that only once. I cannot comprehend what it is like to wander. Don't you feel afraid?"

"Afraid? No. I feel safer among nature than my own people . . ."

Analee's eyes were tinged with bitterness and her voice faltered. Mary sensed a sadness, but also a withdrawal on the part of Analee, as though she did not want to speak further about herself.

"It's something I can't understand, never having known that life," Mary said.

"And you are happy as you are?"

"Well, our family has known much hardship. Once we were, well, wealthy and powerful I suppose you'd say, though it was long before my time. Then our father's brother was in the rebellion in 1715 and was executed. Our mother died when I was born, our uncle died, an exile abroad, and my eldest brother

230

finally managed to find some happiness and married a beautiful girl he had known all his life. They had but ten short months of happiness when she died, too, giving birth to a child . . ."

"And the child?"

"Dead."

"Ah . . ." Analee looked away, not wanting Mary to see the suffering in her own eyes. Then she turned to her again. "And you . . . what is your future?"

Mary's face assumed so suddenly a look of happiness, almost ecstasy, that Analee was taken by surprise. The deep blue eyes became almost purple and a becoming blush suffused her cheeks. Analee laughed outright at such a sudden transformation.

"I see there is someone special for you . . ."

"I am expecting to be married! Any day he could come galloping over those mountains. My brother has gone to fetch him."

"Oh, I am so happy for you. Have you known him long?"

"All my life. He is my cousin; but he never showed any love for me until recently. Last year he was very ill and I nursed him back to health. We fell in love."

"Then why did you not marry last year?"

Mary frowned and studied the ground.

"My family did not fully approve of him. Although he is of noble birth he showed no capacity for settling down, for hard work, and he had no fortune of his own. Of course I didn't mind that," Mary said hastily, noting the expression on Analee's face. "We have never had money, but he also had a reputation as . . . a womanizer." Mary's voice sank to a whisper. "My brother thought him too fickle."

"But all is changed now?" Analee's eyes sparkled at the girl's shyness.

"Oh yes. He has worked hard and been faithful . . . I think, and I expect him any time."

Analee looked at the happy open face gazing into hers and knew a sudden moment of unease, foreboding . . . there seemed to be a cloud between her and this young girl on the verge of marriage. Was it the intervention of her own unhappiness, or was it a foreknowing?

"I must go upstairs," she said quickly, "and see to Nelly."

"What is it, Analee? Have I said something wrong?"

Mary had observed the change in the gypsy's eyes and looked concerned. Analee leaned impulsively over to touch her, then decided not to; Mary might consider her gesture too familiar.

"No, of course not. I was worried that I had neglected Nelly. We cannot stay here long, especially as you are expecting your brother and . . . what is his name, your young man?"

"Mary," a voice came from the wood and Stewart appeared through the trees, "can you come for a minute? I want to talk about the thinning of the coppice with you."

"Ah, I must go," Mary said. "We dine at five, and go to bed very early in these parts."

"I am used to sleeping when it is dark and rising when it is light," Analee said turning toward the house. "In fact I cannot keep awake in the dark."

Stewart who had hoped that the beautiful gypsy would come with them looked disconsolate as she walked toward the house. Mary saw his expression and smiled.

"I think you are smitten," she said.

"A man would not be in his right mind if he were not," Stewart replied. "I don't think I ever saw a woman who struck me more in my life."

"But she is not for you."

"Why?"

"She is a gypsy. A nomad; would you wander too?"

"I was teasing," Stewart said taking her by the arm. "Maybe she will give me a spell to make Emma mine. If she is a real gypsy she should know about the ways of love."

"I am sure she does," Mary said, trembling slightly, for what reason she didn't know. Maybe a chill had sprung up. "I am sure she knows all about them."

Chapter Thirteen

Stewart was at his best at the dinner table that evening, relaxed and full of laughter. In the company of Analee he seemed to bloom, to lose all his reserve. It was the way she looked at him that made him feel so, well . . . manly was the word. Yes, manly, and clever as well. She simply had to smile at him and he wanted to open up and puff out his chest like a strutting turkey-cock. He wanted to please her and impress her; above all he wanted to make her go on looking at him like that.

But when she turned to Mary the look was only subtly changed because Mary was a woman and Stewart was a man. Analee wanted to draw Mary out too, and she did this by her smiles of encouragement, the way she nodded her head, seemed completely absorbed by what was being said. Years fell away from the brother and sister as they responded to the impact Analee made on them. She brought out the best in them, caused them to relive childhood memories, remembering when times were not as hard as they were now, so insecure.

It was almost as though . . . she had cast a spell on them, Stewart thought watching his sister's face as she chatted and sparkled, erupting every now and again into long-forgotten silvery laughter. Could she cast spells, this beautiful gypsy woman who came from nowhere? Was she, perhaps, a witch?

"Mary has been telling me she is about to marry," Analee said suddenly interrupting the flow of childhood nostalgia. "And you, Stewart? Have you no young woman you long to make your bride?"

Stewart looked abashed, less sure of himself. He knew he was blushing, but hoped she did not see it under the brown tan acquired from so many days of chopping trees in the sun.

"Yes, he does have . . ." Mary began impishly, but he looked imploringly at her and she stopped.

"It is true," he said cautiously, "I am enamored of someone; but she will not spare a glance for me. She is younger than I and different, and . . ."

"Then that augurs well," Analee said practically. "It would not do if she were older or exactly the same in temperament."

But she could see that Stewart was not joking; he was not amused. He nursed a hopeless passion for someone who did not love him.

"No, she does not like me enough. Maybe you could give me a spell," Stewart said half in jest, wanting to restore the happy laughing mood of a few moments ago. "Why not? Can you cast spells?"

"No," Analee said slowly. "I do not have the powers. I told you I am not *cohani;* but, well . . . there are one or two ways I do know of trying to capture someone's love."

Stewart leaned forward impressed, despite himself, by her gravity, the sincerity of her tone.

"Then tell it. I will try it."

"Well . . . You must pluck three hairs from the neck of the girl you love, better if you do it while she is sleeping. You then put the hairs in the chink of a tree and as it grows her love will grow for you."

"But," Stewart protested amused, though he could see that Analee did not speak in jest. "She is not here. She lives quite far away and I cannot get the hairs from her head."

"Ah." Analee stared thoughtfully at the table. "You really need a *drabarni,* a drug woman who will give you a potion to put into her food. But there again you need to be with her. To win love from afar, that is more difficult. Look, this will be easy for you. You must go to the lake and pick a leaf from a tree hanging over it. Then with your knife you prick your wrist and smear the leaf with the blood while repeating your name. You then turn the leaf over and smear it on the other side, saying over and over again the name of the girl you want to marry. Her name is . . . ?"

"Emma," Stewart said.

"Then you say 'Emma' over and over again. Then you throw the leaf into the lake and watch it flow away."

She stopped and gazed at Stewart. He was such a handsome, vital young man, looking earnestly at her face. She could tell he was half in love with her. But she did not see happiness for Stewart . . . there was something about this family that bred its own disaster. Looking at brother and sister she could see happiness for neither of them. Neither Stewart nor the girl, not for a long time.

She hoped she was wrong. The mood of gaiety had gone and it was partly her fault. She was not bringing happiness to the house and she wanted to. She felt she already loved this family, the two young vulnerable people who had given her, a rough wandering gypsy woman, so much hospitality. She wanted to help them, to do something for them. But what?

"I must take Nelly some food," she said getting up from the table. "She will be better tomorrow. We will go, and presume no more on your kindness."

"But we like having you here," Stewart said. "We get so few visitors. Besides, where will you go?"

"Ah, that I can't say. We are making for over the mountains, toward the sea. Maybe we will cross the water and go to Ireland."

"You mean you just wander on and on?"

"Yes." Analee tilted her head at Stewart. "You cannot understand it, can you? You have a house and a bed and fresh clothes to put on. You have food at regular times and warmth in your grate. But I, and Nelly, have known nothing else. The earth is our home; the wild hills and forests. We have always done it and it is how we live. I have . . . for some months dwelt in a gypsy camp and I could not abide it. I hated being tied down. I cannot explain it; it is how I am. How my people are."

Stewart thought it thrilling to listen to the somber voice of the gypsy as dark gathered over the lake, and the only light in the room came from the guttering candles on the polished oak table. He thought of her sleeping rough and living like a nomad, no table, no bed. He got up and took her hand and kissed it, noting how fine and smooth it was, the long nails blunted at the ends but not rough or jagged. Although her clothes were poor they were clean and her body was sweet-smelling. She took care of herself.

"I wish you would stay," he said. "At least stay and see Mary married. Rest here awhile. Nelly is not nearly fit to go; see if the spell works. I will try it tomorrow. With you."

Analee laughed into his earnest young eyes. Why not stay a while if he meant it, and it seemed he did? Maybe she could dance at Mary's wedding, reward her like that? She got up and clasped his hand, her eyes shining.

"Well . . . maybe a little longer if you really wish it. Now I must take Nelly her dinner. See how she does. It is late for me to be awake. I am like the birds, as I told you. I will see you tomorrow."

Betty had already taken up Nelly's food and Nelly was asleep when Analee got to their room. She had come slowly up the stairs, along the corridors. She got in beside Nelly and lay for a long time with her hands clasped beneath her head looking out onto the dark sky studded with stars.

Analee thought that, tomorrow or soon, she and Nelly would bed down as they always did beside a ditch or under cover of a rocky crag. Sometimes they found a cave and stayed a day or two if it were cold or wet. Luxury like this she had never known. But, to her surprise, she did not dislike it as much as she thought she would: the feel of the sheets on her bare skin—for she did not wear a chemise as Nelly did—the boards under her bare feet when she got up. The

236

gleaming table at dinner with silver, and flaming wax candles, plates and the smell of hot food.

It was her first real experience of living in a house and she liked it. It was attractive. It appealed to something in Analee she didn't know she possessed.

Suddenly, her head resting on her hands clasped on the fine white flock-filled pillows, Analee thought of the man who had lain in this room recovering from an illness. He would have looked out on the stars as she did; he and Mary had fallen in love; maybe they had lain together in this very bed.

And suddenly, for no reason at all that she could understand, Analee had a clear picture of Brent Delamain, and with his image in her mind she fell asleep.

Brent Delamain had ridden hard since leaving Cockermouth at first light, John close behind him. It had been a glorious morning as they left the valley and began the ascent of the foothills just as the sun broke over Grisedale Pike and the fells, covered with heather and brown bracken, had the rich golden gleam of fresh honey. They toiled up toward Whinlatter and the brown and green fells gave way to the thick forest of tall straight firs through which many a mountain stream cascaded from its source over stones and fallen logs toward Buttermere and Crummock Water.

As it rose the sunlight pierced the trees, dispersing the thick morning mist which spiraled up like smoke through the thick branches. At times Brent's nostrils caught the scent of woodsmoke caused by the charcoal burners who plied a living in the forest.

After a steep descent into Braithwaite they rested, taking bread and ale at the hostelry, and then set off along the narrow bridle paths that meandered through the Newlands Valley by way of Stair and Skelgill and climbed high up to Skelgill Bank and across the top to Catbells. All the way along this last part the lake of Derwentwater gleamed below them, a broad glistening ribbon mirroring the blue sky and clouds, the purple hills that surrounded it and the forest which ran alongside either bank.

From where he waited for John to catch up Brent could see across to Low Moss, Castlerigg Fell and away to Watendlath, and then in the distance the high snowy peaks at the end of Borrowdale.

But below lay the jewel, the prize, its tall chimneys and soft red stone, its gables and mullioned windows reflected in the still lake—Furness Grange and at its core nestled his beloved Mary. He imagined he saw her walking in the grounds and raised his hand to call; but he was too far away. He looked at John who smilingly indicated he should go ahead, and then he dug his heels into his horse and raced down across the fell toward the house.

And indeed it had been Mary walking in the grounds on her way back from taking Stewart and Nat their noonday meal. She clasped her hand over her eyes against the sun as she heard the sound of hooves and there he was towering over her on his horse; and then he had jumped down and she was in his arms.

She could feel his heart beating against her cheek pressed tightly to his chest, and her own arms could scarcely encircle his back he had grown so big. Not fat, she could feel his bones beneath her fingers. He had just developed girth in the months they had been apart. She could feel his mouth in her hair murmuring words of love and then she raised her head, and that face she had seen in so many dreams, that mouth of such gentleness came down on hers, and for Mary Allonby it was the sweetest moment she had ever known in her life. Sweeter than the first kiss, the first embrace; sweeter even than when he had gazed at her breasts and she had been so aware of his desire for her. She knew this was so sweet because it was the prelude to giving herself completely to Brent; to becoming one with him, his wife.

His mouth moved from hers to her throat and, lower down, she could feel his hands trying to slip in between the folds of her bodice. Reality came back and with it thoughts of her brother or the gypsy, maybe, looking out of an upstairs window at them.

"Brent! You have grown so broad."

"Aye, 'tis the good life of the sea." He held her away from him and took in every inch of her precious body.

"And you have grown too, as your brother said. So comely, yes, and a little rounded. Oh Mary, when can we be wed?"

"You still want to be wed, Brent?"

"Can you doubt it? Urgently. Immediately."

"It is what I want, too."

"Despite the war?"

"*Because* of it," Mary said pressing her head against him again, wanting once more to hear that firm steady heartbeat.

Stewart had heard the hooves and, giving time for his sister and cousin to be reunited, joined them where they had remained by the side of the house. It was a relief to him to see them clinging to each other as though they could never bear to be parted. He, too, had wondered what changes the intervening months might have brought, feared the effects on his sister's happiness. But there, they clung to each other and he knew all was well. He held out his hand.

"Brent."

"Oh, Stewart! John is coming more slowly over yonder fell." Brent glanced upward. "I think he wanted to be tactful."

"Aye, he did well. I see you are of the same mind, Brent."

"More than ever. When can we be wed, Stewart?"

"I have told the priest. He is ready to marry you as soon as you wish it."

"Then fetch him to the chapel as quick as you can and let us get wed."

Like many of the old Catholic families the Grange had a small chapel where the priest said Mass when he came by. There was a priest at Keswick, Father Bernard, who lived by staying with one Catholic family, then another. John knew where he was now and had already sent word to him.

"He will be here by tomorrow."

"Then tomorrow we will be wed. Mary?"

"Yes. Tomorrow. Oh, Brent, I can scarcely believe it."

"We are just doing, Mary, what should have happened months ago."

Brent pursed his mouth in the stern expression Mary knew so well.

"Do not be angry, Brent. We have each other now."

"I am not angry, merely sad we wasted so much time."

He kissed her lightly and took her hand.

"I must wash after the journey. Is my room . . . ?"

"Oh, Brent, we have two guests. I'm sure they will bring us luck. They are gypsies and one of them hurt her foot. I'm afraid they are in your old room . . ."

"Never mind," Brent said, "soon I will be in *yours*."

"I put you next to Stewart, that is the room *next* to mine."

"I'll go and wash and change my clothes and be with you soon, sweetheart."

Brent waved and went into the house as John clattered up and, eyes shining with happiness, Mary turned to greet him.

The hot noon sun gleamed on the stairs. Huge beams, in which the dust rose, shone in from the long mullioned windows that illuminated the staircase, panes of blue and rose and yellow making the sun spots glisten with a thousand colors. Brent loved the old house, the smell of beeswax and candles. He leapt up the stairs four at a time and then went quickly along the gallery that ran the length of the hall.

And there she was, coming toward him as in a dream. The dark hair, the supple body, the face that he knew so well but which had remained shadowy for him, became clear. The most beautiful woman in the world; the goddess always seen in moonlight or in the myriad beams of the dancing colored sun. Dancing;

she was a dancer and her quick, sure-footed steps, her lithe, graceful body with upraised arms clicking her castanets were as vivid at that moment as when he had last seen her. She saw him; but still she came on and he thought she was a vision, a ghost and would walk straight through him. But she stopped just in front of him and he could smell her tantalizing body smells, a haunting heady perfume that became dear and familiar to him as the mist that had obscured his memory finally dispersed.

"Analee," he said.

So this was the *gadjo,* this was Mary's betrothed, the man she had fallen in love with as he lay recovering from an illness. Of course he was her cousin, a relation by blood; they even looked too much alike. In a way she realized, she had always known it. The feel of the house, the familiarity, the peace, the sense of home-coming that was so unusual. She had slept in Brent's bed; had looked on the view that had given him so much pleasure as Mary had brought him back to life —to a life of which Randal had nearly deprived him.

"It *is* you," she said.

He tried to reach out for her but she stepped back. It was much too dangerous she knew; besides he had easily forgotten her, fallen into the arms of another. Yet the look on his face . . . it was as though something had come to him from a long way away, something strange.

How could he explain how he had forgotten her? Brent gazed at her and saw the bewilderment on her face. He now remembered everything; his first meeting with her, his search for her, hunting her, possessing her. He remembered her dance in the tavern, the way she had danced just for him.

"Analee, how could I have forgotten you?"

"Then you did forget?"

"Everything. Until now, until I saw you."

"You were very ill," she said gently. "After the blow on the head?"

"I remembered nothing."

"And fell in love with Mary. She is very sweet . . ."

Mary. Brent closed his eyes. Mary . . .

"I . . ."

"She loves you, Brent; loves you so much she can't wait to marry you."

"But I . . ."

"You can't go back on her now. It would kill her. I know her; in a short time I have become her friend."

He had such a desperate look on his face that she began to suffer too.

"Besides, I am married as well," she said. "It cannot be for us again."

Brent's face seemed to swell with an awful rage and he tried to grab her shoulder, but still she backed away from him.

"*You* married! Then you didn't remember either."

"Oh, I remembered, but I had no choice. The man who nearly killed you captured me. It is a gypsy tradition that if you capture a bride she must marry you whether she wants to or not."

"Then you are not really married; not in your heart. It is not too late."

She began to walk away from him, slowly back down the corridor and he followed her.

"It is too late, much much too late. Make your life again . . ."

"Of course I can't make my life again now I have found you. You *are* my life. Analee, let us go now. Let us . . ."

Sadly Analee shook her head.

"No, no . . . abuse the hospitality of the sweet people here? I love them, Brent, and they like and trust me. Mary is a lovely girl, *your* sort of girl . . ."

"She's my cousin . . ."

"*Your* people. We are not meant to live as normal people, Brent. There is something about you and I that is doomed. You would never forgive yourself as a man if you deserted Mary now. We could never be happy in a life built on such sorrow. You would soon tire of the wandering life, Brent; life with me . . ."

"I've been a wanderer too on the seas, Analee. Let

us go somewhere and talk about this. There *is* some solution."

He gazed at her and she knew the solution lay with her. She nodded, as if agreeing with him.

"We will meet later, after dinner. We will find a solution." He grasped her hand, and the thrill of the feel of her flesh was like nothing he had known before or since, not with Mary, not with anyone.

"No," he said desperately. "Let us now . . ."

"After dinner," she said. "Behave normally now. Do as you would do."

She gazed up at him, her *gadjo,* Morella's father, and gently let her hand pass across his face as though to etch his features on her palm. Then she turned into the room she shared with Nelly.

Brent Delamain, his mind in a turmoil, waited for the dinner to begin. How could he guard his expression when Analee came into the room, avoid showing that, for him, she was the only woman in the world—the one it seemed to him he had always sought. In every other woman he had been trying to find Analee, and when he had found her he had lost her, and then found her again . . . and now he was being told it was too late.

He had wanted to follow her into her room, but she shut the door and he stood gazing at it helplessly for some time before finding the one meant for him and throwing himself on the bed. "Womanizer!" they would all say. "Brent Delamain never changes. He came to marry Mary and made off with someone else."

No one would ever trust him again. They would say he was fickle, undependable. Above all, they would say he was not fit to serve the Prince. All these thoughts and more warred with his own desire. They fought within him, so that when at last he appeared downstairs Mary, running up to greet her beloved and seeing his expression, had asked if he were ill? She had expected him down hours before, anticipating him running into her arms. But he told her he was merely tired and then his eyes had wandered over her head looking for something. He was looking for something now, Mary thought, or someone—his eyes kept staring at the door. He looked ill at ease, unhappy. The relaxed lover she had greeted only hours before looked now like some sort of fugitive; his face pale, his eyes restless. Was he in trouble?

But Stewart and John appeared not to notice and happily discussed the nuptials that would take place on the morrow as soon as the priest arrived.

"We had best begin," John said at last. "I know not where our guest is. How is she called?"

"Analee."

Analee . . . Brent closed his eyes. Oh, that word "Analee"—it rang in his mind with all the force of an echo that had been lost and forgotten and now resounded louder than ever. "ANALEE . . ."

"She is very beautiful," Mary said, glancing slyly at Brent. "All the men fall madly in love with her."

"Ah, really?" Brent tried to be jocular. "Well, give us the chance then. Pray, where *is* this Analee?"

"Betty has gone up to fetch her. Maybe she is shy with the company." Any moment Analee would come through the door, Brent thought. And she would stand and stare and he would . . .

"Miss, she has gone!" Betty flurried into the room carrying the large tureen of soup. "Gypsies! Made off with the family plate for all we know."

"Gone?"

Mary looked up suddenly, but it was not Mary who had spoken. It was Brent. He even seemed half to rise from his seat and then thought better of it.

"How 'gone,' Betty?" Mary said calmly. "And Nelly, too?"

"Both, miss, and the room as clean as a whistle and the bed turned back."

"How very unusual," John said offhandedly reaching for the soup ladle. "As you say, gypsies I suppose, Betty."

Stewart too seemed disturbed. He had been so looking forward to wandering in the garden after dinner with Analee, maybe casting the spell together with her by the lake.

"But they were not *like* that!" Mary said, her mind preoccupied by the mystery, but above all by the stricken look on Brent's face, the way he had half risen at Betty's news. "At least Analee was not. What can have sent them away?"

"Very impolite," John said. "Soup, Brent?"

"Please. Maybe they came to some harm?" Brent was trying to control his voice, his emotions, still the pounding of his heart. He wanted to get up and run from the room, mount his horse; they could not have gone far . . . He felt panic rising and subsiding in waves, like a terrible fear that is felt and repelled in turns.

"Harm? What sort of harm? No, they have had enough and gone. Never mind." John passed Brent his soup bowl and turned with a question to Mary.

"Please." Mary nodded at her brother, "but I *am* sad about it. I so like Analee. I hoped she would be here for our wedding."

Wedding. Brent felt a tremor run from head to foot. It was as though he was passing through a nightmare. He was going to marry Mary tomorrow. Analee had betrayed him.

"What is it with thee, Brent? I think you are still fatigued."

Stewart too had been observing the strange behavior of his cousin; how restless and anxious he seemed, how he wriggled about in his seat. How pale and haggard he was after appearing so comely and well on his arrival.

"I hope you are not ill," Stewart added, thinking of the outbreak of the pox that had occurred recently in Keswick.

"No. Naught ails me at all. Maybe weary with the journey."

"Or nervous with excitement, I'll swear," John said smiling broadly. "A bridegroom at last, eh, Brent?"

Brent took a spoon to his soup. The nightmare showed no signs of ending; indeed it was worsening.

245

Every moment Analee was getting further and further away. He put down his spoon and said with pretended calm:

"Maybe we should seek the gypsies lest they have come to some harm in this light. 'Tis dark outside."

"Aye." Stewart got up. "I do not think Analee would behave thus. I agree with Brent. Excuse us, Mary."

He grabbed a candle from the table and, followed by Brent, hastened through the hall up the stairs. The candle fluttered, lighting up the dark corridor as they passed along, throwing great shadows on the wall. The door of the room was open and, as soon as they entered, it was obvious that it was empty—it had that deserted air such as a room does when the inhabitant has packed up and gone away.

Stewart cast the candle into every corner, then went to the window.

"No, they simply got up and left." He looked dejected. "I would like to have seen her again. Well . . ."

He turned away and went out of the room.

"Shall we search the fell?"

"Aye, if you like. But they have not come to harm, Brent. They have left of their own free will."

"We should just see."

Brent knew he had to keep moving; the one thing he could not do was sit still. Stewart shrugged and followed, noting how Brent preceded him to take the lead. In fact Brent had started to run ahead toward the stable not waiting for Stewart to light his way.

Stewart, although puzzled and upset himself, was intrigued by his cousin's behavior, having observed his agitated manner at table. Could it be that Brent *knew* Analee . . . or had he met her briefly in the house and become instantly obsessed by her? It was not impossible, having a mind to Analee's looks and Brent's reputation. He followed his cousin more slowly. He came to the stable door and stood behind Brent who feverishly seized the candle and held it above his head.

"My nag has gone. The one I borrowed from Ambrose to ride over here today."

"Then they *are* thieves," Stewart said, contempt in his voice.

"Nay . . ." Brent swung round, and saw the expression on Stewart's face.

"You know her, Brent, don't you? You know Analee. You've met her before?"

Brent said nothing, turned away as though he had hardly heard.

"She could ride well," he murmured, "we know not which direction she may have taken. Aye . . ." He looked despairingly at Stewart. "She is well away by now."

"You *did* know her. Brent?"

"Aye." Brent looked toward the distant hills obscured now by the dark.

"There was talk of gypsies when you were injured . . ."

"Yes."

Brent met his cousin's gaze. What was the use of concealment now?

"She came here to see *you?*"

"No! 'Twas pure chance. I tell you I had forgot all about her. The memory of her was knocked out of my head by the blow. I swear to you, Stewart, I never recalled Analee again until today. I fell in love with Mary and wanted to marry her. And then today I saw Analee in the corridor. I thought she was a ghost and then, suddenly, I remembered. I remembered everything."

Stewart was staring grimly at his cousin trying to suppress the contempt he felt for him.

"It *is* true what they say about you, Brent. You are an incorrigible womanizer. It . . ."

"Pray spare me, cousin, your thoughts on this matter," Brent said wearily. "It is not as you think."

He turned to go back to the house when he felt himself seized violently by the shoulder. Stewart spun him around and pressed him against the wall. Brent could feel the prick of steel at his windpipe and, by the faint moonlight, see Stewart's face very close to his. He felt his warm breath and observed the whites of his eyes.

247

"I'll not have it, Brent—this womanizing. You marry my sister as soon as the priest comes or, by God, you won't live to see Analee or any other woman again. I promise you . . ."

Brent gazed unflinchingly into his cousin's eyes.

"Do not distress yourself, cousin. I will wed Mary tomorrow. I have given my word and I will do it. That was what Analee intended by leaving me. She wants me to do my duty and tells me so in her own way. I will wed Mary because I have given my word; but as for loving her . . . that I can never do!"

Stewart pricked Brent's flesh gently with his knife so that a rivulet of blood went onto his shirt.

"You . . . will . . . love . . . Mary . . . and . . . make . . . her . . . happy. Do you hear, Brent Delamain? You distress my sister, who has suffered so much already, and I will kill you with my own hand. You hear?"

Brent said nothing. He was not afraid of Stewart. Indeed his knife could have provided an end to his ills, for he no longer felt like living. With Analee gone he wished death would come soon.

Mary lay quietly in the bed not knowing whether Brent slept or not. She stared into the dark and tried to understand; to lie with a man and yet not with him. She knew this was not what had been meant by marriage; what had been promised her by Brent in the chapel that morning: "With my body I thee worship."

What had happened to Brent? What had come between them? Ever since the gypsy had left, Brent had not been the same as before. Yet he swore he didn't know her. Mary didn't know whether to believe him or not. Only that his attitude had changed after he had entered the house, and soon afterward Analee and her companion had apparently left. Had she cast a spell on the house? Had she been a witch? To bring more evil and misery to the Allonby family?

They had gone through the ceremony, through the family meal afterward, with a stiffness and formality that was so different to what Mary had dreamed would be the case. Her ardent wooer had become like a man who walked in a dream.

"Brent. Are you asleep?"

"No."

"If it is not the gypsy, is it that you did not want to be tied down? Did not want to marry me after all?"

"No."

He groped for her hand in the dark. He wanted to love her, to keep his promise to her; but all he could think of was the tilt of the proud gypsy head, the gleam in the black eyes. When he'd looked at his bride it was to see again a cousin, a familial, not a mistress. Someone he wanted to protect and love but could not adore as he adored Analee. He didn't want to sink his flesh into hers and make her his as he did Analee. He had tried but he couldn't do it.

He had lain upon her and kissed her and tried to desire her and be a husband to her, but it hadn't happened. He had felt her flesh stirring, quivering under his, her legs open with anticipation, her back arched for him . . .

It had been terrible. Terrible for him and terrible for Mary. She had felt humiliated and unwanted, spurned by her husband, her lover, unable to arouse him. He had given up and, instead, had taken her tenderly in his arms trying to soothe her weeping, explain to her that sometimes it didn't happen. It was not always possible for a man to behave in that way; if he was tired, or upset . . .

But still she couldn't understand. She didn't know that his mind was miles away galloping from Furness Grange—whither? To Keswick or Borrowdale, or Carlisle, or south to Windermere? How could he know which way she had gone? And why, why hadn't she spoken to him, just one last time?

In the dark he was aware that Mary had started to weep again, her face pressed into the pillow. He yearned to take her as she wanted, just to soothe her, to please her; but he could not. He let his hand caress her breasts, feel her slim waist, her rounded thighs, the cavern between her legs . . . all things that in the past would have been enough to drive him mad with desire. He would have mounted the maid and ravished her ten times over. But nothing happened.

It was the first time he had failed a woman, let alone such a nubile desirable one, lying by his side. Mary stopped weeping while Brent's hands ran over her; she turned her mouth to his to kiss, her slender body quivering with desire as his fingers explored those intimate secret parts of her. She held her breath, hoping that . . .

His hands ceased their exploration and she was aware that he leaned over her in the dark, his face gazing down on hers, his expression abject. He was teasing her, tormenting her! She flung herself on her face and, pressing it into the pillow, gave herself once more to a torrent of silent weeping . . . for she did not want her sorrow, her shame, to be known through the house.

"It will be all right tomorrow," Brent whispered, and he tenderly stroked her wet face.

How could she know that the fault did not lie with her or her beautiful body? That he, Brent Delamain, had been bewitched by a gypsy?

Chapter Fourteen

Stewart Allonby looked into the face of his cousin Emma and remembered the gypsy's spell. But although Emma's eyes were bright and welcoming there was no expression in them of love such as Stewart had half hoped to see. It was too fanciful. And yet he had done as the gypsy had bidden him and put his blood on one side of a leaf, then on another, repeating their names. Then he had cast the leaf on the water and watched it float toward Keswick.

How long ago it seemed, that foolish day in late September when he had gone stealthily to the water's edge to practice the magic love rite prescribed by the gypsy. As he looked at Emma he realized that, despite its foolishness, he had hoped that in the intervening month the magic had had time to work. Then as he looked he smiled at her, aware of his folly. Emma, who always found her Allonby cousin very worthy but dull, was unexpectedly intrigued by the smile and wondered if, after all, he were maybe not as dull as she had supposed. She'd never noticed it before—perhaps because one was conditioned to think of the Allonbys as poor, unsuccessful and not likely to enhance the fortunes or awake the emotions of a pretty young girl.

Unlike many of the young men she had met recently who had pale complexions, well-kept hands and elegant bodies fitted out in the latest fashion, whose hair was concealed in a light periwig or who, if they wore their own, had it beautifully waved about their ears, Stewart Allonby's body was thick-set and sturdy and his face browned by exposure to the elements. He was a smaller, stockier version of her brother Brent. Suddenly Emma thought he was attractive. Really the elegant young men wearied her with their small talk and self-absorption. They danced beautifully and they were not lacking in wit or fine manners, but . . .

"How well you look, Stewart."

Stewart had seen the change in Emma's expression from a rather bored indifference to a quickening of interest and involuntarily preened himself, realizing that she was looking at him in a more intimate and particular kind of way to the one he was used to.

"And you, Emma, a young lady now. Changed since I saw you last, a year ago I think."

"Yes, it was when we came over to Furness for the betrothal of Brent and Mary. How sorry I was to miss the wedding; but it was so sudden and I was in London staying with Henrietta's parents. How go my brother and his wife?"

"Well . . ." Stewart began guardedly; but Emma was not deceived by the inflection in his voice.

"You seem uncertain."

"Well, they are in Whitehaven. After the wedding Brent and Mary left for the coast where Brent works for Ambrose Rigg. I reason they are well enough."

Emma decided that Stewart's lack of enthusiasm was due perhaps to shyness in discussing the relationship of a newly married couple. On the other hand the Allonby brothers had never really approved of Brent. Had they not insisted on a long courtship so that he could prove himself worthy?

Stewart had arrived at Delamain Castle earlier in the day on his way to Carlisle to join the Prince. Because of the nature of his mission Stewart had realized it was unwise to stop over at Delamain, but the presence of Emma was too much of a draw as he made his way toward the city where the Prince was expected any day.

Now he was glad he had come; something in Emma *had* changed toward him. And she was a beauty, grown more imperious perhaps, taller certainly and, yes, voluptuous, why not admit it? Stewart was no connoisseur of woman, but to him Emma Delamain outshone any of his acquaintance. But what chance had he got, an impoverished first cousin? A Catholic, a Royalist? Her brother would be looking for a finer match for his only sister than Stewart Allonby. The only chance was a Royalist victory . . . *then* let George see which way the wind blew.

It was nearly dusk and servants were running through the castle lighting candles and fixing lights in brackets on the walls. From the kitchen came the smell of roast meat and Stewart realized that he was hungry, having left Keswick at dawn. He had yet to meet George and his wife. The bailiff had greeted him on his arrival at the castle and given him a room in the wing reserved for guests. His first thought had been to stay with his aunt, but she was not prepared for him and he felt awkward intruding on her hospitality.

Now Emma had entered the drawing room just as he was standing admiring the view from the window of rolling dales and tree-covered hills. Why, as far as the eye could see the land belonged to the Delamains and George grew more prosperous and important every day.

"You have not met my sister-in-law, have you, Stewart?" Emma said as the drawing-room door opened and a woman of medium height stood looking at Stewart in some surprise.

"Henrietta, may I present our cousin Stewart Allonby? Stewart, Lady Delamain."

George's wife. Well, she was no beauty, as he'd heard; distinctly plain, Stewart thought, as she advanced slowly into the room and gave him her hand. She was plump, not comely but fat. Decidedly fat and because of the fashionable dress she was wearing, which allowed a fair amount of décollatage, her short neck and round stumpy head reminded him of a squat toadstool. In some ways she had a good face, large green eyes and a retroussé nose; but her mouth was small and pursed, as she looked at him now, into a tight little bow as though she did not altogether approve of what she saw. No smile lightened her features as he bowed to kiss her hand; instead he was aware of her bright eyes calculatedly appraising him.

"Stewart Allonby," she said at last. "Emma's mother's side of the family. She is dining with us tonight and will be joining us shortly. George, did you know to expect your cousin, dearest?"

George Delamain strode into the room and also paused in some astonishment at the sight of his cousin; an unwelcome sight, he thought. He reminded him of Tom and Brent and the fact that he had been unable to prise from any of them a modicum of information about the activities of the Pretender who was now threatening invasion of England. It had almost jeopardized his chances of a match with Henrietta when he had reported failure to his future father-in-law.

Luckily for him Henrietta had already made up her mind to be Lady Delamain, and what success George had as a government spy interested her not at all.

And the marriage had worked very well, so far. They were each protected by mutual self interest so that in time their needs were found to be converging. Henrietta had wanted a title, a husband and a landed estate, roughly in that order. She knew she was plain and unattractive to men; she would be wanted for what she could offer, apart from her looks, and thanks to her mother that was a large fortune.

As for George, she knew he had wanted an entrée into London society, a place in the political hierarchy and, being George, there could never be enough money to expand his estates. Lord Dacre was well placed at Court to bring this about and indeed he already had in part.

The village of Little Dacre was being given to George as a rotten borough and he was standing for Parliament at the next election. He and Henrietta had been received at Court, and had entertained already, in the short time since their marriage, personalities well known in the political and social life of London.

Henrietta looked fondly at her husband who, in her opinion, contrasted so well with his cousin who seemed to her to have the airs and manners of a country bumpkin. He had grabbed her hand and put it to his lips in a style that would be ridiculed in the salons of London—grasping the whole hand rather than the tips of the fingers. And then his clothes—heavy broadcloth, not particularly well cut, thick serviceable shoes and she doubted whether he had ever worn a periwig in his life. His thick fair hair was pulled roughly back from his forehead and secured at the nape of the neck by a ribbon. She thought he looked like some kind of menial, not an aristocrat, as she had heard, down on his luck.

"This is unexpected, cousin," George said, not trying to conceal his displeasure. "Did you send word of your intention to honor us with your company?"

"No, George. I was riding to Penrith when I realized I should not get there before nightfall, so I took the liberty of begging your hospitality."

"Penrith?" George said sharply. "Pray, have you business in Penrith?"

"Yes, cousin, I am buying saplings for reforestation of our woods."

"Ah." George looked instantly suspicious. Everyone knew of the impending invasion of England by the Prince. He himself was taking a leading part in the local militia and permitting them to train in his courtyard. "Your business has nothing to do with that ruffian Charles Edward Stuart?"

Stewart, who found it almost impossible to dissemble or conceal his true feelings, had expected this question from his cousin and knew that on this occasion it was essential to lie.

"How can that be, George? His Highness as far as I know abides in Scotland."

"His *Highness* indeed! Scoundrel is what he is, with a price of £30,000 on his head."

"And I believe he put the same price on the Hanoverian Elector," Stewart said mildly. "You know, George, we differ . . ."

"Aye and a mighty difference it is," George said threateningly. "You realize you could be hanged for joining the rebels? Like your uncle in the '15. I'll wager you are hell bent on the same path, Stewart Allonby."

"You should not discuss this," a tired voice said in the background. "When families foregather it should be in friendship not enmity."

Stewart turned to greet his aunt who, he thought, had aged in the past year. Her hair was now almost completely white and she walked with difficulty. He knew she was not old and her appearance distressed him.

"Aunt Susan," he went up to her and kissed first her hand and then her cheek.

"Do you bring news?"

She took a chair and gazed eagerly up at Stewart.

"News?" He was aghast, did she imagine they could

openly discuss the Prince in this house? She saw his bewilderment and nodded understandingly.

"Of Brent and Mary."

"Oh . . . No. I have not seen them since the wedding."

"But have you heard how they are? Sarah must write, someone must keep in touch. Certainly Brent does not write to me, his own mother."

"I imagine he has a lot on his mind," George said darkly. "I hear he is working hard for his wife's brother-in-law. A fishing hand! Imagine, Henrietta, did you think to marry into a family where your brother-in-law worked on the deck of a fishing smack!"

Henrietta tittered at her husband.

"Thank heaven you have your own pursuits, dearest, or I wager I would not be received at court."

Sir George and Lady Delamain giggled together, apparently unaware that those in the room were unamused by their derision of another member of the family.

Stewart however was relieved. This scorn of Brent seemed to indicate that George did not really know what Brent was up to. So far the secret had remained safe.

"I daresay Brent would not distress you, ma'am, if you met him," Stewart said stiffly. "You would not find him unworthy as a brother-in-law."

"Well, *that's* as may be," George said extending an arm. "Mother, shall we dine? Stewart, would you give your arm to my wife? Emma, would you follow us?"

The little procession walked formally to the dining room where, as always, George Delamain kept a good board and Stewart ate well and appreciatively. His mind, however, was not so much on his food as to be indifferent to the glances over the table of his young cousin. Could it be that the gypsy's spell had worked? No, it was absurd; but there she was glancing at him under her lashes and every time he looked directly at her the smile she gave him was, at the very least, provocative.

Stewart began to feel a painful constriction in his chest. Was it possible that the beautiful, worldly Emma Delamain, surrounded as she was by eager young men with fortunes and fine manners, could be tilting her bonnet, so to speak, at him?

Stewart had always been aware of the irony that he and his sister loved their Delamain cousins and that that love was not returned by them, until Brent had had a change of heart and declared for Mary. Stewart's thoughts grew sober. But *had* he made Mary happy? There had been nothing joyous about the couple after their wedding, and John had sworn that he'd heard tears from the room of the newly marrieds, not just once, but night after night until they left.

John had even gone so far as to draw Mary to one side and ask if she were happy, if aught was amiss? But, although seeming to him on the verge of tears, she had vigorously denied that she was anything but blissfully happy. Yet her pale face and lusterless air had not deceived John, or Stewart who more than likely knew the reason for it. He was glad to see them go. Brent was too valuable to the Cause for Stewart to want to have to carry out his threat.

George talked all the time at dinner about his role in the local militia of which he was commander and what they would do to the Jacobites should they so much as see the whites of their eyes. His wife listened to him with approval but the rest of his family were silent. Emma in particular had become contemptuous of George. She thought he took the attitude he did to curry favor with Lord Dacre and his cronies. She had seen too much of their activities in London to feel any admiration for them. To her, half Allonby that she was, there was something stirring about the stories told of Prince Charles. How he had landed with but seven old and ailing men and how, in a matter of weeks, he had captured the hearts of almost every man in Scotland—well, maybe not every man, but certainly every woman. Stories had traveled to London about the charm of the Prince, his handsome looks and kingly bearing so different from the bumptious, overweight Hanoverians. All the women were in love with him, so much so that some even turned the allegiances of their husbands and forced them to declare for the Prince. There were even reports of husbands and wives being split and supporting different sides.

Emma Delamain had returned north a dissatisfied girl, aware that there was more to life than pretty manners and dancing feet. The scorn heaped upon the Stuarts by her young friends and admirers had angered her. Had not Robert Allonby perished on the scaffold? Guy Delamain, her own father, had cared enough to live abroad as a wearied impoverished exile and die for the Cause. And there were her Allonby cousins, her own brothers Brent and Tom . . . all hardy, robust supporters of the Stuarts. Beside them her friends looked foppish, their ideas superficial and their hopes frankly mercenary and self-centered.

Henrietta Dacre, her sister-in-law, typified everything that Emma had grown to dislike about London society and the Hanoverian court. She was empty-headed, mean-minded and selfish. She and Emma shared not the slightest thing in common and here she was casting derogatory glances at Stewart, eyeing him with contempt.

Stewart had unexpectedly appeared to Emma, meeting him again after a year, in an entirely new light. She could see how angry he was as George and Henrietta between them dominated the talk with their hatred of the Stuarts, their scorn for the Cause; how the muscles of his jaw worked and his eyes smoldered. Suddenly Emma was afraid for Stewart. What was his purpose in Penrith?

She drew him aside afterward in the drawing-room as Henrietta prepared to play the piano for them and entertain them with some of her excruciating songs, boringly rendered in a monotonous voice. George sat beside his mother eyeing indulgently the talented little wife of whom he was growing so unexpectedly fond. True she was ugly and had apparently little to offer in the way of charm, but in the dark between the sheets she was just another woman's body

258

and a surprisingly accommodating one at that. Although George still kept a mistress in London he had begun to see less of her, and even to prefer the physical comforts provided by his own enterprising wife.

"Do you really go to buy wood?" Emma whispered to Stewart who sat next to her some distance away from her mother.

"Why, do you think I do not?"

Stewart was intrigued by his cousin's question. Could it be . . . He turned and looked at her and his heart missed a beat. Could it be that she *pretended* to be attracted by him, to have changed her mind so as to draw information from him? He remembered the visit of brother George a year ago. George and Emma had always been considered by the Allonbys to have much in common, certainly as far as Hanoverian sympathies were concerned.

On the other hand Emma had always been close to her mother. Would she really betray her mother's family? As though wanting to prise the truth from her he leaned his face closer to hers and his eyes met hers, daring her to flinch. Emma regarded him steadily, aware of his warm breath close to her face, the hard rugged masculinity of his sun-bronzed face.

"I am not of the mind of my brother George in case you thought it. *Or* my sister-in-law. A season in London would have changed me if I ever had been. They think of nothing but trivialities. Besides I hear the Prince is *so* handsome." She dimpled flirtatiously and then Stewart realized that he loved Emma Delamain, truly and deeply. It was not something that was just occasioned by her youth or beauty; it would not pass.

"Aye, that's what's won you, is it?"

Emma clasped her hands, her shining eyes reflecting the attitude of half if not more of the women in the kingdom.

"Oh, is he not *remarkable?* He is so young, about your age, Stewart, and yet he controls an army. He must succeed, must he not?"

"Aye, if I have aught to do wi' it."

"Then you are going to join him?"

"You knew it already?"

"I guessed it. I guessed you would not pass this way merely to purchase wood! I know you, Stewart Allonby. You know our brother Tom is part of the entourage of the Prince?"

"Yes, I have heard from Tom directly."

"That is why my mother is so worn, so pale. She thinks of Brent and Tom, and you and John. She expects you all to be killed."

"But why should *we* fail? Why not George?"

Emma looked over to where George sat lounging beside their mother, his legs stretched before him, one arm draped across the back of the sofa.

"There is something about George that is indestructible, don't you think?"

Stewart smiled. Looking at George, Emma's words seemed very apt.

"George maybe, but not what he stands for."

"Can I come with you?"

"To Carlisle?"

"To wherever you are going to meet the Prince."

"Of course not, dear girl! It is fraught with danger at this instant."

"But in Perth and Edinburgh he gave balls and soirees."

"Not in Carlisle or Lancaster. Here it will be business until he reaches London."

"Oh, is it possible, Stewart?"

"Of course, it's possible. It will happen."

Suddenly Henrietta's singing was interrupted by the arrival of a liveried servant who whispered into her ear. She got up closing the music with a flutter and hurried over to her husband.

"George! It is my cousin who has arrived unexpectedly. George, go quickly to welcome him; he awaits in the hall."

But before George had time to move the door was again thrown open hurriedly by a servant and a tall well-built man resplendent in his military uniform strode into the room, his hands extended.

"Henrietta!"

"Angus."

The small woman was scooped up by the stranger who embraced her and then turned to survey the room with a quizzing glass.

"George, dearest, may I present my cousin the Marquess of Falconer." George bowed and shook the proffered hand.

"Delighted, my lord. Lord Dacre was only telling me recently of your exploits in France with his Grace the Duke of Cumberland."

"And it is on the Duke's business that I am here, Sir George. I am part of an advance party to meet the rebels at the border, if they do not take us by surprise and get there before we are ready. His Grace will stop with Lord Lonsdale at Lowther Castle but I sought leave to find my quarters with you, dear cousin, if you so permit it." He bowed toward Henrietta.

"Oh, Angus, 'tis an honor. May I present my sister-in-law Emma and my husband's first cousin Stewart Allonby."

Lord Falconer strode across and kissed Emma's hand, pausing as he raised his head to stare boldly into her eyes. What she saw did not displease her. The Marquess was a man in the Allonby mold, tall and broad but, unlike them, very dark and swarthy with a long rather beaked nose, a firm broad mouth and a deeply cleft chin which jutted at a determined angle—a man used to commanding and being obeyed. He wore no periwig and his thick black hair was tied by a ribbon at the nape of his neck, some straying curls falling over his high forehead to give him an air of brooding authority.

His eyes were of a curious brown-green, like his cousin Henrietta's, but otherwise he did not resemble her at all, being so startlingly handsome, whereas she was small and very plain. He wore the red uniform of a colonel with gleaming epaulettes and a row of medals, and a long sword at his waist touched the top of his shining black boots.

261

She liked everything about him except that he was a member of the Duke of Cumberland's army.

"Ma'am," Lord Falconer rose and turned to Stewart, bowed and took his hand.

"Mr.?"

"Allonby," Stewart said clearly. "Allonby of Furness."

"Ah. I think I recall the name," the Marquess's eyes narrowed. " 'Tis well known, I believe, in *certain* circles, Mr. Allonby."

"Indeed, sir. I believe it is."

"But in this house you are obviously of the same opinion as your cousin."

"It is so, my lord," George said angrily, strolling over. "In this house my cousin is a gentleman, a farmer and noises no political opinions abroad at all."

"And has Mr. Allonby any *purpose* in being here?" his lordship said swinging his quizzing glass and looking appreciatively at Emma again.

"What purpose other than to see my cousin?"

"I hear the Pretender is not far from the border. Know you aught about this?"

"Nothing, my lord."

"Ah, 'tis well." The Marquess turned to Henrietta and smiled. "I know you would not harbor traitors under your roof, my dear. Is there aught for me to sup on?"

"Oh, Angus, of course."

"I have ridden hard all day. My men are downstairs being attended to, I believe, in the kitchen. Tomorrow I must ride on, and pray where do you go to, Mr. Allonby?"

"Penrith," Stewart said slowly. "I am buying wood saplings for my forests around Lake Derwentwater."

"Ah, I shall be in the opposite direction, I fear. I have completed my reconnoiter of the border and go back to His Grace who has been recalled from the south to take his position up here. I saw naught to alert me on the Scottish border yet, and Carlisle is very solidly for His Majesty. I have my home on the border," Lord Falconer explained to Emma who was

262

clearly bedazzled by this splendid creature in his gleaming uniform.

"Your dinner is ready, my lord," a servant bowed and the Marquess, with a wave, took his cousin's arm and left the room followed by George. For some moments Susan Delamain sat gazing after them until she was joined by Emma and Stewart.

"So that is the Marquess of Falconer. I have heard much about him. He is a very famous, very fierce soldier, known as the Falcon after his family's emblem which is the bird of prey. See, his beaked nose? They say he swoops on his enemies, and once he has his claws on them will not let them go. He is much feared, and hated by some. I think he will have no truck with our Prince and his army . . ."

"Not even the Falcon will rout them," Stewart said bitterly. "I too have heard how his lordship is called; but I believe there is more substance in the name than his deeds."

Susan Delamain shook her head and her hand plucked worriedly at the silk of her dress, "That is not what I hear. He has spent many years abroad fighting the French. 'Tis where he got his nickname, and earned it too by all accounts."

Emma shivered.

"He is certainly very awe-inspiring. Why, I think he is vaster than any of the men in our family and they are all good broad, hulking fellows. What a pity he favors the Hanoverians and not our side. I hear he is a disinterested politician; more keen on his soldierly duties but, yes, a convinced Hanoverian."

"Enough of the Falcon. I must be gone before dawn," Stewart said, "for I am to proceed as soon as I can to Carlisle. It is true, Aunt, Emma . . ." Stewart paused, and his voice dropped to a whisper, "that the Prince marches toward England and I go to join him."

*

Carlisle surrendered to Prince Charles Edward on 14 November after some days of siege. The inhabitants of the town had thought themselves surrounded by a large army instead of a few thousand men, and also they were in mortal terror of the Highlanders whose reputation for savagery had preceded them. But once inside, the Highlanders surprised everyone by the mildness of their manners and the Prince, as usual, charmed the masses with his fair-mindedness and sense of justice.

On arrival at Carlisle Stewart Allonby had noticed the siege at the Penrith Gate and watched it in the fog and damp along with the rest. But, on hearing that the Prince was at Brampton seven miles away awaiting an encounter with General Wade's army, he rode there and at once encountered his cousin Tom in the throng surrounding the Prince.

Tom looked gaunt and tired, there were deep shadows under his eyes and his cheeks were cavernous. He immediately asked for news of Brent.

"He is to join us here, as I understand it, as soon as he has made rendezvous with Lord Derwentwater who is bringing arms from France. The enemy is already entrenched in Whitehaven with big cannon pointing over the sea."

"Aye. I wonder if Brent would be better off where he is—the supplies are vital."

"I think Brent would not stay. He yearns to fight with the Prince."

"Then he will meet us when we have taken Carlisle. Let me take you to his Highness."

Stewart could see the crowd in the distance gathered around the Prince who was preparing to dine, but at that point a commotion began in front of the Prince's tent and it was announced that a deputation had arrived from Carlisle to treat with his Highness for surrender. Stewart's interview was postponed and the following day Charles Edward Stuart entered Carlisle and immediately set to making plans with his commanders for the occupation of England.

From the very first Stewart was aware of discord in the Prince's ranks. There were so many Highland companies swearing different allegiances that their rivalry seemed more important than the Cause. Many of the Highlanders had been reluctant to cross the border and had returned to their homes, and those who had forded the River Esk had turned as a man and pointed their swords toward their homeland when they reached the English side. But more important and damaging was the fact that the Prince was quarreling with the commander of half of his Army, Lord George Murray, who was reported to have offered his resignation which the Prince had accepted.

The Duke of Perth was now in sole command of the Army, but the restlessness continued down the ranks to the foot soldiers, many of whom still wanted to go home. Tom told how many commanders were putting pressure on the Prince to reinstate Lord George and eventually this was done, but permanent rancor remained between the Prince and his commander and sustained the unease among the men.

Thus instead of being elated Stewart was depressed and it was not until Brent arrived the following day that he began to take heart again.

For Brent this was the culmination of his life, the purpose for which he felt he had been born. He had ridden hard from Cockermouth where he had left Mary in the care of her sister and now here he was, the bustle and excitement of the Jacobite Army about him at last. As soon as he'd heard that the Prince had crossed the border he reminded Ambrose Rigg of their bargain and had put away his sailor's clothes. The very sight of Brent's rapturous face cheered Stewart and the two cousins embraced.

"Where is Tom?"

"He is with the Duke of Perth. The Prince I learn is not too happy to be attended by a Catholic clergyman; he has to maintain the image of religious indifference because of the possibility he may come to the throne."

"But the Prince *is* a Catholic!"

"Aye; but 'tis not *political* to mention religion until King James is established in London. How goes it with Mary, Brent, and Sarah?"

Stewart avoided looking at Brent as he asked him and turned to the window of his lodgings overlooking market street. Their host was a friend of the Allonbys and his house had been the place appointed for Stewart and Brent to meet.

"They do well enough, anxious for the Cause."

"And Mary is . . . happy?"

"I think so, why should she not be?"

Stewart did not reply, for at that moment the door burst open and Tom wrapped his arms round his younger brother.

"Oh, Brent, 'tis good to see you. I thought it would never happen. All the months we plotted and planned. How is the leg?"

"It troubles me hardly at all. I have had many months at sea and this has toughened my sinews."

"And your wife? A married man, Brent!"

"Aye."

Tom looked searchingly at Brent, aware of the way he avoided his eyes. He glanced at Stewart who, too, was looking away. All was not well there. The marriage had surprised Tom who knew the unstable romantic nature of his brother. Well, to all appearances, it had not altered him.

"Come, I will take you to the Prince. He is to have you as part of his very own company."

The Prince had just finished a council of war and looked preoccupied as Brent and Stewart were led into his presence.

"Your Royal Highness may I present my brother, Brent Delamain, and my cousin, Stewart Allonby—a family well known to your Royal Highness." The three men bowed and a smile appeared on the Prince's tired face.

"Indeed it is. The name Delamain is well known to us and you, sir, are well called after my own, Stewart."

"Your Royal Highness."

Stewart bowed low, too overcome to speak. There was indeed a magic about the Prince; to be in his presence was to be aware of something awesome and mysterious. The Prince, he noted, was tall and slim, his face round and brown from his exposure to all kinds of weather. He had a small but full mouth and lively eyes. Altogether he was very well proportioned and his appeal to the ladies was easy to discern. But he also inspired fierce loyalty in his men, and this was because of his regal manner combined with an easygoing informality that seemed to get the best out of them. The Prince lived as his men, did as they did and he was always cheerful and courteous and imbued with an optimistic and resolute air that it was impossible not to be carried away by.

"You are to serve in my company, as your brother may have told you, both as lieutenants. I am grateful to you, Mr. Delamain, for the service you have rendered providing arms for us. Your work is appreciated by us."

"My honor, your Royal Highness."

"Thank you, gentlemen, and God remain with us."

The Prince looked preoccupied again and, turning from them, was immediately surrounded by his commanders.

"They are discussing what to do next," Tom whispered as they left the audience chamber. "The enemy are approaching on all sides."

"God grant I get my sword at them," Stewart growled, his patriotism kindled anew by the encounter with his Prince. "Let us harry them ahead of us to London."

But although the Army began its march south almost at once there was no harrying to be done, no encounter with the enemy who were always to one side or the other, or ahead. The Duke of Cumberland himself blocked their path to London, and the Prince eventually halted at Derby.

There he had to take the hard and, to him, indefensible decision to retreat. There were three Hanoverian armies poised to attack his small numbers. There was no sign of the massive rising he had expected in England or of the French landing promised by his brother Henry. The Prince had done everything in his power to persuade his commanders to go on, but all had voted against him. They thought to continue would mean annihilation of the Jacobite Army and, with it, the Jacobite Cause. Better to retreat and try again. Yet only Charles, possibly, knew the full importance of what they had decided, as on 6 December 1745 the Army started to go back the way it had come so triumphantly and with such hope.

For Brent and Stewart it was a bitter moment when they were told, with their fellow officers, in advance of the men, that they were going backward rather than forward. Orders to move had been given at first light and it was not until they were some miles north of Derby that the rest of the army realized what had happened. The officers were hard put to explain to the men, so near to London, the reason for the retreat and the day was spent in recriminations and expressions of discontent.

But the worst thing was the way the whole complexion of the operation changed, even the character of the Prince. From being so cheerful and always in the vanguard he now sulked and kept behind. The mood of the population in the countryside through which they had marched victoriously only a few days before changed quickly to hostility, and the Highlanders who had held themselves hitherto in commendable restraint now set to pillaging, looting and despoiling everything in their path.

To the English officers like Brent and Stewart and others who had joined them—Manchester had provided a complete regiment—it was a horrible sight to see these men, half savages some of them, reverting to their former reputation. And the Prince, although he knew what was afoot, did nothing to try and stop them. Lord George Murray did all he could to keep the Army together but his fellow commander, the Duke of Perth, was now a sick man and the officers discontented and dispirited.

Stewart and Brent who had not once been engaged in battle or even a skirmish, who had not been part of the force that so triumphantly conquered Scotland, felt this disillusion as much if not more than most.

Having spent such a large part of their lives preparing for this event it was now unbearable to see it all founder without exchanging a single blow against the enemy. It was galling; it was humiliating.

"They say we will regroup in Scotland," Brent said one night as they tried to sleep, having been pursued out of Manchester by a hostile crowd. What was more they knew that General Oglethorpe's army, sent ahead by the Duke of Cumberland to harry them, was not far behind.

"Nay, we are done for," Stewart sighed. He felt ill and coughed frequently. The weather was terrible; it was cold and it never stopped raining. There was not enough to eat and, now that the local people had turned against them, nowhere warm to lay their heads at night.

"Will you leave the Army when we reach Carlisle?"

"No. I'll stay to the bitter end. But we are done for, Brent. The Stuarts are finished."

"Hush," Brent looked anxiously around though it was dark, "people will hear you. You will be split in half by a claymore as you sleep."

"They know. Everyone knows. The Prince knows. It was ill planned, this expedition. Five thousand men in all and they say in *each* of the Hanoverian armies awaiting us there were 30,000 men. In each. The country has not risen to the Stuarts."

"Aye, that is the reason," Tom said. "That is the real reason. People are too content as they are. They do not want change; they do not want the Stuarts and the Catholic church back again."

They had hardly seen Tom. He spent his time tending the sick or cheering the faint-hearted. But now as he sat with them, trying like them to keep warm against the bitter night, he nodded.

"That is the truth. The English people will not tolerate Catholicism. It is too foreign to them; it smacks of the French and the arbitrary rule of James I and Charles I. They hate the Pope and that is that. The Stuarts have become alien to them and we did not realize it. We were too distant and our spies did not rightly detect the mood of the people."

"What will you do, Tom?"

"Oh, stay to the bitter end, like you; but we are done for. I agree."

From Preston on 11 December Charles despatched the Duke of Perth to try and rally forces in Scotland. The Duke was mortally sick and had to travel by coach. Charles announced that he would stay in Preston and await reinforcements from Scotland; but the hooves of General Oglethorpe's soldiers could almost be heard outside the walls, and the dispirited Jacobite army took refuge in Lancaster.

Charles vainly tried to make a stand there to assure people he was merely retiring and not fleeing, but the Duke of Cumberland was said to have arrived in Wigan with 1000 cavalry. Charles set off for Kendal and then more trouble began as the men had difficulty negotiating the heavy ammunition carts on the steep hills in the terrible relentless weather. Charles and Lord George were at loggerheads again. The Prince had gone ahead and peremptorily ordered Lord George not to leave anything behind, not even a cannon-ball. His lordship, who brought up the rear, was said to be angered by this command, being aware of the temper of his men and the state of their health. Disease was rampant. In the end he gave his soldiers sixpence a head to carry the cannon-balls over Shap. It was at this point that Brent and Stewart were divided, Stewart going ahead to join the Prince in Penrith and Brent staying behind with Lord George Murray and the rearguard. And it was here that the first chance of action came, unexpectedly, at Clifton near Penrith.

All day Lord George Murray had been aware of enemy activity. They were in the neighborhood of Lowther Castle and knew that the Duke of Cumberland was expected there. Lord George sent to the Prince at Penrith to ask for assistance, but Charles sent word that he was proceeding to Carlisle and Lord George should follow him there.

Brent could see the distress on Lord George's face at the latest difference between the Prince and his commander. Lord George was a tall robust man, legendary for his bravery; but the weeks of marching, the indecision and unrest had wearied him. He was said to be aloof and haughty, to dislike receiving orders but now his face looked worn and his uniform was bespattered with mud like everyone else's. The rain came down in a seemingly endless stream and the news of the enemy's whereabouts was conflicting. Some said they were a cannonshot away on Clifton Moor drawn up in two lines, and others said they had dispersed and were heading toward Penrith after the Prince.

As night fell Brent, who had remained close by Lord George, taking his commands and issuing them down the line, was sure that they would not engage the enemy who could now clearly be seen on the moorside. Some dragoons dismounted and came down the hill ready for action, their swords drawn. Lord George conversed closely with Colonel Cluny Macpherson, then a signal was given to the men to align themselves in the shelter of a hedge. Brent lay shivering on the ground, listening to the exchange of gunfire, his clothes sodden, his eyes caked with mud. He gripped his sword in his hand and prayed to God, aware of the blood pounding in his head. The smell of battle was all around and he knew now for sure that for the first time he would engage the enemy.

Suddenly at a signal from Colonel Macpherson the Highlanders from his clan uttered their blood-curdling cry that was said by some to freeze the hearts of an enemy before battle commenced, to frighten them to death in advance. With one accord the force leapt over the hedge and fell on the dragoons who, taken completely by surprise despite their drawn swords, put up little resistance.

Brent could hardly see for the rain and the dusk that had fallen so quickly. The blade of his broadsword flashed about him and as he felt it encounter solid flesh he experienced a feeling not of pity for his victim, but of exultation that at last he was drawing blood for the Cause. Maybe after all the tide would turn; maybe . . .

Suddenly Brent felt a stab of pain in his arm and was aware that he had been hit. He put his hand in the spot and felt it warm with blood; but, though painful, the arm was still usable, and he continued advancing, plunging his good broadsword to the right and to the left, echoing the savage cries of the Highlanders.

The rain began to lessen and, in the intermittent moonlight which appeared through the clouds, Brent could see that the enemy, outnumbered and terrified by the ferocity of the Highlanders, were in flight.

Around them on the sloping moorside the dead and wounded lay, men of both sides, but many more dragoons than Jacobites. The stench of sweat and blood engendered even by the brief skirmish was overwhelming and the cries of the injured pitiful to hear. The broadswords did terrible damage, limbs and heads were hacked off and bodies disemboweled.

Yet in all the carnage, his own arm bleeding freely, his stained sword still in his hand, Brent felt a joyous, fierce elation. The fact that here were dead men who moments before had lived and breathed disturbed him not at all.

As the retreat sounded he saw the Highlanders creep over the scrub putting the injured enemy unceremoniously to the sword and moving their own wounded to the shelter of the hedge. Brent placed his sword on the ground and, bending down, tore the shirt from the still warm body of a dragoon and began to bind his wound with it. The blood would not staunch and the bandage was soaked. But Brent did not mind. He had been bloodied in battle; he had killed or maybe wounded fellow men. He was no more a talker, a plotter. He was a doer, a man of action. This was a war and he was a soldier, and war was about valor and courage and indifference to death.

Brent knew that life and his attitude to it could never be the same again. More than all the riding, fencing and athletics, all the womanizing, smuggling and heaving huge smelly barrels of fish in rough seas, the skirmish at Clifton had made him a man.

Chapter Fifteen

Analee opened her eyes and saw it was dawn. Usually birdsong awakened her, but this day it seemed as though the very birds themselves were too chilled to warble. Nelly still lay asleep pressed up against her for warmth, but even in her sleep her slender frame shook with cold. They had found a large overhanging hill beneath whose shelter they had bedded down for the night, making a screen with loose stones and branches to protect them from the wind and rain.

In all her years on the road Analee never remembered such biting cold, such pitiless weather. And the countryside was alive with other dangers; wandering soldiers who had deserted from the Jacobite ranks and who told of disease and defeat. But not only this; they also had to combat the hostility of the population who had so readily turned against them once the Prince's cause was lost.

Some were trying to make their way to Scotland, others to slink back to their Lakeland homes before the terror that was sure to follow the ultimate Jacobite defeat which they knew could not be long delayed. The men were hungry and savage. Rape as well as looting was on their minds as Analee well knew, as she and Nelly hid in a ditch or under the bare hedgerows as the angry, hungry soldiers passed by. One time she had reluctantly given her favors, and told Nelly to do the same, to two ferocious Highlanders in order to protect themselves from rape and, possibly— almost inevitably—murder to follow. Wicked dirks had gleamed in their belts. But after an hour of pleasure, voluntarily given in a barn, both men had fallen asleep satiated, and afforded Analee and Nelly the opportunity to escape. Nelly even expressed her own satisfaction with the encounter and seemed reluctant to take her leave of the lustful Highlander as he lay snoring, replete, on his back.

But Analee had no desire for any such alliance, nor did she wish to linger. Since the Prince had crossed the border and war had been on everyone's mind there was only one thought which drove her on; to reach the Buckland camp which lay directly in the Army's route, to see her baby safe.

For Morella was all Analee felt she had in the world now that she had lost Randal and given up Brent. For she could have had Brent; she knew it. It would have been so easy to have said "yes," and to have slipped out of the house with him and ridden away. But the sight of the two lovers embracing in the grounds at the grange had decided her. Brent and Mary did love each other and they should have a chance to enjoy that love. It was shocking for Analee, dreaming as much of Brent as she had after leaving the camp, to see that it was *he* who was the betrothed, the object of Mary's love. And then it seemed inevitable—of course he had told her he had cousins in Derwentwater; the sick man nursed to health; the family likeness which she had perceived only too late . . .

. . . Until she saw him wait for her in the corridor and knew from his eyes that his love, his true love was not for Mary. It was still for her. It always would be; the gypsy in Analee knew that. But Mary whom in such a short time she had come to love and admire, who had suffered for so many years . . . to deny Mary that happiness would be evil and Analee had made up her mind and acted accordingly.

Many times she had regretted it as they tramped

along the rough uneven paths to Carlisle or left the road altogether and climbed over the mountain ranges, either to shelter from the weather or the bands of marauding soldiers who passed by.

Her baby. Yes, she was going back to get her. She should never have left her; that one comfort to her life, that sole memento of her love for the aristocratic *gadjo*. And how beautiful he'd looked that day with the shimmering lake in the background, tall and bronzed, with his fair hair turned golden in the sun and his massive frame . . . and his arms encircling another woman! It had been too much as she'd looked down and seen the tenderness of their embrace, the smile on Brent's face as he'd gazed into Mary's eyes. Analee knew that smile too . . .

No, she must put the memory from her mind. It was not intended; it was not to be. Besides this was a country at war and Brent had meant to go to the war too. What would happen to him and the Allonbys now that their glorious Prince was so near defeat?

Nelly opened her eyes and saw that, as usual, Analee was gazing at some distant spot on the horizon. Analee daydreamed a lot these days; her mind was always far away. There was a sadness in her that distressed Nelly, who loved her and wanted to protect her from the harshness of the world. She had begged her not to leave the *gadjo* when she had found him again, to think of herself, to take the happiness owed to her. But no. All Analee could think of was the joy of the young girl, Mary, when she had seen Brent ride into the grounds; the tearful happiness of her brave young face turned trustingly upward to his.

"I cannot build my life on destruction," Analee had said turning from the window; and that had been that. Nothing that Nelly could say, no arguments she could put forward, could convince Analee otherwise.

In a way it made Nelly love and admire Analee more. Such nobility, such sacrifice had convinced Nelly that Analee was more than a mere gypsy; she was someone very special, a queen among women. And she had understood Analee's reason for abandoning her plans to go to the coast and wanting to get back to her baby. Analee should never have given the baby up at all, never been forced to. Nelly could not easily forget the sight of Analee and the expression on her face as the baby suckled so contentedly at her breast.

Now Analee was pinched and cold, her thin bones stuck out from her rags; but her beautiful lustrous eyes remained the same and her body was still round enough to attract the men as they roamed about looking for plunder. There was something about the way Analee held her head as she walked; something disdainful yet provocative, and no man failed to turn his head or quicken his step, however leaden it had been, as she passed by.

Analee smiled at Nelly clinging to her against the cold.

"Come, let us start walking and get the blood going again. Today we should reach the camp."

"We have been so long on the road and you keep saying that. How do you know this time for sure?"

"Because I know. There are more soldiers heading for the border and Carlisle is very near Scotland; besides, I recognize some of the landmarks."

They had come a long way; a long roundabout way, since leaving Keswick. They had kept away from the road and skirted Skiddaw and the Lonscale Crags, Saddleback and Bannerdale by bridle paths. They had sight of the River Calder at Tarn Crags and then followed it, saying goodbye to the Lakeland mountains which had provided them with some hard climbs, but also given them shelter in its warm caves protected from the icy blasts of midwinter.

The valley of the Calder was flat, though lush pastureland had afforded more food than the bleak high peaks over which they had come. But as she walked Analee would often glance back at those magical hills which grew smaller as, just before Carlisle, they reached the busy road which ran down to Penrith.

Analee got up and shook herself like a dog. It was hard to stand, as though her limbs had been petrified by the cold. Indeed one leg she could hardly feel at all and she shook it to make life return to it again. She still wondered that she and Nelly were alive, having slept out every night in this terrible winter except for the mountain caves and the barn they'd once shared with some soldiers. She wondered if they owed their lives to the fact that they had each other through the long cold nights?

Already there were one or two carts on the road, although it was not yet dawn, and groups of people mostly hurrying southwards. Analee and Nelly set off on their way north aware of the rumbling in their bellies and wondering when they would get something to eat. There were no berries at this time of the year, and cold and damp had long deprived them of wild animals. Sometimes a family eating by the roadside would give them a crust; but this morning everyone seemed in too much of a hurry, people with carts and sometimes horses, seemingly laden with all their possessions, appeared to have no time to stop and share bread.

Analee was puzzled. As the morning advanced the numbers seemed to increase, only they were all going in one direction and she and Nelly in another. Finally she stopped by a group who had paused to try and straighten a crooked wheel on a cart. The whole family clustered anxiously about the cart on which were piled bedding, eating utensils and even small pieces of furniture.

"Pray," Analee said to the woman who looked like the mother of the family, "could you tell me why there is all this activity on the road to Penrith?"

The woman looked nervously at her husband mending the wheel, bidding him to hasten, before replying to Analee.

"Have you not heard? The Jacobite army is abroad plundering and looting; it has already entered Carlisle and plans to lay waste to the city. We are some of the last allowed out of the gate. They entered after nightfall and terrible tales of pillage are told. The Prince has lost all interest or all control over his men, and a more savage band of murderers you never saw."

"Then Carlisle is not safe?"

"Nay, the gates are shut and bolted. You will not be allowed in. The Hanoverian army is chasing the rebels and people fear a long battle. We are bound for Keswick in the hope of escaping destruction. You had best turn back."

The wheel was given a final knock into place and the harassed-looking family set off at a brisk pace along the road. Nelly tugged at her skirt and looked wistfully after the departing family, but Analee shook her head, her heart already cold with fear.

"We cannot turn back. Did you hear them? Pillage and plunder. What will happen to the gypsies who are right in their path? Maybe we are already too late."

What was left of the Buckland camp still lay smoldering despite the rain. Everything was blackened and no single tent, cart or hut remained standing. The few who had survived the slaughter had fled in all directions and now only the bodies of the dead littered the field: men, women, children, animals and even horses.

It was such a terrible sight that Analee had frozen in her tracks on seeing it; even when she felt she could move she did not. Nelly walked around, braver than she, knowing that her family would have moved on long since, though God knew what had happened to them. Slowly Analee walked through the field to join Nelly, not wishing to see what she knew she must see.

First was Rebecca lying on her back, an old woman who had lived over a hundred years, now cruelly despatched with a dirk through her chest and another in her shoulder. Maybe she had started to run, but what chance had she against soldiers in their prime? But she had been lucky, perhaps her great age had saved her for, unlike the other women, she did not lie with her skirts drawn over her stomach, her naked legs stretched wide, the victims of rape before the final hideous slaughter.

The stench was awful and Analee's ears filled with the pounding of hooves, the screams of the women as they clutched their children and ran. This is what she had heard so long ago; it was what she had dreamt. She had known what the war would bring. There, some way from Rebecca, was Lancelot, or so it appeared. His eyes had been gouged out and one could only judge it was him because of his age. Analee shut her eyes but no tears came, just a choking in her throat, a pain in her chest that threatened to cut off her breathing.

And the children . . . the little ones, it was too awful, too pathetic and dreadful a sight. How could men . . . There were babies too, clutched tightly in their mothers' arms. But although she dreaded to find what she sought Analee knew, after an hour of searching—the most gruesome task she had ever undertaken in her life—that neither the baby nor Reyora were here. The *cohani* had kept her promise to look after Morella.

Analee's heart filled with gratitude as she looked at the sky. Morella was safe, for that at least thanks to God. It had stopped raining and a weak wintry sun struggled to penetrate the thick clouds. Suddenly Analee heard a groan, an awful sound in that dreadful silent waste. It came from the far corner of the field and she had already been past the bodies which lay in a stricken heap beside the main part of the camp. She hurried over and peered at the faces which stared, some with awful sightlessness, up at the merciless heaven. The groan came again and one of the bodies, slightly under the rest, moved. She bent over and, putting out a hand, clasped the shoulder, gently turning the face toward her. The eyes that looked at her were red and glazed with pain, the mouth a rictus of fear.

Randal.

Randal Buckland still lived. Analee's heart cried out with pity at the sight of the man who was still her husband reduced to such pitiful straits.

"Oh Randal, Randal . . . Can you hear me? It is I. Analee."

Randal seemed neither to hear nor see her; his eyes stared beyond her and then they closed and his head dropped, but he still breathed and started pathetically to try and crawl away from the mass of dead bodies piled near or on top of his.

"Nelly, help me!" Analee cried and, as Nelly ran over, she told her to take Randal's legs and detach them from the mangled limbs that surrounded him.

Nelly, her tearstained face shocked from the awful sight, gently took hold of Randal's legs and Analee flinched to see that one was nearly severed at the knee. In fact the blood had almost congealed; even with this massive wound he had lived through the night.

They stumbled over the field and carried Randal to the shadow of the hedge that ran by the side of the road.

"They might come back," Analee said fearfully, "God forbid, but let us try and remain out of sight."

Nelly looked about, pointing to a barn that still, surprisingly, had its roof on although most of the half-burnt timbers swayed in the wind. It was where the gypsies had stored their grain, and this too had been looted by the plunderers.

"Let us take him over there; it provides some shelter." Once again they made the slow journey across dead bodies and Randal, racked by pain, fell into merciful unconsciousness. His head lolled on his chest as they half-carried, half-dragged him across the field.

But it was better inside the barn. It was dry and sheltered from the strong wind and there was still some grain left to make a soft bed for Randal. Analee sent Nelly to the stream for water while she did what she could to make him comfortable and to see the extent of his wounds. She soon realized she could do nothing.

They were terrible; apart from his almost severed leg he had sword and dirk marks all over his body as though someone had been using it for target practice. His face though was unmarked and even, deathly pale, bloody and dirty as it was, Analee saw the remnants of the dark, handsome gypsy boy with whom she had so many times made passionate love.

She knew he could not survive. Even now his breathing was faint, but he opened his eyes as Nelly brought water and the feel of its cleansing coolness on his body seemed to restore him and recognition dawned.

"Analee."

"Randal. I have come back."

"Too late," Randal gasped sipping the water Nelly offered him to drink. "Too late."

"What happened?"

Randal shook his head, tried to speak but could not. His lips hung slack and his eyes began to roll in their sockets.

"The army? The Highlanders?"

Randal nodded.

"They swept through the camp like, like . . ." Words failed him and his head sagged on his chest. "At dusk, as we were eating . . ."

"Randal, what happened to Reyora . . . the *baby?*" Analee's voice faltered as she saw the jealous spark come into Randal's eyes even in this pitiful and desperate condition.

"I don't know . . . never saw . . . Reyora . . ."

He drank again and made another effort, drawing large painful breaths.

"Forgive . . . Analee. Always . . . loved you . . ."

Analee's eyes filled with tears as his cracked swollen mouth uttered words that were obviously deeply felt. She bent down to him and, her lips brushing his cheek, she whispered in his ear:

"Forgive me, too . . ."

"If we could start again . . ."

"We will. You will get better."

But Randal shook his head and his eyes half closed in another spasm of pain.

"Done for, Analee . . . done for."

Randal suddenly opened his eyes wide and stared at her and, for a moment, it looked to Analee as though he had a sudden resurgence of strength and might, incredibly, recover. But the eyes went on staring and it was then she realized he was dead. Tenderly she laid his head back on the floor and closed his eyelids, gently planting a kiss on each one. She gazed

281

at him for a long long time as tears rolled down her cheeks. Randal Buckland, her husband.

" 'Twas better thus," Nelly whispered. "He had the happiness of seeing you again, asking your forgiveness, and you kissed his eyelids in death. It would never really have done . . ."

Analee tried to choke back her sobs, but could not. They racked her body as she lay against Randal, mourning not so much a husband as a lover and the embodiment of a vigorous young gypsy male, cruelly struck down in the prime of life.

"Hist!"

Nelly sat up, her eyes wide with fear. Analee, even as her face lay on Randal's body, could hear the thunder of hooves and then voices, and then a clatter of swords being drawn. She stiffened herself and closed her eyes. This was the moment.

Let them kill her, too; she would die with her people. But let death be quick, let not . . . she thought of the skirts over the heads of the gypsy women and shuddered.

"What have we here?" a voice said briskly.

"Two gypsy women, sir, with the body of a man."

"Ah."

Analee looked up and saw an imperious dark face gazing down at her. Eyes used to such scenes glittered angrily and his full, rather cruel-looking mouth was set in a stern thin line. He was enormously tall and broad and beneath his cloak she saw a red coat and a chest full of medals. She dusted her hands on her skirt and, getting up, dropped a quick curtsey. This splendid man was clearly a general at the very least.

"Do not kill us, sir . . ."

"Kill!" The man thundered in a deep voice to match his forbidding stature. "*I* am not here to kill, my good woman! This was done by the barbarian Highlanders, not by soldiers of His Majesty King George such as we are. Luckily you were spared." He looked around, his face grimacing in disgust at the scene, the stench. "This man some relation?" He pointed with his stick impatiently at the mangled body of poor Randal.

"My husband, sir, Randal Buckland. This," she gestured with her arms, "this was once the camp of the proud Buckland family." She started to weep afresh. Desolation all around her, and death had never seemed so immediate, so close, so disgusting in its harshness. At her feet Nelly still crouched in an attitude of supplication.

"Get her to her feet," the officer touched her lightly with the point of a well-polished boot. "God knows what we shall do with them."

"They look starved to death sir." The soldier who was with him, clearly an inferior, bore an expression more compassionate than that of his superior.

"Are you hungry, woman?"

"Aye, sir. Famished."

"Then get them to our camp and fill them with victuals. After that put them on their way. We want no gypsy camp-followers!"

The officer spun round angrily and walked off to where the body of his men waited at the entrance to the camp. At a brisk command from him they began to disperse across the field, gathering the bodies into piles for burial.

Analee looked at Randal and in his dead face she could see no hope for her, no future. Where was her baby?

"You'll have to leave him," the young soldier said kindly. "The Colonel wants us to be clearing here and then on our way after the rebels."

"What will happen to . . . the bodies?"

"Oh, they will be decently buried. His lordship is a harsh man but just; he will send the chaplain to bury them properly. Now come on quick before he changes his mind about your dinner. The camp is only half a mile away. Can you manage?"

"I expect we can, for some food."

Analee pulled her cloak about her and dropped once more on her knees to gaze into Randal's face. She hadn't loved him and he had treated her badly; but for a time, a little while, they had shared something that was good and life-giving and her pity was

283

for a young healthy man killed before his time—a tribute to the host of murdered Bucklands. She took his cold hand in hers and put it to her lips.

"Come."

Nelly was gently tugging at her shoulder. Analee got up and, leaning heavily on Nelly, they walked after the soldier through the bodies that littered the ground.

At the gate Analee glanced around for the last time at the camp, once her home, and saw that the imposing commanding officer had stopped in his tracks and was gazing after her. When he saw her looking at him he turned sharply away and started to bark fierce, angry commands.

Analee shivered from something other than cold; was it apprehension, fear? There was a keen, penetrating look in the commander's eyes—a tawny green under thick black brows as she could not help observing when he'd looked down at her beside Randal's body. They were eyes that were compassionate yet chilling—compassionate, maybe, because she was a woman and chilling because he was a soldier and this was a war. But the look at the gate had another, more lingering meaning and she caught her breath.

"How is your commander called?"

The soldier drew himself up and puffed out his chest.

"That, woman, is the Marquess of Falconer, no less. Colonel of our regiment. You were honored that he so much as noticed you, let alone talked to you."

"He seems a very stern man. Powerful."

"Aye, he is. Very. Some say he has a gentle side to him but I have rarely seen it myself. I am his servant, McNeath. He is keen on strict discipline for his men and absolute obedience to his commands. As for the enemy . . . why, his name is enough to make them tremble with fear. He is called the Falcon not only after his family name, but because they say he swoops down like a falcon and once he gets his claws in a foe he will not let go.

"They gave him his name in France—'Le Faucon!'

284

they would cry and rush to be out of his way. I tell you I observed it with my own eyes.

"Now hurry so you can be off before his lordship returns. You heard what he said about followers and it would not do for you if he turned his ire toward you. You would see what was meant by the Falcon then."

His arm bandaged and in a sling, his coat sleeve hanging by his side, Brent rode slowly in the rear of the retreating army. They had reached Penrith after Clifton only to find that the Prince had gone and left orders for them to follow on to Carlisle. The army were weary after days of difficult hill marching and, despite the skirmish at Clifton, the inevitability of ultimate defeat. They all knew the Hanoverian forces had not properly deployed themselves at Clifton, perhaps not expecting a night-time attack, and thus they were vulnerable to the Highlanders' surprise assault. They knew that with the vast government army massing against them they were hopelessly outnumbered, and now they had lost the support of the people.

Setting off at first light Brent had thought longingly of Delamain Castle only a few miles away, but he knew that to so much as show himself to his brother was tantamount to surrender. He would be handed over to the authorities immediately. Brent didn't want to defect; the die was cast. He only longed for some rest, a real bed and good hot food, some balsam for his aching limbs. His brother officers riding with him did not talk or laugh among themselves as they had on the journey south. Some had only joined it at Manchester. It was a silent, apprehensive group, occasionally shouting a command to the weary foot soldiers to keep in line.

But the soldiers were angry and restless; their eyes looked haunted and bitter; they roamed around restlessly for the sight of plunder. Thus when they saw the small hunted group of people coming toward them they cheered. Such misery, such dejection would be

285

good sport. It never occurred to them to feel pity for people even worse off than they.

Brent saw the commotion first, heard the screams. A cart fell over on its side and the pathetic bundle of goods inside it tumbled out onto the path. The men started to kick these remnants of whatever worldly goods someone had possessed as though in sport and already one of the Highlanders had thrust a young woman into a ditch and was tearing at her skirts.

It still horrified Brent, this savagery of the Highlanders whom he knew basically to be good men with wives and families of their own. Despite their reputation they had done little to deserve it on the march south; now it was a very different story. This was why he traveled well to the rear of the force. Lord George Murray ahead would know nothing of this.

Brent drew his sword with his good arm and bore down on the marauding men scattering them.

"Pick it up. Pick it up!" he yelled, pointing to the cart. Meanwhile a member of the Manchester Regiment, Matthew Somerset, was hauling the lustful soldier off the shivering body of the nearly naked woman in the ditch. There were one or two women with children but the rest were old, old men and old women. They looked like gypsies. He turned to one younger woman who stared at him, sheltering a bundle in her arms. As he approached her she shrank back and clutched the tiny body more tightly to her.

"Where are all your young men?" Brent asked her.

"Dead, sir. Killed by the soldiers."

Brent closed his eyes in an involuntary spasm of nausea.

"What . . . what soldiers?"

The woman pointed around her.

"Dressed like these; the Scots. They came to our camp the evening before last just before dusk and pillaged, raped and plundered before setting the whole place alight. We only escaped because we were on the edge of the camp. We did not wait."

Brent leaned over to look at the bundle in her arms.

286

He drew back the ragged blanket which covered it and looked kindly at the woman.

"Don't be frightened. I'll not harm you."

"The baby is ill sir. I fear she will not last the day. She has the fever and it is no way to travel without warmth or food in this weather."

Brent found he was staring at a beautiful fair-skinned baby with golden hair, so unlike the dark gypsy who held it in her arms. The baby's eyes were shut, and her pale face shook with fever.

"You have not stolen this child, have you?" Brent said glancing suspiciously at the woman.

"Oh no, sir. Saved her. Her mother is fled and her father dead—killed by your soldiers."

"She doesn't look like a gypsy baby."

Reyora looked at the tall fair soldier with the kindly face who was staring down at the baby. The father would have been someone just like this *gadjo*. Reyora wondered where Analee was now; how had she fared?

"The mother was one of our gypsies, sir. The father . . ." Reyora gestured expressively, "I am not sure."

Brent felt the stirrings of some peculiar and unexpected emotion inside him as he looked at the baby. A tenderness for the poor little outcast in a harsh world; what chance did she have? Abandoned by father and mother.

"She is a very beautiful baby."

"Oh she is, my lord. And a lovely nature."

"Look," Brent said impulsively. "My home is not far distant. Have naught to do with my brother, Sir George Delamain, but my mother is a compassionate woman. Tell her you met me and I sent my love and asked her to give you shelter until the baby is well."

"Oh but, sir, I am with the remnant of my tribe . . ." Reyora glanced about her and saw how, standing in a pathetic group, their eyes appealed to her.

"My mother could not give hospitality to all even if she wanted to. But for the baby . . . ? Could you not join them when she is better? They cannot go far. The soldiers are all about the place and who knows that the government troops are any better than our own? You are directly in the line of pursuit."

Reyora's eyes grew speculative.

"Maybe they could camp somewhere in these parts, and I, for the baby's sake, will seek refuge. You are very kind, my lord," Reyora looked into his eyes, "kind to a poor gypsy woman and a baby. You will never regret this kindness. I, the gypsy woman, tell you it will only bring you happiness."

Brent looked at her and the tall lissom body, the lovely face of Analee suddenly danced in imagination before his eyes.

"I owe the gypsies a kindness," he said suddenly.

"Maybe you loved a gypsy once, sir?"

Reyora looked at him slyly, but a curious thought had come into her mind. This soldier was being unusually kind . . . she remembered the blond *gadjo* who had loved Analee. Could it be . . . could this possibly be Morella's father? Reyora shut her eyes and tried to conjure up her *cohani* powers of divination, but she was too tired and hungry, weary with shock and numb with exhaustion. This *gadjo* offered rest and it was all she wanted; warmth and rest for the baby. The *cohani* powers told her nothing and she opened her eyes to see the *gadjo* waving to his men.

"I am summoned. I must go. I am sorry for the behavior of our troops toward your people. Yes, I did once know a gypsy; but I cannot talk of that now, except to say that for her people I will do all I can. Listen, Delamain Castle is just a few leagues south of Penrith, and my mother, Mrs. Delamain, lives in the dower house there. Ask your way in the town. You can see it from the hill there in the distance, surrounded by trees. Your people can scatter in the forest and rest for a while if they wish, but take care you or they do not go near the castle for my brother Sir George Delamain would take a very harsh view of gypsies, and I believe he is active with the militia."

Reyora looked startled as Brent curled his lip and put her hand protectively about the baby's head. "Oh do not fear; my mother's house is well hidden from the castle and he never goes near her. She is a kind and compassionate woman and will help you if you say I sent you and also my love. Tell her it was her son, Brent, to whom you spoke. Speak only to her or my sister Emma and stay with her until the baby is well. God go with you."

Weary and sick as he was, Brent's voice broke and he looked longingly back the way he had come, toward the hill on which Penrith lay. Would he could go with them and find succor, too. His mother would not betray him. But it was not to be. Whatever his destiny was, he had to follow it and, however reluctantly, ride on.

Reyora dropped a deep curtsey.

"And with you, my lord, and bless you for your graciousness. See, the baby has opened her eyes and smiles at you."

And indeed Morella had opened her big blue eyes and gazed, without either of them being in the least aware of it, at her father. But even though he was ignorant of the fact, Brent's heart was filled with emotion as the beautiful baby girl looked at him and a little smile tugged at her lips. She gurgled and held up a hand and he took it and smiled into her eyes and stifled a desire to kiss her soft little cheeks.

"How is she called?"

"Her mother called her Morella, sir. It is the secret name given by a gypsy's mother, but I kept it as a talisman for her daughter."

"Morella," Brent said. "I will remember it. May only good things happen to you, kind woman."

Brent remounted and gazed at the strange gypsy woman and the lovely baby. Suddenly Reyora darted up to him and, taking his hand, kissed it.

"My lord, sir. You will suffer many things, but you will not die although you will come close to it. In the end you will find happiness, though there are dark days ahead. Remember it is the gypsy woman, Reyora the *cohani,* who told you these things."

Brent nodded at her gravely, his eyes unsmiling.

"I will remember it."

His companions had now separated gypsies and soldiers and sent the latter marching on their way. The sad gypsy remnant stood back from the road as he rode past them; they bowed to him and put up their hands in blessing. Ahead was his struggling, defeated army, but he turned in his saddle before he caught up with them and gazed back to where the gypsy woman Reyora stood a little apart from the others clasping the baby Morella. Brent Delamain stared at them for a long time. Then he put up a hand and waved farewell.

Chapter Sixteen

Even though such scenes as he had witnessed at the gypsy camp were not unfamiliar to him, Lord Falconer was still sufficiently affected by them to have his temper severely stretched. It was thus in something of a rage that he rode back to his camp and berated his men for their sluggishness and idleness, and bade them clean their muskets and shine their boots for they were hotly to pursue the rebels who were now holed up in Carlisle.

"Rabble!" his lordship muttered angrily as McNeath helped him off with his boots and asked if he were ready for his dinner. "Aye, though who could eat after that sight, and the stench . . ." The Marquess screwed up his aristocratic nose in a grimace of distaste. "Tell me did the gypsy women have aught to eat?"

"Yes, sir."

"And are they on their way?"

"No sir . . ."

"*What?*" His commander rose to his feet gazing threateningly at his servant. "Don't tell me the men . . ."

"Oh no, sir, I told them expressly not to touch the women, on your orders, sir. They are about to depart, but the older woman, Analee, would like to thank your lordship for your kindness."

The Marquess waved his hand in a gesture of dismissal and poured himself some wine.

"Oh no, send them off, send them off. I want no gypsy woman hanging about, nor gratitude."

But as he looked up Analee stood at the entrance to his tent and he grudgingly told her to enter.

"We shall not 'hang about,' my lord," Analee told him with quiet dignity. "I merely wished to thank your lordship for your humanity toward the gypsies and kindness in feeding us and offering us warmth. We are rested and ready to depart."

The Marquess of Falconer lowered his glass and looked thoughtfully at the gypsy girl. Now that she was cleaned up and rested he confirmed what he had already suspected on the field—she was uncommonly pretty. She was thin, even scraggy—God knew it had been a hard winter and she must have had little to eat —but as she'd walked off the field he had been struck by the proud tilt of her head, the graceful way she carried herself, the sway of her hips that was distinctly alluring.

"What will you do now, woman?" he inquired quietly, turning to refill his glass. "Where will you go?"

"Why, sir, we are nomads . . ."

"But the place is swarming with soldiers. What chance do you and the girl with you think you will have of escaping rape seven times a day even if you do not lose your lives? Have you not heard about the Highlanders? Have you not *seen* . . ."

Analee shuddered and covered her eyes.

"Ah, pray do not, sir. Pray do not remind me of that terrible scene. We will go westward, away from the army . . ."

She was aware that the Falcon was standing directly in front of her and she looked up to see him towering over her, his thin mouth pursed in a cruel sneer, his eyes gleaming.

"The army are *everywhere*. A force of ours has gone to Whitehaven to detach the big cannon there to subdue Carlisle; they're to the south, east, north and west. I doubt if you will live the week out. Still, no matter, I have done all I can." He made a gesture of dismissal.

"Thank you, sir."

Analee curtseyed and turned to Nelly who stood sobbing behind her.

"Come, Nelly . . ."

"Oh, Analee, what is to become of us?"

"Hush, girl," Analee said clasping her arm, "we have survived before. We shall again. Thank his lordship and come on. He is a very busy man."

As Nelly started to sob her thanks Lord Falconer lifted his head and gazed at the roof of the tent.

"I am prepared to help you find shelter. My home is not far distant, on the border, and if you go there you can find board and lodging in exchange for some services. You can clean, can you not, and . . ."

"Oh yes, sir," Nelly said, the flow of tears instantly ceasing. "And cook and help in the house . . ."

"Nelly!" Analee said quickly. "Thank you, my lord, but we will be safe. We are used to wandering . . ."

" 'Tis of no concern to me," his lordship said, turning to where his dinner was being put on the table. "You will not survive the week. Go and get killed. Ah, thank you, McNeath, and uncork some claret for me. I have an uncommon thirst after that hideous scene."

"But, Analee. *I* want . . ."

"You see," the Falcon observed to Analee with the trace of a smile, "your companion is not of the same mind as yourself. She would like shelter for some days. Is it not so? How are you called, woman?"

"Nelly, sir. Nelly Driver."

"Well, Nelly, you go by yourself and present my

compliments to my housekeeper. McNeath will set you on your way."

"I could take her on my horse, my lord," McNeath said quickly, "if your lordship will allow it. It will be safer and quicker."

"Aye," his lordship said eating his soup. "Well you may do that, McNeath, and you two women had better say goodbye to each other."

Quivering, Analee stood looking at the Colonel of the regiment. She was sure she had not misread the insolent light in his eyes as they had run over her body, the appreciative smirk on his face. "Some services" indeed, "cooking and cleaning" . . . a likely story! If Analee was not mistaken, or deceived about the nature of men, these services would include some of a more intimate nature. Well . . . Analee looked at the Colonel unconcernedly spooning his soup and then at Nelly trembling with fear. She felt too drained to care over much either about the desires of the one or the fears of the other and, yes, it would be nice to have a roof over their heads, regular food and shelter from the marauding bands of savage Highlanders. At least if she were going to be raped the Falcon would do it in style, whereas the Highlanders . . . she had seen too recently the results of their debauchery.

Nelly by this time was hanging on to Analee's shoulder sobbing, and Analee impulsively clasped her and patted her back.

"There . . ."

"Ah, Analee, *please* come . . ."

"All right, I will if his lordship allows it. I cannot lose my companion, can I?" She stood back from Nelly and smiled encouragingly. Lord Falconer, closely observing her behavior, thought to himself that she was indeed no ordinary gypsy. Here was a woman with style. His heart gave a little satisfied lurch. This was the only good thing that had happened all day. The beautiful gypsy was going to lodge under his roof and she would have every reason to be grateful to him.

"Take both the women on your horse to Falcon's Keep," the Marquess said with pretended indifference, "and enough of those female blatherings. And be quick back, McNeath, d'ye hear? Make sure my castle is well protected, but I think the Highlanders will avoid it on their way north. Be off now."

And the Marquess returned to his soup without another glance at the women who, after curtseying once more, were ushered out of the tent by a respectful and delighted McNeath. If he was not mistaken, the servant thought he had seen a singularly saucy look in the eyes of young Nelly as she had eagerly scoffed up her soup and meat, casting him grateful glances.

At Carlisle where his farm regrouped on 19 December, Prince Charles once again set about quarreling with his commanders. He was gracious enough to congratulate Lord George Murray on his victory at Clifton. This brief period of amity was disrupted however when the Prince announced that he would pull out of Carlisle but leave a garrison there for its defense. His Highness was anxious now to return to Scotland where Lord John Drummond, the brother of the Duke of Perth, awaited him with fresh forces brought from France. From here he would launch another and, he felt, more successful attack on England which would take him to London.

Lord George Murray, still deathly tired after his days in the saddle, tried to argue with his leader, but he was not supported by the other officers even though they privately agreed with him that Carlisle was not capable of being defended. Since the retreat from Derby the officers had grown wary of the Prince whose sudden violent and petty moods, whose long periods of silence and dejection, when he refused to talk to anybody, were so much at variance with his erstwhile good humor. No one liked to anger the Prince further at this stage by publicly disagreeing with him.

Accordingly, telling them that as soon as he had reformed his army he would return and relieve them, the Prince left a garrison of about 400 men and marched with the rest to the border which he crossed on 20 December, his twenty-fifth birthday. As he turned from the swirling waters of the Esk and looked back onto English soil little did he know he would never return to it again, at least at the head of any army.

Among those left behind to defend the town was Stewart Allonby. As many of the Highlanders as possible had been taken with the army because of their unpopularity with the townspeople, and most of the men who formed the garrison were English, either local men or men from the Manchester regiment. Many remained at their own wish, being reluctant to cross the border to Scotland.

Stewart was depressed about his chances of survival but determined to do his duty.

"I would dearly love to come with you, Brent, for I think we shall be massacred here."

"And I would like to stay," Brent replied, clasping his cousin's hand. "But it is not to be. Farewell, cousin, we shall soon return to relieve you."

"Will you?" Stewart said bitterly, sitting on an upturned box in the bare room of his billet. The townspeople had set themselves resolutely against the Jacobites and there were few comforts to be had. The kindly host who had formerly been only too glad to accommodate Stewart now barred him. "I doubt it. The Prince will not see England again. Can't you see now, Brent, he never had a chance? Why, everything about him is un-English, even his accent, which he cannot help because he was born and brought up abroad."

"Aye, but they say King George in London speaks with a German accent," Brent replied dryly.

"It is his manner, his dress. Always the plaid, the kilt . . . you can see how the English people would not take our army seriously, even though some of us are English and wear not the kilt. Very few."

"We must not give in, Stewart," Brent replied sternly. "We have committed our lot to the Prince."

"Aye, 'tis too late," Stewart said. "Too late."

The bugle sounded in the yard below and Brent saw the ranks of tired dispirited soldiers forming. The Prince and Lord George Murray were at opposite sides, the one looking proud yet and determined, the other bitter, but his haughty head raised higher than ever.

"They never got on, those two," Brent said, shaking his head. "You may contribute much of our defeat to that fact. 'Twas disastrous."

Stewart stood behind his cousin and clapped him on the back.

"You said not to talk of defeat, Brent. Now you do it. Go with them and fight, man, and we shall hold out until you return."

But the small outnumbered garrison had no hope of holding out, as everyone knew. The big cannon from Whitehaven were rolled up to Carlisle and the Duke of Cumberland himself directed the bombardment of the city. Beside the massed ranks of the enemy without the walls, the garrison knew that not only was the populace not on their side but the government forces outnumbered them by about five to one. When the guns did arrive they knew they had no chance and on 30 December the governor, Mr. Hamilton, hung out the white flag.

There was some pretense at bargaining for the lives of the garrison and the Duke of Cumberland concurred, only because he was anxious to go back to the south where he had been urgently sent for to command an anti-invasion force on the coast. But he agreed to the terms to save unnecessary expenditure of lives of his own soldiers and in the sure knowledge that his father the King would mete out justice "as they have no sort of claim to the King's mercy and I sincerely hope will meet with none."

The townspeople went wild with joy as the disciplined Hanoverian army reoccupied the town and the ragged remnant of the Jacobite army, some having gone without sleep for nights on end, were herded into the dungeons of Carlisle Castle—Stewart Allonby, bleeding from a wound in the head, among them.

Colonel Lord Falconer was well pleased with the swift capitulation of Carlisle, although to his mind ten days in taking the town had been ten days too long. It was not really until the 18-pounders arrived under his escort from Whitehaven that he knew the end was near.

The Marquess had campaigned hard all year and he was anxious for a rest. He had scarcely left the side of the Duke of Cumberland, a man with whom he had little in common though he admired his qualities as a commander and a soldier. Many times had he personally witnessed the King's younger son's bravery on the field of battle in the Continental wars.

Although the Duke was exactly the same age as his adversary Prince Charles he was very different to look at, being grossly overweight and having the Hanoverian proclivity for self-indulgence. However he was popular with the men who served under him and had given him the name "Bluff Bill" for his easygoing ways. The Falcon sought an audience with the Duke before he returned to London and asked if he might have leave to visit his estates. The Duke had just enjoyed an excellent meal of fish, five kinds of meat and several bottles of wine provided by the grateful citizenry, and was sitting with his jacket undone over his corpulent stomach picking his teeth when Lord Falconer stood before him with his request. The Duke eyed one of his best commanders indulgently.

"Why, I see no reason not to grant your request, my dear Marquess," the Duke said in his guttural German-accented voice. Though he had indeed been born in England, German was still widely spoken at the court. "But hurry south won't you, soon? For I shall need you to keep the French away from our shores. You know how they fear Le Faucon!" The Duke grinned.

"Surely they will not attempt this now, your Royal Highness?"

Cumberland shrugged his podgy shoulders and screwed up his small pig-like eyes.

"The brother of the Young Pretender, Henry, is active in France on behalf of his father. Let us hope now they will not consider such wastage of men worthwhile."

The Duke belched and summoned a servant.

"A glass of wine for his lordship!"

The servant hurried over and poured some claret into a crystal glass. The Duke raised his glass and bowed to his colonel.

"You will be well rewarded for your help to me in this campaign, Angus. After I have reported to the King my father, I hope he will consent to have you gazetted a lieutenant-general!"

The Falcon bowed very low. He was not a soldier for the honors it brought, but to have his qualities so well regarded was very rewarding. It had never occurred to him for a moment that the Hanoverians might be defeated or the Prince victorious. But now the thought did cross his mind that, had things gone a different way, he would be languishing in the dungeons below this very room where the Duke and himself, glasses raised, were drinking a toast to his Majesty King George II.

The Marquess of Falconer stretched his long legs before a roaring fire and reflected that it was good to be home. It had not taken long to send the Jacobites packing, but the weather had been wretched and his quarters uncomfortable. He was a soldier and used to any amount of hardship, but there was a lot to be said for a warm fire, a comfortable bed, and . . . He thoughtfully got up and pulled the bell rope by the fire.

The gypsy had served him at table, the tall good-looking gypsy, that is: he neither knew nor cared what happened to the smaller, plain one. And what a woman she was, this gypsy as, clad only in her simple skirt and bodice with nothing on her feet, she had plied silently between table and kitchen under the direction of the major-domo.

He had tried to engage her eyes, but to no avail. Her long lids were lowered over her eyes so that he could not see their expression. No matter. To look at her was good enough; he had no need to see her eyes or hear her speak. Her breasts thrust hard against her bodice which was but carelessly laced, and the sight of them swelling above her neat décolletage almost put him off his food. But not quite. Food was just as important as dallying with a woman, or nearly as so. For instance it gave one the strength to employ one's amorous powers to good effect. McNeath entered silently, bowing to his master.

"Your wish, my lord?"

"Fetch me some brandy, McNeath, and you can ask that gypsy girl to come here . . . you know, the tall one. The one who served me at table."

McNeath raised an eyebrow but said nothing. He understood quite well to which girl his master was referring. Knowing his master's inclinations, he himself had made sure she had waited at dinner. He had seen how his master had observed her when he'd first seen Analee, kneeling beside her dead husband.

"Yes, tell her to fetch me the brandy," Angus winked and settled in his chair feeling a stirring in his loins at the prospect before him. He leaned his head back and half closed his eyes, remembering her dark, almost savage beauty. He wondered where she came from. And then he heard a movement and, opening his eyes, saw her before him carrying a tray on which there was a decanter and a heavy crystal glass.

"Pour for me, will you? How are you called, did you say?"

"Analee, my lord."

"And have you settled down here, Analee?"

Analee didn't reply and his lordship turned to glance at her.

"Well?"

"I do not wish to stay here, sir. I am a gypsy girl, not happy in a house."

"Well, if you want to go into the cold with marauding bands about it is up to you." Lord Falconer turned and, with pretended indifference, settled in the chair.

"The Highlanders have returned to Scotland, sir."

"Only for a short time, they hope. Come here, girl."

Analee placed the tray on a nearby table and stood for some time looking at it without moving. She had lain with worse men than Lord Falconer, far worse; but there was something about his easygoing assurance that she objected to.

"You feel you have 'bought' me, my lord?" she said pointedly, remaining where she was.

"*Bought* you?" Lord Falconer wondered whether he could believe his aristocratic ears.

"With the warmth and food, the shelter from marauding soldiers." Analee dwelt heavily on the word "marauding" for the benefit of his lordship. "So unlike yourself, my lord. They will pillage and rape regardless, whereas you," she turned and stared at him derisively, "wish only to rape in the comfort of your own home."

His lordship jerked back his head. He was annoyed, indeed dumbfounded. Who did this creature imagine she was?

"I wish no such thing. Leave immediately if you so desire."

"Thank you, my lord. I will."

Analee was about to take the tray and leave the room when his lordship sprang from the chair and within two bounds stood before her.

"Here, wait. What did you say your name was?"

"*Analee,* my lord, as I have said."

"I thought it was maybe *Lady* Analee such is the haughty tone of your speech. How dare you talk to me like that?"

"I apologize, my lord, if I misunderstood your intention."

The Falcon felt himself flush, while the commotion in his loins engendered by his previously lewd thoughts grew more persistent. The girl, the gypsy brat was looking at him with the most tantalizing, provocative air, her black eyes blazing with scorn and her lips half parted. Curse her!

He gave a deep breath but, unable to maintain control, seized hold of her shoulders and crushed his mouth down on hers. At the same time he got a knee between her legs and pushed her against the broad sofa that stood alongside the window. She put out her arms to prevent herself from falling and thus lost all means of protecting herself so that his lordship was able, unresisted, to rip open her bodice with one hand and grope roughly under her skirts with the other. All the time, relentlessly, unyieldingly his mouth bore harshly down on hers thrusting her head backward.

His lordship raised her skirts well above her thighs and began to straddle her on the sofa, one hand moving to unfasten his breeches. Analee was aware of the enormous strength and power of the man, but although she was angry she was not frightened. There was something so deft, so expert about his lordship's actions, that she realized she was in the grip of a practiced seducer and marveled at the skill with which he had maneuvered her into this position.

With one hand he caressed her exposed breasts and the exquisite touch, the feel of her naked thighs between his, caused his lordship to release her mouth so that he could give vent to a gasp of satisfaction and desire. It was almost like a growl and, glancing up at him, Analee was reminded of some great untamed savage with his dark looks and thick black hair falling over his face.

Looking down at her, completely in his power, Angus saw a face not contorted with fear, but one in command of itself, angry, but not as angry as he would have expected, almost . . . could one *possibly* say, half amused?

The expression, totally unexpected in one about to be raped, stopped his lordship in his tracks and though he still straddled her, her breasts fell free as he put his hand on his hip, gazing at her with astonishment. Analee smiled.

"Must you *rape,* my lord, when you can take me to my pleasure as well as your own?"

The dignity, the charm with which she spoke, reminded Angus of a London courtesan of his acquaintance who had begun life as the daughter of a French nobleman, but who had taken to whoring when her family were faced with destitution.

She was still a gracious lady, but had completely

abandoned herself to carnal delights and her conversation was as witty as her style elegant. She was, it was said, making a fortune so much were her talents appreciated by those gentlemen who liked their love to be amusing and sophisticated, if ephemeral.

"*Your* pleasure?" his lordship said. "You mean you will not resist?"

"Does it please you more if I do?"

"Of course not."

The Marquess of Falconer began to feel rather foolish and backed away from the half recumbent form of Analee, hastily fastening his breeches and smoothing down her skirts as he did, not without a passing regret, so delightful had been the sight of her exposed flesh. It had whetted his appetite for more; but he put out a hand and helped her to her feet tantalized by the sight of her swaying bare breasts, the mocking curve of her mouth.

Still clasping her hand he pulled her gently over toward him. Her eyes were wide and, as she offered her half parted mouth to him, he could see in them a desire similar to his own. The thought excited him beyond reason and he crushed her body in his arms.

Slowly they sank to the floor and lay there on the thick Persian rug that his late father had bought in the east many years ago. The Marquess was delightfully aware that Analee's hand was exploring under his shirt, too, as he relieved her of her torn bodice completely, and drew one of her luscious breasts to his mouth. At the same time he eased Analee's skirt down over her hips so that he could see again what had so enchanted him before, a soft belly crowned with silky black hair and firm but ample thighs the color of ivory.

When she was completely naked he lay close to her, still kissing her, and allowed her to help him divest himself of his clothes until their naked bodies, still entwined by their kissing, lay against each other. He put a bare leg between hers and very gently intruded himself, delighted by the willingness with which she allowed him to by parting her legs wide and, with a sigh of satisfaction, settling her rump squarely and comfortably on the floor.

For a moment Analee saw this great man, torso covered with thick, black hair crouch over her then, with an exclamation of joy, he plunged himself deep inside her. She thrust out her legs to grasp him better, and reached eagerly for his head wanting to feel his mouth once again on hers.

He spent himself very quickly, such was the torment of her body, his overpowering desire for her, the length of time he had been without a woman. As he looked at her he could see she had enjoyed it too, just as the courtesan in London did, the excellent Marie-Claire. She expressed great satisfaction with lovemaking and always declared how much it pleasured her, unlike some of his mistresses who never ever admitted to anything other than that they were rendering him a supreme favor.

He opened his eyes and saw Analee's black ones looking into his.

"Better than rape, my lord?"

"Much," he gasped. "How did you learn this art?"

"I am a sorceress."

"I can believe you."

The place where his body had entered hers was sticky and shiny and her thighs were gleaming with sweat. It was hot from the fire and a film of moisture clung to the top of her lip. She was breathing fast and deeply, her beautiful breasts rising and falling. Angus got up and stood over her like a colossus astride a victim; the feeling of power that he had when he'd possessed a woman, especially one he scarcely knew, showing in his stance, the pride in his eyes. He went to the table and poured more brandy, then brought the glass over to where Analee lay still spreadeagled on the rug, and sat down beside her.

"Drink?"

"Thank you, my lord." She sat up and took the glass, sipping delicately from it. He saw that her body, though thin, was without blemish and her skin shone with health despite the vicissitudes she must have en-

303

dured. Her dark hair hung about her face as she drank and the long elegant curve of her breasts reached toward the fire, the nipples glowing darkly.

"You are a mystery," he said. "You have just lost a husband and yet . . ."

Analee shook her head.

"It is not as you think. He was my husband but I deserted him many months ago. That is why I was not in the Buckland camp. I had wandered from it and when the war began I decided to return."

"And Nelly?"

"A companion, a poor woman like myself."

"Why did you desert your husband?"

"It is too long a story now, my lord," Analee looked at him and he could see her eyes were sad. "One I might tell you some day."

"Some would despise you for what you did just now," Angus said harshly, "lying so easily with a man."

"Do *you* despise me?"

"I . . ." His lordship was again surprised by Analee. "No . . . but I am a man of the world. I have known many women; but you, Analee, you remind me of a very remarkable woman of my acquaintance in London whom some would call a whore; but . . ." Angus shook his head, "in some curious way she transcends whoring. I never think of her as a whore though I pay her well for her services."

"She likes love," Analee said simply. "I am like that. I understand it. I need men as much as any man needs a woman. That is why I wanted to turn rape to love, because I knew you needed me and would have me and I . . ." she looked solemnly at him, "I did not want to have to hate you. I cannot forget the dead gypsy women in the camp with their skirts above their buttocks."

"No," Angus took the glass from her and drained it. "I can see that. It was vile. Unfortunately I see it often in war. Violence excites men's passions. The same thing can be both horrible and beautiful."

Analee smiled and moved closer to the black giant.

"Your manservant told us that some said you could be gentle, but he scarcely ever saw it. I think those people who do are mostly women?"

"Aye," Angus laughed, conscious of her warm body pressed up against his. "I am a soldier used to war and giving commands. Certainly few of my men consider me gentle. I am glad you do, Analee. I am glad I did not take you by force." He leaned over to her and kissed her shoulder, aware that she turned toward him and nestled her cheek against his. "Can I take you to my bed and we can do this nice thing again in comfort?"

"I think it comfortable here by the fire, but I will do as you say, my lord."

She smiled at him with mock humility and slowly stood up so that her thighs were level with his eyes, and the glistening jewel he so much wanted to possess again was close to his lips.

Chapter Seventeen

Analee sat looking out at the snow which fell on the Cheviot Hills surrounding Falcon's Keep. The lair of the Falcon . . . She shivered. Although Lord Falconer's lovemaking was breathtaking, there was something menacing about him as well. She had no objection to the fact that he used her as an object, as a servant she expected nothing more, but his overpowering strength had at times frightened even her, a woman used to the ways of men.

He had also introduced her to a savagery that was new to her, a violence that sometimes went out of control and he would throw her to the floor and beat her. But afterwards he was so contrite, so eager to atone, that the lovemaking that followed these episodes was better than ever. It did much to make up for the bruises and swellings which Nelly had had to dress on various parts of her body when, exhausted, Analee crawled to her bed in the attic at dawn.

"He is a violent man," Analee had gasped wincing with pain as Nelly rubbed some ointment on the sore places, "he admits it. He is a soldier used to war and has never really known a gentle home life. His mother died when he was a boy and he went for the army as an ensign when he was eighteen."

"I see he tells you everything to gain your pity," Nelly had said sarcastically, noting the red bruise on the breast, the savage teeth marks on the buttock.

"But he can be so tender and loving . . ." Analee had sighed and turned painfully on to her back. "I think I am more than intrigued by Lord Falconer."

Her eyes sparkled and Nelly marveled that one so knocked about could still appear so enamored. Analee felt that here truly was a man; the cruelty in him appealed to some deep instinct in her that she had not known she possessed. In a way she resented it, that he could use her body so violently, cause her pain; but at times his stern administrations induced in her a sort of ecstasy that made her obtain pleasure on her own which drove him to renewed frenzy.

Analee seldom had the chance to sit down, and she crouched by her bed looking out of the narrow attic window. Due to his lordship's ministrations she had not slept at all until he had unceremoniously ejected her from his bed at dawn and she had crawled upstairs to try and snatch half an hour before the bustle of the castle began again.

Mrs. Ardoine, the housekeeper, had disliked Analee on sight and delighted in giving her the most menial of tasks; grate blacking, floor scrubbing, anything that involved hard dirty work. Even some of the tasks that were normally done by boys Mrs. Ardoine gave to Analee, and that morning she had cleaned and laid the fires in the grates of all the main rooms, staggering along by herself with great piles of logs.

Nelly spent almost all of her time at the sink, her arms in water to the elbows. In a great house such as Falcon's Keep there were many mouths to feed, and different hours for the many classes of people who lived there—the family, guests, then the servant hierarchy beginning with the housekeeper, the major domo, the head butler and so on right down to the meanest skivvy like Nelly and herself who were not even allowed to sit at a table but groveled on the floor for what they could get.

It was a mean, terrible existence and Analee looking out longed for the open spaces again where she was her own mistress, alone and free. And now that the master of the house had taken her to his bed? What could she expect but further humiliation, maybe even serious harm once his lordship had tired of her? Analee thought this was one of the darkest times of her life, her subjugation to the house and its master, the almost total tyranny that he and it exercised over her.

Her eyes searched the bare harsh mountains for a path that would lead her away from the house, out of sight of the narrow road that approached it. Maybe when the thaw came and there was no snow to betray her tracks?

"Analee! Analee!"

Nelly came rushing in nearly tripping herself up in her haste. "Oh, Analee, you are there! Mrs. Ardoine says she will whip the hide off you when she finds you. What ails you, Analee?"

Nelly knelt down looking anxiously into the eyes of her beloved friend. She knew what hour Analee had come to bed; how she had scarcely eased her aching body on to her pallet or closed her eyes when they were harshly awakened. Nelly was fearful for Analee now that the dreaded Falcon, the master of the house, had chosen her as his prey. Why, he was such a terrifying man he would surely treat her even more cruelly and once he had had his way cast her aside, maybe with child, uncaring as to what would become of her. Nelly had been unable to believe that Analee had spent all night with Lord Falconer until, recovering her humor, she had described to Nelly the vastness of the master's bed and how at times she thought she would lose herself in it, but his lordship always seemed to be able to find her again!

But there was no humor in Analee's eyes now, only tiredness and a kind of despair as she returned Nelly's gaze.

"I was so tired after doing the grates, I thought I would faint. I had to come here for some rest." Nelly tugged anxiously at her arm.

"Oh come down, I beg you, Analee. She knows you are missing and has gone to look for her birch."

"I will not be birched," Analee said standing up and straightening her skirts. "I will birch *her*."

Nelly clutched at Analee's arm dragging her toward the door.

"Oh Analee, pray do not vex Mrs. Ardoine. Say you are sorry and . . ."

"Nelly, I am going to *quit* this place!" Analee hissed before they were out of the door. "I cannot stand it. I am the most menial of servants, hated by Mrs. Ardoine, lusted after by the men and now ravished by his lordship. Although he is a vigorous lover and capable I know of giving a woman great pleasure, he has some ruthless ways. He will always think first of himself, and then he will toss me aside and go off to the wars. Nelly, I must go and find my baby! The thought of her whereabouts haunts me. Maybe she and Reyora were captured by the soldiers. I am going to cross the border into Scotland and find where they may be now."

"They will not have taken a woman and a baby. They . . ." Nelly avoided Analee's eyes.

"They did not kill them," Analee whispered, "they were not there . . ."

"No of course not. They fled. They must have gone south, back to Penrith . . ."

"Then I will go to Penrith."

Analee and Nelly were tumbling down the narrow dark staircase that led to the servants' quarters whispering as they went, but when they came to the large stone kitchen which was full of bustle, steam and smoke they fell silent. The awful Mrs. Ardoine was standing by the stairs, her arms akimbo, a thick bundle of fine twigs clasped in one hand which she beat against her ample hips. Although she was a large, comely woman who looked as though she might at one time have been a beauty, many years of hard work and disappointment, the loss of all her children in childbirth or infancy, had soured her and she wore a cruel expression on her thin twisted lips.

"Now do we have the servants skulking upstairs away from their duties!" Mrs. Ardoine roared so loudly that it penetrated the clamor of the kitchen and a few who scurried about stopped in their tracks to listen and observe. "Put up your skirts, girl, and bend over that chair." Mrs. Ardoine pointed authoritatively. "I will administer to thee such a sound thrashing that your buttocks will be raw like rumpsteak! And I care not who sees thee," she said gesturing toward the male servants who stood gawking hopefully.

Mrs. Ardoine seized Analee by the shoulder, her eyes glistening with malice, and threw her across the room. Analee fell heavily but, before the termagant had time to advance on her to administer further humiliation, she nimbly sprang up and faced her persecutor.

"You lay the canes on me and I will thrash you six times as bad even though you *kill* me for it!"

Mrs. Ardoine faltered in her steps, observing the way Analee's lips curled showing her fine white teeth bared in a snarl, so that she had the look of a fierce beast. That blaze in her eyes, the heaving of her breast convinced the housekeeper that the gypsy meant what she said; but it infuriated her the more and she raised her birch to bring it across Analee's face when her arm was arrested in mid-air and the birch roughly wrested from her hand.

McNeath stood towering over her, a foul curse on his lips.

"Damn you to hell, woman! Would you mark the face of someone who is enjoying his lordship's favors? A small price I'd give for your continued existence here if that were the case."

McNeath threw the birch on the floor and gestured to Analee who was still staring with some surprise at her savior, while Nelly gazed with adoring eyes at their liberator for she had no doubt that her turn would have come to bare her buttocks to Mrs. Ardoine's birch.

"His *lordship* . . ."

Mrs. Ardoine stepped back, her face white with terror.

"Exactly. His *lordship* has pleasured this young woman all night and wishes her to serve his breakfast. *Now* do you understand, you old faggot? A mark on her face and I dread to think of his lordship's wrath . . . Analee! Smart now to the pantry where one of the footmen is preparing a tray for his lordship who will take his breakfast in his bedroom. You are to follow the footman and serve him yourself. Do you understand?"

There was no misunderstanding McNeath's leer or the chagrin on the face of Mrs. Ardoine. Analee tossed her head, thrust out her bosom and pushed past the housekeeper, giving her a little nudge as she did so as if to say "so there."

McNeath was looking at Nelly, noting the becoming bloom to her face caused by the heat of the kitchen. She did not have the figure or the presence of her friend, but what she lacked in physical attributes maybe she would make up for in enthusiasm? Besides, her waif-like appearance appealed to him. He winked at her.

"Maybe I should follow my master's path, if you understand me?" Nelly pretended not to and raised an inquiring eyebrow.

"Forge a furrow for myself." McNeath looked at her meaningfully.

Nelly blushed and looked away, her heart beating furiously. Could this handsome, vigorous McNeath possibly desire *her?* He was almost as tall as his master but fair with a red face and sandy hair, fierce blue eyes and ginger whiskers that covered almost all the lower part of his face.

"I will see thee later," McNeath whispered to her. "Meanwhile keep out of the way of the dragon and I will see that my master is properly served his breakfast."

McNeath hurried after Analee and the footman who were already climbing the several staircases to his lordship's rooms. The footman carried a large tray and Analee a smaller one with a pot of coffee and the claret that his lordship sometimes took with his breakfast chops. McNeath ran up behind her and put a hand under her skirts and, from her position on the stair above him, she administered a vigorous sideways kick and hissed, "If thy master knew thy foul hands had laid hold of me he would cut thy throat!"

McNeath and his master had often shared a woman, but only in the harsh conditions of war when they were few and far between. Sometimes the whole garrison had had to make do with merely one or two poor wenches, but his lordship always had them first, when they were fresh and untainted by the other men. His lordship was very particular about cleanliness and had quaint ideas like that. However, McNeath did not think that this was one of the occasions when his lordship would be passing the wench on. Something both about Analee's manner and the enthusiasm with which the Falcon had called for her so soon after waking made him think his master was unusually struck.

The Falcon was sitting in a chair by the huge fire that roared up the chimney. He wore a scarlet silk morning gown tied round the waist with a black silk sash, the long loose sleeves rolled back at the wrists. His long bare legs were stretched out before him. He looked up as the procession entered and put down a volume he was reading, carefully marking the place before he did. It was nearly noon and the sun streamed into his room lighting up the rich carpet and the folds of the carelessly tossed back sheets. Analee glanced at the bed on which she and her master had tumbled so freely that night and then she looked over at him and caught his eye. His lordship was thinking exactly the same thing.

The footman placed the tray carefully on the table by his lordship's side and bade Analee place the coffee pot and bottle of wine by it. McNeath hovered about, stoked the fire and put on another log.

"Thank you, McNeath," the Falcon nodded and waved a hand. "The gentlemen may leave us. This woman here will serve me very well."

His lordship smiled and the men withdrew as Analee took the covers from the dishes, marveling at what one man was offered for breakfast. The smell assailed her nostrils and reminded her that she had had nothing but some dry bread and water, having declined stale ale.

"Well, wench?"

His lordship leaned back easily in his chair raising his arms above his head and stretching.

"Did you sleep well, my lord?"

"Eventually, yes. Thanks to you."

"Steak *and* chops, my lord?"

"Both," said his lordship, "and pour me some claret. You have given me a fine appetite, Analee. I like you very well."

Analee filled his lordship's plate and laid it before him, shaking the damask napkin and placing it on his lap. He trapped her hand and held it to the bulky part of him that was already hard and swelling beneath her palm.

"See. I am ready for you again, Analee."

"First you should eat, my lord." Analee swayed. The smell of the food was too enticing; it reminded her of the pain that always gnawed inside her belly.

His lordship threw down his napkin and stood up taking her by the shoulder.

"Why, girl what is it? Are you with child that you are nearly fainting?"

"No, *no,* my lord. You are the first man I have lain with for many a long day. I am tired, my lord, and . . ."

"And, Analee?"

The Falcon tipped her chin and looked into her eyes and she saw there, to her surprise, an expression of tenderness, almost concern.

"I am frightened, my lord. I was nearly thrashed."

"Thrashed!" the Falconer roared, "and by whom? In my house? Here sit down, girl, and tell me."

His lordship led her to a sofa and laid her along it so that her body was propped up by cushions. Then he sat beside her.

"I dare not tell you, my lord. I feel I must go from here."

"Tell me. I command it!"

Analee bit her lips but knew she must obey. Those knowing green eyes, that stern, scowling brow daunted her. Really he was the most fearsome man she had ever met in her life.

"Mrs. Ardoine, your housekeeper, sir. I was away from my duties and it vexed her. I was tired, sir. I have much to do in the house, the grates to clean and all the fires to lay, and the floors to scrub, and with your lordship's need of me last night . . ."

Analee leaned her head back and closed her eyes. This was really like heaven. But it would not last, lying back on silk cushions, the hands of a Marquess —no, not just a Marquess but *the* Falcon, the scourge of the Jacobites—protectively about her, his warm breath on her cheeks. She opened her eyes and saw that his face was very close to hers.

"You poor girl. We do not understand, do we? We lords and masters know not what goes on in our own houses. Are servants often whipped, I wonder? I suppose they are. I never thought. And was I cruel to you last night? Did my ardor make me too harsh? Believe me I did not mean it. 'Twas my passion got the better of me. I have thought of you a lot, Ana-

lee. I dreamt about you and your face haunted me
as soon as I woke so I sent for you. And you scrub
and clean and black grates . . . my poor little Analee." His lordship held up her hand and looked at it.

"Yes, I see your skin is harsh and red, and you
have such fine long fingers, Analee; they are those of
a lady not a servant. Tell me about yourself. 'Twas
something," his lordship gave a little cough and
smiled, " 'twas something we did not have the time
for last night."

His lordship slipped a hand beneath her bodice and
cupped it over her breast massaging her nipple with
his strong fingers so that, despite her weariness, Analee already felt a resurgence of desire.

"Nor will have now, my lord . . ."

"Ah, that is my Analee. See the blood is returning
to your face, and your heart . . . yes, I can feel it
beating strongly beneath my hand." His lordship's
large palm on her bare flesh excited Analee to no
ordinary degree. She gazed up at him and he bent
closer to her until his tongue flicked over her lips pris-
ing them gently apart and she caught it teasingly with
her teeth before allowing its passage into the deeper
caverns of her mouth. His lordship eased her skirts
over her hips, his desire knowing no bounds as he
saw once more the ample ivory thighs parting now for
him, the enticing richness of her dark body hair. He
undid the sash at his waist letting his morning gown
fall open and she marveled at the vigor and the size
of him, and how ready he was for her. He positioned
her buttocks comfortably on the sofa and, standing,
straddled the sofa and rode her as though he were
seated on his horse, charging into battle.

"Your breakfast will get cold, my lord."

"Then I shall warm it on you," the Falcon said,
bearing down on her and smothering further words
with his mouth.

"Your breakfast *is* stone cold, my lord."

The chops were congealed on the plate, the steak
curled a little at the edges. Even the fire had died in

the grate. His lordship was stretched face down on the sofa and Analee, having extricated herself from beneath him, prodded the cold food with a finger.

Then she went over to the washbasin that stood on the tallboy and pouring water into it set it on the floor and squatted over it, dowsing her hot flesh with the delicious cold water and working away inside with her fingers so as to eliminate as much as possible of his lordship's residue. She looked up to see that he had turned his face and was looking at her.

"What are you doing, you wench?"

"Cleaning myself, my lord. It is how to prevent a child. We gypsies know other ways but this is the easiest; to clean out the seed before it has time to sprout."

Lord Falconer rolled off the couch and onto the floor with laughter; he rolled and rolled about and the great guffaws echoed around the room.

"Oh, Analee, Analee. You are a jewel, my jewel. You are the most extraordinary, basic, lovable creature . . . Is *this* what women do?"

"My lord did not know it?" Analee said with some surprise, rising from her squatting position and rubbing herself vigorously with one of his lordship's towels.

"Well we men do not have to think of that kind of thing. 'Tis not our concern. I often wondered what women did. I declare, the ladies I usually make love to are either too grand or too ignorant to do it in front of me."

"You never saw a woman wash herself before?"

Analee looked at the Marquess in astonishment and then glanced at herself in the mirror by his bed. Her face and shoulders were still flushed, the nipples still erect on her breasts, her hair tousled.

"I would Mrs. Ardoine could see me now," she murmured.

"What is that? Come here, my witch."

The Falcon, still on the floor, rolled over toward her and caught her ankles, gazing up at her wonderingly.

"Witch, my lord? I am no witch."

"You have bewitched me."

She stared down at the enormous soldier lying on

the floor at her feet, his torso almost covered with fine, black hair, his face clean shaven but bearing a night's bristle on his chin. His dark hair fell over his brow and she decided it was his thick, black eyebrows almost concealing his eyelids, that gave him an expression of such severity. But again the tenderness in his eyes as he gazed at her took her by surprise. Or rather it was a compound of lust and tenderness because his eyes would look at the spot directly above his head where he had gained his most intimate knowledge of her, and then they would roam upward over her breasts until his eyes met hers.

"Come, Analee," he reached for a hand and drew her down. Naked they sat side by side and then he leaned over and put a log on the fire and they watched it catch and flare up. She shivered and he looked protectively at her and reached for his gown which he wrapped about her shoulders.

"My lord is most attentive. Are you not cold, sir?"

"No. I am warmed by your love, Analee. I am anxious for some dinner and we shall dine together. How's that?"

"*Dine*, sir? What will the servants think?"

"Curse what the servants think," his lordship snarled and leaping up dangled the bell beside the fireplace.

The dinner for Lord Falconer and Analee was served with some surprise but without comment by the footman who, several hours before, had brought up the breakfast which, untouched as it was, he now removed. Now, composed and dressed, Analee sat by the fire and his lordship, also washed, dressed and shaved, strode up and down the room, a glass of sherry in his hand.

Neither McNeath nor the footman betrayed by so much as a flicker of the eye that they thought there was anything untoward in his lordship dining with a servant who, only that morning had been blacking the grate and nearly had her backside scorched by Mrs. Ardoine into the bargain. To McNeath it was quite unique to see his lordship so enamored by a common passing wench as to do her the honor of dining with her in his bedroom! This distinction was usually re-served for fine ladies, sometimes the wives of fellow officers whose husbands were absent on maneuvers. Not only this, but the Falcon was doing her every honor, bowing to her as he assisted her to her place at table, and insisting that she was served before himself.

And what a feat it was to delight the palate of no-bleman and gypsy alike—partridge, roast venison, beef, lean succulent ham, quails' eggs, quinces, tarts and jellies. Dish after dish was laid before them in lavish profusion, and different wines were poured in crystal goblets by an under footman called in to help.

Here was Analee, dining with a lord and waited on deferentially by three servants to each of whom she smiled and nodded graciously as they served her, watched carefully by the Falcon.

At the end of dinner he signified that they should be left alone after McNeath had lit his pipe and placed a decanter of brandy by his side. Outside it was dark; the snow had started to fall again and a thin piercing wind howled round the great house.

Analee belched and gazed at his lordship, noting how seldom his eyes had left her face. The Falcon smiled.

"Analee, ladies do not break wind in public."

"I am no lady, my lord."

The Falcon leaned back and twirled his quizzing glass, thoughtfully drawing at the same time on his pipe. He wore a powdered periwig over his dark hair and whereas before he had looked awesome and dis-tinguished now he looked aloof and aristocratic as well. He wore a suit of dark blue silk, and a cravat made of snowy Bruges lace gleamed at his neck. On the little finger of his left hand was a huge ring of solid gold engraved with the family crest—a solitary falcon. But on the middle fingers he wore more elaborate rings of gleaming sapphires and rubies, emeralds and dia-monds.

"You were going to tell me about yourself, Analee,"

his lordship twiddled the gold signet ring on his finger, "how you come to have an air of such breeding and refinement yet call yourself a common gypsy. True, you make love like a whore, but it is to my taste."

"I enjoy it, sir."

"I can see that you do."

"As to my origins, I know not, my lord. I am dark skinned like my people. My mother's family came from beyond the seas, I think they call it Transylvania. My father . . ." She lowered her head. "I know naught about my father."

"Ah," his lordship leaned forward. "I wager he was no gypsy then. Maybe a little peccadillo on your mother's part, eh?"

"My mother died when I was born, sir. I know no more; naught about my father, little about her. But I am a true gypsy, Lord Falconer. I am not a lady."

"Maybe I will make you one," the Falcon said thoughtfully. "I can see you gracing my salons in London, Analee, clothed in fine silks and satins and bedecked with jewels. How now girl . . . why look away?"

Analee had turned her head sharply to one side, avoiding his gaze. When she looked at him again her eyes glinted.

"Do not mock me, my lord. I am a gypsy. A scullery maid in your home. Have your pleasure with me, do as you will; but do not jest. When your lordship is tired of me you will do what you have done with other women . . . maybe given them a sovereign and told them to be off. Besides, Lord Falconer, I am not made for finery, silks and satins. I am a wandering girl, a vagabond."

Analee looked up to see a shadow pass over the floor and his lordship, the great bulk of him, stood by her side.

"I do not mock you, Analee. Is it false to say that I am in love? Can it happen in so short a time? Is it possible?"

"With *me,* my lord?"

"With whom else? I have seen no other woman in

the last two days and with you I am besotted, Analee. You are no common gypsy, no whore. No ordinary woman at all. With you I have enjoyed love such as I have seldom known before and I believe it was the same with you too, was it not?"

Analee met the Falcon's gaze and nodded. Yes, it was the same with her, like no man before, not even Brent, not even her first love. Even now to look upon his lordship filled her with no ordinary emotion—not mere lust, not love, yet . . . Fascination was perhaps the word.

"I will make you my mistress, Analee, and take you to London when the war is over. You will be a woman of importance, live in a fine house. I will set you up proper and see you well married in the end. I do not mistreat those I have loved."

"Oh, my lord . . ."

The Falcon leaned over to her twisting the ring on his little finger. His lips brushed her cheek and she felt herself trembling. He drew her up and stood facing her, towering over her, tall as she was. Then he put a glass into her hand brimming over with white wine and took one from the table for himself. He raised his glass.

"To us."

The Falcon drank and Analee drank but to what she knew not. A house in London, satins and brocades. Was this what she wanted? She looked over to the window but the curtains were drawn. Outside in the thick snow the foxes would be prowling, the squirrels asleep in their burrows. Somewhere there would be gypsies sleeping in caves, in sheltered ditches. Somewhere there would be Reyora and her baby, her Morella. Analee turned and looked at the proud form of the Falcon as he gazed at her, his glass still raised. She shook her head.

"It cannot be, my lord. I cannot see myself in silks and satins, shoes even . . . the mistress of a nobleman."

"People will honor you, Analee. It will be no shame."

"It is not the shame. I cannot do it. I belong in the wild."

Lord Falconer fell to his knees and seized Analee's slender hand.

"Analee, I am making a passionate declaration of love! I *want* you. I will have you! You will be my mistress and I your humble slave. We will have such a time together, Analee . . . so much loving . . ."

He drew her hand to his lips and kissed it, then he put his arms round her waist and drew her to him kissing her tenderly on the mouth. She felt something slip into her hand and her fingers closed over the heavy solid gold ring he had worn on his little finger. She opened her palm and gazed at it. There it lay . . . big, much too big for her, gleaming dully, the outline of the Falcon, sturdy and proud, with the obdurate expression on its face that she also observed on her lord's.

She grasped the ring and stared up at him.

"You have only just met me, my lord."

"I have known you forever, Analee. I knew even when we met on the field 'twas no ordinary encounter. How you struck me, standing ragged and barefoot as you were among all that death and horror, afflicted and grief stricken and yet . . . proud and untouched and invincible. Ah, well I remember that day, Analee. It was destined that we should meet. You are mine and this gift I give you is the symbol of my troth.

"See, the color of the gold? 'Tis called Falcon Gold and the story of how this came about is a strange one. One of my ancestors, Sir Beyrick Falconer, was a companion of Sir Francis Drake, a sort of brigand who plundered the Spanish Main in the name of Queen Elizabeth. He was captured by the Spaniards and taken to South America where he contrived to escape and have all manner of adventures among the Indians, so much so that they gave him the name of the Falcon because he was so swift and savage.

"So great were his exploits that he was held in veneration by the Indians. Much of what he did is lost in legend, but he became very wealthy by the discovery of a rich vein of gold that was so fine, so pure, so light that they called it Falcon Gold after my ancestor.

"After that he sailed home, the holds of his ship full

of booty and plunder and of course of the rich gold he had found. Much of it he gave to the Queen who made him an Earl in her gratitude ('twas Beyrick's son who became a statesman, and the first Marquess of Falconer). But enough of the gold and booty was left to him by the gracious Queen so that he could extend the rough castle on the Scottish border, from which he and his ancestors had also plundered both Scots and English by turn when it suited them.

"It was called Falconer's Keep because 'twas but a fortified tower such as were built in olden days by the Marcher Barons from whom my family is descended. Beyrick, now an Earl and become respectable due to the trust placed in him by Her Majesty, tore down the fortress and began the gracious mansion we have here today, and he changed its name to Falcon's Keep because 'twas the gold from South America, the Falcon gold, that made his ennoblement, his good fortune possible.

"Much of the gold that was not retained to swell Queen Elizabeth's coffers was made into our family plate from which we dine on great occasions, and some was made into rings and ornaments. This ring that I wear has descended from father to eldest son since the original Falcon, my ancestor Beyrick.

"And in time my son shall wear it too; but now it is for you. The ring of the Falcon is the symbol of his patronage, that he will protect you and look after you. Your life will never be the same again."

Analee slipped the ring on her middle finger, but it was too large for her even though the Marquess had worn it on his little finger. Falcon gold. The word of the Falcon was law; his command was to obey.

"But it is too big for me, my lord."

"That I know." The Falcon held up a chain of fine gold filigree and, taking the ring off Analee's finger, threaded the chain through it. "This chain too is made of Falcon gold and belonged to my mother; see how it matches the ring? 'Tis almost white, the color unique. We have it on our crest, on our banners and everyone knows it as Falcon Gold. Now my love let us dally again, and I promise you rest in a fine bed and in a while some sleep to make up for your lack of it last night in the arms of your impatient wooer.

"Never again will you go to the servant's hall, Analee. From this moment you are my established mistress and the gold of the Falconers is your talisman. Wear it between your breasts because I shall think of them often when I am far from you in the war, and know that my talisman is safe and warm and a symbol of our love."

Analee fingered the ring then tucked it into the deep cleavage of her bosom so that all that was seen was the chain around her neck.

"And when you want it back, sir? For another?"

"I have never given it before. Methinks I never shall again."

Analee heard the cry of an owl, or thought she did. Beside her his lordship, having vigorously spent himself despite his promise of sleep, had at last succumbed, his legs still entwined in hers, his arm across her belly. He had surprised her by the degree of consideration he showed her. Gone was the savagery of the previous night and instead he enveloped her in a warmth and tenderness that made him not only the most ardent but in some mysterious way the most profound, the most meaningful of all her lovers. She gazed at him with regret. She was loath to tear herself away.

Analee stared into the dark and thought of the owl on the cold snowy branches of the tree and of the gypsies huddled on the hillside; the dead bodies of the Buckland gypsies under the ground. She belonged to the earth, to the soil. She wanted to feel the ground under her bare feet, the feel of grass in the spring.

She fingered the heavy gold ring that lay on her breast; it seemed to thud against her chest like a second heart. It was the symbol of his love, his desire, his possession. It was his yoke. She had to wear it always. Falcon gold.

But she did not belong to the Falcon, nor in fine salons, gracing the arm of a nobleman. Analee gently, regretfully freed her leg and his lordship murmured in his sleep, reaching for her, as though to keep her with him. In the dying embers of the fire she could see his face and the glow of his limbs, the strong chest, the long muscular legs. The periwig was cast aside now and the dark hair lay loosely on the pillow. He *was* like a falcon with his aquiline nose and proud forehead.

How well he suited her, as a lover and as a man. As her thigh had gripped his body pressing him to her she felt he belonged with her, in her. But it was not to be. She gently kissed the forehead of the Falcon and he murmured again; but he was deeply asleep. She got carefully out of the huge bed so as not to disturb him and covered his nakedness with the bedclothes, looking regretfully for the last time on that which lay inert now, but which in its strength had given her such intense pleasure.

She dressed quietly and quickly. Then she stood before the fire to warm herself and yet again fingered the gold ring round her neck. Reluctantly she unfastened the chain and put it with the ring on the table where they had supped. He would know what she meant when he awoke. She was his no longer.

Analee swiftly made her way upstairs to the attic she shared with Nelly. She paused at the door and opened it softly. To her consternation she heard loud masculine snores and saw that Nelly had a companion in the narrow bed with her, mostly obscuring her . . . the great bulk of McNeath.

But Nelly, used to the open life, where danger often lurked, was a light sleeper and as soon as Analee crept into the room she peered out from under the form of her comatose lover. She could hardly move her slender body such was the weight of his over hers, having fallen fast asleep after spending himself in love.

"Analee," Nelly whispered and Analee ran lightly to her side, "Are you all right?"

"Nelly? Will he wake?"

"No; he is drunk as well as fuddled with love. Hear how he snores. But I cannot move. He has wedged me. What is it, Analee?"

"Nelly, I am going from here."

"Has his lordship . . ."

"No, it is nothing his lordship has done. It is what he wants to do."

"Oh!" Nelly said with alarm.

"Nothing unpleasant," Analee smiled in the dark. "He is not a monster . . . on the contrary. I feel I perhaps could love him, and he wants me, Nelly. He wants to set me up and give me a fine home. But, Nelly, 'tis not what I want. I must find Morella. I must know if she is all right. Nelly, I must."

"But *surely* his lordship . . ."

"His lordship is thinking of romance, not babies! He would not help me find her. I must know what has happened to my baby, Nelly. You must see that! If he takes me to London as he says he will I shall never return again. Besides . . ."

McNeath gave a loud snore and embedded himself more deeply on top of poor Nelly who felt as if she were being slowly stifled to death.

"I am not meant to be a lady, Nell. It is not the life for me and while I am with him I cannot make his lordship see it. I am going now, Nell. Farewell . . ."

"Oh, Analee. Let me come with you."

"Not this time, Nelly. It is too cold, too dangerous. Whether or not we shall meet again I know not. But it is something I must do. Tell my lord . . . say it was not that I did not care . . ."

McNeath snorted again and appeared to be waking up. The enticing feeling of female flesh beneath his own seemed to him like a pleasing dream too good not to be taken advantage of. He was well wedged already between Nelly's thighs. Nelly felt divided between her own lustful longings and her love for Analee. But even if she wanted to move she could not.

"I think he is waking," she whispered timorously. "He is moving already against me."

"Then I will not be an onlooker." Despite her agitation Analee smiled in the dark, "and mind what I told you about washing well. His lordship will protect you. He is a good man; he knows about Mrs. Ardoine so do not let her touch you. Farewell, Nell."

Analee swiftly implanted a kiss on the cheek of her friend, and brushed it gently with her hand.

Then once more she put her few things together in the familiar bundle and, clasping her cloak firmly about her to ward off the cold, made her way to the stairs.

Chapter Eighteen

Nelly cowered before the Marquess of Falconer, her head hung abjectly on her chest. She had scarcely had time to recover from the delights of her night with McNeath when she was unceremoniously torn from her bed and rushed before his angry lordship. Fully dressed, striding up and down the Falcon fulminated with wrath.

"Just went out into the night in this weather!" his lordship howled looking out of the window where snow had turned to sleet and dashed against the window panes. "I believe it not! There was a reason. Tell it me!"

Nelly looked even more abject, were that possible, and gazed at her feet. Suddenly a hefty blow sent her spinning to the floor. She looked up and saw his lordship, his fist raised against her, about to strike her again. The sight of his glowering face, the brooding menace in his eyes struck fear into the girl and she knelt before him, her hands raised in prayer. She remembered the bruise on Analee's back.

"I beg your lordship . . ."

The Falcon's fist trembled and then he went to the tassle by the fireplace and pulled it so sharply it nearly came away from its fastening.

"I am not one to hit a woman in anger, God help me. But I know one who will. I will fetch Mrs. Ardoine to administer such a beating that you . . ."

The thought of Mrs. Ardoine's terrible birch struck fear into the trembling girl and she fell on her face.

"I beseech your lordship. I know nothing."

The footman summoned to the door was despatched to fetch the housekeeper and her birch while Nelly wept wildly protesting her innocence.

"I only want to know where she is gone, girl! I will not harm her."

The Falcon looked out of the window and thought of his misery on waking, of moving a hand across the bed to embrace his beloved, of finding it empty. And then of the evidence that she had left him . . . the gold ring with the head of the falcon beside the chain on the table where the remnants of their dinner still stood.

Why, why had Analee done this to him? His emotions were torn between anger and misery as the door opened and the housekeeper, clutching the evil looking bundle of thin sticks, came in and curtseyed before her master.

"Madam, I want you to administer a punishing to this young woman," his lordship snarled pointing to the groveling Nelly. "Whip her until she begs for mercy."

"With pleasure, my lord."

His lordship strolled to the window, his hands behind his back while, with a smile of anticipation on her face, Mrs. Ardoine flecked her cane and applied it sharply to Nelly's legs.

"That is a foretaste, my girl. Now get across that chair and pull up your skirts."

"Oh, ma'am, I beg . . ."

Mrs. Ardoine seized Nelly by the shoulder and pulled her to her feet. Then, administering another whipping to the legs, she caught at Nelly's skirts and pushed her across a chair raising them over her head to expose her naked backside.

Sobbing wildly Nelly covered her face with her hands, begging for mercy, her whole body taut, waiting for the sharp sting across her buttocks.

"Stop!" His lordship strode up to Nelly and abruptly pulled her skirts back over her legs. "I cannot see it done, not to a woman, not even to a sniveling lying wench like this."

Mrs. Ardoine stepped back, her face a picture of frustration. She liked nothing better than administering a good beating, seeing flesh wobble and bleed under her cane.

"Pray leave us," his lordship said sharply to his housekeeper. "Methinks you are too enamored of the birch, ma'am. One day someone will apply it to you."

She groveled at the menace in Lord Falconer's tone and backed out of the room while Nelly straightened her skirts with as much dignity as she could muster, and looked apprehensively about her. She was wiping her nose on the back of her hand when his lordship came up to her and surprised her by the expression on his face. Gone was the menace, the threat; instead it was replaced by a look of yearning and sorrow that drew pity from Nelly's heart.

"Nelly, will you not tell me where my Analee has gone? Only a few days did I know her, Nelly, and yet she has a place in my heart none has had before. What is it about Analee? Is she a witch?"

Nelly smiled and looked timorously up at his lordship.

"Nay, sir, she is no witch. But she does have a powerful effect on the hearts of men."

"Ah, I thought so," his lordship turned away and looked into the fire. "By her art alone I know I am by no means the first, but I thought I was an important one. How *could* she leave me, having captured my heart?"

Moved by the sight of the arrogant nobleman reduced to such misery Nelly was more prone to confide in him than if she had been beaten to pulp. The gypsy in Nelly was used to hardship; kindness was something else.

"I will tell you, your worship, for I see you are much moved. It is not that Analee does not love you, my lord. She asked me to say it was not that she did not care."

"She said that?" The Falcon looked up eagerly grasping at any hope.

"Yes, my lord, when she came to take leave of me. 'Tell him it is not that I did not care,' she said. My lord, there is something else that occupies Analee's heart, a great sorrow."

"Tell it me. What is it?"

Nelly sighed and wondered if she was doing the right thing. Analee had not told the Marquess, so why should she? Would it destroy his love forever?

"Analee has a child, your lordship. A small baby who was taken from her soon after it was born. She was looking for the baby when she found the Buckland camp so cruelly destroyed. The child was not there."

"Analee has a baby? But why did she not tell me?"

Nelly hung her head. "I know not, my lord. It was the child of her husband, Randal Buckland, and Analee never found favor with the Buckland tribe."

"Ah, I see it now."

"The baby was brought up by the *cohani*, Reyora, and Analee fled from the camp."

"So. It is clear to me now. Oh poor girl, if only she had confided in me."

"Analee was honored by the attention paid to her by your lordship. She felt that if . . ."

"I knew about the baby I would not love her. Foolish girl! I would have helped her to find it. I think Analee did not apprehend how much she has moved my heart, Nelly."

"No, your lordship."

"And I *will* find her. I will go after her, with your aid, and fetch her back here. Then I will help her find her baby. Now, my girl, there is no time to lose.

328

She cannot have gone far in this weather. Where would she go?"

"She thought the gypsies fled south, my lord, away from the fighting."

"True, they would—those who survived. Toward Penrith?"

"Aye, my lord."

"Can you ride a horse, Nelly?"

"Not well, my lord . . ."

"Then you can mount behind McNeath. We will go after Analee this instant. Fetch your cloak and be quick!"

His lordship strode to the fireplace and jerked the tassle again, this time so strongly that it did come away in his hands; but the effect produced a bevy of servants swarming about and quickly he gave orders.

The snow had begun to melt in the early dawn as Analee set out from Falcon's Keep, careful to stay in the shadow of the hedgerows. She knew by the way the light was breaking in the eastern sky which direction she should take and, despite the cold, she felt an exhilaration at being on the road again, even with the sleet beating in her face, the wet earth squelching under her bare feet.

But as she trudged her thoughts became a confusion of emotions. On the one hand she thought of the strapping body and warm lips of the Falcon, on the other the blond hair and blue eyes of her baby Morella. What would she do with Morella when she found her? What life was it for a wandering gypsy and her child?

The rapturous hours she and Lord Falconer had spent together were something Analee had never known before. The ease and comfort of a large feather bed, and the abundance of wine and good things to eat. For one who had always tossed on the ground or, at best, in a loft of hay, such comfort had enhanced the delights of lovemaking and introduced her to a dimension that was new and wholly pleasurable.

She thought making love in a bed made a lot of difference. Instead of the hard earth against your back you sank deliciously down beneath the weight of your lover. All sorts of contortions and variations were then possible that on the hard earth resulted only in bruised buttocks and a sore back.

It was an episode in her life. It was over. As the gray, wintry day grew brighter Analee sighed and, keeping the low mountain range of the Pennine chain to her left, moved steadily south through the valleys and byways of the border country toward Carlisle.

She encountered no wandering bands as she had before, no straggling soldiers. The armies had moved into Scotland where doubtless Lord Falconer would soon join them and forget all about her.

But Lord Falconer had not forgotten. All day he rode hard south with McNeath and another servant William behind him keeping a sharp eye for that figure that had come to mean so much to him. But the weather was against any hopes he had of success. A mist rose from the fells battling with the steady rain and hung about them all day. Soon the mountains became invisible and he was hard put to keep his bearings and those of his companions.

In the early afternoon he stopped and alighted from his panting horse. He bade McNeath dismount with William and wipe down the sweating beasts.

"Curse this mist. We have lost her. She is miles behind. We will return the way we came and look more closely, scouring every path."

"Would it not be better, my lord, to await her in Penrith?" McNeath ventured, stepping forward. "We know she will be bound thither, and it is a small town. It grows dark, my lord."

"Aye," the Falcon looked about him, "and I am hungry. You are right, McNeath. We shall lodge with my cousin Lady Delamain, and then set forth tomorrow for Penrith. William, you will go back to Falcon's Keep and report my whereabouts, for I am daily expecting a summons to rejoin the army."

"Aye, my lord."

William's stomach was rumbling, but an empty belly was part of the price one frequently had to pay in the employ of the Falcon who rarely thought of himself or others when engaged on service, and this was service of a kind.

"Off now, William, and if you should chance upon Analee apprehend her and fetch her straight to me. Understand?"

"Aye, my lord."

William mounted his tired horse and wearily turned his way back the twenty miles or so they had come, while the Falcon and his diminished party set their face once more southward.

Sir George Delamain was honored at the unexpected arrival of the Marquess of Falconer and sent his servants into a spin of preparations for a sumptuous dinner. Maidservants were despatched with warming pans to prepare his lordship's bed and Nelly and McNeath were sent to the servants' hall.

It was a sad and divided home that Angus Falconer found. Emma was grieving for Stewart Allonby, still confined in Carlisle Castle, and her brother George was too ashamed to mention his fate or that of Brent, bragging only about his own deeds.

"I was very active with the militia in routing the brigands, my lord. When your lordship assisted in the final relief of Carlisle I helped to send them packing across the border."

"And your brother?" his lordship said with a trace of sarcasm. "He is well?"

"Brent, my lord. I . . ."

"Your cousin likewise is clapped in Carlisle gaol, I hear, waiting to hang."

Sir George flushed and took a draft of wine while his wife cast him a glance of disdain.

"You know, cousin, that George has naught to do with the rebels. He distinguished himself on the side of His Majesty's militia. We cannot help it if our family is divided."

331

Henrietta looked witheringly at Emma who was gazing in front of her.

"My family, too, is divided, cousin," the Falcon replied gently, looking at Emma. "I have many members of it on the side of the Stuarts, including two ducal cousins! There are now two Dukes of Athol, a Hanoverian one and a Jacobite one!"

The Falcon laughed and smiled kindly at Emma as if guessing the secret of her heart. Emma had already visited Stewart in Carlisle Castle, seeking to encourage him and give him hope.

Now that he was rested and had eaten well Henrietta ventured to ask her cousin the reason for his journey.

"I would not ask it, cousin, for it is surely on His Majesty's business, were you not accompanied by a serving girl as well as your servant."

"Ah."

The Falcon's eyes sparkled and he twisted the stem of his wine glass winking into its ruby depths.

"I am bewitched by a gypsy. A beautiful woman whom I intend to make my mistress. She has already given me her favors, but I wish to establish her in style. I offered her everything, jewels, silks, the gold of the Falconers; but she has run away from me."

Emma looked up from her sad reverie at the mention of the word "gypsy." Drawn to her brother's wife by shared sorrow she knew full well the story of Brent's involvement with a gypsy enchantress. Was it possible that a witch was again abroad in Lakeland?

George Delamain sighed and avoided his guest's eyes. These noblemen and their indiscretions! He would never have boasted about pursuing a mistress; he had just very discreetly paid his last one off for fear Henrietta should become suspicious. Henrietta was beginning to show a pleasing fullness in the figure and he was expecting good news about an heir from her soon. Besides there was a sharpness to Henrietta that made him nervous of displeasing her. After all, the Dacre fortune was no small consideration.

"Really, Angus!" Henrietta said, not one to mince

her words, "a man of your eminence sporting with a gypsy!"

"No ordinary gypsy, my dear. I wager she has noble blood in her veins. She is a temptress, an enchantress."

Emma said nothing. Neither her brother nor sister-in-law knew about Brent and his gypsy love; but it was an odd coincidence nevertheless.

"And how will you find your gypsy, Angus?"

"By roving the country for her. I think she is coming south to Penrith, and tomorrow I will wait for her there . . ."

Suddenly there was a commotion at the door and McNeath burst in followed by William who had left them only hours before.

"My lord," McNeath bowed to Lady Delamain and approached his master, "William scarcely arrived back when a message came post haste from His Grace of Cumberland who would have you rejoin the army in Scotland. The barbarians are fighting back."

"Curses!" Lord Falconer jumped up, " 'twas a summons I expected but not so soon. Where is His Grace?"

He began to question the exhausted William while Henrietta gave directions to her own servants.

"I will leave at first light," Lord Falconer said, "my duty to my King comes first. McNeath will journey with me, but Nelly and William will continue the search. If you permit us to stay the night, cousin?"

"Of course. I would be offended if you left before you had passed a peaceful night. Your room is prepared."

"Then I will go straight to my bed."

The Falcon bowed and glanced at Emma.

"Good night, Miss Delamain. May you be luckier in your next choice of a sweetheart."

"There will be no next choice," Emma said thrusting out her chin defiantly. There was something odious about Lord Falconer; arrogant and imperious. She had been about to ask him discreet questions concerning his gypsy but now decided not to. Besides, it was no concern of hers. She was intrigued though to know the identity of this gypsy who had such a powerful attraction over men. She thought of the maidservant who had come with the Marquess, and slipped quietly down to the kitchen where Nelly, recovered from her ordeal, was ogling McNeath across the table where they were enjoying a good meal.

"I am looking for an escort to take me to my mother's house. Will you come with me?" she asked Nelly. "I have heard what a harrowing journey you had this day. Maybe this fine soldier will see you safe back here?"

Nelly jumped up and dropped a low curtsey. She had never seen a fine lady in the kitchen premises before, and this girl was both elegant and beautiful, but she wore an expression of sadness as though she had been bereaved.

"I am Emma Delamain," Emma said, smiling at Nelly. "In fact," she whispered, "there is something I would ask you."

Intrigued, Nelly pushed her plate away and, nodding to McNeath, went to get her cloak and then followed Emma through the long subterranean corridors of the castle into the cold night air.

"Tell me," Emma whispered, guiding her along the narrow path to the lodge, "what is the name of the gypsy so sought after by the Marquess of Falconer?"

Nelly stopped in the dark and McNeath, following close behind, nearly cannoned into her.

"Why, miss?"

"I assure you 'twill be a secret. Can you tell it me?"

"Could you not ask his lordship, miss?"

"There are reasons I cannot. Is she called Analee?"

There was no moon and Nelly felt confused and uncomfortable in the darkness, uncertain what to say. She saw they were approaching the house and the glow of candles flickered through the thin rain. The door opened and Emma's mother peered anxiously into the darkness.

"Emma, is it you?"

"Yes, Mama. Lord Falconer has arrived at the castle and his servants very kindly brought me home.

Please," Emma whispered urgently, *"tell* me her name."

Suddenly Nelly heard the sharp cry of a baby and Mrs. Delamain disappeared back inside the house. Emma ran forward followed by Nelly and McNeath, who thus found themselves all assembled together in the hallway.

"It is all right," Mrs. Delamain smiled. "She has the colic. We have a baby, you see," she looked at Nelly, "the most darling little child, do come and see her."

She put a hand to her lip and crept up the stairs followed by a very puzzled Nelly. To whom did the baby belong? Would Miss Delamain have a *baby?* It was quite a common occurrence for unmarried gypsy girls, but among the gentry . . .

Emma was behind her but McNeath, awkward in this company, stayed on the doorstep. Inside the nursery Nelly could see a nurse fussing over the crib.

"Come see our baby," Mrs. Delamain said, "she has transformed our bleak lives. A gift from God, the darling . . ."

Nelly leaned forward, a candle held high for her by Emma who was also smiling.

"Is she not perfect?" Emma said, "she was found quite by chance."

Nelly leaned over and looked into the face of Morella, little changed since she had last seen her. She was bigger and chubbier, but had the same flaxen hair, the same large blue eyes and cupid's bow mouth as the baby that Analee had given birth to that awful night three months before. Was it only three months? It seemed like a lifetime. Comforted, the baby had stopped crying and gazed earnestly up into the eyes of the girl who had helped to deliver her.

Nelly gazed for a long time at Morella, her mind in a whirl. She turned to look at the nurse expecting to see Reyora, but a stranger returned her gaze.

"She is lovely," Nelly said at last, nervously stepping back, "is she yours, miss?"

"Mine?" Emma laughed. "I am unwed! No she is not mine, would that she were! She was found by

chance, and ailing, among a crowd of gypsies fleeing from the war. My mother gave shelter to the woman who had saved her—her mother and father had been killed by the soldiers. Then this woman wanted to go and rejoin her tribe, but my mother begged to be allowed to keep the baby. Seeing that in these hard times she would be well looked after, the woman reluctantly agreed. Her name is Morella."

Nelly knew her name; she knew everything about her, her mother and her father. How such an extraordinary circumstance had come about that Morella was in the care of her lawful grandmother she could not guess. She could only attribute it to the will of God.

One thing she knew. She must find Analee and tell her her baby was safe. Only then would Analee have peace.

Nelly looked once more at Morella, noticing the fine lawn of her nightgown, the linen on her crib, the soft shawls and blankets. The room was richly furnished and a fire glowed in the grate. The nurse's only task was to look after her. Morella could not be better cared for. Nelly knew what she must do.

She gave Morella her finger to clutch for a moment, then murmured a silent blessing on her head and stepped back.

"I must get back to the castle, miss. McNeath will be waiting for me."

Emma followed her down and saw her to the porch. She held the candle high and looked earnestly into Nelly's face.

"I must know," she said, *"was* she called Analee?"

Nelly stared at Emma, her open country girl's face wide-eyed and innocent.

"Oh no, miss, nothing like that. I've never heard that name to tell you the honest truth."

Emma searched Nelly's face, but found there only honesty and simplicity. Surely such a girl would not lie? Would have no need to lie?

"Thank God," Emma said stepping back into the hall. "I thought for a moment it might have been a woman also loved by my brother. He cannot forget her either."

Guessing that her lover might try and find her, Analee avoided the roads and kept instead to the hillsides and valleys. She skirted Penrith, it was too full of memories for her; the wood high on the hill was where she had made love to Brent, where Morella was conceived. But once close by Penrith the hills of Lakeland appeared out of the mist in the west and she was drawn towards them as one seeking shelter from an angry and hostile world. Maybe Reyora, fleeing from the armies, would have found refuge in these hills? Almost instinctively Analee set out in the direction of Keswick, scarcely knowing why she did.

As the days passed the weather improved. Although the cold was biting, the rain had ceased and occasionally the sun shone. The nearer she got to the vale of Derwentwater the higher loomed the mountains on either side of the busy road on which plenty of traffic—carts, horses, sometimes a fine carriage and walkers like herself—plied between Penrith and Keswick.

Analee savored the peace and beauty of the scene around her. Here in the hedgerows, among the pine forests she had found brief happiness. Thinking as she did constantly of the lover she had left and the baby she had lost, the magnificent countryside was a balm to her tired soul. But although she saw many people on their way to market at Penrith, drovers with sheep or cattle, farmers with their produce, the odd peddler, she saw no gypsies. No one had seen a gypsy tribe; no one a gypsy woman and a fair-haired baby. Of everyone she saw and stopped, she asked the same question.

But the answer was always a smile and a regretful shake of the head.

The purple range of Blencathra and giant Skiddaw on her right, Helvellyn and the distant mountains surrounding Ullswater to her left, Analee finally saw in the distance the ribbon of blue that was Derwentwater enclosed by its hills. Just as she saw it the sun broke through the clouds lowering over the mountains, and the purple clad hills were ahead in the gentle light of early morning. Suddenly in her mind's eye Analee saw the house on the side of the lake, pink stoned and surrounded by water, almost hidden in the forest of pines.

Would they receive her? Welcome her? Did she dare? At least she would know what had happened to Brent, Morella's father.

Purple Skiddaw now loomed above her and the wide expanse of Derwentwater ahead of her glittered. The mountain tops covered with snow stretched like sentinels of uneven height guarding the entrance to a magic kingdom.

Analee took a path to the right before she reached the town nestling in the valley. At once she began to climb through a forest and when she emerged the hills towered about her, their purples, browns and greens a kaleidoscope of color while below her stretched a much longer, wider vista of the lake, cerulean in the sunlight. Her heart quickened as she rounded a hill and there, perched on a promontory, was Furness Grange, its pink stone and black beams reflected in the still waters of the lake. Analee began to descend until she reached the wood and then she saw the jetty where the boat landed and the small crofter's cottage that nestled against the mountain side, wood smoke spiraling upward through the trees.

Analee approached the lakeside and sat on a stone. She pulled up her torn skirts to her knees and rubbed her sore calloused feet. She was very weary. Five days had passed since she had left Falcon's Keep, and now it seemed that even her mind was numbed by the harsh winds that wrapped around her at night instead of the warm blankets she had become used to.

Used? Analee sat up and stared at the distant peaks. Had she become used to the easy life, even the attic at Falcon's Keep? A roof over her head and food, however humble, however roughly thrown at her, to eat?

But the master had offered her much more. He had offered her untold wealth and security, a place of honor and status by his side.

Analee shook her head. It was not for her. She let her feet soak in the clear water even though it was icy cold and stared at the pebbles sparkling beneath. Yes, her belly was empty; she was cold and almost permanently damp. Maybe the Allonbys would let her spend a night in their barn? After all, she had not harmed them.

She rose and, picking up her bundle, walked round to the kitchen entrance from which came the good smell of baking bread. Maybe Betty would be there and . . . Suddenly she stopped. A woman was staring at her from the window; a woman whose face she recognized, but whose expression was hostile, even frightened.

Mary Allonby had on her face a look of such bitterness that Analee stepped back and shielded her eyes from the morning sun to be sure she was not deceived.

"Hey!" a voice called out and Betty Hardcastle stood at the door of the kitchen, her arms on her hips. "We want no vagabonds . . . why?" She went up, her eyes screwed against the sun which had risen over Walla Crag, and stared at Analee. "Were you not a gypsy that was here?"

Analee nodded, half smiling, half afraid.

"Then get thee off quick. Thou art not welcome here."

"But why?"

Analee backed away, frightened and dejected. What had she done?

"Let her stay." Mary Allonby stood behind Betty, gazing at Analee. Then she brushed past Betty and went over to her, her face a mixture of emotions— pity and anger and curiosity. " 'Twas not her fault he preferred her to me."

"Me?" Analee faltered. Then gradually, intuitively, she understood what Mary was talking about.

"He is not here?"

"You had better come inside." Mary turned and Analee followed her through the kitchen into the hall, then into the room overlooking the lake she remembered so well. And there was Charles the Martyr on the wall and the heads of all the Allonby ancestors looking, it seemed, down at her.

"I see you are cold and wet," Mary said. "Sit by the fire and Betty will bring you some nourishment. But what are you doing, Analee? What has happened to you?"

"I left a baby when I came here, driven out by the Buckland gypsies. Then when the war started I knew I had done wrong. I wanted to know what had happened to her, where she was. I found the Buckland camp pillaged and half the tribe dead . . ."

"The baby . . ."

Analee shook her head. For once in her life she felt close to tears.

"No. I have sought her. I have not found her. Some escaped. I think they went further south, maybe to Lancaster. I only ask for a night's rest in the warm barn and I shall turn back the way I came . . ."

She stopped and looked at Mary, aware of the things that were unspoken between them.

"I am not welcome here, am I? Is it because . . ."

Mary's eyes filled with tears. "He does not love me, but you. He went mad when you disappeared, tried to follow you."

"But did you not wed?"

"Oh, we *wed*," Mary said bitterly. "My brother held a knife at his throat though I only discovered that afterward. It was the gentlemanly thing to do, anyway, Brent knew that. But he does not love me, Analee, he cannot. Although three months wed I am still a maid."

Mary bit her lip and looked anxiously at Analee.

"He has tried but he cannot. He was glad to go to the war, glad to get away from me."

"And that is where he is?"

"Aye, with the Prince. If not dead. He was

340

wounded at Clifton; but he avoided capture at Carlisle although my brother Stewart is now imprisoned in the gaol there, awaiting death."

Analee saw the tears stealing down Mary's face and her heart filled with compassion. She got up and gently put her arm around the weeping girl.

"May I, Mary? Do you forgive me? I liked you so much when I was here before; you were so good to me, so kind. I lay with Brent but once; 'twas a circumstance . . ." She faltered. Mary nodded.

"He told me. He said it was magical, the moonlight, the forest. He said you bewitched him."

Analee laughed derisively. "I am no witch."

The memory of Brent, or Randal, or her first faraway love, seemed so remote now. She thought of her latest love, the Falcon. Her heart lurched at the memory of his vigor, the strange power he exercised over her, the compelling, riveting look in his hooded eyes. Truly she was half afraid of him, half—dare she think it—in love? Yes, she did have a power over men; but it was not sorcery.

"When you and Brent meet again, Mary, I will be far away. I will go south back to where I came from, maybe find my own tribe."

"Can you not release Brent from your spell?"

"I have *no* spell, Mary."

"But Stewart said . . ."

"Oh, that was folly."

"But she *did* fall in love with him! Emma, our cousin, the one he loved. She said she suddenly seemed to see him with new eyes."

Analee was aware that she was cold despite the warmth of the fire. She shivered. The power of the *cohani* . . .

"Well," she shrugged, "maybe there *is* something we can try . . ." She stopped at the sound of a footstep and stern-faced John Allonby stood at the door.

"John, this is . . ." Mary stepped forward but John brushed her aside.

"I know who it is. Betty told me. Don't you think you have done enough harm, you *gypsy* . . ."

"John, do not speak to her like that! She is not to blame if she is beautiful . . ."

" 'Tis not beauty, 'tis sorcery. She should be burnt like others of her kind."

"John, how can you be so cruel? They have not burnt witches for many years in these parts. Analee is my friend."

"*And* with the rest of her tribe," John said contemptuously. "See, more are gathered outside."

Analee ran to the window, her eyes scarcely able to believe what they saw.

" 'Tis Nelly. Oh, Mary, 'tis *Nelly!* I thought I would never see her again."

Nelly sobbed as soon as she saw Analee, and it was a long time before she could explain why she had come. The stout William who had brought her on his horse eagerly quaffed from the tankard of ale he was offered.

"We were on our way back, having waited at Penrith and scoured the countryside, I asking after you constantly, when someone remembered seeing a gypsy of particular beauty," Nelly looked shyly at Analee, "on the way toward Keswick. I remembered the house here, and on the chance . . . Analee, you are to come back! His lordship is pining for you. He has had to return to the Army . . ."

Mary and John were looking with astonishment at Nelly and Analee, embarrassed and realizing they had no idea what Nelly was talking about, put a hand on her arm saying: "Shh, desist."

"His lordship?" John said abruptly. "Lord who?"

"Lord Falconer, sir," Nelly bobbed, "he is very smitten with Analee."

"The Falcon," John thundered, "the terror of the Jacobites. *You* and him?"

Analee met his eye boldly, nodding her head.

"His lordship found me when the gypsy camp had been overrun and despoiled by *your* soldiers, sir. The Jacobites for sure it was. He had me taken to his home as a servant and . . . he did me the honor of . . ."

Analee, seldom at a loss for words, couldn't for

once think quite how to put it. Mary felt her hatred for the gypsy woman evaporating. After all, she had suffered much, too. How tired and worn she looked.

"He fell in love with you obviously," Mary said with a sad smile, "as other men have. My brother Stewart half fell in love with you, too."

Mary looked at John and saw how, despite his initial hostility, even his face had grown softer after some time in Analee's company. John, whose heart had turned to stone on the death of his young wife.

"The Marquess of Falconer," John murmured disbelieving. "He swoops on his foe like a falcon, is feared and hated . . ."

"He is not as bad as he might appear," Analee said defensively. *"Once* you get to know him."

"He saved me from a flogging," Nelly said supportively, "mind you he ordered it in the first place, then he changed his mind. Oh, I can see how he could appeal to a woman."

Nelly was nevertheless thinking of the lusty McNeath whom she personally preferred. She sighed at the very thought of him away at the war.

"Then, Analee, will you go back since you are sent for?"

"I? No. I will find my baby and maybe take her to the south away from here, to my tribe. His lordship would have me set up in style as his mistress, but I am not that sort. I am a vagabond, and so I shall remain. As for Nelly, what she will do I know not; but if you will give us a day's rest in your barn we shall be on our way. Eh, Nelly? On the road again?"

Nelly had become extremely attached to McNeath in the short time she had known him and the thought of not seeing him again was almost more than she could bear to contemplate. She stared in alarm at Analee and then said quietly:

"First I have to discuss something with thee. Something very important."

"Analee, you and Nelly will have your old room overlooking the lake. Yes, I insist, and that you dine with us at table. You must tell us what you have seen of the war. I cannot believe the terrible things you speak of our soldiers. Now you and Nelly go upstairs and I will have Betty fetch hot water for the tub and some fresh clothes for you. No, I am adamant . . ."

Analee was overcome by such kindness on the part of someone she had so unwittingly wronged. Despite her protests, though, she and Nelly were taken firmly in hand and ushered up the broad staircase of Furness Grange.

That night Analee and Nelly snuggled down together in the large bed in the room overlooking the lake. The moonlight rippled along the water, as though moved by a mysterious current and Analee had spent a long time at the window looking at the broad sweep of Derwentwater, from Keswick nestling under massive Skiddaw in the east right to the jaws of Borrowdale in the west. It was a cold night and snow had started to fall again. Analee thought of the Falcon preparing, perhaps, to do battle against Brent, against the people the Allonbys supported and loved.

Analee sighed and Nelly put her arms around her hugging her, her hand stroking the smooth silky flesh of her back.

"Come, you will not make love to me!" Analee protested laughingly. Nelly blushed in the dark.

"Nay, it is not like that. I do not love you as a man; but I love you, Analee, you know that. I missed you so much. I feared I would never find you."

"Aye. I thought we had seen the last of each other."

"Analee, will you not return to his lordship? He . . ."

"No." Analee lay on her back, her head resting on her hands. "I am a gypsy. I will find Morella and go south. We . . ."

"Analee . . ."

Timidly, nervously Nelly put her hand on Analee's shoulder. She put a hand up to stroke her cheek, tilting Analee's face toward her.

"What is it, Nell?" Analee was aware of something troubling her friend.

"Analee, I have found the baby . . . Morella."

"What is it you say?" Analee sat upright in the bed. "You what? Oh Nell, she is . . ."

"No, no . . . she is alive, she is well. Analee, she was found by Brent on his way to Penrith, he not knowing who she was, sick and ailing with Reyora. Being a kindly man he sent her to his mother at Delamain Castle nearby. The mother took a fancy to the baby, not knowing it was her granddaughter, and has kept her. Is it not a miracle? Reyora had just left when we arrived."

"And you said . . ."

"I said nothing, Analee. His lordship, who had gone to the castle, had told everyone that he was seeking a beautiful gypsy girl—see how proud he is of you, Analee? He does not hide you at all—Emma Delamain was reminded of the story of Brent and the gypsy. She asked me if she were the same person. Thank God I did not reply until I had seen the baby and when I had, I said no."

"She knew my name?"

"Yes. She had it from Mary Allonby."

Analee leaned back against the pillow, her eyes full of tears.

"How is . . . Morella?"

"Oh, Analee, she is so beautiful, a big bonny baby. Her hair is golden and her eyes so round and blue, just like her father's I'll warrant."

"Yes, they were."

"She chuckles and laughs, she has that dimple on each cheek, do you remember, Analee?"

"I remember. I shall fetch her, Nelly, and . . ."

Nelly pressed Analee's shoulder trying to comfort her. "Analee, what I have to say is this. Is it right that you should take Morella? She was so ill on the road, nearly died of cold and hunger, and now she is so pampered and cosseted. She has her own room and a soft crib and fine linen; beautiful lawn nightdresses and her very own nursemaid. She smells of sweet oils and unguents and a fire glows in the grate to warm her."

"You're saying, Nelly . . ." Analee gripped Nelly's hand. "You're saying I should *leave* Morella?"

"Yes, Analee; she is with her family, her own grandmother. In time, especially if you went back to his lordship, you may have the means to claim Morella. But as a wandering gypsy . . . Is it right, Analee?"

"But I am her mother."

"What can you give her except hardship and maybe death? She will grow to be a fine lady, and you, too, Analee. As his lordship's favorite . . . in time, who knows? But I think now you must give up thoughts of claiming Morella, leave her where she is. You owe it to her, Analee."

Analee threw herself on Nelly, weeping copiously. Nelly stroked her long hair and her back, hugging her in her arms.

"Analee, you are a young woman. You will have other babies. With his lordship's protection . . ."

"I am *not* going back to his lordship!" Analee thumped the bed. "I am a gypsy, a vagabond. I want no jewels and silks."

"But you loved him, didn't you?" Nelly murmured softly. "Was your love not as instant as his own; just as urgent? Even that day on the field when you met?"

"Aye, his lordship has a powerful attraction. He is a fine strong handsome man. Whether 'tis love . . . No, Nelly. My mind is made up. Tomorrow, whatever you decide, I will go from hence and make my way south to where I came from."

"And Morella? Will you take her, too?"

Analee was silent, the tears still flowing quietly in the dark.

Chapter Nineteen

To the surprise of everyone—most people having considered them defeated—the Jacobite fortunes improved despite the persistent bickering that still dogged the commanders, and the many desertions as disillusioned Highlanders made their way to their homes. Reinforcements had arrived to swell the Jacobite army to about 8000 men and a new mood of confidence swept through the Prince's followers.

But the Hanoverians had regrouped too, and sent for reinforcements from the South. These began to foregather in large numbers in Scotland under General Handyside and General Hawley.

Lord Falconer, not yet gazetted lieutenant-general, was sent to join General Hawley's command and arrived in Edinburgh just as his troops were leaving to march to Linlithgow.

Hawley was a severe, unpopular man rumored to be a natural son of George II and thus half-brother to the Duke of Cumberland. However, he and Angus Falconer found much in common. They were both tough disciplinarians and the Marquess did not share the men's opinion that Hawley was a poor military strategist. Hawley was pleased to see Falconer and immediately drew him into his counsel with his second-in-command General Huske.

The objective was to relieve Sterling, which was being besieged by the Jacobites. An advance party, however, under Lord George Murray came upon the government army, and the Prince's soldiers were thus withdrawn from Sterling and drawn up around Bannockburn in anticipation of an attack being made.

But the attack never came. Hawley spent much time in council with his commanders and decided to wait for the Jacobites to expend themselves. He was convinced that the rebel army was a contemptible bunch of rascals, and could never withstand well trained and disciplined soldiers such as his own, the victors of Dettigen and Fontenoy. He did, however, warn his men about the Highlanders' barbarian tactics in order to prepare them and allay their fears.

As the Falcon—eyes hooded ready to pounce on the foe—waited at the head of his men for the Jacobite charge that they knew must come he was possessed by an unaccustomed feeling of unease. He didn't like the fact that the Jacobite army had formed a superior position on the barren moorland ahead of him known as the hill of Falkirk. Moreover, part of the government army had unexpectedly taken off under the impression that the Jacobites were moving south, and now that it had been reported as a false alarm, maneuvered by Lord John Drummond, Falconer realized how clever the Jacobite reasoning was. Half the government army was still absent, including its commander Hawley who was last seen dining well as a guest of Lady Kilmarnock at Callender House. Falconer had refused the invitation to accompany his commander. He knew Lady Kilmarnock supported her husband who was with the Prince's troops and suspected her motives in offering such lavish entertainment to a government commander.

It was cold and the Falcon shivered in the wind as the storm clouds gathered. Suddenly a bugle sounded and the Jacobite army was observed not a mile and a half away, moving up in the direction of Falkirk Muir.

There was still no sign of Hawley, and Falconer and his fellow commanders began making agitated signals to disperse their troops in order to confront the enemy. Suddenly Hawley, red faced, his jacket still undone, appeared at the gallop and ordered the dragoon regiments to march up the hill before the Highlanders got there; but as the command was given the clouds broke and rain lashed down in the face of the government army, almost obscuring their sight of the enemy.

Lord Falconer's foreboding increased as he ordered his men to draw their swords and advance slowly. Ahead he could see the government forces with their cannon struggling up the hill right in the face of the gale which the Jacobites had to their backs. The cannon stuck in the mud and Angus urged his men forward to assist the foot soldiers. An order came from Hawley, however, for Lord Falconer's dragoons to break into a trot and as the run toward the enemy began the Marquess forgot his foreboding and plunged into the thick of the fight, swirling his sword about his head regardless of the onslaught of enemy fire.

But the fire took others by surprise and two regiments of dragoons on their right flank wheeled about and fled the field. The Falcon shouted to his men and, spurring his horse, dived regardless into the line of Highlanders confronting him. Savagely he began trampling them underfoot, his sword flaying to right and left.

The storm gathered momentum and dusk began to fall but, impelled by a new savagery, even for him, Falconer penetrated the heart of the enemy line relishing the crunch of bones as the men fell under his horse's hooves. Even the wild cries of the Highlanders did not disturb him, and he was well into the enemy ranks when suddenly his horse trembled and fell, and a huge Scot, looming out of the gloom, struck Lord Falconer a blow with his broadsword that felled him. As his head crashed to the ground his lordship's last thoughts were that this was the end.

McNeath, perceiving what had happened to his master, rushed to him just as the large Highlander was about to administer a mortal blow, and practically severed the man's head from his shoulders. From under the Falcon's horse another Highlander crawled out and McNeath, in white fury at seeing his lord so badly

349

injured, despatched him to hell as well. By this time more of Falconer's officers had come to McNeath's assistance and, even though they thought their commander was dead, they removed him from the height of battle to the side of a nearby stream. Then they returned to the fray while McNeath tried to unloose his lordship's tight clothes and see whether he breathed or not.

His lordship breathed, but erratically. McNeath saw, to his consternation, that the Jacobite army was triumphant in the field and that many of the dragoons were fleeing in terror at the bloody frenzy of the Highlanders. Even now some of the Jacobite troops were stripping the bodies of the enemy dead for loot. McNeath thought that if he left his master as he was, he was as good as dead, so he heaved him onto his back and lumbered with him into the shelter of the neighboring forest. There he remained until nightfall when he was able to emerge, and seek fresh help.

Both sides claimed victory at Falkirk, but for Hawley it was a bitter blow and he was to wreak vengeance on his own men by the savagery of his actions to those who he thought had been guilty of cowardice.

The Marquess of Falconer meanwhile knew nothing of this. He remained unconscious and only came to the following day in the bed of a government sympathizer who lived nearby. He had a terrible pain in his head and difficulty in focusing his eyes, and he could hardly move his body. McNeath and his hostess hovered anxiously by and General Hawley, who had personally observed Falconer's bravery, sent word to inquire after him.

"Those beggardly Highlanders pierced the belly of your horse from under you, your lordship, as you passed overhead," McNeath muttered. "They did the same to a number of officers, most of whom are dead. Their dirks dug in the animal's belly. Many of them that did it were crushed beneath, but they cared not."

The Falcon nodded, scarcely able to reply. He looked toward the window and everything blurred. He thought he was done for. He was going to die as he had seen many men do; despatched from the world and forgotten. And who would remember him? His brother James would succeed to his title. His family would mourn for him for a while, but what had he really achieved? What had he to leave behind? No family of his own, no loving wife to mourn his passing, no children.

Suddenly Angus opened his eyes and saw very clearly the face of Analee looking at him, her deep black eyes tender and passionate. She came nearer to him and her lips parted to kiss him, revealing her splendid even white teeth.

"Analee . . ." he opened his mouth to return the kiss, but she was no longer there.

"Sir?"

"I saw Analee, McNeath, the gypsy woman. Is she here?"

"No sir."

"Ah. It was so clear. I am dying then. 'Twas like a vision of an angel. Farewell, Analee, my love."

Angus' head sank back on the pillow. He had seen her. She had come to visit him; but maybe, after all, to tell him he would recover. Her face had not looked sad. She was a witch, a sorceress. He felt better already. The pain was less severe and when he focused his eyes on the window he could clearly see the skeletal trees outside and the dark, stormy clouds hovering above. He closed his eyes and Analee came to him in a vision again, her body naked and her belly swollen with child. His child. He put his hands on the belly and kissed it and the child inside moved. Analee was going to have his child: he would have a child to leave to the world. He would be remembered.

His lordship opened his eyes and looked at the ceiling, his face puckered in a frown. Then he lost consciousness again.

As Analee and Nelly lay in bed at Furness Grange clasped together, half waking, half sleeping, talking through the night, the snow had continued to fall and

351

by the following day a white blanket feet thick cloaked the moors and fells of Lakeland.

Mary Delamain had refused to hear of Analee's departure but William, however, insisted on attempting to make the journey, fearing the wrath of the Falcon if he did not return. With trepidation they watched him set out, snow half way up his horse's legs. And still it fell. Considering the circumstances Mary was kindness itself to her guest. The two women resumed the friendship only briefly begun months past. Mary talked about Brent and the Stuart tragedy while Analee, without saying what she knew from Nelly, talked about the baby so cruelly taken from her, as though listening to her own words comforted her.

Nelly set to helping in the house and the kitchen, and the days they spent isolated from the world in that beautiful part of Lakeland were to remain in the minds of all for many a long day. The lake froze over so that even the boat could not reach them, and the hardy Herdwick sheep had to fend for themselves on the bleak snow-covered fells. But the cows could be milked and there were provisions in the larder sufficient to prevent the family and the guests from starving.

One morning Analee woke to see that the thaw had set in and, although still bitterly cold, only traces of the snow remained on the ground. The high peaks around them were still thickly covered and, outlined against the blue sky and tinged by the rosy morning sun, looked like some promised land upon which Analee knew she must turn back, perhaps forever. She shook Nelly awake.

"Nelly! The snow has almost gone. And I am going, too. These good people have been so kind, but it is time I left."

Nelly shivered in her comfortable bed. The thought of a life on the road again, scratching about for food and sleeping in ditches . . .

"Analee, *must* we go?"

"I am going, Nell. You could make your way back to Falcon's Keep or . . ."

"No. No. I will not be welcome there without you. His lordship will have me well and truly whipped! I will go with you, Analee, be with you where you are. We will find a way together. Besides you will need help with Morella . . ."

Analee stood very still in the act of fastening the laces of her bodice. She looked out of the window for a long time and then at Nelly.

"No. I will not fetch Morella. I have often talked about her with Mary these last few days and, although Mary does not know Morella is my baby, she has told me how well looked after the baby is, how much her aunt dotes on her, like a second daughter. It is all the comfort the poor woman has in the world after the tragedies of these past months. There Morella is loved and protected. What right have I to claim her?"

The tears began again to fall down Analee's cheeks and she quickly finished her toilet and, yet again, started to collect her few things together.

The Allonbys, early risers, were already at breakfast as Nelly and Analee descended the stairs. Mary looked at the bundle and the expression on Analee's face and jumped up.

"Oh, you are not going?"

"Yes, the snow has cleared. You have been so kind to us Mary, dear Mary, more kind than I can ever say or forget. You have helped me more than you know . . ."

Mary looked for a long time into the clear eyes of Analee, trying to fathom there the mystery of a woman who intrigued her more the more she knew about her. Was it not strange that Analee had lost a baby and Aunt Susan had found one? But the baby was fair, not dark, not a gypsy baby, not like Analee at all. Analee had seemed so persistent in talking about little Morella, in wanting to know everything about her. Maybe, Mary decided, to comfort her for the loss of her own.

"Are you sure, Analee? You are welcome here. Betty will miss Nelly in the kitchen, and I talking to you. We are like sisters."

"I think we shall meet again," Analee said gravely. "How or when I know not, but in my bones I feel it."

They both looked up sharply at the clatter of hooves descending the hill toward the house. There were two men and Nelly ran to the window.

"Oh, Analee, 'tis McNeath. McNeath with William. Oh, he must bring word . . ."

Nelly flew to the door followed by the others. In the courtyard McNeath had descended from his horse which stood snorting and steaming after a rough ride. McNeath's face was red and he was panting hard.

"Ah . . . Analee. William and I have ridden all night. 'Tis his lordship. He is dying and he would see you before he breathes his last. Pray go to him, I beg you!"

McNeath who loved his master almost fell on his knees, his face creased in supplication. Analee's hand flew to her heart and for a moment she thought she would swoon. The world seemed to turn upside down, so that the earth was over her head, the sky under her feet. She leaned against the doorway.

"Dying?"

"Aye, badly wounded in battle. We brought him home, but he has not rallied. His days are numbered. He asks for you all the time. William brought word of your whereabouts, but we have not dared tell the master you refused to return. Oh, Analee, you must come home, even to see him breathe his last."

Analee thought of the mighty, powerful Falcon lying on his deathbed. They had shared so much pleasure, such rapture. But more than that she could not forget him. His presence haunted her mind and his image seemed constantly to hover before her. Now she had no doubt what she must do.

"I will come," she said quietly and turned to Nelly whose face was alight with joy at seeing her beloved again.

"Nelly? You get up with McNeath. I'll go behind William." Analee paused and gazed solemnly at McNeath. "McNeath, this is not a trick to lure me back. You are sure?"

354

"Oh, Madam, would it were," the soldier said brokenly. "Even as we talk my master may be dead."

The room was very quiet, the curtains half drawn to keep the light out of his eyes. Only his heavy uneven breathing disturbed the silence. His face was ashen and covered with sweat, his great beaked nose and closed eyes already resembled a mask of death.

Analee stood by his side and gazed at him. They had ridden all day and she still wore her cloak, her face grimy with dust. They had not even paused to eat, negotiating the narrow tracks with an ease born of desperation. Lord Falconer was considered to have very little time to live. The servants already crept about as in a house of death.

Analee placed a cool hand on his brow. She closed her eyes and willed him to live; that the life force should pass through her own vibrant living body into his. She pressed her hand on his forehead and murmured the only gypsy blessing she knew. If ever she had *cohani* powers she used them now, summoned every force in her being to invoke the spirits of her Romany ancestors.

But the Falcon did not stir. She drew her hand away and saw her palm was covered with the moisture from his brow. Analee knelt by the side of the bed and took between hers the hands that had already been placed crosswise on his breast, in an attitude of resignation to death. She leaned over and kissed his cheek letting her lips brush over his, sending the message of life and vitality.

"Do not die, my lord," she whispered. "There are so many good things yet to do."

Suddenly his eyelids flickered and those standing near gasped. Then they saw his pain-wracked eyes gazing at Analee. He looked at her face for a long time and slowly she saw the color beginning to creep back to his ashen cheeks. She smiled.

"Am I in heaven?" he whispered.

"Not yet, my lord. I think they would not have you there."

Analee pressed his hands again and put her lips to his cheek.

"It is real? Is it *you,* Analee?"

"They have brought you home and I have come to you. You are going to get better. I have willed it."

"You *are* a witch," the Falcon murmured weakly. But there was a trace of a smile on his lips as he closed his eyes again and fell into a peaceful, more natural sleep.

There were those who had witnessed the miracle they said Analee had performed on the dying nobleman, and went in awe of her from that day. That she had supernatural powers very few doubted. For the Marquess began to recover and from then on Analee never left his side. At night she slept by his bed on the floor. Nelly brought her fresh clothes and she and McNeath supervised the serving of the food, the broths and coddled eggs needed to restore his lordship to health.

He spoke little. In the days that followed Analee's return he could hardly speak at all. But when his eyes were opened they gazed at her, and always when he closed them he smiled as though he were dreaming of her.

The doctors thought it was a miracle; they had given his lordship only hours to live. His wounds were not only severe, but infected with pus. Now even the wounds were beginning to heal. The gypsy woman would go herself into the grounds and, even in the depths of winter, return with herbs and plants which she mixed with her own blood, urine and spittle to lay on his wounds. These she refreshed herself every day. The doctors were horrified by the evidence of this sorcery. She was certainly a witch, otherwise the Marquess of Falconer would be dead.

Analee knew that the powers had flowed from her to her lord. It had felt almost as though her own life was draining away and passing to him. One day they were alone together and, in weariness, she stretched on the bed beside him. She could feel his regular breathing beside her, the pulse growing stronger every day, the healthy complexion returning to his face.

She awoke to feel a hand caressing her naked breast and as she turned saw that Lord Falconer's eyes were wide open and gazing at her. As she slept he had unlaced her bodice, exposing her breasts.

"I think you are recovering fast, my lord."

The Falcon said nothing but turned her toward him so that her breasts were level with his face. Like a baby he took first one nipple in his mouth and then another, suckling her. A feeling of exquisite ecstasy swept through Analee, as though he was drawing life from her even though it was four months since she had suckled her own baby and the milk had long since dried up.

His lordship's mouth was moist with the nourishment and she perceived that his eyes were alight with desire. His hand slipped inside her skirt and she quickly slid out of it so that she lay naked by his side. He put his hand between her thighs and she pressed them tightly to warm him.

Timorously her own hand reached under his nightshirt and she felt that already he was strong and vibrant, the powerful body awakening beneath her touch.

The Falcon released her breasts, which glowed from his caress, the nipples dripping with fluid.

"It is not possible," she murmured, feeling her breasts aching, "I have not suckled for months."

"Anything is possible with you," the Falcon said, his lips reaching for hers. His strong hands drew her body close to his so that her womanly parts, her full breasts and soft round belly, delighted in the sensation of intimate contact with his firm body, his thick body hair, the urgent summons from his groin.

She caressed his cheeks and his neck, smothering her face in his chest, her tongue darting out to kiss his small pink erect nipples, the deep impress of his navel, his taut lean stomach and the wide generous expanse of his groin. She felt him trembling at her light expert touch, as she gently took his manly part, caressing it as it grew and throbbed until it poured its richness into her mouth. Then, satisfied, she lay her head on his belly relishing the smell of him, listening to the quick healthy pounding of his heart, knowing that his seed still flowed strongly and well.

Analee had restored the Falcon to life.

A week later Lord Falconer was able to sit up in bed, resting against cushions piled high behind him. Analee now slept by his side every night because he would not be parted from her; but she got up before he woke and made sure his food was ready to be served.

Then when he had eaten she washed him all over with perfumed soap, drying him and rubbing oils of fresh pine, lavender and herbs into his skin. She then put on him a clean fresh nightshirt and combed his long hair back from his head, noting the new found vigor in his fine eyes, the healthy flush of his skin. He had lost a lot of weight, but he had always taken such care of his body that his illness appeared to have done him no lasting harm. He was wiry like a young man. His thin face still handsome with the long aquiline nose and the thick brows, the clean shaven cheeks and the ruthless mouth, whose harsh lines were softened by Analee's presence and, more often than not, curled up in amusement at something she had said or done.

For Analee was not only a lover but a companion to him. She entertained him and amused him. Her character delighted him and he made her go over and over again the story of her life, the myths and legends of Romany love. He found her knowledgeable, even profound, and they would discuss life and its deeper meanings, of which both felt they had recently acquired harsh knowledge.

Sometimes after her ministrations, washing and dressing him, his lordship felt amorously inclined and they often caressed each other and, if he felt strong enough, began to make love.

At first Analee had to be very patient with her lover as he rediscovered his powers so long in disuse. But because she wished to please him in all things she found new and ingenious ways to make him desire her without causing him distress or discomfort, or too much exertion. And he thought she was a marvel, the way she enticed and tempted him; her gleaming naked body, her willing mouth and pliant subtle hands pleasing him in all kinds of ways until he was able to achieve full use of his former vigor and powers.

Analee sat by his bedside all day talking or watching him as he slept, for he had still to regain his strength. As he sat there on this day, propped up, the Marquees looked at the woman who daily became more precious to him.

"Analee, do you not get bored here with me all day?"

"Bored, my lord? I?"

"Can you not read?"

"No sir. I was never taught."

The Marquess laughed and told her to fetch him a travel book from the case by the side of his bed. She snuggled up beside him and he carefully turned over the thick pages, slowly enunciating the words and getting her to repeat them after him.

The printed word was meaningless to Analee but she stared at the pages as he turned them, obediently repeating after him what he said.

"You must be able to read to be a fine lady," her lover said, kissing her ear.

"I? A fine lady?"

"You cannot leave me now, Analee."

"No, my lord."

"Say 'my love.' "

"My love." She looked at him.

"Do you mean it?"

"Of course I mean it."

"I know about your baby, Analee. I have known a long time. When I am well I will help you to find her; but I never want you to leave me. Do you understand?"

"Yes, my lord."

"My love."

"My love."

"Angus. Say Angus."

"Angus."

"There."

"Angus." Analee reached out a finger and stroked his chin. "I know my baby is well and cared for. Do not ask me how but I do. She is happy where she is. Better off. I am content."

Lord Falconer put a hand under her skirt and stroked her rounded belly. Then he lifted the skirt and gazed at it, bending his lips to kiss her.

"When I was so ill near death I dreamt I saw you, and your belly was swollen with my child. I wanted you to have my child, Analee. I wish it so, strongly . . ."

"But, sir . . . Angus."

"I thought a lot about my life and as I have struggled to stay alive I have come to realize how frail we mortals are. I am thirty-six. I have no progeny that I know of though I have loved many women. Nothing to leave, to carry my name. You have become much more than a love to me. I want you to have my children. Do you wish it, too, Analee?" Analee looked at him gravely.

"Now I wish anything that you wish, my lord, Angus. Once it was not so. I thought I was a gypsy, a vagabond: my life was in the wilds. But now in these past weeks seeing you near death, helping you to recover, I have felt otherwise. I know that for as long as you wish it, I belong to you. If you wish it I am content to do as you say, be your mistress, bear your children. I . . ."

There was a knock on the door whereupon Analee hastily straightened her skirts and jumped up from the bed. Both Mrs. Ardoine and Nelly had bundles in their arms and, at the direction of his lordship, who was clearly expecting them, laid on the bed dresses of lavish silks and brocades and undergarments, hoops, petticoats and bodices, pentelairs and stomachers.

His lordship was looking at the array with satisfaction; Analee with amazement and alarm.

"There, my love. I cannot have you as my mistress without fine clothes. See, Mrs. Ardoine and Nelly have been to Carlisle to purchase the best they can. In time the finest dressmakers will be called to serve you. There, take no notice of me. Mrs. Ardoine and Nelly will assist you to dress."

"May I not pull the curtain, my lord?" Analee said with unaccustomed modesty.

"Well, if you insist!" His lordship smiled and took up the book he had been reading with Analee. Then she drew the heavy curtain across his bed and allowed Nelly to help her out of the simple gypsy bodice and skirt which was all she had ever worn.

Nelly was having a fit of giggles as she held up one undergarment after the other.

"Mrs. Ardoine, leave us please," Analee said noticing the curious, prurient gaze of the older woman as she stood naked. She had never liked the housekeeper, but since the attempt to whip her she loathed her. Moreover she knew she was jealous of her position with Lord Falconer.

"But . . ."

Mrs. Ardoine cast a glance at her master's bed, futilely hoping for his intervention. Then with a tilt of her chin she left the room, slamming the door behind her. Analee smiled.

"I think I will soon show her who is mistress here. What are those?"

Nelly was holding up a pair of frilly drawers and Analee, unused to wearing such a garment, held it against her and began to laugh.

"You step into them," observed his lordship, his face peeping out from the curtain. "A lady is never without her drawers, except on certain occasions."

"I pray you, don't look," Analee said to him laughing. "Put your head away!"

She stepped into the drawers and then Nelly produced a cage-like structure made of whalebone which narrowed at the waist and had laces at the back.

"This is the corset . . ."

"But I *cannot* wear it . . ."

361

"It will pull your waist in and accentuate the fullness of your breasts," his lordship said, peeping again. "My dear Analee, it does me so much good to see you in such finery . . ."

"I cannot wear that!"

But Nelly was already putting her arms through it and pulling hard at the laces.

"Now the hoop," said his lordship, throwing the curtain right back and settling down to enjoy himself. "I can see you two women are unfamiliar with such garments."

"And I see you are only *too* familiar," Analee retorted glancing at him over her shoulder. "Ouch, not too tight, Nell."

The hoop was made of buckram, distended by hoops of whalebone and tied at the waist by running strings, upon which Nelly firmly tugged, following his lordship's instructions.

"Now the petticoat," ordered his lordship.

Analee gasped as the most beautiful garment of white quilted satin was pulled over her head settling on the hoop, so that it was carried out horizontally from the waist and then hung vertically all round. Nelly was already struggling with an open robe of heavy blue silk damask embroidered with flowers.

"First the stomacher," instructed the Falcon putting away his book and the pretense of reading. This was made of dark blue ribbon and silver lace with a decolleté neckline edged with lace flounces. Already Analee could see the transformation in the mirror, how slender her waist had grown and how full her bust. Everything fitted so beautifully. She exclaimed as Nelly put over her head the damask robe which opened down the front to reveal the fold of the stiff white petticoat and the beribboned stomacher. It had graceful winged cuffs also edged with lace and stood out at either side.

She turned for approval to the Marquess who nodded and smiled.

"I said you would make a fine lady. Finer than I thought. Always keep your head high."

"Now the stockings," Nelly said.

"Stockings!" exclaimed Analee. "I never wore stockings in my life."

"Nor a dress like that neither," Nelly grunted.

"The stockings should have been put on first," murmured his lordship, "first to put on and first to take off. No matter."

"But I cannot wear *stockings!*"

"Why, my love, you will be a lady in damask and silk but with bare feet? Come."

"You see, Analee, you put your foot in this," Nelly explained holding out the white silk stocking and looking at it doubtfully. "I must say I never saw the like of it myself."

Analee sat on the bed and, watched approvingly by his lordship, stretched first one long leg and then the other encasing them in the unfamiliar hose, which ended just above her knee.

"Garters, I believe," his lordship said, "have been forgotten."

"Oh no, sir. Mrs. Ardoine remembered *these*." Nelly held up a pair of colored ribbons with rosettes and proceeded to tie them around Analee's legs.

"That will be my privilege when I am well," his lordship observed. "In fact I feel better already at the sight of the clothes to take off you, my love. 'Tis part of the attraction of dressing up, to get undressed again. Not that you needed adornment . . ."

"The pumps," Nelly said, holding up a pair of elegant high heeled shoes made of the same material as the dress and embroidered with silver braid like the stomacher. "We were not sure of the fit . . ."

Analee gazed uncertainly, almost with hostility at the shoes as though they symbolized the final surrender of her freedom. Then she tentatively put first one foot in and then the other, held up her rich skirts and gazed at them.

"You are so much taller!" his lordship laughed. "I wager you will be higher than me. See yourself in the mirror."

Analee turned slowly and, hands on her waist,

gazed at herself, slowly pirouetting and turning her hear as she did. Indeed it was a complete transformation from the short bodice she was used to and simple skirt which hung without artificial aids. She felt cramped and stifled in her whalebone corset, tight stomacher and large hoop. She pulled herself up, her eyes on the Falcon, and walked slowly over to him. His eyes glinted with admiration and he reached for her hand and kissed it.

"My lady . . ." he murmured "I have but one thing left to give you. No, two . . ."

His lordship put a hand under his pillow and took from it a small case which he opened to show a huge ring of diamonds and sapphires set in gold. He placed it on Analee's long, slender forefinger and she held out her hand unable to believe her eyes.

She remembered all the gewgaws and baubles she had gazed at on the market stalls, all the silks and brocades she had allowed to run through her hands.

"It is . . . mine?"

"Forever. It is a gift; but this . . . this is more precious to me. It is what you left behind and I want you to wear it for me for as long as we love each other. It is more precious to me than all the diamonds, all the sapphires and jewels I could have given you."

The falcon took also from his pillow the massive gold ring at the sight of which Analee hung her head. It had engraved on it the head of the falcon, the bird of prey, and the gold was white as though it had been freshly mined.

She had left it on the table the night she fled—a symbolic gesture that she and the Marquess were no longer bound together as he had wished, no longer one. Now all had changed.

He held it up for her to look at, and then he put it to his eye and peered through it.

"I see you, Analee, my mistress. Mine. Remember this ring? Made of the purest Falcon gold brought from South America? A ring is round and has no join; that is why it is symbolic between two people—love cannot be broken. You must never take it off again

364

Analee, or at least not leave it as you did before. Well I knew what you meant when I saw that ring gleaming so brightly at me on that dull morning. Now I give it to you again." Analee bent her head and he slipped the chain around it, himself settling the object between her breasts, against her heart. "Now it is even more precious because I wore it at Falkirk, and perhaps it saved my life; the talisman of our family. People say I resemble the great Beyrick because I am warlike and ruthless with my enemies. Maybe the French knew about him when they dubbed me "Le Faucon" and my troops took it up; or maybe it suited my style. I know not and now it matters not. The ring is yours. No other gold matches Falcon gold. No other woman, in my eyes, can match you. Like it, you are beyond price. And when our son is born and grows to manhood the ring will be his, and I will have a medallion fashioned for you also of this precious gold. But until he is of age, it is yours."

Analee felt the heavy ring rest on her bosom. Her eyes had filled with tears which she brushed quickly away not wishing her lord to see how much his words had moved her, how grieved she was to have hurt him by leaving it behind. That she meant as much to him as this was proof that he loved her and would not lightly cast her aside. He was even talking of their children. What could more solidly weld together their flesh?

But his lordship saw her tears and put his arm about her shoulder clasping her to him.

"My Analee. You did not think I loved you so much?"

"A great lord . . ."

"What you have given me is great, too—life. My doctors say but for you I would be dead; they know not how you did it. But I know. It is not sorcery, not magic. It is love. Pure love, as pure as the Falcon gold . . . the white unalloyed gold from South America. Now my love, I am tired. I must rest in order to regain my vigor and provide you with sons. Go with Nelly and play with your fine new clothes. You will soon get used to them; the constriction will not worry you. You will learn how to carry yourself as the daughters of noblemen do. You must be a credit to me in what you wear and what you do—for what you are yourself honors me already.

"I myself will teach you to read and write for I see you are an adept pupil, and you will be taught to embroider, and the finest of teachers will instruct you in the pianoforte.

"But the gypsy skirt is gone forever, Analee, and that part of you that was at one with the fields and the meadows and sleeping under the hedgerows. Promise me it is gone?'

Analee turned her face away and looked out of the window to where the bough of a tree, heavy with buds, swayed in the gusty wind of an early spring day. How could she promise him anything else? She loved him, so completely that any former love, even the very first, seemed like a childish whim. She had brought the Falcon through death and given him life. Her life had gone into him just as one day his seed would root in her, bringing yet more life. Life renewed itself again and again.

"I promise," she said meeting his gaze and fingering the heavy gold ring at her neck. "But your lordship will bear with me if at times I kick off my shoes and run about in the grass, for my gypsy ways are hard to lose, and I was born in the wild. I will find it hard to be a lady."

The Falcon sank back against his pillows and took her hands between his, kissing the tips of the fingers one by one.

"Wild lady," his lordship murmured, "I think it will be an irresistible combination. One that I shall find fascinating forever."

Chapter Twenty

By the month of May all the snows had disappeared
from the Cheviot Hills and the trees in the great park
of Falcon's Keep were dressed with tiny green leaves.
Angus Falconer, whose arm had been all but severed
from his shoulder, still walked with difficulty but under
Analee's care he had grown fit and strong. His recovery had been hastened by the burgeoning of the deep
love between them, the understanding of each other's
minds and bodies that the long weeks together had
only strengthened.

Angus never ceased to be amazed by the accom-
plishment and intelligence of Analee who, because of
his careful tutelage, could nearly read and write. She
had even taken over the running of the household after
gladly despatching Mrs. Ardoine back to her native
Edinburgh.

Dressmakers were sent from Carlisle and a whole
wardrobe made for Analee consisting of ornate dresses
for evening, simpler gowns for morning, cloaks, a riding habit and the ball dresses which Angus insisted
she would need when he took her to London.

At times Analee would slip off her shoes and stockings and relish again the feel of the bare earth under
her feet; she would wander in the park far from the
house and some little yearning would flutter in her
heart for the old life. She would finger the silk of her
dress and touch the rings on her fingers looking toward
the hills, and some part of her would feel like a
trapped bird that yearned to take flight.

But then she remembered the heavy gold ring round her neck, and she clasped it and rubbed it between her fingers. The heavy ring of white Falcon gold would remind her of her lover and with it came the realization that her true existence lay in him and the old days were indeed gone forever. She had kept her promise.

The servants at the castle quickly got used to the dominance of one who had once been among their numbers. For Analee did not lord it over them or give herself airs. She was firm and authoritative, but always smiling and gentle. Her commands were softly spoken and accompanied by a smile. It was as though she had been born to it.

One day Analee had slipped away to think, removing first her shoes and stockings and carrying them in her hand; it was a gentle spring day warm enough to be without a cloak. She looked toward the sky and thought of Morella. She wondered if she would ever see her again, and then she remembered what she had just learned and a soft smile illuminated her face. It gave her hope and strength for the future and impulsively she turned toward the house to find Angus and break the news to him.

But his lordship was coming toward her, across the broad lawn between the house and the lake, walking slowly with a stick as he still did, the sleeve of his coat flapping loosely from his left arm which was still inert and strapped to his body. He waved his stick when he saw her and quickened his pace. She waited for him under a tree, her face dappled by the shadows made by the leaves against the sun.

She was so lovely, Angus thought, approaching her slowly so that he could savor the moment of seeing her under the tree, the dark green of her gown merging with the lighter color of the soft young leaves. He saw the smile on her lips and the light in her eyes and . . .

"Analee! You have still got bare feet!" he roared.

Analee dug her feet into the grass and curled up her toes in a gesture of stubbornness. Then she tossed her shoes on the ground in front of her and laughed as her lover caught her in his arms and gently molded his lips against hers.

"You are incorrigible . . ."

"What means that, my lord?'

"You will never be a lady. Not a true lady."

Analee leaned back, flushed from his kiss, and smiled enticingly at the Falcon.

"Will you cast me aside then?"

The Falcon groaned and pushed her gently against the tree pulling up her skirts so that he could feel her bare thighs.

"And, Analee, you wear no drawers!"

"I have so little need of them sir. They are the sort of garment I cannot get used to. They constrict one."

"Nor no corset," he murmured, caressing her waist, his hand moving down across her belly until it rested snugly between her thighs. Glancing round and perceiving that they were hidden from the house by the overhanging branches of the willow, his lordship cast his stick to the ground and began to unfasten his breeches with his good hand. Aware, from his trembling, of his intention and inflamed by the sight of his ardor, the circumstances of their meeting and the heady spring day Analee eagerly assisted him by spreading her legs wide against the tree and, clasped her hands tight around his buttocks, pressing him hard into her.

After weeks of making love in the comfort of a bed, the feeling of hard wood against her back and the thrusting, panting energy of her lover restored to full vigor, quickly aroused in Analee a state of ecstasy which coincided with the peak of his lordship's passion and, sighing and moaning with satisfaction, they sank exhausted to the ground.

There, the shadows of the leaves still providing them with cover, the delightful sward of fresh-smelling tender green grass beneath them, they lay for some time as they had fallen, still entwined, until his lordship raised himself and straightened his dress. Even then he was unable to take his eyes from his mistress who still lay with her skirts over her thighs in an attitude of complete abandonment.

"Thou art a very saucy wench," his lordship whispered gazing at her, "I perceive the reason you do not wear drawers and corsets . . . for a contingency such as this." He lowered his head and kissed the dimpled pit of her navel, the soft rounded belly.

Analee looked at him, their eyes meeting. She put a hand on her belly and then stroked his lordship's face which still rested on it.

"This is the reason, Angus. Here." She pointed to her stomach.

He put a hand on hers and understood. He felt the soft flesh, the rounded contours, the full hips.

"The Master of Falcon's Keep," he said and kissed the place where his hand had been.

"Angus?" Analee cocked a head on one side not fully understanding.

"My heir. You are carrying my child?"

Analee nodded.

"The heir to the Marquess of Falconer is the Earl of Blair . . ."

"It may be a girl," Analee said slyly.

"Then she will be Lady whatever-her-name-is Blair. Oh, Analee, you make me very, very happy. I care not if it is a girl, so long as she resembles you in *every* respect."

His lordship kissed her again and laid her head on the grass, lying beside her. He arranged her skirts decorously lest a servant should come across them, and put his good arm round her waist, leaning over her. His eyes looked over toward the house, the hooded eyes of the Falcon, the sharp imperious beak sniffing the air.

"But first you must be Lady Falconer."

Analee struggled to sit up.

"I?"

"Why not? 'Tis only a name. You cannot bear my children and *not* be married to me, Analee. 'Twould not be legal. They could not inherit. I swear I meant to ask you before you told me this. I decided I could

370

not take the risk of you running away again. Every time you are out of my sight I grow anxious. Will you have me?"

His lordship bent his head, his eyes an inch from hers, his expression grave.

"If I will have your children I will have you," Analee said. "But I will *still* not wear shoes when I do not wish it, even though I be a lady. A proper one."

Analee became the Marchioness of Falconer at a simple ceremony carried out in the chapel a few weeks after the proposal in the park. Although her condition was not so far advanced as to be noticeable his lordship judged it judicious to have the ceremony quickly and, because he was not fully restored to health, a long and elaborate ceremony was thought unwise. His lordship, looking upright and handsome despite the fact that he still used a stick, was married in the scarlet uniform of a lieutenant-general, with gold epaulettes and several rows of medals. Analee wore a gown of gold brocade richly embroidered with silver thread over a large hoop; her slippers were gold, and jewels and diamonds glittered on her fingers.

Her hair was simply dressed without adornment, her natural ringlets falling over her shoulders and she carried a posy of fresh summer flowers in her hands. But on her bosom between her breasts was the solitary ring on the fine gold chain, the symbol of the love of the lordly Falcon for the gypsy girl.

After the final defeat of the Jacobite army at Culloden in April of that year, 1746, the Duke of Cumberland's affectionate name of "Bluff Bill" was swiftly changed to "Butcher Cumberland." So terrible was the vengeance wreaked on the defeated Highlanders and their allies, that the deeds perpetrated by the government troops on enemy soldiers and civilians alike went down into history for their perfidy, brutality and inhumanity.

When Lord Falconer subsequently heard the details of the Battle of Culloden, even he was glad he had not been there to share in the doubtful glory of the butchery and savagery that had followed it—Cumberland being determined to put an end to the Rebellion once and for all.

Prince Charles escaped from the field and some of his commanders, incurably optimistic, regrouped to meet in another place and plan to rally. But the Prince was done for. He, with scant thanks for all they had done, bade his supporters disperse while he became a fugitive with a price on his head.

For weeks after Culloden Brent Delamain found it impossible to rid his mind of the sounds of the battle, the screams of the wounded, the savage cries of the Highlanders trying to resist defeat, the relentless sound of gunfire and of steel upon steel. As a special category prisoner Brent had been cast into the dungeons of Edinburgh Castle; special because he had been so close to the Prince, a captain in his Life Guards. Brent had served in all the encounters since Clifton and battle had taken its toll of him; he was a silent man, a man of iron and bitterness. He blamed the undisciplined Highlanders and the personality of the Prince, whose spirits were either up or down but never seemed capable of maintaining that balance, that detachment, that was so essential for a successful military commander. His temperament was too mercurial, too uneven and, in fact, it only flourished at its best when he was hunted as a fugitive although Brent at that time could not know this.

Brent was lucky to be alive. His brother Tom was dead, killed very early in the battle, as the waves of government soldiers bore down upon the tired and grossly outnumbered Jacobite army. Brent had seen the way the wounded were dealt with as he waited to be led away, sabred or shot to death where they lay, just as his men had dealt with the wounded Hanoverians in other engagements.

It was sickening and horrible and now that it was over he was glad to be out of it, although he knew that death inevitably awaited him because of the degree of guilt attributed to him. The majority of prisoners taken at Culloden had been sent to Inverness for shipment to London, and dreadful stories had come back of the conditions in the transport ships in which the men were confined, many of whom died of untreated wounds and disease.

But Brent was incarcerated in Edinburgh Castle along with other gentlemen and members of the nobility including the Earl of Kelly, the Duchess of Perth, Lady Ogilvy and, most important of all, Murray of Broughton who had been so instrumental in bringing the Prince to Scotland. Those who were in prison in Scotland did not expect to remain there long. It was known that the English victors would not attempt to hold trials in Scotland and, uncertain of his fate, Brent nevertheless prepared himself for the end. Whatever happened to him the Cause was lost indeed.

Stewart Allonby, in prison in Carlisle, had waited much longer for his sentence. The lots that had been cast among the ordinary soldiers to stand trial did not apply to officers and Stewart had been sent to London for trial at Southwark. After the vengeance taken on the men of Manchester Regiment, all of whom had been sentenced to death and barbarously executed on Kennington Common in July, Stewart expected no mercy. But to his surprise his cousin George Delamain, urged on by Emma, spoke for him. It was submitted that he was only a half-hearted supporter of the Young Pretender and that, moreover, he had not drawn sword or fired a gun in battle, which was true, his duties at Carlisle keeping him off the ramparts.

Worn out by months of waiting and repeated bouts of gaol fever Stewart did not deny his lack of fervor, and was rewarded with a sentence to be deported to His Majesty's Colonies and to remain there for the rest of his life. He was then returned to Carlisle to await shipment from Liverpool and, dazed, he still did not know whether it was better to have died or to be forced to live forever so far from the home, the country which he loved.

Two days after his return Stewart was summoned

before Carruthers, the Keeper of Carlisle Gaol, and told he had a visitor. Carruthers was aware of the importance of Sir George Delamain's evidence in securing leniency for Mr. Allonby and smiled on him kindly.

"You were lucky, Mr. Allonby, in that your cousin spoke for you." Stewart looked at the floor. He was not proud of George's intervention. He had also been surprised by it.

"I know not whether I prefer death to a life of exile."

"Oh come, sir. They say his Majesty will extend a general pardon once all is cleared away. You will not be gone long. In the meantime I have a surprise for you. Miss Delamain who accompanied her brother to your trial is here to see you."

"Emma?"

Stewart's eyes, sunk deep in his head with suffering, momentarily brightened.

"Emma was *there?*"

"You did not observe her in the crowd?"

"I have been in prison six months, Mr. Keeper. It does not make the senses alert. That and the prison fodder."

The Keeper turned away and shuffled some papers. He had expected very few to survive their trials, certainly not Stewart Allonby. The prisoners from Carlisle had been very harshly dealt with. The Manchester Regiment who, after all, had played very little part in the war had been savagely butchered. The behavior of the Scots was considered more forgivable than that of the English who had turned against their King. Carruthers was sorry that he had not treated Mr. Allonby better. He was now trying to make amends.

"You may use my room to see Miss Delamain, sir. I will have her brought to you."

Stewart turned his back and gazed out of the window. He was uncertain whether he wanted to see Emma; how he felt about her. He heard her come softly into the room but still he did not turn.

"Stewart?"

Stewart closed his eyes, his jaw working hard to hold back his emotion. He felt her hand on his arm, her fingers slowly tightening.

"I look awful, deathly pale . . ."

"I know. I saw you in court. But alive! You are *alive*, Stewart. You have a chance."

"Thanks to George."

He felt Emma remove her hand and her voice was low.

"I knew you would be bitter. But I did not care. I know how you felt about the Prince, how disillusioned you had become with the Cause. You told me in your letters. Not to *die* for him now, Stewart."

"Oh, Emma . . ."

Stewart turned toward her and she threw herself into his arms. He was so weak that he could hardly support her and for a while they leaned on each other. How beautiful she looked, he thought, stroking her hair, seeing the tears cascading down her cheeks. Weeping for *him?* What had he done to deserve it?

"I am not worth the tears, Emma. I am not a hero, not even a brave man, not even dedicated."

"But you are alive and I love you."

It was the first time she had told him. She looked up into his eyes; pale gaunt man that he was, tired and disillusioned. He had lost stones in weight and dark shadows framed his eyes. But she loved him, had come to love him through his letters from prison, his need of her.

"How can you love *me?*"

He pressed her close to him again scarcely believing.

"I do. And I will stay with you, Stewart, wherever you go—to the West Indies or America—I will join you as soon as I can. Whatever your circumstances I will be by your side."

So it was worth it. He had lost a cause, but gained the love of a woman he had always cherished. Was it true, after all, that good did come out of evil?

"Oh, Emma, Emma, I do not deserve you. I do not deserve this."

He hugged her again then pushed her gently from him and warily went to sit on a chair. He felt his legs could scarcely support him any longer.

"Unless I recover my strength I shall not survive the voyage. I shall die like those poor men in the transports in Tilbury."

"Don't worry. I have the measure of Carruthers. He is anxious to please, seeing George is so powerful. You will be well fed."

"And Brent? What news of Brent?"

Emma's proud noble frame, so upright in front of her lover, seemed to shrink.

"For some reason the authorities are treating Brent with severity. There are reports that he was ruthless in battle against the English, his own countrymen. He was seen to strike many down at Falkirk and Culloden. It is this that tells against Brent more than anything else. When he was in London George made inquiries in the highest of circles; he even had an interview with the Duke of Newcastle himself. But the English Jacobites are not popular with the Hanoverian Court—hated even worse than the Scots."

"Then it is hopeless for Brent?"

Emma gazed at her beloved and her eyes again filled with tears. Would they could both be safe— lover and brother. It was too much to expect, too much to hope for. Brent would be hanged and Stewart live out a life of bitterness and misery in the undeveloped American colonies, far from home.

"Our family has suffered too much for the Stuarts," she said, nodding her head in reply to Stewart's question. "They have lost everything. They do not even have the advantage of admiration for the Prince although he is hunted all over the Highlands, a price of £30,000 on his head and none betray him."

"He inspires great loyalty, he has such charm." Stewart reached up and took Emma's hand, putting it to his lips. "But he was not a good commander. He would not have made a good king. He was overfond of his own way, his own opinion. Nay, I'm disillusioned, I'll admit. The Stuarts are surely gone forever and Hanover firmly entrenched on the throne of England. Would I were at my home on Lake Derwentwater, going out to hew wood. Would all this had never happened. The Cause lost and I humiliated by my cousin having to plead for me. Now Tom is dead, killed in battle and Brent sure to hang."

Emma's eyes were wet with tears and she pressed Stewart's hand tightly.

"I didn't know Tom so well, of course; he was older than I and always lived abroad. Mother said he wanted to die if he could not win."

"How does your mother bear up to all this?"

"She is very brave; also she has had comfort during the past months. The most curious thing, Stewart. Brent sent a gypsy woman with a sick baby to take shelter with us and mother has become very fond of the baby. The gypsy woman, who was not the mother, has gone on her way and mother has taken over the baby."

"Your mother has taken a gypsy baby?"

"She thinks it is not. She is a dear little thing, very blonde with blue eyes, called Morella. She could almost be a Delamain. Mother mourns, of course, for Tom and Brent and you. But, Stewart, listen, there is the oddest story I have to tell you that Mary told me. And here I have hope for Brent."

"And that is?"

"Before they were married a gypsy came to your home, do you remember?"

"I do," Stewart said bitterly. "Well I remember her."

"It seems my brother was once enamored of her."

"Mary knows that?"

"Brent told her after the wedding. However the gypsy, Analee, has, by the most curious chain of circumstances, married my sister-in-law Henrietta's cousin, Angus Falconer. They met in the war or something, I know not quite what."

"Lord Falconer has married *Analee?*"

Stewart could not keep the incredulity out of his voice.

"He was much taken by her and cared not what people thought. Now she is always at his side. It is rumored her strange gypsy powers even saved his life."

"So, what is the plan?"

"Mary has gone to Falcon's Keep to plead with Analee whom she got to know well, to intercede with her husband to save Brent."

" 'Tis a slim chance."

Emma nodded. There was a knock on the door. Emma took Stewart's hand and looked into his eyes. They had never made love, never even kissed. Now Emma felt she wanted this thin defeated prisoner more than anything in life.

"Stewart," she said quietly. "I will follow you. I will find where you are and get a boat as soon as I can."

"But the conditions . . ."

"No matter what they are I will share them with you. I love you too much to let you go."

Stewart looked down at her and took her tenderly in his arms. The moment he'd always waited for had come too late.

"How can I say no?" he said brokenly. "Even though I have nothing at all to offer you."

And for the first time they kissed, before the door swung open and the gaoler came to take Stewart back to his cell.

The Marchioness of Falconer sat at her escritoire in her own salon on the first floor of the mansion which overlooked the elaborate gardens and the lake in the far distance. Beyond that was the uneven range of the Cheviot Hills. She wore a simple pentelair that now suited her more ample figure. It had a round décolletage which emphasized her magnificent bosom and she wore it with a plain petticoat of the same dark green silk which rested on a domed hoop. Like a simple countrywoman a handerchief was tied round her neck and she wore no rings or jewels except for her necklace which she never removed.

Her feet were bare and tucked under her chair as

she tried to grasp the simple arithmetic of her household accounts which she prepared under the tutelage of his lordship.

Analee had taken to her new status with a natural dignity which impressed all who met her—the local worthies and the members of his majesty's army who called to pay their respects to his lordship and wish him health and happiness. At night she entertained regally, dressed in the latest mode, her hair dressed and ablaze with jewels. But by day she wore simple clothes and on retiring she lay, as she always had, naked except for the close companionship of her loving husband.

Analee, looking forward to the future, aware of the child quickening inside her, the heir to the Falconer estates and fortune if it were a boy, thought only sporadically of her former life and the happier she became the less she missed it.

She still loved to wander barefoot around the estate, and she and Nelly would talk of the old times, sometimes with laughter and occasionally with tears when they thought of the fate of the Buckland gypsies, the harshness the war had brought to so many people.

But although Analee often thought of Morella she never spoke of her. She knew she was well looked after and that her future was as good as any she could give her. She felt she owed it to the Falcon to start a new life with him and, apart from telling him that the baby was safe, she had told him no more and he never inquired.

Mrs. Ardoine had been replaced by a new and younger housekeeper and with her Analee took care to see that the staff, even the meanest, were well housed with ample food, that no one was ill treated or subject to cruel whippings. Analee infused the large household with her own vibrant personality and it became a happy laughing place full of vigor and good cheer.

Analee found it hard on this particular day in July, with the sky outside a clear blue and the birds singing in the park, to concentrate on her work and was gazing out of the window, when a voice cried:

"My lady! My lady!"

Analee, still unused to her new title, looked about her as though to see who could be meant, when Nelly burst in without ceremony, her face alight.

"Oh, ma'am, who do you think is *here?*"

Analee's face was alight with excitement and she jumped up, relieved to leave the accounts, and seized Nelly's hand.

"Who, Nelly? Who?"

No one was more delighted than Nelly at the elevation of her beloved Analee to the peerage or at her own promotion as personal maid to a Marchioness, but she still maintained the informality of their earlier relationship, at least when they were alone together. In public Lord Falconer insisted that his wife be treated with all the deference due to her station and then Nelly never spoke out of turn, or betrayed their intimacy in any way. "Analee, it is Mary—Mary Delamain and her brother John Allonby."

"Mary and John here!"

"Oh, Mary is so excited to see you; but she looks sad and drawn . . . I think the business is to do with her husband."

Analee took Nelly's hand and made quickly for the door running along the corridor and down the stairs, brushing aside the servant who hastily tried to open the door into the main drawing room.

She opened her arms as soon as she saw Mary and the two women embraced, Mary with tears in her eyes.

"Oh, Analee . . . your ladyship . . . I . . ."

Analee put up a hand.

"*Analee,* Mary, no ladyship from you! I am Analee the gypsy and always will be . . ."

Analee stepped back and gestured toward herself, her simple morning dress, her lack of adornment. Mary threw back her head and laughed.

"Analee, what does his lordship say about his wife's bare feet?"

"Oh." Analee clasped a hand to her mouth. "That was a mistake. I am allowed to do it, but only if no one is about. Nelly, fetch me my stockings and shoes please."

Nelly bobbed, stifling a giggle.

"And Nelly is with you! Oh, Analee, I am so happy for you. I heard, we heard, about his lordship's serious illness and his recovery . . ."

John Allonby had stood in the background and now came forward bowing stiffly.

"Your ladyship, my felicitations on your husband's recovery and your good fortune. May you be very happy . . ."

"We are, Mr. Allonby." Analee, who had never known this dour man well, took his hand and smiled briefly. "Now what brings you here? Not bad news?"

John nodded and Mary cast her eyes to the floor.

"We are here to invoke the compassion of Lord Falconer, your husband, hoping that he will help a distant member of his family now in dire straits."

"His family?" Analee's gaze went from Mary to John.

"Brent, my lady. Brent Delamain, related to his lordship's cousin by marriage, is in mortal danger. He is to be sent to London from Edinburgh to stand trial, and it is certain he will be sentenced to death. The record against him is black. He served in the Prince's elite corps of Life Guards and he killed many of his own countrymen in battle. His cousin Stewart Allonby has been spared the extreme penalty and is sentenced to deportation; but there is little hope for Brent."

"But how can my husband help? He has no influence at court." Analee looked distressed.

"*The* Falcon, ma'am? The bravest of soldiers, newly gazetted general? Surely well favored by the King?"

"Or is it that he would not *want* to help?" Mary moved over to Analee who impulsively grasped her hand.

"Oh, Mary, worry not that Angus knows anything about Brent and myself. That is a secret and forever will be. No, it is simply that his lordship has no time

381

for the rebels, I fear. He says they put the country to a lot of trouble and suffering. He remembers well the gypsy camp . . ."

"But that was not Brent!"

"Of course it was not. He knows in his heart that there were many fine and upright men on the Jacobite side, though you would not think it to hear him talk. But my lord is," Analee inclined her head as though searching for the right word, "he is not an *easy* man. He is personally a kind man and a wonderful husband; but . . . stubborn."

"Not the Falcon for nothing," John Allonby murmured.

"He has strong views on loyalty."

"It is a matter of ideals, Analee."

"I know, Mary; but Angus, for right or wrong, believes the Jacobites to be traitors to the rightful King of England. I know he will do nothing." She shrugged. "However, we can try. I will ask him. Unfortunately he has still not recovered from his serious wound which nearly killed him, and lies abed until nearly dinnertime. But you will stay with us and see him then."

Mary shook her head.

"We must go at once. There is no time to lose. If only to say goodbye . . ."

Mary leaned her head on Analee's breast and gave herself up to a torrent of weeping. "Oh, Analee, and to know that he does not even love me. That he thinks only . . ."

"Shhh." Analee patted her shoulder looking at John who nodded and moved toward the door just as Nelly entered with Analee's shoes and hose.

"My lady . . ."

"Take Mr. Allonby into the garden, Nelly. He wishes to take some air."

Left alone Analee took Mary to the sofa and sat beside her.

"There, my dear, cry to your heart's content. How unhappy I am that Brent has behaved to you as he has; it spoils my own happiness. But if he could see, if he could know how happy his lordship has made me!" She put a hand on her stomach, "and we are to have a child, Mary, to solder our love. I am nearly five months gone."

Analee saw the expression on Mary's face and smiled.

"Are you shocked, little one? We have been married only two months I know. But his lordship and I were always meant for each other; there was never any question . . ."

Mary looked at the gypsy, now no longer a gypsy girl despite what she said. Analee had in some subtle way changed; she had the air and regality of a lady. With her customary sorcery Analee had already achieved the part. Why, there she was, a real marchioness with one of the great lords of the land for a husband. Yet it seemed perfectly natural for her. It was not only the way Analee looked—it was her bearing and the way she held herself; a dignity as though she had been somehow born to it.

"If Brent lives, Analee, can you use your powers to free him from your spell? *Can* you?"

"Mary, I have told you I have no extraordinary powers. I am no *cohani*, no witch. But, yes, if Brent lives I will do what I can. Why . . . here is my lord."

The door opened and the Falcon came slowly in, his eyes searching.

"Ah, Analee, they told me you were here. My dear . . ." His gaze fell on Mary and he stopped.

"My lord, Angus, this is Mary Delamain who was so kind to me when I was snowbound."

The Marquess walked over to Mary and bowed over her hand.

"You are very welcome, ma'am, and thank you for your hospitality to my wife. How long will you stop here?"

Analee got up and took her lord's arm.

"Angus, Mary is the wife of *Brent* Delamain, your distant cousin by marriage."

"Ah," his lordship cried, understanding dawning.

"That will be why she is here. I understand he is on the list for trial in London and almost certain to be condemned. His is one of the names of those thought most culpable."

"You know it, my lord?"

"Aye. I heard it yesterday from Colonel Worth who stopped here on his way back to London. He knew we were very distantly related."

"Oh Angus, cannot you do something for your cousin!"

His lordship thumped the floor with his stick.

"No, I cannot and pray do not ask me. You know how I feel about the rebels. There is nothing I can do anyway. His Majesty is determined to punish them and stamp them out by his example. I know it."

The Falcon shook his head and moved to the window. Analee could see from his stormy gaze that he was angry; that brooding Falcon stare that had struck terror into the hearts of so many, friend and foe. But now it was never directed at her; the only expression she ever saw on the face of her husband was one of love and tenderness. She went over to him and leaned her head against his arm stroking his sleeve. The Marquess fidgeted with his stick and tried to move away.

"Analee, pray do not. It is no use . . ."

"My lord, Angus, did you never have anything you felt very passionately about?"

"Only you," he whispered, so that Mary could not hear.

"Very well. You defied society to marry me. But only supposing it had been against the law? Would you have done it then?"

"You know it. I would have defied everyone and everything to have you as my wife."

"Then think how Brent Delamain and those like him felt. They are zealots. They are not criminals."

Reluctantly Lord Falconer, who was still tantalized by the proximity of his wife even though he knew her so well, freed his arm.

"My dear Analee . . . even if I wanted to I can do nothing. I am powerless. There!"

"Can we not contrive to *rescue* Brent before he is sent?" Analee said quietly. "There must be a way. Even Lord Nithsdale escaped from the Tower of London itself after the '15 Rebellion. It is a famous tale. Can it not be done from Edinburgh Castle?"

"No, it cannot!" his lordship thundered. "You want me to lose my titles? Forfeit my commission in His Majesty's regiment? We are undone, Analee, if we so much as lift a finger to help these traitors! I will not risk my life, my inheritance, the inheritance of our child, for something in which I do not believe. *You* I do believe in, but the Stuarts no!"

There was a silence only broken occasionally by the sound of Mary weeping. Analee gazed stormily at her husband.

"When you are married, my lord, do you not take on obligations owed by your spouse?"

"You have obligations to Brent Delamain?" his lordship said incredulously.

In Analee's mind there flashed the thought of a moonlit scene; a handsome blond god—a beautiful baby girl. She found she was trembling, but she tried to hide her emotion. Much as she knew Angus loved her he was not ready now to hear about Morella, if he ever would be which she somehow doubted. He was too jealous, too single-minded to countenance hearing about her relationship with Brent, to know about their child. It would not make him want to help Brent; he would probably volunteer to hang him with his own hands. Her lord was much too savage for magnanimity at this stage in their relationship, which was still so dependent on physical passion. No, she would not tell her husband the truth. Even Mary did not know the whole truth.

"I have obligations to the family of Allonby. They were very kind to me and Nelly and offered us shelter when we needed it on two occasions. I would like to do a favor for Mary, more particularly than Brent. As you love me, sir, so does she love her husband and would have him by her side."

"But they would be exiles, outlaws . . ."

"No matter," Analee said firmly, "they would be alive and together. For *me*, my lord, won't you help?"

For answer his lordship shook his head angrily and stumped out of the room.

Mary turned her ashen, tear-stained face to Analee who, she was surprised to see, was smiling.

"I think he will do something," Lady Falconer said. "I know my lord."

"If my name is ever brought into this plan," his lordship said over dinner when the room was cleared of servants, "I and future generations of my family will curse the name of Delamain . . . and Allonby," he added scowling fiercely. "I am doing this solely for my wife, whom I adore. It is much against my better judgment. It is a token of my love for her; she has asked it and I will do it. I know she will not be ungrateful and will show me so in many ways; thus my motives are not altogether without self-interest . . ." Lord Falconer paused and looked meaningfully at his wife who bent her head and suppressed a smile, her eyes shining. "We shall vigorously deny any connection with the plan to free Brent Delamain and say our name was used basely because of my relationship to the family. 'Tis all I have to say. D'ye hear?"

John Allonby was gazing with open admiration at the man he had hated; the Falcon. Not only had a committed Hanoverian and a member of the government army to boot consented to help free his cousin, but the plan was so simple it was perfect.

"You are a born strategist, my lord," John said respectfully.

"Aye," his lordship replied modestly, "I have that reputation, which is why I am today a General in His Majesty's regiment. You see then why my name must never become associated with this, even though you are put to the rack . . ."

"Never, sir. I swear," John got up and bowed to his host.

"And you *may* be racked, Mr. Allonby, or worse.

You will be the one left behind in your cousin's place. Maybe they will take your head instead of his."

"They are welcome to it, sir, if they so decide," John said slowly. "Do not think it has not occurred to me . . ."

"Oh no, John . . ." Mary, who had been so happy as the plan was revealed, looked aghast.

"Yes, Mary. I have done no wrong that they know: I have not fought with the Prince; but . . . I shall have contrived to help a traitor escape. However, my love, do not grieve if it is so. I shall die cheerful. I am a single man and you and Brent have all life and all happiness in the world before you. I am half dead since Charlotte died, anyway. Furness Grange may be sequestrated and sold . . . but you will be free, starting a new life, maybe overseas in the Indies or Africa."

" 'Tis nobly spoke," Lord Falconer said. "Now to the details of the plan. For if you are to be in time you cannot delay a moment. They are despatching the criminals like hens in a farmyard I hear."

Chapter Twenty-one

The governor of Edinburgh Castle, Colonel Guest, was a stern man. He ruled his castle and its garrison with a fist of iron and gave little quarter. He shared with the Tolbooth and Canongate prisons responsibility for the large number of captured Jacobites who had supported the Prince, in battle or otherwise. He had many noblewomen in his castle who had rallied to the Prince —either by raising bodies of fighting men themselves or by selling their jewels or by defying reluctant husbands.

Most of his prisoners were of the rank and file and in batches they left the castle to be taken for trial at Carlisle, Chester, York or Lancaster. Once in England lots were cast among the men for those who were to be tried, one in twenty. The rest were deported or, ultimately, pardoned and freed according to the degree of guilt. Colonel Guest cared little as to what happened to any of them.

He had one or two special prisoners, like Murray of Broughton and Brent Delamain, whose offenses were deemed enough to hang them. These were kept apart from the rest while a strong escort was awaited to take them to London.

An orderly stood at the door and the Governor, who had been studying papers, looked up.

"A Mrs. Delamain to see her husband, sir. She has come from Keswick and knows he is soon to be taken to England."

"Is there permission?"

"From General Hawley himself, sir," the orderly handed the governor a note which he barely glanced at. He had no time for these sentimental gestures on the part of the authorities. In his opinion rogues like Delamain should be denied all privileges.

"It may be the last time she sees him, sir. She is said to be unwell and her brother has accompanied her."

"Is *he* to be admitted, too?"

" 'Tis on the order, sir."

"Oh get it over. See 'tis kept short. Traitors have no rights in my opinion; they all deserve the gallows. Have the prisoner Delamain brought up."

Mary stood trembling in the small room near the entrance to the prison. Even though John was with her she was terrified. Lord Falconer's plan had seemed so simple in the shelter of Falcon's Keep; but here it seemed impossible. As they waited John tightly held her hand and she pressed it, unable to speak.

She hardly recognized her husband when he was

388

brought in. He was so thin and gaunt and he dragged his leg with pain. He blinked his eyes against the light and scarcely seemed able to recognize her.

"Brent, it is Mary."

"Aye, so I heard. Why did you come, Mary, to distress yourself thus? I have not been a good husband to you. Start life again . . ."

John moved quickly over to Brent and seized his arm.

"Do not waste time talking. Remove your clothes." Brent stared at him and held up his arms.

"How can I remove my clothes in chains?"

Curse, they had forgotten that!

"Then your breeches merely. My jacket will conceal the chains."

"You are . . ." Brent gazed at him in amazement.

"Rescuing you. I am taking your place. We are the same color, the same build . . ."

John had not reckoned with Brent's emaciated appearance; but it was too late now. The best laid plans always misfired so he had heard. He was prepared to brazen it out now, whatever happened.

"Haste, man. We have no time to tarry."

"But they will try you in my place."

"We think not; but it is a chance I must take."

John had removed most of his clothes and kept glancing anxiously at the door. As if accepting the inevitability of what was happening, Brent stumped out of his breeches with Mary's help and donned John's clothes.

"We will never get away with it."

"We might. 'Tis dark in here. Here now, my hat, pull it well over your face which has a ghastly prison pallor. There. Good-bye, sweet sister. Brent, come!"

"John, I cannot . . ."

John gazed at his cousin, at his sister.

"It is all I have done for the Cause, Brent. Is it too much to ask I be allowed my contribution? Even if I die I die happy; but I think I will not. Even the Hanoverians do not kill innocent men . . . at least officially. Now call the guard. It is important he does

389

not come in first. Say Mary is too upset and I will tarry here until they come for me. Mary must create a commotion with her weeping. 'Tis part of the plan. Quick."

Mary began to wail loudly and Brent limped over to the door. John observed the limp and bit his lip. How they had ever hoped to get away with this . . .

The door opened and the guard peered into the gloom.

"What is it?"

"My sister is greatly distressed and her husband would have us go."

"Ah . . ." the guard shrugged and opened wide the door, glancing at the prisoner slumped dejectedly by the window. He had seen it happen so often lately as all the men were being sent to England; it was a sorry business. He locked the door and shepherded the weeping woman to the gate having little regard for the man who walked slowly behind her. He knew only one woman had come in and only one woman had gone out. No one had warned them to take much notice of the men. He saw the weeping woman through the gate and returned to the darkness of the prison. He would just finish his game of dice before taking the prisoner back to the dungeons. There was no hurry.

Analee sat in the carriage holding tightly to Nelly's hand. She stared anxiously at the castle gate and shared with those inside it the strong conviction that the plan would not succeed. Now that it had happened it seemed idiotic to suspect it would. Forging General Hawley's signature had been foolhardy, though Angus had a letter from him and they tried to copy his hand. They were being a long time and she stared anxiously at Nelly.

"It has gone wrong!"

"Hush," Nelly comforted, "you are too impatient. They have only been gone a few moments. There is the governor to see and all sorts of things."

Lord Falconer had not wished his wife to accompany Mary and John; after all, what had she to do with it? And if she was discovered? He had been foolish enough as it was. But the Falcon, if he did not know it before, was becoming aware of the stubbornness of the woman he had married. She would not take "no" for an answer. If she wanted a thing she would get it. The only place he found her at all submissive was in bed, and even there she also seemed subtly to exercise her own particular kind of dominance. She was remarkable. He had let her go after warning her not to expect a visit from him when she was lodged in the castle as a prisoner of His Majesty along with Lady Strathallan and Lady Ogilvy.

But Analee had felt she owed it to Mary to see that she got Brent back; and she wanted to talk to Brent. They had stayed the night on the way with Jacobite friends of the Allonbys who had so far been spared persecution by the government, and they would stop there on the way back. After that Analee would return to her husband and see Brent no more.

The gate of the castle swung back and she clasped Nelly's hand and closed her eyes.

"Oh, Nelly . . ."

"Aye, 'tis them. 'Tis Mary and . . . why, Analee, it *is* Brent. There is no doubt for he drags a leg and Mr. John walked in quite firm and straight."

Nelly tumbled out of the carriage at the same time as McNeath jumped from the box. They had thought to effect the escape in a light coach driven by McNeath so as to involve no further members of the household. Nelly ran up to Mary and put her arm about her, but, as planned, McNeath stayed by the coach. To anyone looking on, any guard or soldier, they must appear to be merely a sorrowing family, not the escort for the escape of an important Jacobite prisoner.

Yes, it was Brent, but how changed. So changed, so unlike John except in height that Analee wondered how they had achieved it. She leaned forward and held the door open, clasping Mary as she stumbled in. Then Brent followed and almost before they had sat down and closed the door McNeath had whipped his horses into a fast trot down the hill from Edinburgh Castle into the teeming streets of the town clustered in its shadow.

Everyone was breathing hard and now Nelly was also crying. Analee had tears in her eyes as she looked at the face of the exhausted man, his head back on his seat, his eyes closed. Analee studied the face to see whether she felt any emotion . . . tired or starved or ill or whatever, he was still Brent, her onetime lover, Morella's father. Yes, there were traces of the handsome man he had been, eyes made even finer now by suffering, the curve of the mouth, the fine arch of the brow . . .

Brent opened his eyes and looked straight into those of Analee; then he quickly shut them again. He reopened them cautiously as one does when expecting a shock. She smiled at him reassuringly.

"Yes, Brent. It is I, Analee. I have contrived to help your escape."

"Analee . . ." Brent leaned his head back and closed his eyes again. Analee. Was it possible? But she did not look like Analee in those fine clothes, that gorgeous cloak, the elegant hat with a plume.

Analee with a *hat?* Brent opened his eyes and looked again. It was not Analee, could not be. Why this person undoubtedly had her eyes and resembled Analee; but . . . she wore shoes, and carried a bag and her hands were gloved. No it could not be Analee, the wild gypsy he had loved.

"It *is* I, Brent," Analee said gently knowing full well what was going on in his mind, "but I am married now to a man of substance, a lord . . ."

"The Marquess of Falconer," Nelly said firmly, "*General* The Marquess of Falconer."

Brent opened his eyes and his lips trembled in a faint laugh.

"The Falcon? This is a joke someone is playing on me. He is a Hanoverian soldier, a man known for his mercilessness in battle. I thought he was killed at Falkirk and we all said 'good riddance.' Why should he be married to Analee? No, I am dead and this is a dream."

"It is no dream, Brent, and we shall explain all by and by. For the moment rest and be thankful that you are alive."

Rory Macintoch had fought with Brent in all the Scottish battles. He had escaped from Culloden and was overjoyed to see him again. They were to spend the night together in the priest's hole in the house because they were loyal Catholics as well as Jacobites. Servants kept a twenty-four hour guard in the grounds of the house; but even during the day Rory kept out of sight.

Luckily in this remote part of Scotland few people outside the house would even be aware of the visit of Mrs. Delamain and her brother, nor would it be noted as exceptional. Fiona Macintoch and Mary Allonby were old friends.

Fiona was a girl very like Mary in upbringing. She had known deprivation all her life, though it was especially bad for her family since the Act of Union. Up to that time Scotland had had its own Parliament; after that the country was ruled from London. At least Queen Anne, in whose reign the union took place, had been a Stuart; but after her death and the German Elector of Hanover usurped the English throne—according to her family's view of things— there was no going back. The English were hated and opposed at every turn. If the Allonbys thought they had martyrs to the Cause the Macintochs had more. In the present rising alone Fiona had lost another brother, killed, and a father who was in hiding with Cluny Macpherson in his cave in the highlands.

But to see Brent alive, even if he looked far from well . . . And to hear the part played by Lady Falconer, of all people. But Fiona was sworn to secrecy; that was a trust she would never betray. Like many Scots people near the border she had heard of Lord Falconer's sudden marriage to a fascinating gypsy— the Falcon was a law to himself, so everyone expected him to do something different. But a gypsy! How would *she* be received at the court of George II?

Fiona had taken to the new bride immediately, sensing her warmth and concern for the Allonby family. She had also trusted her. There was a strength about Analee that had convinced Fiona that if anyone could pull off the audacious coup she could. Mary jokingly said she was a witch but would not admit it.

Seeing Brent now among them and hearing how it was carried out, of the forged letter and the risky plan that had succeeded, Fiona was convinced Analee *was* a witch. How otherwise could she possibly have succeeded?

What was more the Marchioness, despite her beautiful clothes, was not the one to stand on ceremony. She knew that the Macintochs were poor and what servants there were patrolled the grounds of the house. Her ladyship set to in the kitchen and insisted on helping Fiona prepare the dinner while Mary, still shocked, rested in her room and Brent was put to sleep in the priest's hole after his sore leg had been bathed and his chains cut off, with some difficulty, by McNeath.

"My lady, I insist you should not come into the kitchen."

"Nonsense," Analee said. "You know I am a simple gypsy woman?"

Fiona, a bonny girl of nineteen with auburn hair, smiled.

"I have *heard* it said, your ladyship. I do not know I believe it."

" 'Tis true," said Analee, "now tell me what I have to do and I will do it. Do you have meat to carve? Bread to cut?"

She stared at Fiona noting her amazed expression.

"I see you do not think I am a gypsy. Is not my face dark and my eyes black? If I could show you my feet through these fine stockings you would see that I spent most of my life barefoot. It is the one thing my lord complains of, the scratch of my feet in bed. He says it is as though I wore boots!"

Fiona threw up her hands and laughed.

"Oh, Lady Falconer . . . you are very droll. Still Mary did say that you were a gypsy; she saw you as one. She says you have magical powers."

"I have not; but we gypsies have a certain . . . way with us you know. Maybe it is that. Now let us eat, girl, for I must be away at first light to my husband. You will see that Brent and Mary go on from here?"

"That is the plan. They will travel on horseback to Cockermouth where Mr. Rigg has agreed to give Brent shelter until a boat may be found to take him to Ireland. Mary will stay for a while with Mr. Rigg and her sister . . ."

"Mary must go with her husband," Analee said firmly. "I will speak to him about it."

At dinner Brent could not take his eyes off Analee; everyone noticed it, especially his wife. Yes, it was his Analee, the same. But married to another . . . Her gypsy husband had died and she had married the scourge of the Jacobites . . . the Falcon himself! It was incredible. But he still loved her; he always would. He looked into her eyes unaware of Mary next to him, unaware of anyone except Analee . . . But Analee seemed unconcerned and ate heartily as though she had spent a tiring day which in fact she felt she had. She spared Brent no special glances and entertained the company with stories of her wandering life as a gypsy and how his lordship had found her at last and taken her to his home.

"And do you miss the life, Lady Falconer?" Fiona, very much taken by her guest, had listened, her chin propped on her hands, her eyes shining. To her it sounded like a fairy story.

"I can't say I miss it now," Analee replied truthfully. "It was a hard life; but sometimes, yes, I look about me and see the trees burgeoning and the hard winter earth breaking open with life. Then I recall that special kinship with nature that I had when I was not the wife of the Marquess and a very different sort of world is now before me."

395

"But how did you come to be up here?" Mary said, also caught by Analee's spell, "so far from home? What made you come to the north?"

Analee drew from her bosom where it rested between her breasts the talisman of her husband's love, the ring of Falcon gold, twisting it thoughtfully in her fingers as she often did. Yes, today she was dressed like a marchioness with a corset and hoop, underclothes of lace and fine cambric and a one piece gown made of crimson brocade. She glanced at the rings on her fingers, the diamond and sapphire Angus had first given her and a rich ruby on her little finger. Although she had not married him for them she loved fine things. She'd fingered silks and baubles on the market stalls of the towns through which she had passed whenever she had the chance. She remembered the vision she'd had that one day she would be a grand lady.

She knew they were looking at her and admiring her, the set of her hair, the elegance of her dress, the glitter of her jewels. The ring of Falcon gold was like a lucky charm to her and she rubbed it between finger and thumb. What should she say? The truth? At last?

She looked at the young faces gazing at her—Rory Macintoch and Brent Delamain who had fought in battle, Mary and Fiona who had known suffering and deprivation and the agony of waiting for their men to return. Maybe she did owe them something, the knowledge that out of much misery happiness could come, that victory could take the place of disaster.

She leaned her chin on to the palm of her long brown bejewelled hand which glistened in the light of the guttering candles so that the audience knew not which dazzled them more, the diamonds and rubies on her fingers or the blazing dark eyes set in the imperious, beautiful face.

"I will tell you," Analee said at last sighing deeply, "though it is a secret few know. Not even my husband knows, though of course I will tell him in time. I tell it you now because you all have suffered much in recent times—you have gambled and appear to have lost. You, dear Mary and Brent, will be exiles in a foreign land, maybe forever. You, Rory and Fiona —who knows where you will be in a twelvemonth? I tell you this little tale because it may give you hope and show that out of bad times good things can come, as I pray they will for you.

"It so happened that I was orphaned at birth and brought up by my grandmother. We were wandering gypsies, part of a nomadic tribe, not stationary as were the Buckland gypsies, into whom I eventually married. We rested sometimes for days, sometimes months, and from being a maid, I knew that I interested men a good deal and they me.

"My grandmother wanted to preserve my purity and marry me to a good gypsy boy because she could see, even at fourteen, how developed I was, how interested in love.

"But I was willful and didn't heed my grandmother. I flirted with the boys and teased them and earned a name for myself for fickleness and inconstancy. I loved to dance and enjoy myself as young girls do; but I liked all the boys who admired me and my grandmother despaired.

"My grandfather was already dead and then one day when I was seventeen my grandmother took a chill and died, and I found I was on my own. I had no near relations and no one really cared for me or was concerned about me, and I passed many months in depair until one day I met a gypsy boy who was far more serious minded than any I had known before. He was a fine horseman and taught me to ride expertly, and he had many skills which he wanted to develop only he lacked the education and means to do it. Oh he was such a fine, handsome, proud young man only a little older than I, and with such promise. He taught me really how to love and he cared for me and I was his woman. That was how it remained until one day we met up with another crowd of traveling gypsies and among them was a brilliant dancer with whom I discovered an immediate affinity. He was taller and more beautiful than my man and such a wonderful dancer that whenever I was with him I felt lost to the world.

"We continued with this group on the road and I soon realized I was in love with two men, or fancied I was. I was happy with both. My lover, by whom I was now expecting a child, became savagely jealous and this only spurred the dancer to flirt with me anew although he merely did it to anger my love.

"I know not what got into me at the time. I was young, and although I loved my man best and wanted his child, some devil in me made me pay more attention to the dancer and I flaunted myself in front of him, pretending to prefer him to the other.

"One day my lover, insane with jealousy though I was too blind to see it, asked me outright if *he* was indeed the father of my child. I smiled and played and teased and then shook my head and, before I knew what had happened, my love had drawn a knife and plunged it into the heart of the dancer who, even then, was looking incredulous at what I had said. For we had never even lain together, and deep in my heart I had kept constancy for my man.

"I shall never forget the look in his eyes as that beautiful youth lay dying, the bewilderment and the silent way he rebuked me, for he was incapable of speech. And then, turning to my love and seeing the jealousy and hatred die and turn to remorse, I threw myself into his arms and said I had merely teased him.

"'Twas too late. The authorities took him and hanged him and no one pleaded his cause. I waited by the gaol, but I was not even allowed to see him again, beg his mercy. We gypsies have always been treated as a low form of human life.

"Meanwhile the winter came on and I was alone and friendless, big with child and prey to a remorse that all but killed me. Would that it had, I thought at the time. My baby was born before term and died immediately for lack of care, and I had no one but a strange woman to comfort me and take away my dead child . . ."

Analee paused, her eyes glistening with the sharpness of the memory. She saw that Fiona was silently weeping; that Mary had her eyes on the table, and Rory gazed at the floor, the muscles in his jaw working. Only Brent, who still loved her, met her eyes, gazing at her with the stormy jealousy she had once seen on the face of her lover, the one who had been hanged. She had, he now knew, borne another's child—what if he knew she had borne his, too? She gazed at him tenderly and smiled.

"So I wandered on, forever trying to rid myself of the dreadful memory of what my wanton flirtatiousness had done. Two men cut off in their prime on account of me. I often dreamed that my lover came back and asked the truth, but however much I told him that the child was his he did not believe me and he would vanish, crying reproaches in the wind.

"Because it is my nature to love and to want to be admired I consoled myself with other men, in time. Randal Buckland who forced me to marry him I did not love at first, but I grew attached to him because of the nature of our lovemaking. It is inevitable between a man and a woman that if that goes well everything will be well. It is the most important thing.

"And now at last I have found my *true* love; my husband, Lord Falconer. I did not marry him for his title or wealth, but because we too had grown to know and love each other through the pleasures of the body and also, more deeply, through suffering shared after he was nearly mortally wounded at Falkirk. I knew his reputation but he is not a bad man. He is a soldier and an aristocrat. A strong man. The man for me."

Analee looked at Brent, saw the pain and suffering in his eyes, and then at the gentle unloved Mary so long denied the bodily joys for which she yearned, which she had a right to expect from her husband.

Analee felt with all her heart that she wanted to make things go well for them before she returned to her own life of happiness with the husband who so anxiously awaited her at Falcon's Keep.

After dinner Analee indicated that she would like to speak to Brent alone. The table was cleared and they were left in the dining-room, one on either side of the fire. Already rested and in fresh clothes Brent looked better. He would soon be the tall, upright, well-built man she remembered.

"Analee . . ." he said to her as the door closed and came quickly to her side, but she put out a hand to stay him and he was surprised by the distant expression on her face.

"Come no nearer, Brent Delamain."

"But, Analee . . . you did this for me. Took this risk."

"I did it for your *wife,* for Mary and the Allonby family whom I love."

Brent dropped his arms, extended to take Analee, and turned away.

"She is not my wife. I cannot love her. I have tried but I think only of you. You bewitch me, Analee. Even though you have told this tale tonight of your love for another man—I speak not only of Lord Falconer but of your first love—even though you emphasize that you have lain with so many of whom I am merely one, I still love you and want you, and I always shall. You pretend you are a strumpet but you are not. You are *my* Analee! Thinking of you prevents me from even performing the act of love with anyone else."

Analee sat down and placed her hands in her lap. She pursed her beautiful full mouth into an expression of severity and looked at Brent.

"Why, sir, I am surprised to hear that a vigorous man like yourself is unable to give pleasure to a woman even if his thoughts lie with another. But, Brent, you must get over this fixation you imagine you have for me. I confess that for me you were *not* someone casual; you were someone very special, Brent, and always will be."

She remembered their blonde daughter and her eyes momentarily clouded with thoughts of a happiness that was now lost but which might have been. Yes, she did love Brent; he was part of her. Morella was part of them both; but it was a love that lay in the past, encapsulated in time. She wanted to take the stricken youth in her arms and tell him how much she had loved him, what she had done for him, suffered for him. Instead she gazed at him, her imperious head, beautifully coiffured, tilted to one side, her eyes masked to hide her true feelings.

"Brent," she said slowly, softly, "I am married to the Marquess of Falconer, a man of fascination who dominates me body and soul. What happened between you and me is in the past and will never occur again. Let us remember it as a beautiful moment, captured forever in the moonlight. My husband is a masterful, jealous man and expects much from me. Compared to my love for him my feelings for you were like that of a young infatuated girl. Angus and I have a very deep bond. See . . ." she shook the chain around her neck and showed him the ring of palest gold with the head of the falcon engraved on it. "Angus gave me this as a symbol of our enduring love—a ring of purest gold, Falcon gold it is called. Our love is binding like this gold, eternal like the ring." Analee dropped the ring back into her bodice and folded her hands on her lap. "You and I are not for each other, Brent, whatever you say. If I ever thought it, I think it not now."

"You may think what you like," Brent said. "If the Falcon has captured you now, so be it; but it will not last and when it ends I will be waiting for you as I was meant to do, as I should have done before. My life of suffering these past months has made me realize what a fool I was to give you up, to put someone's happiness before mine. Not only was I not happy; but I made Mary desperately unhappy. I could not be a husband to her, not a man . . ."

"I know," Analee said with some asperity. "I am surprised at you, Brent, losing your ability to make love. I and my husband do very well, I can assure you."

The blood rushed to Brent's face and he felt a savage fury at the very thought of Falconer and his beloved together. He raised a fist and shook it. "I'll not hear about him! I'll . . ."

"You'll do naught," Analee said quietly. "You are a fugitive and are bound for Ireland and, Brent, I want to ask you this and tell it you at the same time. Be a husband to Mary. Forget me, for you can can never have me again. As Mary nursed you, I nursed him to health and that way my love for him was cemented. I love Angus much more that I ever loved you. I can't tell you why but 'tis so, and now . . ." Analee crossed her hands meekly over her stomach and gazed at Brent, "I am carrying his child and his blood runs with mine. It is final . . . It is settled. It is done. We are to raise a family and I am to become a fine lady with a house in London." She smiled mischievously.

"My husband is teaching me nice manners, how to conduct myself like a lady and how to read and write. You might not believe it, but I have taken to the life far better than I expected. Although I am always Analee the gypsy, nothing can change that, I am also the Marchioness of Falconer—and nothing can change that either, or will." Her ladyship patted her stomach and gazed complacently at Brent.

Brent's face, still contorted, was more livid than ever.

"I don't care whose child you are carrying or how many more you have!" he shouted. "You are my Analee . . . *my* gypsy and you always will be."

Analee lowered her eyes and felt a sickening moment of defeat. She got up and walked slowly to the door, turning at the threshold, her hand on the doorknob. "I will see you no more, Brent, and I can say no more; but if you love me then do as I ask. God bless you."

She saw that tears had come into his eyes, as there were in hers, as she quietly shut the door behind her.

Then she went to find Brent's wife. There was only one thing left to try and do.

Mary had heard everything. Even down the corridors Brent's shouts had penetrated. She wept as Analee came to her room, sat on her bed, took her hand.

"It is no good, Analee. He has eyes only for you."

"Now listen," Analee said practically. "I have done all I can; there is still something *you* can do."

"I? What can I do?"

"Well, the only thing left is a gypsy spell . . . oh I know I have denied magical powers; but some things are passed down in gypsy lore and I have known them since I was a little girl, they came from my grandmother who was foreign. Whether they work or not depends often on the intention of the one who wants to win the man's love. You *must* believe it. Well, Stewart was successful was he not?"

"Yes, but you said . . ."

"Maybe I was wrong? Maybe it *was* the spell? We can only try. Now listen, this is what I want you to do. It is simple and you must repeat it after me. Will you do it?"

"I will do anything to win Brent's love."

Analee squeezed Mary's hand and leaned forward.

"Now when you have your woman's time I want you to take some of the blood and add it to the powdered pips of apples and pears, quinces and berries, and fruits you have in your sister's garden or wherever you are. These you must previously have burnt and ground to a powder. This you add to the little phial of blood you have procured and then you get some pieces of Brent's hair or, if you can, parings from his nails and add these to the mixture which you must then put in his food. Oh do not wince . . . It sounds unpleasant but 'tis tasteless if the food is well flavored. You can add this mixture to his food up to three times, after that . . ."

Analee got up.

"I have told Brent I am with child by my lord and want naught more to do with him. We are building our own life together, we and our children, which Angus urgently desires. He is of the government, bound for important duties in the army, at court perhaps. Our lives must sunder, Mary. But I will always have a place for you in my heart. I hope you escape to happiness and wish you and your family well. Now I am going. . ."

"But it is dark . . ."

"No matter. McNeath will drive carefully and we shall lodge at the first hostelry we come to. When Brent finds I am gone you will see he will soon realize how lucky he is to find such a wife as yourself. And you *will* be happy, Mary. I know it. You have remembered the spell? Say it again."

Mary nodded and repeated it until Analee was happy. Her eyes were on Analee the enchantress, the witch.

Moments later she heard the rattle of the coach, the barking of dogs.

The Marchioness of Falconer was returning to her lord, to the great mansion of Falcon's Keep in the heart of the Cheviot Hills. The Cheviots marked the end of the Pennine Range so that Analee had in some sense finished her journey. The past was behind her. Like the Allonbys, the Delamains, the defeated Jacobites and their fugitive Prince, she, Analee the gypsy, was beginning life again.

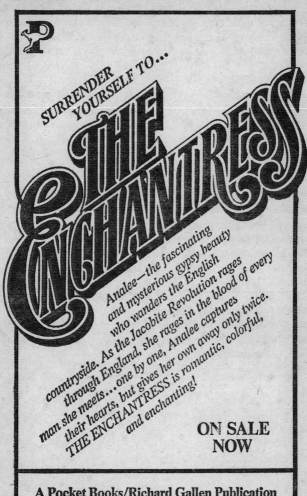